THE SURGEON'S CINDERELLA

BY
SUSAN CARLISLE

SAVED BY DOCTOR DREAMY

BY
DIANNE DRAKE

KT-501-323

MILLS & BOON

Susan Carlisle's love affair with books began in the sixth grade, when she made a bad grade in mathematics. Not allowed to watch TV until she'd brought the grade up, Susan filled her time with books. She turned her love of reading into a passion for writing, and now has over ten Medical Romances published through Mills & Boon. She writes about hot, sexy docs and the strong women who captivate them. Visit SusanCarlisle.com.

Starting with non-fiction, **Dianne Drake** penned hundreds of articles and seven books under the name JJ Despain. In 2001 she began her romance-writing career with *The Doctor Dilemma*. In 2005 Dianne's first Medical Romance, *Nurse in Recovery*, was published, and with more than 20 novels to her credit she has enjoyed writing ever since.

THE SURGEON'S CINDERELLA

BY
SUSAN CARLISLE

MILLS & BOON

Published in Great Britain 2017
By Mills & Boon, an imprint of HarperCollins*Publishers*
1 London Bridge Street, London, SE1 9GF

© 2017 Susan Carlisle

ISBN: 978-0-263-92650-7

Our policy is to use papers that are natural, renewable and recyclable
products and made from wood grown in sustainable forests. The logging
and manufacturing processes conform to the legal environmental
regulations of the country of origin.

Printed and bound in Spain
by CPI, Barcelona

Dear Reader,

I never know where a story idea is going to come from. This one literally came from the sky. While I was on a plane, reading the airline magazine, I noticed an advertisement for a matchmaker who specialised in helping the busy professional. A spark of an idea was born, and that became Whitney and Tanner's story.

This was a fun one to write—especially when this couple finds out that what they want is right under their noses. The setting isn't bad either— San Francisco and Napa Valley.

I hope you enjoy the journey that Whitney and Tanner take on their way to finding true love. Hearing from my readers is one of my greatest joys. You can contact me at SusanCarlisle.com.

Happy reading,

Susan

To Eric.
Everyone should have a son-in-law like you.

Books by Susan Carlisle

Mills & Boon Medical Romance

Summer Brides

White Wedding for a Southern Belle

Midwives On-Call

His Best Friend's Baby

Heart of Mississippi

The Maverick Who Ruled Her Heart
The Doctor Who Made Her Love Again

Married for the Boss's Baby
The Doctor's Sleigh Bell Proposal

Visit the Author Profile page
at millsandboon.co.uk for more titles.

CHAPTER ONE

TANNER LOCKE NEEDED a matchmaker's help.

Two days earlier Whitney Thomason's hand had quivered slightly as she'd held the phone. He was certainly a blast from the past. Why would someone like Tanner require her help?

An hour earlier he had texted her that he needed to change their arrangements and asked her to meet him at a small airport outside San Francisco. As the owner of Professional Matchmaking, Whitney had made concessions for clients on more than one occasion, but this was the first time she'd been asked to meet one at an airport at dusk.

Tanner had said something had come up and that he couldn't join her at her office. He would appreciate her meeting him at the airport. If she hadn't been familiar with his status in the community she wouldn't have considered such a plan. She wasn't acquainted with the small airport but had agreed to do as he'd requested.

Having *the* Dr. Tanner Locke's name on her client list would be good for business. Even though it was unethical to publicize his name, she could say that an eminent doctor in the city had used her services. Who knew? He might even send her referrals. Either of those would make it worth her drive to meet him.

As the "big man on campus" when they'd been at Berkeley, all the girls had had a crush on Tanner, including herself. But she hadn't been his style. He had been into thin, blonde, preppy sorority girls while she had been the heavy, dark-haired, mousy nobody. At least she already knew his type.

In the past couple of years she'd seen Tanner's name in the news a few times. He was an up-and-coming surgeon in the heart transplant field. So why did someone as good-looking and eligible as Tanner need her help in finding a mate?

Whitney chuckled drily. For the same reasons her other clients did. They didn't have the time or energy to weed out the unsuitable. She handled the nitty-gritty work of finding people with similar backgrounds so they only connected with the people most appropriate for them. It was a one-and-done process.

She rolled through the gate of the airfield minutes before she was due to meet Tanner. Would he recognize her? Why should he? She'd just been one of those people who had been a filler in a couple of his classes. Plus she'd changed a great deal since then. At least on the outside. She'd lost fifty pounds. She'd long outgrown having a crush on Tanner. Heavens, she didn't even really know him.

Pulling into a parking spot in the lot next to a red single-story, cement-block building, she turned off the engine. A gleaming white jet sat on the tarmac in front of the terminal. There were a couple of men working around it. Was Tanner going somewhere? Probably off to Hawaii for the weekend.

Normally Whitney liked to have her initial interview in a neutral and laid-back place. A local café, the park. Out of the client's high-pressure work world so that they were more relaxed, less distracted. She found that even though people's favorite subject was themselves, when it came to their personal life they weren't as forthcoming. Men tended toward telling about half of what she needed to know. The more successful her client was, the more insecure or demanding or both they were about their choices for mates.

At the sound of an ambulance siren, she glanced into the rearview mirror. The noise abruptly ended as the vehicle rolled through the gate at a normal speed and continued until the ambulance stopped close to the plane. A group of people dressed in green scrubs exited the back.

What was going on?

One of the men in the party broke away from the group and started toward her. That must be Tanner. It had been years since she'd seen him. He'd changed as well. His shoulders had broadened and his face had lost its youthfulness, having matured into sharper angles. He was still an extremely handsome man. Maybe even more so now.

With a wide stride that spoke of a person who controlled his realm and was confident to do so, he approached her. She stepped out of the car, closed the door and waited.

"Whitney?"

He didn't recognize her. Was she relieved or disappointed? She extended her hand when he was within arm's reach.

"Whitney Thomason."

Tanner took her hand and pulled her to him, giving her a hug.

What was he doing?

Her face was pressed into the curve of his shoulder. He smelled not of hospital antiseptic but of clean, warm male. Whitney was so surprised her hands fluttered at his waist. What was going on? She was released almost as quickly as he had grabbed her.

Tanner glanced over his shoulder. "Please just go along with me. First names only. No titles."

She looked beyond him to see the others in his party watching them. He made their meeting sound like a covert operation. She took a small step away from him. "Okay. I'm Whitney."

"I'm Tanner. I would prefer we keep my request between the two of us." His dark brown eyes beseeched her.

"I understand. I assure you I am discreet." Most professionals she worked with wanted their interactions with her to remain low-key. Either they didn't want others to know they needed help in their personal life or were just embarrassed they couldn't find someone on their own. Whatever it was, she respected their desires. But no one had gone to the extent that Tanner was to keep his secret.

So why was he meeting her in front of his colleagues? "Then why here?" She nodded her head toward the group at the plane.

"I didn't know I was going to have to go after a heart and I wanted you to get started on this right away."

"After a heart?" Her voice rose.

"I'm a heart transplant surgeon. I'm in the process of retrieving a heart."

"Oh." He made it sound like that was commonplace. For him it might be, but for her it was a little unnerving.

He looked over his shoulder as the jet engines roared to life. "So what do you need from me?"

And he wants to do this right now, right here?

"It usually takes an hour or so for me to get enough information from a client to form a good idea of the type of woman they are best suited to."

Tanner glanced back to where the others were loading the plane. "I don't have an hour. I have a patient who needs a new heart."

"Then I suggest we postpone this meeting." Whitney reached for her car door handle.

"I'd like to get the process started. I'm up for a promotion and the board is breathing down my neck to settle down. I've got to do something right away about finding a wife. But with my caseload I don't know when I'll be able to sit down and talk anytime soon." His voice held a note of desperation that she was confident didn't appear often. "What I'm looking for is someone who takes care of herself, is good in social situations, wants to be a mother and would be supportive of my career."

Really? That's all he wanted? He hadn't said anything about love. This would be a tough order to fill. "Those are pretty broad requirements. I like to know my clients well enough that I don't waste their or their potential partner's time."

"Hey, Tanner," the last man getting on the plane called. "We gotta go. This heart won't wait on us."

Tanner looked back to her. "I've got a patient that's been waiting for months for this heart. I have to see that he gets it. Look, I've heard you're the best in town. Do your thing. I'm sure you can find someone for me. Here's my contact information." He handed her a business card. "Call when you have something. Don't pull away. I'm going to give you a quick kiss on the cheek. I need for these guys—" he nodded toward the plane "—to think that you're my girlfriend."

Before Whitney could agree or disagree, his lips brushed her face and he jogged away.

The man's nerve knew no bounds!

Minutes later Whitney watched as the plane lifted off the ground and flew into the darkening sky. Somehow tonight the Tanner she'd had such a crush on and worshipped in college from afar had become a mortal man. The thing was she really didn't know this Tanner any better than she knew the old Tanner. If she did manage to find him a match, would he take the time to get to know the woman or just expect her to bow to his list of requirements? Whitney's goal was to find love matches, and Tanner had said nothing about wanting that.

And while they worked together there would be no more physical contact. She was a professional.

Tanner looked down from his window seat of the plane at the woman still standing beside her small practical compact car. She looked like a matchmaker. Simply dressed. Nothing sexy or suggestive about her clothing—he'd even characterize her style as unappealing. Her hair was pulled back into a band at her nape.

He didn't go around kissing strangers but he had kissed her. Little Ms. Matchmaker had the softest skin he'd ever felt. She was nothing like the women he was attracted to yet he found her no-nonsense, straight-to-the-point personality interesting. People generally didn't speak to him so frankly.

Did he know her from somewhere? Maybe she'd been a member of one of his former patients' families? But she'd said nothing about knowing him. He was good with faces. It could be her smile that drew him. It was one of the nicest he'd ever seen. Reached her eyes.

He hoped he'd made the right decision in calling her. There had been noises made by the powers-that-be at the hospital that he might be in line for the head of department position when Dr. Kurosawa retired. A subtle suggestion had been made that a settled married man looked more appealing on the vita than a bachelor.

For a moment he'd thought about doing the online dating thing but couldn't bring himself to enter his name. He didn't have the time or inclination to wade through all the possible dates. Make the dates and remake dates. The speed-dating idea came close to making him feel physically sick. Being thought pathetic because he used a dating service also disturbed him. The fewer people who knew what he was doing the better. Truthfully, he was uncomfortable having others know he needed hired help to find a partner. Even employing a matchmaker made him uneasy. But he'd done it. He wanted that directorship.

Finding women to date was no problem for him, but he had never found someone who met his requirements for a lifelong commitment. Tanner wasn't interested in a love match but in a relationship based on mutual life goals. Maybe with the help of an outsider, an impartial one, he could find a woman who wanted the same things he did? The search would be handled like a business, a study of pros and cons.

One thing he did know was that love wouldn't be the deciding factor. He'd already seen what that did to a person. His mother had loved his father but his father had not felt the same. In fact, she'd doted on him, but he'd stayed away more than he'd been at home. Each time he'd left she'd cried and begged him not to go. When he'd leave again she'd be depressed until she learned that he was coming home. Then she'd go into manic mode, buying a new dress and spending hours "fixing herself up." His father had never stayed long. Leaving two boys to watch their mother's misery as he'd disappeared down the drive. Finally he'd divorced her. Tanner refused to have any kind of relationship like that. His career demanded his time and focus. He had to have a wife who could handle that.

Maybe the executive matchmaker could help him find what he needed in a woman. If that woman was happy with what he could offer outside of giving his heart then she would suit him.

"Hey, Tanner," the kidney team surgeon said after a tap to his arm, "who was the woman you were talking to? Did you have to break a hot date?"

He shrugged. "Just a woman I met."

"You know one day you're going to have to settle down. Hospital boards like to have their department heads going home to a family at night. I've got a friend of a friend with a sister. Pretty, I heard."

"I'm good, Charlie."

He grinned. "I'm just saying…"

Tanner was tired of being fixed up by friends and family. Everyone wanted their daughter or friend to marry a doctor.

He looked over at the nurse sitting beside Charlie. She was talking to a member of the liver team. They'd been out a number of times but nothing had really clicked. Tanner didn't want to date out of the nursing pool anymore. He wanted to go home to someone who wasn't caught up in the high adrenaline rush of medical work. A woman who gave him a peaceful haven where he could unwind.

He expected Whitney Thomason to find that person for him.

By the next morning, Tanner had put in over twenty-four hours at the hospital, but his patient, who had been at death's door, was now doing well in CICU. The life-giving gift of a heart transplant never ceased to amaze him. He was humbled by his part in the process.

Thankfully he'd managed to catch a couple of hours' sleep on the plane to and from the hospital where his team had retrieved the heart. Now he had morning rounds to make and then he was headed home to bed. His sched-uled surgeries had been moved back a day or postponed. Sleep was the only thing on his agenda for today.

Knocking on the door of Room 223 of the step-down unit, he slowly pushed it open. "Mr. Vincent?"

"Come in." The man's voice was strong.

Tanner entered and moved to the bed. "How're you feeling today, Mr. Vincent?"

"I'd be lying if I said I wasn't sore."

Tanner smiled. Mr. Vincent was only a week out from transplant. Where he'd hardly been able to walk down the hall in the weeks before his surgery, now he could do it back and forth with confidence. Transplants were amazing things. "Sorry about that but it's just part of the process. It should get better every day." Tanner looked around the room. "Mrs. Vincent here?"

"Naw. She had a hair appointment. She doesn't like to miss them." He sounded resigned to his wife's actions. "She'll be here soon, though."

"The plan is for you to go home tomorrow. There are a number of things that the nurses will need to go over with you both."

"Cindy doesn't like blood and all this hospital stuff."

"She'll need to help with your care or you'll have to find another family member to do it. Otherwise home health should be called in."

Mrs. Vincent's self-centeredness was just the type of thing that Tanner couldn't tolerate. This man's wife was so focused on her own needs that she couldn't be both-ered to support her husband's return to good health. Her actions reminded him too much of his father's.

"I need to give you a listen, Mr. Vincent." Tanner re-moved his stethoscope from his neck. After inserting the earpieces in his ears, he placed the listening end on the man's chest. There was a steady, strong beat where one hadn't existed before the transplant.

"Can you sit forward, Mr. Vincent?"

"I can but I won't like it much." The middle-aged man shifted in the bed.

Tanner was listening to the man's lungs when a platinum blonde strolled through the door. She stopped short as if she was surprised to see Tanner.

"Hello, Dr. Locke," she said in a syrupy thick voice.

Tanner had only met Mrs. Vincent a couple of times but each time he had the prickly feeling that she was coming on to him. This time was no different. At least twenty years younger than her husband, she was overdressed and too absorbed in herself for someone who should have been concerned about a husband who had recently been at death's door. Wearing a tight top and pants a size too small, she sauntered up to the bedside, leaning over. Tanner had a view of her cleavage that had no business being shared with anyone but her husband.

More than once Tanner had seen his mother act the same way toward his father. The action then and now made him feel uncomfortable.

"Hi, sweetie. It's nice to see you." Mr. Vincent gave her an adoring smile.

"So how's the patient doing?" she cooed, not looking at her husband. His mother had used that same tone of voice when she'd spoken to his father.

"He's ready to go home after we make sure you both understand his care." Tanner wrapped his stethoscope around his neck.

"I'm not sure I can do that. I'm no nurse. I'm not good with blood and stuff." She gave him a wide, bright, red-painted-lips smile.

Tanner stepped toward the door. "I'm sure the nurses

can help you practice so that you become comfortable with what you need to do."

"Cindy, sweetie, we'll figure it out together." Mr. Vincent took her manicured hand and gave her a pleading look. Just the way Tanner's mother had looked at his father before he'd left for weeks.

"I'll let the nurse know that you're ready for her instructions." Tanner went out the door.

The Vincents' marriage was exactly the type he didn't want. The one-sided kind. Tanner was afraid he would be too much like his mother. Give his heart and have it stomped on. A relationship where one of the partners couldn't see past their love for the other while the other cared about nothing but themselves. A bond based on mutual respect would be far more satisfying in the long run. With his executive matchmaker contacts, that should be just the type of arrangement he'd manage to find.

The censoring look in Whitney's eyes when he'd given his list of requirements had him questioning that she might have expected something more.

Whitney had spent the last two days working through her database in search of women who fit the description of what Tanner wanted. She had five names she thought might be of interest to him. Now she had to pin him down for a meeting so they could start the process.

She picked up the card he'd handed her and tapped it on her desk.

Why couldn't Tanner find his own mate? What was his deal with the passionless list of requirements? He had nothing in common with her in that regard. She was looking for true love. The kind of love that endured forever, no matter what the hardships. The till-death-do-us-part kind that her parents and grandparents had. She'd built her business on that idea. Believed her clients should have that as well.

Once she'd thought she'd had it. That love. With a business degree in hand, she'd taken a job in a corporation. There she'd met Steve. He'd worked in an adjoining department and had seemed not to care that she'd been heavy. That had been a first for her. She'd had no dates in high school and very few in college. When Steve had started giving her attention she'd been ecstatic. For once in her life someone had been interested. After dating for over a year, they'd started planning a wedding.

Two weeks before the ceremony he'd called and told her he'd found someone else. The woman had turned out to be thin and pretty.

Whitney had been devastated. Again that inferiority she'd felt in high school and college had come flooding back. To fight the pain, she'd done whatever she could to keep busy. She'd spent her time walking whenever she'd been alone to prevent dwelling on her broken heart. After a while she'd become interested in wellness nutrition and had adopted a healthy lifestyle. Soon she'd joined an over-eating support group and continued to slim down. Men had started paying attention to her but she'd not yet found one that she trusted to stick with her. She wanted a man who cared about her and not just her looks. Those faded.

In college she'd introduced a number of friends to other classmates. The majority of those relationships had become long-term ones and many of the couples had gone on to marry. Whitney had gained the reputation of being a matchmaker. When her boss had confided in her that she was having trouble dating, Whitney had introduced her to a friend of her family. They too had married. A few years later, when the company she'd worked for had downsized and Whitney had been let go, she'd decided that if she couldn't find someone for herself she could at least help others find the right person. Opening Professional Matchmaking had been her answer.

Despite her own disappointments, she still believed that there was a soul mate for everyone. So what had happened in Tanner's life to make him not believe in love? Could she convince him it was necessary for him too? But that wasn't what he was paying her to do. He wanted the best mate possible and it was her job to see that she found that person, not change his requirements.

Whitney punched in Tanner's number from the card. Now it was time to help him do just that.

On the second ring he answered. "Locke."

"This is Whitney Thomason."

"Who?" His voice became muffled, as if he was speaking to someone else.

"Whitney Thomason of Professional Matchmaking."

"Uh, yeah. Just a minute."

She waited while he spoke to the other person, giving orders about what should be done for a patient.

Even with his abrupt speech he had a nice voice. Sort of warm and creamy. The kind a woman liked to hear in her ear when a man rolled toward her in the middle of the night. Heavens, that wasn't a thought she should be having about her newest client.

Seconds later the background noise quieted.

"I only have a few seconds. What can I do for you?"

She understood about being busy but he was the one requesting her help. "I have compiled a list of possible matches for you. I'd like to get together and discuss them. Start setting up some socials."

"Socials? I'm not interested in, neither do I have time for, tea parties."

That's why he didn't have anyone. He wouldn't put in

the effort it took to develop a relationship. "Socials are when you have your first meeting with a potential mate. Before I can set those up we need to talk and sort out who you'd like to consider first."

"Can't you just take care of that?" He already sounded distracted. Maybe he was the same self-centered guy she'd known in college.

"Tanner, are you sure you want to do this?" Her voice took on a hard note. "You have to put some time and effort into finding the right person. Maybe you aren't ready yet."

There was a pause then a sigh of resignation. "What do you want me to do?"

"Can you meet me at Café Lombard at six this evening?"

"I'll be there." There was a click on the line as he ended the call.

Had she made him mad? Her time was valuable too. Tanner had come to her for help. He was going to have to meet her halfway, do his part to help find the perfect match for him. That required energy. If their conversation at the café didn't go well, she'd just tell him that he needed to go elsewhere for assistance.

Café Lombard was a small establishment at the bottom of Lombard Street, which was famous for being the curviest street in the world. Flowers bloomed between each of the curves, making it a fun street to look at but not to drive along. Tanner wasn't a fan of quaintness and this was one of the most picturesque places in San Francisco. When he arrived right at six, he spotted Whitney sitting at a table for two in the patio area.

Again her shoulder-length hair was primly pulled back into a controlled mass at the nape of her neck. She wore a simple blouse that gave little hint of her body shape and with that were a pair of black pants and flat shoes. There was nothing flamboyant about her. She looked as if she wanted to blend in, go unnoticed.

He started across the street toward her. She glanced up. A smile came to her lips as she waved at him. Now that expression stood out. It encouraged him to return it and he did.

Tanner joined her at the table.

"You're not going to grab me, are you?" She put a chair between them.

"Not unless you want me to. Look, I'm sorry about that. I just didn't want my colleagues asking a lot of questions. It was easier to pretend you were my girlfriend."

"I guess I can understand that."

He dropped into the chair across from her.

"Would you like something to drink or eat? It's on me, of course," Whitney offered.

She seemed to have already forgotten his invasion of her personal space. She was a good sport. "Thank you. I'm starved. But I can get my own."

The waiter came to their table.

"I'll have a cob salad and a water," Whitney said.

"And I'll have a steak sandwich with fries with a large lemonade."

The waiter left. Whitney quirked a corner of her mouth up as if perplexed by something.

"What?" Tanner asked.

"Lemonade? You seem more like a beer guy."

"I am, but I'm on call."

"Ah, that makes sense." She appeared to approve.

He leaned forward and crossed his arms on the table. "I'm sorry I was so abrupt with you on the phone. I've just been super busy this month. Under a lot of pressure."

She smiled. "I understand. I'll try to keep this short and sweet."

"So what did you need to see me about?"

"I've found some potential dates I think you might be interested in. I'd like you to review their files and see what you think. Then I'll set up a social with the one you like best." Whitney pushed a pink folder toward him.

Pink seemed an appropriate color for a matchmaker. At least her office supplies had some flair. Tanner opened the folder to find a printed page with the name of a woman at the top and information about her. He looked at Whitney. "No picture? I don't get to see what they look like?"

"Not until you meet them. I think a lasting relationship should be based on something more than looks. I want my clients to see beyond the surface."

"Interesting." Was there something peculiar about that belief? She no doubt believed in true love and happily-ever-after. He'd learned long ago not to believe in fairy tales. He flipped through the other pages. The women seemed interesting but a couple of them owned their own businesses. He picked up their sheets. "These don't look like they would have time to devote to children, take on social obligations."

"They both assure me that they would be willing to change their lifestyle for the right person. We can put them at the bottom of the list, if you wish, however."

"Have you spoken to them about me?" He didn't relish the idea of being discussed like a piece of merchandise. Yet he was doing the same thing in regards to those women.

She took the women's profiles from him and placed the open file on the table between them both. "I didn't disclose your name or picture but, yes, they have reviewed your profile as well."

"So this is how it works."

"Yes."

The waiter returned with their meals. Neither of them said anything until he left.

Whitney leaned forward with a reassuring smile on her lips. "It's not as painful as you might think. All my clients are interested in finding the same thing. Happiness with someone."

She made it sound like this was about a love match. A ride off into a beautiful sunset. "I'm more interested in someone who's compatible and interested in the same things as I am."

"I think if you spend some time reading this information—" she tapped the folder with her well-manicured, unpolished index finger "—you'll find these are all women worth meeting. They're all very lovely people."

Tanner took a bite out of his sandwich as he flipped the pages back and forth. He continued to eat and review the women's information. A couple of them sounded like they might work. He glanced at Whitney. She was sitting straight with one hand in her lap, eating her salad. Her manners were excellent.

He pushed two sheets toward her. "I think I would like to start with these."

She put her fork down and looked at the papers then nodded. "These are good choices. I'll see about setting up socials. I'll let you know when and where to meet."

"How will I know them?"

There was that reassuring lift of the lips again. "I'll be there to introduce you. It's very uncomfortable to wait for a person you don't know so I'll make the introductions and then leave you to get to know each other."

"So that's all there is to it?" He closed the folder and nudged it back toward her.

She moved her half-eaten salad away and took the folder. "That's it, except for the bill."

He raised a brow and grinned. "I thought you were getting the meal."

"I am, but there's the charge for my services so far." Whitney reached into her purse, removed an envelope and handed it to him.

"Did you add extra for meeting me at the airport and the hug and kiss?"

Whitney pushed the chair back. She looked dead serious when she said, "No. That came for free—once. Next time it will cost you."

"I hope it isn't necessary again. I'll have this in the mail tomorrow." He stuffed the envelope into his pants pocket.

Again she dug into her purse, came out with a couple of green bills and placed them on the table. "Thank you for that. Now, if you'll excuse me, I'll get started on setting up those socials. I'll be in touch soon."

Tanner watched her leave the patio and cross the street. Interesting person. Combination of quiet firmness and solid businesswoman. He grinned. She'd become a little flustered when he'd mentioned that hug and kiss again. There was a softness under that businesswoman tough exterior. His gaze moved to the swing of her shapely hips. That wasn't bad either.

CHAPTER TWO

It HAD BEEN two days since Whitney had spoken briefly to Tanner about the social she had set up for him today. He'd assured her he would be there but he'd yet to show. She'd always had one of her clients meet her early so that they were waiting for the other one when he or she arrived.

Whitney looked around the coffee shop again. Still no Tanner. Picking up her phone, she texted him.

"Were you worried that I wouldn't show?" a deep voice asked from behind her.

She looked around and into Tanner's dark, twinkling eyes. He had nice eyes. Eyes she suspected saw more than he let on. "I was more worried about your tardiness hurting your chances with Michelle Watkins. After all, we're doing this for you."

"And I appreciate that. It's the reason I am here. So I'm going to be meeting Michelle. Five-six, brown hair, educated at UCLA and likes the outdoors." He came around the table and took the chair across from her.

"I see you remember your facts."

"So what happens now?" He leaned toward her as if what she was going to say was super important. She'd bet he had a great bedside manner.

"When Michelle arrives, I'll introduce you to each other, then I'll leave you to charm her."

His focus didn't waver. "How do you know I can do that?"

Tanner's intense attention made her nerves jump. She'd said more than she'd intended. Would he see the weakness and insecurity she worked to keep at bay? Since he hadn't remembered her she hadn't planned on bringing up their college years. Now she either lied to him or admitted she'd recognized him. She wasn't a liar. With her ex, Steve, she'd lived a lie and wouldn't ever treat anyone that way. "You and I had a few classes together at Berkeley."

He looked truly surprised. Cocking his head to the side, he asked, "We did?"

"Yeah. They were lower-level classes." From there she'd gone into business classes, he into sciences. She'd still seen him around campus, though.

He appeared to give that thought, as if searching back through his memories of those days. "I'm sorry, I don't remember you."

His tone led her to believe he was sincere. "There's no reason that you would."

Tanner leaned back in his chair and studied her. "So how does a woman with an education from Berkeley become a matchmaker?"

"Mostly by accident. I helped some people in college meet someone and then later did the same thing for my boss, and the rest is history."

He nodded sagely. "Just that easily you started a business matching people up?"

"It wasn't all that easy at first. But the word got around that I am discreet and, most of all, successful."

She glanced toward the front door then raised her hand, drawing Michelle Watkins's attention.

Tanner looked over his shoulder then quickly stood. Whitney gave him points for being a gentleman. But she wasn't the one he needed to impress. Michelle was. She was smiling, which was encouraging.

When the woman reached them Whitney introduced them. "Michelle, I'd like you to meet Tanner Locke."

Tanner offered Michelle his hand, along with a warm smile that Whitney recognized from their college days when he'd been charming a crowd of women. "It's a pleasure to meet you, Michelle. Please, join us."

Michelle couldn't seem to keep her eyes off Tanner. Was she already bowled over by him? Whitney was tempted to roll her eyes. The man's magic knew no bounds.

"Thank you," Michelle cooed, and took the chair Tanner held for her.

"Why don't I order us all something to drink?" Whitney suggested as a waitress came to the table.

"That would be nice," Michelle agreed, not taking her gaze off Tanner.

Whitney placed the order and the waitress left.

Tanner looked at Michelle. "I understand you like the outdoors."

"Yes," Michelle simpered. "I love to hike when I have the time."

Whitney sat back and listened as the two traded stories about their favorite hikes. They seemed to have forgotten she was there, something that had happened to her more than once in her life. She'd learned to live with it. This time it was part of her business.

The waitress brought their drinks, which swung Tanner's attention back to her. "Thank you for the lemonade.

I'll get these this time," he said to Whitney, then his attention returned to Michelle.

Whitney took a long swallow of the cool, tart liquid. Setting the glass on the table, she said, "I'll leave you both to get to know each other better. I'll be in touch."

Tanner nodded.

Michelle said, "Thank you, Whitney," before her attention went straight back to Tanner.

Whitney walked to the front door. She looked back at them. They made a nice-looking pair. Two dark-haired, well-groomed, professional people who looked as if they were enjoying each other's company.

That was what her matchmaking was all about. So why couldn't she do that for herself?

Two days later, Whitney answered the phone.

"We need to talk."

Whitney didn't have to question who she was speaking to. She knew that voice at the first roll of a vowel. This time it wasn't warm and creamy. It was icy and sharp.

"Tanner, is something wrong?" She kept her voice low and even. She didn't often have to talk a client down after a social or a date.

"Michelle won't do. We need to meet again. Bring that file."

Whitney stiffened. She wasn't one of his OR nurses to be ordered around. "What's wrong?"

"I don't have time to talk about it now."

And he thinks I do?

"Let me see. How about the coffeehouse on Market Street tomorrow morning around nine?"

"I have surgery then. Could you come to the hospital in about an hour?"

What? She wasn't at his beck and call. She'd already

gone out of her way for him once and now he wanted her to drop what she was doing and drive downtown. "I don't know. That isn't how I like to conduct business. I thought you didn't want anyone to know you were using my services. Aren't you afraid someone might ask you questions?"

"They might but I don't have to answer. Whitney, it would really help me out if you could come here. I'm tied up with cases but I'd really like to get this other stuff rolling along."

Other stuff rolling along.

Was that how he thought of the woman who would share the rest of his life? She was glad she didn't fit his list.

Unfortunately, she didn't really have a good excuse why she couldn't help him out. "Okay, but I won't be doing this again."

"Great. Just give me a call when you get here." He hung up.

Tanner hadn't even said goodbye. It was time to have a heart-to-heart with him about whether or not he was really interested in doing the work needed to find a soul mate.

The traffic was light so she made good time going up and down the hills of San Francisco. The city could be difficult to drive in but the views of the bay made it worth it. She was just sorry a streetcar didn't run close enough to the hospital for her to take one of those.

She found a parking spot in the high-rise lot next to the hospital. Crossing the street, she entered the towering hospital. In the lobby, she pulled out her phone and called Tanner's number. Never in her wildest dreams would she ever have imagined having it at her fingertips. She and Tanner didn't move in the same circles and never would.

He answered as he had before. There was an arrogance to how he responded but the crisp sound of his last name seemed to suit him.

"It's Whitney."

"Hey." His tone changed as if he was glad to hear from her. She liked that idea too much. Obviously since he'd gotten his way he had calmed down. "From the main lobby door continue down the long hallway to the second bank of elevators on your right. They'll be about halfway down the hall. Take one of them. Come up to the fifth floor. I'll meet you at the elevator."

Tanner didn't wait for her to answer before closing the connection. That she wasn't as accepting of. She'd rather be told goodbye.

Whitney found the bank of elevators and took the next available car. At the correct floor she stepped off. As good as his word, Tanner stood there, talking to another man also dressed in scrubs. When he saw her he left the man and strolled over to her.

He was the epitome of the tall, dark and handsome doctor. He still had the looks that drew women's attention. What had happened between him and Michelle she couldn't fathom.

Michelle had called yesterday morning all but glowing about the social and the date they'd had the night before. How she could have seen it as being so wonderful while Tanner was so unhappy was a mystery to Whitney.

"Thanks for coming." Tanner ran his hand over his hair. "I know it wasn't what you wanted to do. I had to come in last night to do an emergency surgery. I just couldn't get away today. I have one more patient to see. Would you mind hanging out for a little bit?"

If he'd asked her that in college she might have fainted. Now Whitney only saw him as a man who needed her services. "Sure. I wouldn't mind watching what you do. It might help me better understand you, which would assist me in matching you."

"All business, all the time."

"You're one to be talking," she quipped.

He grinned. "You're not the first person to say that. After I see this patient we'll go to my office to talk."

They walked down a hall until they came to double doors. Tanner scanned a card and the doors opened from the middle out. They entered a hallway with patients' rooms. He stopped at the third doorway along the passage. "This is Mr. Wilcox. Let me get permission for you to come in."

"I don't mind waiting out here."

Tanner touched her arm when she started to move to the other side of the hall. A zing of awareness traveled up her arm. "He's rather lonely. He'd like to have the company. See a face that has nothing to do with the hospital."

That was a side of Tanner she hadn't expected. Compassion beyond the medicine. "Then I'll be glad to say hi."

Tanner raised his hand to knock on the door but turned back to her. "He has a lot of pumps and drips hooked to him. That stuff doesn't bother you, does it?"

She smiled. "No, I promise not to faint or stare."

"Good." Tanner appeared pleased with her answer. Had other women he'd known acted negatively to what he did for a living? He knocked on the door and stuck his head around it. There was a rumble of voices, then Tanner waved her toward him.

"We'll need to wear masks." He pulled a yellow paper one from a box on a table outside the door and handed it to her before entering the room. She followed.

Mr. Wilcox was about her father's age, but his skin

was an ash gray. Beside him was a bank of machines with lights. There was a whish of air coming from one. A clear rubber tube circled both the man's ears and came around to fit under his nose.

"Mr. Wilcox, I brought you a visitor," Tanner said.

The man's dull eyes brightened for a second as he looked at her.

"Whitney Thomason, I'd like you to meet Jim Wilcox."

"Nice to meet you, young lady," Mr. Wilcox wheezed as he raised a hand weakly toward her.

"You too, Mr. Wilcox." Whitney stepped closer to the bed.

"So how're you feeling?" Tanner asked, leaning forward, concern written on his face.

Whitney was impressed with the lower timbre of his voice, which sounded as if he truly wished to know. She could grow to admire this Tanner.

"Oh, about the same. This contraption—" Mr. Wilcox nodded toward the swishing machine beside him "—is keeping me alive but I'm still stuck in this bed."

"Well, maybe there'll be a heart soon."

"That's what you've been telling me for weeks now. I'm starting to think you're holding out on me." Mr. Wilcox offered a small smile and perked up when he looked at her. "At least you were kind enough today to bring me something pretty to look at."

Whitney blushed. "Thanks but—"

"Aw, don't start all that stuttering and blustering. I have a feeling your beauty goes more than skin deep."

Whitney really did feel heat in her cheeks then. "I think that might be the nicest compliment I've ever received."

Tanner's eyes met hers and held. Did he agree with Mr. Wilcox? Did he see something that others didn't?

The older man cleared his throat.

Tanner's attention returned to him. "Okay, Romeo. I need to give you a listen." He pulled his stethoscope from around his neck. "I might have done a bad thing by inviting Whitney in."

"If I promise to be nice, will you bring her back again?" Mr. Wilcox asked with enthusiasm in every word.

Whitney touched the older man's arm. "Don't worry, he doesn't have to invite me for me to come again."

She felt more than saw Tanner glance at her.

"Then I'll look forward to it. So tell me how you know this quack over here?" Mr. Wilcox indicated Tanner.

Her gaze met Tanner's. There was panic in his gaze. He probably didn't want the man to know she was helping him find a wife. "Oh, we were in college together."

Tanner's brows rose. He nodded as if he was pleased with her response.

"Where'd you go?" Mr. Wilcox rasped.

"Berkeley," she told him.

"Then you got a fine education."

Tanner interrupted them with, "So, are you having any chest pains?"

Mr. Wilcox paused. "No."

"That's good. You seem to be holding your own." Tanner flipped through the chart he'd brought in with him and laid it on the bed tray. "You need to be eating more. You have to keep your energy up."

"I'll try but nothing tastes good." Mr. Wilcox pushed at the bed table as if there was something offensive on it.

"Not even ice cream?" Tanner asked.

"I've eaten all those little cups I can stand. I'd like a

good old-fashioned banana split that I could share with someone like your young lady."

Tanner chuckled. "When you get your heart and are out of here I'll see if I can get Whitney to come back and bring you a fat-free split."

"Fat-free," he spat.

"That's it," Tanner said with a grin.

"Well, if Whitney shares it with me maybe I can live with it. She has nice eyes. Windows to the soul, they say." Mr. Wilcox smiled.

"That she does," Tanner agreed.

Whitney looked at Tanner. Did he really mean that? She'd had no indication that he'd noticed anything about her.

"So is she your girlfriend?"

"Just friends," she and Tanner said at the same time.

Whitney wasn't sure that their professional association qualified as friendship. Tanner wanted his personal business kept private, so "friends" seemed the right thing to say. Could they be friends? She didn't know. What she did recognize was that she liked the Tanner who was concerned enough about his patient's loneliness to invite her to meet him just to cut the monotony of being in the hospital day after day. That was a Tanner she could find a match for. Sad that the other Tanner wouldn't let this one show up more often.

"Even behind that mask I can tell she's pretty enough to be your girlfriend. You can always tell a special woman by her eyes. My wife, Milly, had beautiful eyes."

Tanner put his hand on the man's shoulder. "I think we'd better be going."

Whitney touched Mr. Wilcox's arm briefly. "I hope to see you again soon. It was nice to meet you."

He lifted a hand and waved as she reached the door. "You too. You're welcome to my abode anytime."

Whitney smiled. She liked Mr. Wilcox. "Bye, now."

Tanner joined her. "See you soon, Mr. Wilcox."

"You too, Doc."

Whitney stepped out into the hall and Tanner followed, pulling the door closed behind him.

As they removed their masks Tanner said, "I'm sorry if he made you feel uncomfortable in there or put you on the spot about being with me. Mr. Wilcox can be pretty cheeky."

"I didn't mind. He seems like a nice guy who's lonely."

"He is. As a doctor I'm not supposed to have favorites but I really like the man. He's been waiting too long."

She watched for his reaction as she said, "That's why you took me to see him. You knew he needed something to prick his interest. You didn't mind him assuming I was your girlfriend because that would give him something to figure out, live for."

"Why, Ms. Thomason, you are smart."

Whitney couldn't deny her pleasure at his praise. She also couldn't help but ask, "I know you can't tell me details, but what's going on with Mr. Wilcox?"

Tanner's eyes took on a haunted look. "Most of it you heard. He's waiting for a heart. He needs one pretty quickly."

"Or he'll die," she said quietly.

Tanner's eyes took on a shadowed look. "Yeah."

"You seem to take that in your stride." She sounded as if she was condemning him even to her own ears.

"It's a part of what I do. Medical School 101. But that doesn't mean I like it." His retort was crisp. He started down the hall and she followed. At the desk he handed a nurse Mr. Wilcox's chart and continued on. "My office is this way. I'm on call tonight."

Whitney had to hurry to keep up with him. They walked down a couple of hallways to a nondescript door. Again Tanner swiped his card. There was a click. He turned the doorknob and entered. She trailed him down a short hall to a small sterile-looking office. It became even smaller when Tanner stepped in.

There was a metal desk with a black high-backed chair behind it and a metal chair in front. What struck her as most interesting was the absence of pictures. Didn't he have family? Nieces or nephews? A dog?

"Please, come in." Tanner walked around the desk and settled into the chair. Was his home this cold as well? Could he open his life enough to have a wife and family?

Whitney sat in the uncomfortable utilitarian chair. Apparently whoever visited wasn't encouraged to stay long. "I understand from Michelle that she had a wonderful time the other night. So what's the problem on your side?"

Tanner picked up a pen and twisted it through his fingers, a sure sign he wasn't comfortable with the question. "She wanted something that I won't give."

There was a chilly breeze in the words. "That is?"

"Let's just say she was already getting more emotionally attached than I want to be. You need to go through your file and find me some women who are interested in security, financial comfort, social status, not whether or not they are loved. I'm looking for something far more solid than love. Companionship."

Whitney felt like she'd been punched in the chest. She'd never heard anything sadder. All the compassion she'd just seen Tanner show Mr. Wilcox was gone. Now all she saw was a shell of a man. For him a heart was nothing more than an organ that pumped blood. Not the center of life she believed it to be. "The women I represent all want to be loved."

He put his elbows on the desk and steepled his fingers, giving her a direct look. "For the amount of money I'm paying you I expect you to find someone who suits my needs. I thought I'd made it clear what I wanted in a relationship. It's your business to find me that match."

If he had slapped her she couldn't have been more insulted. "I assure you I know my business. I'll set up a social with the next client on my list for as soon as possible." She looked him in the eyes. "But you should know, Tanner, it's my experience that most people see marriage less as a business deal and more as an emotional attachment."

Tanner's face turned stern. His voice was firm when he said, "That might be the case but that isn't the type of person I'm looking for. I've made my request and you've stated you can fill it, so that's what I expect."

What had happened to the man? How could he be so compassionate toward his patient but so calculating about the type of wife he wanted? Whitney stood. "I'll be in touch soon."

He got to his feet as well. "Good. If you take a right out of my door you'll come to a set of elevators. It'll take you down to the lobby. Thanks for coming here."

She'd been dismissed. That was fine with her. Whitney turned on her heel and left. Right now she wasn't sure if she should keep Tanner as a client. Truth be known, she wasn't certain she even liked him.

Tanner was at Café Lombard for the "social" before Whitney or the woman he was to meet. When Whitney had left his office the other evening she hadn't been happy. Her lips had been pinched tight and her chin had jutted out. Somehow what he had said she had taken personally. Hadn't he made it clear what he was looking for in a relationship during their earlier interview? Couldn't she understand that he had no interest in a love match?

Those only led to pain, not just between the husband and wife but for the children as well. He and his brother were a prime example of that. They hadn't seen each other in years. Tanner wanted a marriage based on something solid and not fleeting, like an emotion.

His date with Michelle had been wonderful. They'd had a number of things in common. They both enjoyed the outdoors, liked baseball and traveling. It wasn't that he didn't like Michelle, but he could tell by her speech and her body language that she was looking for more than he could give. There had been hopeful stars in her eyes. He wanted someone whose expectations were less dreamlike and more firmly rooted in reality.

Statements like "Children should know that their parents care about each other. It makes for a more stable child," or "I want a husband who can be there when I need him," showed him that Michelle needed emotional support that he just couldn't give. Tanner wanted someone who could handle their own ups and downs without involving him.

He looked up to see Whitney entering. The displeased expression she'd worn the other day was gone but there was still a tightness around her lips, indicating she might not be in the best of moods. When had he started being able to read so well someone he hardly knew?

He half stood. She flashed a smile of greeting. It was an all-business tilt of the lips instead of actual gladness to see him. Tanner didn't much care for that. Yet why did it bother him to have her disgruntled with him?

Today Whitney wore a flowing dress with a small pale pink rose pattern on it that reached just past her knees. A sweater was pulled over her shoulders and the sleeves tied across her chest. She was dressed like an old-maid schoolteacher. Why did she wear such nondescript clothing? Did she do it because she thought people believed that was how a matchmaker should dress? She was too young and too attractive not to flaunt it some. What would she look like in a tight, short skirt? He'd be interested to see. Great, would be his guess. But why should it matter to him how she dressed?

"Hello, Tanner." She took the chair across from him. "You're early."

"My last case was canceled due to a fever so I got away from the hospital sooner than I thought I would."

Whitney clasped her hands in her lap and looked directly at him. "I think you work too hard and too many hours." It wasn't an accusation, more a statement of fact. She didn't give him time to respond before she continued. "You're going to meet Racheal today. I think you'll really like her. She has a master's degree in business and loves children."

"I remember reading her profile. Did you make it clear to her what I am looking for?"

"I did. She's interested in a family but doesn't want to give over her freedom just to have that. She's looking for the same type of relationship that you are." Whitney made it sound as if the idea left a bad taste in her mouth.

"Do you have a problem with that?"

She shrugged then leaned back in the chair. "Not if that's what you both want."

He leaned forward, piercing her with a look.

She shifted in the chair.

Tanner crossed his arms on the table. "Tell me what you think this should be about."

Her eyes widened. She did have pretty ones. Like

green grass after spring rain. She blinked. "It isn't about what I think but about what you want."

"Spoken like a true matchmaker, eager to please. Are you married, Whitney?"

Her chin raised a notch. "I don't believe that has anything to do with your case."

"It might not but it gives me an idea of how good you are at this matchmaking business."

She shifted in her chair. "If you don't have any confidence if my ability then I'll be glad to refund your money minus five hundred dollars for the work I've done so far."

He'd hit a touchy spot. "And add the charge for the hug and kiss after all?"

She relaxed and shook her head. "No. I wouldn't do that. This isn't a joke."

He leaned back in the chair and watched her for a long moment. Her direct look challenged his. This was a woman who wouldn't give up until she had succeeded. "You're right—it isn't. I'm not ready to throw in the towel yet."

"Then you do understand that I have the same responsibility to the women I introduce you to as I do to you?"

She had backbone and a moral line. What you saw was what you got with Whitney. That was refreshing. Most women he knew were only really interested in themselves. "I realize that. I'll try to be on my best behavior."

"I'm starting to wonder what that is. I also expect you to give them a fair chance." Her tone had become schoolmarmish.

"You don't think I gave Michelle that?"

She didn't immediately answer. "Truthfully, I'm not sure you did."

It didn't matter to him if she thought so or not. He knew what he wanted better than she did, matchmaker or not. It was his life they were talking about. He'd seen what uninvited and unrequited love did to a person. He wanted none of it. Good, solid, practical thought was what his marriage would be based on.

A blonde woman stepped up to their table. Whitney jerked around as if she'd forgotten all about her joining them. Tanner smiled. She'd been too flustered by his questions to remember why they were there. He liked the idea that he'd rattled Whitney. Too much.

"Hello, Racheal. I'm sorry I didn't see you when you came in." Whitney's voice sounded a little higher than normal.

Once again, Whitney was a contrast to her female client. Racheal had a short haircut and every strand was in its place. Her makeup was flawless and she wore the latest fashion with ease. She certainly looked the part of the woman he thought he would like to share his name. He looked at Whitney and somehow he found her more to his taste. Shaking that thought away, Tanner returned his attention to Racheal.

He stood and offered his hand to her. "Tanner Locke. Thanks for joining us."

He held a chair out for Racheal and she gracefully slipped into it.

"It's nice to meet you." Racheal had a no-nonsense note in her voice.

He looked at Whitney. "I've already ordered drinks."

"Thank you, Tanner. I think I'll leave you and Racheal to get to know each other better. I'll be in touch soon."

Tanner remained standing as she left. A tug of disappointment went through him to see her go. Why?

Whitney hadn't heard from Tanner in three days. Far too often she had found herself wondering how things were

going between him and Racheal. She liked to give her
clients time to get to know each other and digest their
thoughts on the new match before she asked. This time
she was particularly anxious to know.

Racheal had already checked in. She seemed pleased
with Tanner. According to her, they'd had a wonderful
time talking at the social and had enjoyed their first date.
Maybe she had found the right one for Tanner after all.
But she had thought that with Michelle. She would wait
until tomorrow and give him a call. See if he was as
pleased as Racheal.

That evening Whitney was just slipping into bed when
her phone rang. A call this late usually didn't mean good
news. Was her father ill again? "Hello?"

"It's Tanner."

His voice was low and gravelly. There was no apology for calling so late. She wasn't surprised. But with
his schedule he probably thought nothing of it. "Yes?"

"You told me to call and let you know how things
are going."

She had indeed told him that but had assumed he
would do so during business hours. An edgy feeling
washed over her, knowing she was in bed while talking
to Tanner. It seemed far too evocative. She flipped the
covers back and stood beside the bed.

"Racheal seems to be working out. We went out last
night. I have a party on Friday that I've invited her to."
His voice was low and calm, as if he had all the time in
the world to talk.

"I'm glad to hear it. I'll check in with you both next
week. I look forward to hearing how the relationship is
progressing."

"How have you been?" His voice was warm and silky.
Whitney walked to the window. "I'm fine."

"That's good. Goodnight."

Whitney listened to the click on the other end of the line. She returned to her bed and pulled the covers over herself again. Somehow the sheets didn't feel as cool anymore.

Maybe Racheal was it. Had Tanner found the one he wanted? Whitney wished she felt happier about that idea.

Even if he hadn't, he wouldn't look at her that way. Did she want him to? Turning off the light, she settled under the covers, but it took her far too long to fall asleep.

Whitney continued to wonder how things were going between Tanner and Racheal. More than once she'd been tempted to call him but had held back. She'd never had that problem before. Normally she let her couples go without thought or overseeing them, but Tanner's case held too much of her attention.

Whitney was already asleep a week later when the phone rang. She picked up the phone and a man's voice said, "Just what type of women are you introducing me to? You're supposed to be the best at this."

"Tanner, what's going on? Do you know what time it is?"

"Yes. I know what time it is." He sounded angry.

At this point the time didn't matter. She was awake anyway. Despite that, she found herself happy to finally hear from him. "What's the problem?"

"The problem is that Racheal backed out of a weekend we had planned in Napa. It's a hospital retreat and I had already said I would be bringing a guest. I'm trying to make a positive impression on the board. This situation could hurt my chance for a promotion."

"I'm sorry." And she was. He was a good doctor and deserved it, she was sure.

"You should be. I hold you responsible."

"Me!" Whitney squeaked and set up in bed.

"I'm paying you to provide me with women who understand the importance of my job and position."

What was he raving about? "Racheal didn't?"

"I guess not. She agreed to go and now at the last minute she's backed out."

Whitney worked to keep her tone even. "Did she give you a reason?"

"She just said she wasn't ready for this step."

That sounded reasonable to Whitney. "You can't expect her to do something that she isn't comfortable with."

"I damn well can expect her to keep her word."

He had a point there, but what did he imagine she could do about it? She couldn't make Racheal go with him. "I have to honor what my clients feel they need to do."

"And you have to honor our contract. I need someone as my girlfriend this weekend."

It was Thursday. How was she going to find someone who would go away with a perfect stranger on such short notice? "I wish I could help you, Tanner. At this point I don't know what I can do."

"Well, I do. If you can't find me someone then you have to come. At least that way I'll be bringing a guest. I can make up a story about how we broke up later."

What? Is he crazy? Spend a weekend with him?

"That's not possible. It's unethical. You're my client."

"One you're expected to keep happy. You were supposed to vet the women you introduce me to. You failed in determining Racheal's true character. I expect you to meet your professional obligation."

How did that logically extend to her personally replacing a client?

"Look, this weekend is important to my career, just

as finding the right woman is. There will be no expectations on my part except for you to be pleasant and act as if we're a couple." His voice was firm and determined, as if he wouldn't accept no as an answer.

Whitney's heart pounded. Was she seriously going to consider it? "You can't just demand that I spend the weekend with you."

"Sure I can." His voice had turned hard. "We have a contract for services and you need to hold up your end. It was your suggestion that I pick Racheal. She didn't hold up her end so that defaults to you."

Whitney wasn't sure she agreed with his reasoning but she didn't need him bad-mouthing her around town. She'd taken Tanner on as a client to increase her professional profile, not to hurt it. Plus, she hated that he was in a spot.

If she agreed to his demand she couldn't imagine the weekend being anything but long and miserable. She didn't belong in his social group. She was an outsider. Tanner wanted someone who could make a good impression. More than once she'd been judged by her looks. He needed someone who could influence. That wasn't her. She was good with people one on one but not as a member of a house party. To run in Tanner's world…

"I'll pick you up at nine in the morning. What's your address?"

"Tanner, I can't do this."

"Oh, yes, you can," he all but hollered down the phone.

He wasn't going to allow her a way out. Apprehension bubbled in Whitney as she gave him her address.

"You'll need a cocktail dress, swimsuit and casual clothes." There was a click on the other end of the line. Tanner had hung up. Once again.

Whitney lay there. What had just happened? She'd just

gotten press-ganged into a weekend with Tanner as his "plus one." What was he thinking? What *was* she doing?

Those bubbles combined into a heavy mass of dread in her chest. She wasn't part of Tanner's world. What if she made a mistake and embarrassed him?

If she had really changed from that insecure girl from years ago it was time to prove it.

CHAPTER THREE

TANNER DIDN'T KNOW what had gotten into him when he'd insisted that Whitney join him on this weekend retreat. He had been so angry when Racheal had called and told him that she wouldn't be going that he'd picked up the phone and dialed Whitney's number without a thought. But to insist she attend a weekend with him might have been overreacting. Desperation had fueled his demand. He needed a woman on his arm.

Well, it was done now.

For him to have a "significant other" with him for the weekend was an unwritten requirement. Besides, he might have hinted to one or two of the board members that he'd become serious about someone. It mustn't look like he'd been lying or he could kiss that promotion goodbye.

He pulled his car to the curb in front of Whitney's home. To his surprise, he'd known the address. She lived in one of the famous "painted ladies." Whitney stood waiting in front of a light blue Victorian row house with a yellow door and white gingerbread trimmings. Pink flowers grew in pots on the steps. The house was an obvious reflection of Whitney. He'd always liked these old homes. Something about them said life was peaceful inside.

Whitney looked small compared to the towering three-story home. His heart fell. This wasn't good. She wore a full shirt that hung almost to her knees and underneath she wore baggy pajama-style pants and flat slippers. Her hair was pulled back into a bun. Whitney couldn't have looked more nondescript if she had tried. He really couldn't force her to dress better, or could he?

Stepping out of the car, Tanner went to the trunk and opened it.

Whitney joined him with her bags in her hand. "Tanner, I think we should really reconsider this idea."

"I've already done that a couple of times and I don't see another way. I need a girlfriend for this weekend and you are it." Even if her sense of style was missing.

Uncertainty filled her eyes. "This type of thing really isn't me."

"You'll be fine. Sitting by the pool and reading all day works for me. I just need you to attend the dinner this evening and tomorrow evening and all will be good."

She didn't look any more enthused but she let him take her bags and climbed into the car.

Yet again he felt bad about insisting she come with him, but he needed her. The board members would be at this retreat and he had to give them the impression he was getting close to settling down. "Do you mind if I put the top down? It's a beautiful day."

"Not at all. I love a convertible."

Tanner leaned over her to unlock the roof from the windshield. A floral scent that fit her perfectly assaulted his nose. Maybe the weekend wouldn't be so bad. He flipped the other lock above his head. When he pushed a button, the roof slowly folded down behind them.

"I like your car. It suits you," Whitney said.

"Thanks. I grew up wanting one of these and when I finished medical school I bought one."

"I've always loved two-seaters. I'm going to enjoy riding in this one." She gave him a weak smile.

So at least they had that in common. As Tanner started the car, Whitney pulled a long multicolored scarf out of her purse. With deft efficiency she wrapped it around her head and tied it under her chin. Great, now he had Old Mother Hubbard with him. Why did she dress like she did?

"The only complaint I have about having the top down is that it's hard on a hairdo."

He'd never really thought of her as having a hairstyle. Her hair had always been just pulled back behind her neck when he'd seen her. Today was no different. She didn't seem to make any real effort to stand out where her appearance was concerned. What was she hiding from? Now with the scarf around her head she looked drabber than ever. That was with the exception of when she smiled. At those times she captured his attention completely.

It disturbed him on a level he didn't want to examine how much time he'd spent thinking about his matchmaker in the past few weeks. Even when he and Racheal had been dating he'd wondered what Whitney would think about this or that, or what she was doing. These were not things his mind should have been contemplating. Racheal had seemed perfect for him, just what he'd asked for, so why had he been thinking about another woman?

Especially Whitney. There could never be any real interest there. They clearly didn't want the same things out of a relationship. He had no plans to ever love a woman. His parents had seen to that.

Tanner's attention remained on his driving as he made

his way up and down the steep streets of San Francisco lined with houses and businesses. He glanced at Whitney a couple of times. She seemed absorbed in the city life around them. Once he caught her looking at him. She made him feel both uncomfortable and pleased.

As they waited at the toll booth at the Golden Gate Bridge she said, "I love this bridge. It's like this big smiling sentinel standing over the bay, protecting it."

"I've never thought about it like that. For me it's a feat of engineering, from the rock foundation to the suspension towers to the length of the wires."

"Or maybe it's like a big swing. Either way, it's amazing."

Tanner looked at her and grinned. "Agreed."

"Did you know that as soon as they finish painting it they have to start over again?" Whitney had her neck craned back, looking up at one of the three soaring towers.

He smiled. "I did. That's a lot of red paint."

Tanner paid the toll and they started across the bridge.

Halfway over the bay Whitney said, "The thump-thump of the tires reminds me of a heartbeat." A few seconds later she continued, "It's mind-boggling to me that I actually know someone who has held a heart in his hand."

Tanner grinned. "I'm glad I can impress." He wasn't sure he had so far during their acquaintance.

Traffic was heavy, even for a Friday morning, as people were leaving the city for the weekend. The road widened and the driving became easier after they were over the bridge. Tanner had been accused of being a fast driver but Whitney didn't seem bothered by his weaving in and out of traffic. Her hands remained in her lap and her chin up as if she were a flower enjoying the sunshine.

As they headed off the bridge toward the green rolling hills on the way to Napa she asked, "So what's expected of me this weekend?"

"Mostly to act as if you like me."

She met his eyes. "I'll try."

For some reason it disturbed him that she didn't already like him. "I know I've been a little high-handed a couple of times—"

Her brows rose. "A couple? How about all the time?"

Tanner shrugged a shoulder as he changed lanes. "Okay, maybe I deserve that, but I really need your help this weekend."

"You could have asked."

He glanced at her. "Would you have done it?"

"No…" The word trailed off.

Tanner's focus went back to the black sedan he was following. "So I would've had to apply pressure anyway. How about I double your fee for your trouble?"

She shook her head. "Let me think about it. No. That would make me feel like a prostitute."

He didn't like her accusation at all. "Whoa, that isn't what this is about. You won't be expected to sleep with me. In fact, I don't expect you to do anything more than hold on to my arm and pretend to be my girlfriend." Turning left, he followed a sign to Napa.

"Sleeping with you wasn't what I was referring to. I have no intention of doing that."

She made it sound as if he wasn't good enough for her. That was a first for him. Women were usually more than eager to climb into his bed. Why wouldn't she be? Was she holding on to her favors until she found that "love" she was so fond of believing in? Maybe he was just the person to change her mind.

Wait, that wasn't what this weekend was about. He'd

promised sex wouldn't be on the agenda. He had no business thinking that way. Whitney was his matchmaker, and only with him because he had insisted. This wasn't some weekend fling. He had to remember that.

"So what're the sleeping arrangements?" Whitney asked in the matter-of-fact way he'd come to expect from her.

"We'll have to share a room but I'll give you as much privacy as possible. I'll sleep on the floor if necessary." That he wasn't looking forward to. But she was doing him a favor so it was the least he could do to try to make her as comfortable in the situation as possible.

"And what're the other plans for the weekend?"

"There is a round of golf organized for this afternoon and tomorrow." The land flattened as they entered the valley, allowing him to look at Whitney more often.

She met his look. "Do you play golf?"

"Not really. But I'll make a showing just to be a team player." Why did he feel like she was accusing him of being dishonest?

"I wouldn't have thought that was your style. Impressing the board really is important to you, isn't it?"

"It is." Tanner straightened in the seat a little. He wasn't ashamed of it. The promotion meant everything to his career.

"Is the department head position so vital?"

He felt her studying him. "Yes. It's my chance to make a difference in my field. Help people. I can influence the way we do transplants, lead the development of new skills."

"That's to be admired." He heard the approval in her voice.

Tanner glanced at her. He rather liked the glow of respect in her eyes.

* * *

Whitney couldn't keep the sigh of pleasure from rushing out of her as they drove up a long lane lined with neat row after row of vines for as far as she could see. The contrast of the deep brown of the rich dirt, the vivid green of the grape leaves and the tranquil blue of the sky was almost breathtaking. She glanced at Tanner.

And she was spending a weekend here with him. Her life had become surreal. She was off with a man that she hardly knew, pretending to be his serious girlfriend, and in a social situation she wasn't comfortable in. How was she not going to make a mess of it?

"Ever been to Napa?" Tanner asked, without taking his eyes off the road.

"Not really."

"I think you'll like it. We're staying at a vineyard with a hotel attached. One of the board members owns it. I understand there's a pool, tennis courts, a spa and just about anything else you might like. And, of course, there's wine."

He made it sound like she would be on her own most of the time, which suited her just fine. She didn't consider herself much of an actress so trying to convince people of the improbable idea that she and Tanner were a couple was distressing.

Finally they drove out of the vines into an open space where a huge structure that looked like a French château stood. Tall, thin trees flanked it on both sides and a manicured yard begged for Whitney to lie in the emerald-colored grass. If she'd been impressed with the landscape on the drive here, this view made her catch her breath. It was picture-perfect and despite the reason she was there Whitney could hardly wait to see inside.

Tanner leaned over and said close to her ear. "See, it's not going to be all bad, being here with me."

Whitney turned. Her mouth stopped only inches from his. Her heart fluttered. She looked into his velvety brown eyes. They could swallow her up if she let them and she would never know how it had happened. For long moments, though far too short for her, she waited, watched. Dreamed. Tanner's head lowered a fraction. He was going to kiss her. No, this wasn't what this weekend was about.

She blinked and quickly pulled back. She wouldn't be his plaything. She wasn't in his league when it came to casual affairs, she was sure. He would win every time. "I didn't say it was going to be bad. I just don't like being told what I'm going to do."

He leaned back and looked at her. "Noted. With that in mind, I'm asking you, not telling, would you please take off that hideous scarf before someone comes out?"

Whitney didn't have time to reply before the door to the hotel opened and a sophisticatedly dressed woman started their way. Quickly Whitney removed the scarf and the band securing her hair. Shaking it loose, she ran a hand through it. She looked to Tanner. "Better?"

A strange look had come over his face and he said softly, "Much." Seconds later a crease marred his forehead. "Can we keep what you do for a living between ourselves?"

"I won't lie."

His look held hers. "Maybe just evade the question."

A young man in a knit shirt and khaki pants followed close behind the woman. This was a far fancier place than Whitney had expected.

"Hello, Tanner. Welcome to the Garonne Winery," the woman said warmly as Tanner stepped out of the car.

The young man opened Whitney's door for her. She said, "Thank you," and received a warm smile.

"Marie Jarvis, I'd like you to meet Whitney Thomason," Tanner said from the other side of the car.

Marie stepped to Whitney with a well-manicured hand extended. "It's so nice to meet a special friend of Tanner's."

Whitney smiled and took her hand. Marie had no idea just how *special* a friend Whitney was.

Marie waved Tanner away from the trunk of the car. "Kevin will see to your bags and park your car. Just come join us by the pool. We have cool drinks waiting."

"That sounds lovely," Whitney said.

Tanner offered her an encouraging smile. On their way to the door he took her hand. His touch sent a tingle of awareness through her. It was so powerful that for a second she almost jerked away. Remembering they had to pretend they were a couple, she got control of herself. She hadn't counted on her body's reaction to being in such close contact with Tanner. Or how hard she would have to work to remember his touches were just for show. She tried to appear relaxed but her insides were a jumble of knotted nerves. Tanner gave her fingers a squeeze. Did he sense the effect he was having on her?

He allowed her to enter ahead of him through the tall double doors that opened into the cool dimness of the château. The entrance hall was every bit as astounding as the outside. A wrought-iron staircase circled up on both sides of the foyer to a landing. On each side of the landing were large windows with heavy drapes. From there, the stairs climbed again to branch off right and left. To one side of the foyer there was a small Queen Anne–style desk with an attractive young woman seated behind it.

Marie waved in the woman's direction and she smiled

before Marie said to them, "Don't worry about checking in. I've already taken care of everything."

Kevin moved across the gray tile floor past them, laden with baggage, and headed up the stairs.

"The pool is this way." Marie walked toward the back of the building.

As they stepped out into the bright light once more, the scene reminded Whitney of a 1940s picture of a movie star's pool. The men stood in groups, talking, with drinks in their hands while the women sunbathed on loungers.

A flutter of anxiety went through her. She was in over her head. Could she get out of this now? What did she have in common with these people? Tanner expected her to mix and mingle. How was she supposed to do that?

When she would have pulled her hand out of Tanner's he gripped it tighter. Had he read her mind and been afraid she might run? Somehow his clasp gave her confidence. Taking a deep breath, Whitney reminded herself that she was no longer that overweight girl who'd felt inadequate for so long. Or at least she didn't plan to let anyone make her feel that way. She was educated, owned her own business and paid her bills. There was nothing for her to feel ashamed of.

Marie said, "Tanner, why don't you introduce Whitney around then you both can change into your bathing suits and join us."

Whitney scanned the area. Even the women who were twice her age seemed to have better bodies than she did. Stretch marks and extra skin still plagued her, despite the number of years that had passed since she'd lost so much weight. Wearing a swimsuit in front of these people, particularly Tanner, wasn't something she was interested in doing.

Tanner's hand on her waist directed her toward the

closest group of people. She wasn't used to his touch and certainly not to her reaction to it. If the situation didn't make her nervous enough, Tanner's close proximity did. Why? She wasn't even sure she liked him.

As they approached the group the circle opened to include them.

A man with more white than dark hair and a round belly stepped forward. "Tanner, glad you could make it."

"Malcolm, thanks for having us." Tanner gave her a slight nudge. "I'd like you to meet Whitney. Whitney, this is Malcolm Jarvis, the chairman of the hospital board and the owner of the Garonne Winery. Best known, though, as Marie's husband."

"Yes, yes. Good to meet you." Malcolm smiled at her.

Whitney couldn't help but return one of her own. "Nice to meet you as well. You have a beautiful place here."

"Thank you. Please, make yourself at home this week-end. All the hotel amenities are open to you while you're here."

Tanner faced another man. "This is Dr. Russell Karr, the medical chair and my boss."

Dr. Karr offered his hand. She took it and received a firm shake as he said, "Nice to meet you, Whitney. I look forward to getting to know you."

"And I you." To her amazement she'd managed to say that without her voice wavering.

His hand still on the small of her back, which was surprisingly reassuring, Tanner guided her around the pool. He introduced her to each guest, which included Sue Ann, Russell's wife, Ellen and Carlos Gonzales, and Lucy and Rick Hunt.

A woman close to their age, wearing a skimpy yellow bikini, stood as Whitney and Tanner came around the end of the pool toward her lounger. She rushed to Tanner and threw her arms around his neck.

Something about their friendliness said there was history between them. Whitney's radar went off. She wasn't going to like this person. Why should it matter what their relationship had been? Tanner didn't belong to her.

"Hello, Charlotte." Tanner's voice didn't sound as warm as her hug would suggest. He removed her arms and stepped away. "I'd like you to meet my girlfriend, Whitney Thomason."

The word *girlfriend* had rolled off his tongue as if it were the truth. Had he put extra emphasis on the word as well? It took all of Whitney's willpower not to stare at him as he continued, "Whitney, this is Charlotte Rivers. Her fiancé is Max Little and *he* is a member of the board. By the way, where is Max?"

Charlotte looked at Whitney as if she were something she would pull off the bottom of her shoe. "He'll be here later this evening. There was a last-minute case."

Not a good history, would be Whitney's guess.

"I know about those. We're going in to get settled. Maybe be out for a swim later." Again, Tanner's hand came to Whitney's waist. For some reason it gave her a sense of satisfaction to know Tanner was leaving with her. She held her head just a little bit higher.

When they were out of hearing distance from anyone Whitney said, "I don't think Charlotte likes me too much."

"I wouldn't worry about it."

"She's not going to sneak into our room in the middle of the night and take a knife to me and hop into bed with you, is she?"

Tanner stopped walking, threw his head back and let out a huge belly laugh. Hardly able to contain his mirth, he said, "Why, Ms. Matchmaker, I had no idea you had such a sense of the dramatic. I promise to be the one to open the door if anyone knocks. Feel safer now?"

She grinned. "A little." After a moment she dared to ask, "So what's the story with her?"

"Let's just say she doesn't like being turned down when she wants something." Putting his arm around her shoulder, he pulled her to him. This was a friendly action of two people conspiring together.

Maybe they could be friends.

Warmth entered Tanner's voice when he said, "I don't know if I said it but thanks for coming with me this weekend."

"I didn't know that I had a choice."

He held the door as they stepped inside. "I'm afraid you're right about that. But I do hope it isn't too awful for you."

Tanner was pleased with Whitney's reception by his colleagues. They had seemed to like her and she'd handled herself well, even with Charlotte. She had easily read the tension between Charlotte and him and had managed to make a joke out of it. That was a talent he admired. At his guffaw of laughter everyone had looked. To them they must have appeared as two lovers enjoying themselves.

In the house again they passed Kevin going to the front door and he told them what room they were in. Tanner led Whitney up the stairs, to the right and down the hallway to a door at the end. He opened it wide in order to allow her to enter first. When she hesitated he looked back to find her staring at the opening.

"I'm not so sure about this," she said, shaking her head slightly.

"The weekend, the room or staying with me?"

"How about all of it?"

Tanner glanced down the hall. Thank goodness no one was around. "At least come in to talk about it."

He reached for her but she stepped away. His hand fell to his side. After a moment she entered. He joined her and closed the door. Unsure what to do to make her feel more comfortable, he simply waited near the door.

Whitney's attention appeared fixated on the queen-size four-poster bed against the far wall. Thankfully there was a small sofa under one of the windows. That would be his sleeping spot for the next three nights. Not that he was looking forward to it.

"Why don't we have a seat?" He pointed toward the sofa.

She moved as if her shoes were weights. There she sat on the edge of the cushion, looking as if she would run at any moment. Finally she said, "I'm not particularly comfortable with lying to all these people."

A little charm and persuasion was needed here. "Have we lied? I introduced you as a girlfriend. I don't think that's such a stretch."

"We're really more like colleagues, though."

Whitney wouldn't be an easy sale. "Okay, colleagues. Still we can be friends."

"Those usually know more about each other than we do. I know little about you and you know nothing about me."

"Sure I do. You're a businesswoman with the ability to read people. You understand what helps people relax. You know how to put them at ease. And you like nice cars. You did great back there, by the way." Why was she all of a sudden so antsy? She'd seemed confident at the pool. Was she afraid to be alone with him? Did she sense his physical reaction to her?

When he'd initially placed his hand on her waist it had been for show, but as they'd made their way around the pool, and especially in front of Charlotte, it had become a protective action. Whitney pulled at something in him that he had no intention of examining or exploring.

She scooted back on the sofa, resting more easily in the cushions. "If you don't mind, I would rather not go to the pool. I'll just stay here and unpack."

He wouldn't push her. For now he'd just let her get used to the idea of being here with him. "That's fine. I'll see what Marie has planned for this evening and come back to get you."

"Okay."

"Is there anything special you would like to do while we're in Napa? We don't have to be underfoot here all the time." Maybe if they did something she enjoyed she would settle down some. He certainly didn't need her panicking and heading back to San Francisco.

"I don't know." She pursed her lips. "Maybe a tour of the winery?"

"Sounds good to me. If one isn't planned then we'll take one ourselves."

She smiled but it didn't reach her eyes.

"I'll leave you to unpack." He headed for the door. "I'll see you in a little while."

Tanner returned an hour later to find Whitney asleep in the middle of the bed. It was early for a nap. Had she been up the night before, worrying about coming with him this weekend? Through their meetings she'd proved herself intelligent and a woman who took little guff from people, or at least him. So why wouldn't she take the weekend at face value? Was she that distrustful of men or just him? She didn't strike him as insecure.

Why did he care? He had no intention of becoming

emotionally involved with Whitney. The more he knew about her the more invested he would be in her life. He didn't want or need that. In fact, that implied caring and he wasn't going to take that step. Caring equated to hurt. He'd seen that clearly with his parents.

They'd get through this weekend and go back to being matchmaker and client.

Whitney looked so peaceful that he hated to wake her but Marie had made plans for everyone that afternoon. He placed a hand on Whitney's shoulder and gave her a gentle shake. She blinked then her eyes popped wide open. They were pretty eyes, almost as nice as her smile. The kind that saw into a person.

"Hey, the women are going into town for lunch and some shopping while the men go to the club to play golf."

"Is it necessary for me to go?" she asked after a yawn.

"If you don't mind, I wish you would. I wouldn't want to hurt Marie's feelings." Tanner wouldn't make it a demand. He'd made enough of those.

"Oh, of course." Sitting up and trying to unrumple her clothing, she said in a convincingly sincere tone, "I don't want to do that either."

If anything, Whitney had a kind heart. Maybe that was why her business as a matchmaker was so successful.

"I'll tell you what—" he reached for his wallet in his back pocket "—why don't you buy something nice for yourself? It's the least I can do for you helping me out this weekend."

"That's not necessary."

"Maybe not, but I'd like to. You could maybe get a new outfit." He shrugged a shoulder. "Something more fitted."

Whitney raised a brow. "Thank you but I don't need you to buy clothes for me."

"I just thought you might enjoy going more if you could buy something new."

She rolled off the bed and faced him. "I don't need your money."

Tanner held up a hand. "Whoa, whoa. I didn't intend to insult you. Whatever you wear is fine with me. I was just thinking you must be covering up some nice curves under those loose-fitting clothes." He handed her a few bills. "Just take this. Get whatever you want. Or don't. Marie said to meet in the lobby in half an hour. I'll see you later."

He was out the door before she could argue more. Had he touched an exposed nerve?

Whitney stood in the lobby, waiting for the other women. She wasn't looking forward to the foray into town, especially if Charlotte was going. Whitney had known more than her share of Charlotte's type growing up but she refused to revert back to that timid, sensitive girl who had hidden behind her weight. She'd worked too hard to let the Charlottes of the world control her life anymore.

She clutched her purse. The money Tanner had given her was inside. He'd paid enough attention to her that he'd noticed her clothes? Had wondered about her curves? Heat filled her at the idea. But he'd said he wanted her to have something that fit her better. She looked at herself in the large mirror in the grand hallway. Did she have the confidence to wear a tight dress? Have him see her in it? She'd spent so many years covering up, could she let go enough to do that?

Soon she was in a limousine with Marie, Charlotte, Lucy, Ellen and Sue Ann, all of whom she had met at the pool. To Whitney's great distress, Charlotte took a seat next to her.

With her nose pointed down, Charlotte said as if they were new best friends, "So what brought you and Tanner together? You don't seem his type."

Marie came to her rescue. "How about a glass of champagne on our way to town?"

Whitney didn't normally drink much and certainly not in a limo. Still, she gratefully accepted Marie's offered glass of the bubbly liquid.

"So where did you meet Tanner?" Charlotte persisted.

Her tone was far too condescending for Whitney. In the past women like Charlotte had made her life miserable. Now it was happening again. Why she'd ever agreed to this weekend Whitney didn't know. It wouldn't be over soon enough to suit her. She took a sip of champagne in the hope it would fortify her. "We met in college."

Charlotte gave her a sly smile, as if she had set her trap. "Really? I knew Tanner in college as well. I don't remember you."

She wouldn't. People like Charlotte didn't notice people like her unless forced to.

"I was there nonetheless. We had a couple of undergrad classes together."

Thankfully Marie gained everyone's attention, wanting to know where they would like to shop. When Whitney voiced no opinion she said, "Whitney, is there someplace special you would like to go?"

"I've never been to Napa so I really can't say."

"Then is there something you're interested in shopping for?" Marie asked.

After her conversation with Tanner there was. "Yes, I need a new cocktail dress and I didn't have time to get one before I left San Francisco. Do you know of a good place to buy one?"

A large smile came to Marie's lips. "I know just the

boutique." She picked up a phone attached to the side of the car and instructed the driver where to stop. "There's plenty of other places nearby for the rest of us to enjoy while you're getting your dress."

Minutes later they were stepping out of the car in front of a store with two windows on each side of a glass door. In one of the show spaces was a beautiful red dress. The bodice was seamed in panels so that it would fit tightly above the waist, while the skirt flared and flowed around the mannequin's legs. It was so unlike anything Whitney owned yet for some reason she wanted to surprise, even shock, Tanner. What was happening to her? All her life she'd been in the background, had worked hard to stay there, and yet everything about the dress screamed, *Notice me.*

"I can see the red dress has caught your attention. Let's go in and you can try it on." Marie all but pushed her into the store.

The other ladies, including Charlotte, headed down the sidewalk with a wave of their hands. One said, "We'll meet you in an hour at the café for tea."

A small bell tinkled as she and Marie entered the shop. A saleswoman greeted them. Marie wasted no time telling her that Whitney wanted to try on the dress in the window. Minutes later Whitney was standing in front of three mirrors, wondering who she was looking at.

"It's lovely on you." Marie's words were soft and reassuring.

Whitney moved from side to side, watching the folds of the dress sway around her legs. "You don't think it's too much?"

"No. Tanner won't know what's happened to him when he sees you."

Did she want that? They weren't lovers. She was looking for a woman for him, not *to be* his woman.

"Yes, and even better, it'll get Charlotte's goat."

Whitney gave Marie a sharp look. "Why?"

"Because she seems to think she has some claim on him."

Watching Marie's face closely, Whitney responded, "Tanner said she's engaged."

Marie curled her lip in distaste. "She is, but that doesn't seem to mean much to her. Max doesn't spend enough time with her to keep her happy so she goes after other people's husbands."

Had Charlotte gone after Malcolm?

Marie picked out a necklace with a small pearl on the end of a stand on the table near them. "Turn around," she ordered then fastened it on Whitney's neck. "I'd like to see her put in her place. You might just be the person to do that." Marie patted her shoulder. "Perfect. He'll never know what hit him."

Her? She'd never outshined someone like Charlotte. Cautiously Whitney asked, "If you don't mind me being nosy, if you feel that way about her, why is she here?"

"Because she's Max's latest young thing." Marie didn't sound at all pleased. "His wife, Margaret, was my best friend. She died of cancer a couple of years ago."

Whitney touched her arm. "I'm so sorry to hear that."

"Thank you. It was a dreadfully hard time on everyone. Enough of that. Let's get this dress paid for and go have tea." Marie started toward the desk.

Did Whitney dare buy the dress? Tanner's comment about her clothing compelled her to say yes, but she sure didn't want Charlotte goading her into doing something to prove a point. But just this once it would be nice to indulge herself, wear something that made her feel confident, feminine.

"Okay."

It wasn't until she was taking the dress off and looked at the price tag that she almost fainted. It was half her house payment for a month. If she could just find the right woman for Tanner his fee would help her afford it. Even though she had his money in her purse, she wasn't about to use it. Only because of the idea that wearing the dress would give her enough poise to pull off the rest of the weekend and deal with Charlotte's barbs did Whitney have the courage to give the saleswoman her credit card.

She and Marie stepped out into the sunshine again. They gave her dress to the driver, who was waiting nearby, and started down the street. The honk of a car drew their attention. It was Tanner. He pulled into the nearest parking place and got out.

"What're you doing here? I thought you were playing golf." Whitney didn't take the time to examine the little skip of her heart at seeing him.

"Turns out I was odd man out and not needed for a foursome. I tried to catch you before you left but apparently you have your phone off, so I thought I'd drive in and find you. Maybe see if I could join you ladies for lunch."

"Sure. You're welcome," Marie said, then started down the street toward where the others sat on a patio of a café.

Whitney whispered, "So why are you really here?"

"I got to thinking it was unfair of me to throw you to the wolves by pressuring you into coming into town without me to run interference. So when I wasn't needed for golf I came to save you."

"Just like a knight of old," Whitney jested. In reality she found it rather sweet that he'd been anxious about her welfare. Or was he just afraid she might slip up and tell everyone she was his matchmaker? Despite his high-handed method of getting her to come with him, he seemed genuinely concerned for her. It made it hard not to like him.

"Are you making fun of me?"

"I would never do that," Whitney said with pretend sincerity and then followed Marie.

Tanner caught up with her. He took her hand and leaned in close. "We need to make this look good."

A tingle of pleasure rippled through her. Just having him near made her feel warmer than the day indicated. She had to get a handle on her reaction or she would soon be swooning over Tanner like she had in college. That was a stage in her life she wasn't returning to.

Minutes later they had taken a seat at the table on the patio with the other women.

"I don't know if I've ever had afternoon tea. I might do this again soon," Tanner remarked as he picked up a sandwich that almost disappeared between his large fingers.

"You don't know what you've been missing," Whitney said. "It's one of the most relaxing things I do for myself."

"You've had afternoon tea before?" Tanner sounded surprised. Did he think she wasn't interested in anything that cultured?

"Many times."

"I prefer other diversions," Charlotte purred, giving Tanner a speculative look.

He ignored Charlotte and said to Whitney, "I'm going to count on you taking me to your favorite place. My treat."

The look he gave her created a low glow in her. He was putting on a show for the women but she was still enjoying his attention, no matter what the reason.

Tanner was a perfect charmer during lunch. He spread his attention around each of the women, including Charlotte, but he made it clear Whitney was special. Where some men would have felt out of place as the only male at the meal, Tanner seemed to be enjoying himself.

When he wasn't eating, his arm remained across the back of her chair. That element of his personality Whitney had seen when they'd been in college was now very evident during the meal. Occasionally his thumb would drop down and brush her shoulder.

When she shuddered he leaned in too close and asked with his lips just touching her ear, "Are you cold?"

He knew full well she wasn't. If anything, she felt compelled to fan herself.

Tanner entertained with stories of his exploits during med school and shared one very poignant one about a patient. Whitney envied his ability to fit in wherever he was. He even paid for everyone's meal, stating, "That's what a gentleman does."

"So, Marie, what do you have planned for us this evening?" he asked as they were leaving the café.

"Tonight we're having a wine-and-cheese tasting at the winery, then taking a tour and ending with dinner in the wine cellar."

They had arrived at the limousine and the women started taking their seats. When Whitney ducked her head to get in Tanner said, "Aren't you going to ride back with me?"

He almost sounded hurt. "Uh, sure." Whitney joined him on the sidewalk again. They watched the limo move away from the curve.

"Do you need to get anything else while we're in town?" he asked.

"No, I'm good." She already had a stunning dress that Marie would take care of.

"Okay. Then how about a ride through the valley since you've never been to Napa? It's a beautiful day."

Secretly pleased, she admonished, "You know you don't have to entertain me. Don't you need to be hanging out with Malcolm and the other board members?"

"Nope. I have you here and I understand the need to appear ready to settle down, but I'm not going to pander to anyone for a job."

She was glad to hear that Tanner had a moral line that he wouldn't cross.

"Let's take that ride. Do you have a hat?"

"No, but I have a scarf." She gave him her best mischievous grin.

"We're going to find you a hat." He grabbed her hand and pulled her toward a boutique with hats in the window.

A few minutes later, they came out with her wearing a tangerine-colored wide-brimmed hat that was far more attention-getting than anything else she owned. But she loved it. Between it and the dress she was really stepping out of her comfort zone. Somehow Tanner was bringing out her inner diva.

"That color suits you," he said as they settled in the car.

"Thank you. You do know you don't have to compliment me when there's no one around to hear?"

"Has it occurred to you that I might like complimenting you?"

It hadn't, but she had to admit she liked the attention from him.

Over the next couple of hours they just drove at a peaceful speed along the main road through the center of the valley. The vineyards they passed were impeccably groomed and endless. Tanner pulled over at a little roadside stand and bought them bottled drinks.

"This is so beautiful." Whitney stood beside the car, looking off toward the east where the hills created one side of the valley.

Tanner leaned against the car and crossed his ankles. "I was impressed the first time I visited as well. It's like a little piece of France at your back door."

"I would love to visit France one day." Whitney took a sip of her cola.

"I think you would like it. I'd heard so much about Paris that I didn't believe it could live up to the hype, but it was everything I had expected and more."

"Do you travel a lot?" She couldn't help but look at him. Even his body movements captivated her. She was so on the road to trouble. Heart trouble.

"When I can. It takes some reconfiguring for me to get away from the hospital." He didn't sound disappointed, just resigned.

She met his gaze from under the brim of her hat. "So what about this weekend? Who's watching over everything?"

"I'm close enough to be there in an hour or so. I have good staff who will help out until I can get there."

Their lives were so different. Her career almost seemed frivolous compared to his yet he'd asked for her help. No matter what people did in life they wanted to share it with someone. The more she was around Tanner the more she could understand why he would be considered a catch.

But why was he so against a relationship that involved love? She had a feeling he had a lot stored up to give.

They were in the car again and Tanner was about to turn into the road to head back the way they had come when Whitney said, "Thank you for making the afternoon nice for me. It was sweet of you. I would have made it through tea by myself but it was good to have your support."

"You're welcome. If you have any issues with Charlotte, just let me know. Max will be here this evening and most of that will stop."

"Is she always so catty?"

He glanced at her. "Only when she can get away with it."

Whitney watched his capable hands on the wheel. He had nice hands. What would it be like to be intentionally touched by those fingers? That wasn't a safe subject. Charlotte was a more benign one. "She said she was at Berkeley at the same time we were."

"She was. We dated awhile in my senior year." He slowed and let a car go around them.

"I don't remember her."

"She transferred in." Tanner looked up into the rearview mirror.

So that was why she hadn't recognized her. Charlotte had been around during those years she hadn't seen much of Tanner.

They returned to the château around four that afternoon. Whitney pulled off her hat and shook out her hair as they walked toward the main entrance.

"You have beautiful hair. That chestnut color is so unusual."

"Thank you." Oh, yes, the man had charm. And was laying it on thickly.

He pushed a strand off her cheek. "You should wear it down more often."

If she let him keep this up he would have her in bed in the next fifteen minutes. "Tanner, I think we need to make a rule that you only touch me if it's necessary."

"Do I get to decide what's *necessary*?" He fingered her hair.

She stepped out of reach. "No, I think I should make that decision."

"What're you afraid of? That I'll uncover the true Whitney?" He waited for her to join him on the stairs.

Tanner was perceptive, she'd give him that. Was that the part of his character that made him such a good doctor? But he was her client and she had no intention of confessing any of her secrets.

CHAPTER FOUR

TANNER COULDN'T REMEMBER when he'd spent a more relaxing few hours with a woman. Whitney didn't need to be entertained. She seemed happy just being along. Few women he knew would have been glad to spend hours riding in a car. There was something reassuring about having Whitney in the seat next to him. It was an odd feeling. It was nothing like what he'd seen in his mother and father's relationship. He wasn't going into that emotional minefield. They had nothing to do with him and Whitney.

Now she was in the bath, preparing for the evening. He was confident from her no-nonsense personality that he wouldn't be left waiting long. After showering and shaving, he'd given the bathroom over to her. He had no idea what she planned to wear that evening but he was determined that his response would be positive, no matter what her attire.

There was a knock at the door. He opened it to find one of the bellboys.

"Mrs. Jarvis sent this up for Ms. Thomason." The young man handed Tanner a dress bag and was gone before Tanner had time to tip him.

Tanner closed the door. So had Whitney taken his

suggestion and bought something for herself after all? He tapped on the bathroom door. "Marie has sent you something."

Whitney opened the door a crack. Her eyes widened when she saw the bag. "I forgot." She reached out and took the bag. "Thank you."

Seconds later Tanner was left looking at the panel of the door.

It had been twenty minutes since he'd heard anything coming from the bathroom. He checked his watch again. What was Whitney doing? They would be late if she didn't hurry up. He tapped on the door. "Is everything all right in there?"

A muffled sound reached his ears. That wasn't good.

The door barely opened. Her voice held a note of misery. "I can't zip my dress."

So that was what this was all about. "Step out here. I can help with that."

Tanner registered a flash of red as she came only far enough into the room to present him with her back. For a moment his focus was on nothing but the bare V of skin between the two sections of the zipper. Whitney wore no bra. He made himself swallow.

Stepping up to her, Tanner took the tiny pull of the zipper between two fingers. Why were his hands trembling? He'd seen many bare backs. The zipper didn't move when he tugged so he had to hold the material below it snugly, which brought his hand into contact with the curve of her back.

Tanner didn't miss the sharp intake of Whitney's breath. He was breathing harder as well. Getting hard. This simple action of closing a zip was turning into something personal, sensual. With the zip closed Tanner stepped away, shoving his hands into his pants pockets.

What was going on here? He had no particular interest in Whitney. Still, what he wouldn't have given to run the tip of a finger over the exposed creaminess of her back. Or to taste the ridge of her shoulder.

He cleared his throat and stepped back until the backs of his legs touched the bed.

"Thank you," she said as she turned.

That scalding desire Tanner had felt had been fading and now it ignited to explode throughout his body as he took in the full view of Whitney. Her dress was demure by most standards but sexy on Whitney. With a V neckline that only showed a suggestion of cleavage and a length that stopped at her knees, she looked amazing. Just as he had suspected, there were curves under those baggy clothes she usually wore.

Her hair flowed thick and free around her shoulders. Tanner fisted his hands in his pockets so he didn't reach out and grab a handful. "Whitney, you look lovely."

A shy smile covered rose-tinted lips. "Thank you. I'm ready when you are."

His desire intensified. He was ready all right, but not for something that involved anyone but them. He stepped closer to her. "We should be going or we'll be late. But before we do, I think we need to take care of something."

Whitney looked around the room as if she had forgotten something then back at him with a questioning look on her face.

"I know you said only when necessary but I might need to kiss you tonight in front of the others so I think we should practice. Get that first uncomfortable one out of the way. Settle the nerves, so to speak." Yeah, like that was going to happen. Nothing about the reaction she was creating in his body was settling.

"I guess we could do that…"

He found Whitney's lips with his.

They were soft and inviting. Plump and perfect. He pressed more firmly and a shudder went through her. Her fingers gripped his biceps yet she didn't return his kiss. Tanner pulled back and searched her face. Her eyes were wide and she looked dazed.

"It might be more believable if you kissed me back. Should I try again?" He waited. This he wouldn't push.

"Yes, please. I think it's necessary." Her lips hardly moved as the soft words left them.

Tanner chuckled softly. What little taste of Whitney he'd had made him want more. She lifted her mouth to his. This time he placed his hands on her waist and brought her against him. When her lips stirred, his heart drummed faster. Her hands tightened, fisting in his shirtsleeves.

The kiss was quickly moving away from practice to pleasure.

Seconds later, with one sharp movement Whitney broke away, turning her back to him. "I think that was enough practice. We should go." She picked up a shawl from the bed and draped it over her arm. The tightly controlled woman had returned.

Their simple kiss had left him rock hard. Staying where they were was more of what Tanner had in mind. But he was a man of his word. He'd promised not to ask her for anything physical. Their kisses might be considered bending the rule but he'd not push further. Nothing about Whitney struck him as someone who didn't invest emotionally and he certainly wasn't looking for anything that involved his heart.

"I guess we should." Even to his own ears he sounded disappointed.

Tanner's kisses had been sweet and nonthreatening yet they sure had rocked Whitney's world. Even now as they walked across the parking area toward the winery she still trembled. She'd been kissed before but none had been as divine as those Tanner had gifted her with. The problem now was that she wanted more, but she wouldn't let that happen.

She could be in trouble on so many levels. He was her client. He didn't believe in love. He was looking for a wife. She was nothing like what he wanted. He would break her heart. Of that she was confident. She had to get through this weekend and see to it that they returned to their business relationship.

When she stumbled, Tanner's hand was on her elbow to steady her instantly. "I'm sorry, Whitney. I promised nothing physical. I shouldn't have kissed you. It won't happen again. It'll be your call from now on."

Was that statement supposed to make her feel better? It sounded as if he regretted their kisses. Here she was trying to hold herself together while it hadn't had any effect on him. She couldn't have him thinking that she was some ninny who fell apart when a man kissed her.

Long ago she'd learned to cover disappointment and hurt. She'd just do it once more. "Not a problem. I won't hold it against you. It's no big deal."

Had she felt his fingers flinch?

"I'm glad you understand." His hand remained on her arm until they stepped in front of the tasting-room door to the winery. When he let go she felt the loss in more ways than one. That tentative friendship they were building had lost some stones.

"I hope I don't slip up and say anything wrong," she whispered.

"Don't worry about it. Let's just concentrate on having a nice evening."

Tanner seemed far too laid-back for someone who was worried about his friends finding out she was actually his matchmaker. She sure wished her nerves weren't jumping. If it was from Tanner's kisses or her worry over disappointing him, she couldn't say.

He held the large curved door open for her to enter. Inside, the lights were turned low, giving the stone-walled space a cozy feel. It reminded her of pictures of a French farmhouse. To one side there was a bar with a full wine rack behind it. To the other side was a small, tastefully arranged shop area where shelves held wine flutes, cork removers and other paraphernalia. An upright, glass-doored cooler containing small packages of meat and cheese was discreetly positioned in a corner.

Sharing the other half of the room was a grouping of café tables and chairs. Each table was covered in a bright yellow cloth with a white dahlia in a vase. They were a pop of sunlight in the otherwise dark area. Greenery and tiny lights were draped above the doors and along the shelves. Whitney was instantly charmed.

"I love this place." Whitney couldn't help but be impressed. She glanced at Tanner. He was giving her an indulgent look.

"Has anyone ever told you that you have a beautiful smile?"

"No."

He held her gaze as he said softly, "They should have because you do."

Tanner's voice vibrated through her. Had anyone ever looked at her like that before? Like she was the most special thing in the world?

"I think if you continue to look at me that way I'll forget my promises," he said quietly. "Maybe we should join the others? I've been told that the Garonne Winery has a remarkable white."

Whitney didn't drink much but she was in the mood to enjoy some wine with Tanner. She would *not* get any ideas where he was concerned. The only reason he was paying this much attention to her was because he was putting on a show. But that kiss had felt real. That moment just now had felt real too. She was going to enjoy this feeling while she could.

He took her hand and wrapped it around his elbow and they walked toward the others gathered near the bar.

Marie met them, her hands out in welcome and a wide smile on her face. "Whitney, you look wonderful. I knew that dress was just the thing for you." She regarded Tanner. "I hope you told her how beautiful she is."

He nodded. "I did."

"Did he?" Marie looked at her.

Whitney smiled up at Tanner. "He did. He was very complimentary."

Thankfully, Marie didn't waste any time directing them to the bar. "You must try the white."

"Tanner said it was good," Whitney remarked.

Marie smiled with obvious pride. "It's our first award winner."

"Then no wonder you're proud." Whitney watched as the middle-aged man behind the bar dressed in a white shirt, black vest and pants poured the liquid into a glass.

"I must check on our meal. The tour will begin in a few minutes," Marie said, and whirled away.

The bartender handed Tanner a tall fluted glass and he gave it to her, then took his own. He tapped his glass against hers. "To a nice weekend."

Their looks held as they took a sip of wine.

"Nice," Tanner said. "What did you think?"

"I'm not much of a wine connoisseur so I can't really say." Once again she was out of her element.

"That's okay. You either like it or not."

She paused a moment. Was he talking about more than wine? "I like it."

Tanner smiled. "Was that so hard?"

"No."

"Would you like a lesson on how to taste wine?" He made it sound like it was something intimate between them.

"I'm always willing to learn something new." Had she really said something that flirtatious?

Tanner's eyes darkened but his grin was an easy one. "That's good to know. Okay, let me show you. First, you look at it." He brought his glass up so that it caught the light. "Then swirl it gently so that you can get the bouquet." Tanner put his nose to the rim.

Whitney followed his lead, doing exactly as he did.

"Next you take a sip in your mouth and swish it around, letting each taste bud have its turn."

Whitney watched, enthralled, as Tanner's lips moved against the edge of the glass. Those same lips had just touched hers. She had tasted their fullness and she wanted more.

"Appreciate the richness of it. Then swallow."

She watched the long length of his neck as he drank. He was making the process a seduction. Heaven help her, he was a temptation she was having a hard time resisting. She no longer needed her wrap in the cool, dark room.

It had turned far too warm for her. Tanner had an effect on her like no other male. He wasn't what she needed but she couldn't seem to stay away.

His gaze met hers. Tanner asked in a low raspy voice, "Do you still like it?"

He wasn't referring to the wine. The innuendo was clear. She licked her bottom lip.

Tanner's nostrils flared. He looked as if he might grab her. This time the kiss wouldn't be a practice one, she was sure.

The moment was shattered when Malcolm slapped him on the back. "Tanner, how're you doing this evening? We missed you on the course. I'd hoped we would get a chance to talk."

Tanner's attention went to Malcolm and that suited Whitney fine. She wasn't sure she could have handled the intensity she'd seen in Tanner's eyes if they had continued uninterrupted.

The two men talked about general hospital business and Whitney stood by listening but not really understanding the nuances of the conversation. Still, she enjoyed the rumble of Tanner's voice as it became animated about an issue. She was content to just listen to him. Mercy, she had it bad. Just like trying to return a cork to a bottle once it was out, there was no going back. She was falling for Tanner.

Marie had just touched Malcolm's arm, reminding him it was time for the tour, when Charlotte, hanging on the arm of a distinguished-looking man with snow-white hair, entered the room. Everyone in the room looked in their direction. The atmosphere took on a tense air.

"Well, it looks like we can start now that all the guests are here." The distaste in Marie's voice was unmistakable.

"Yes, it's time," Malcolm said in a pacifying voice

as he took her hand. "Ladies and gentlemen, I believe
they're ready to show us the winery now."

As if on cue, a young man dressed identically to the
bartender came to stand at Malcolm's side.

"Please follow me," the young man said as he opened
a wrought-iron door and walked along a passage. Whitney, Tanner's hand at her elbow, followed the other members of their small group through the stone opening into
a modernized cement-floored room with large alumi-
num vats.

The guide began telling them how the grapes were
harvested and pressed. Charlotte and her partner, who
Whitney hadn't been introduced to, came to stand beside her and Tanner. The entire time the guide was talking Charlotte was busy whispering in the man's ear and
giggling. Once Whitney saw him give her butt a squeeze
and was disgusted by the display. It was as if Charlotte
wanted everyone to pay attention to them. A few times
she noticed Tanner glancing in their direction. Did this
show bother him as well? Was Charlotte putting it on for
Tanner? As if he knew what she was thinking, his arm
came around her waist and brought her close.

"Now, if you'll follow me," their guide announced,
"we'll go into the cellar where the wine is stored in oak
barrels to let time create our award-winning vintages."

They entered another room where barrel after wooden
barrel were piled on top of each other in ranks. They were
stacked well above Tanner's head.

Whitney pulled at her shawl, trying to bring it up over
her bare shoulders as the coolness of the windowless
wine cellar surrounded her. Tanner's fingertips brushed
her arm. Why did she have to love his touch so much?
The wrap was lifted off her. Seconds later, it came to rest
across her shoulders.

"Thank you."

"You're welcome." His voice warmed her as much as the material around her.

They continued down the wide aisle until they came to an area where three formally dressed tables were set for dinner. A single candle flickered in the center of each.

"Everyone." Marie gained their attention. "This is where we'll be having dinner tonight.

"Charlotte and Max, you'll be at this table." She pointed to one to her right. "Ellen, you and Carlos will be joining them. Lucy and Rick, you'll be at this table with Whitney and Tanner." She touched the table closest to her. "Sue Ann and Russell, you'll join Malcolm and I here." She indicated the table off to the right.

Whitney couldn't deny she was relieved not to have to spend the entire dinner with Charlotte. The woman rubbed her up the wrong way for more than one reason. What Tanner had ever seen in her Whitney couldn't imagine.

Tanner held the chair for her to sit. His hand brushed her neck as he moved to take the chair at her left. A shiver of pleasure went through her. Had he done that on purpose? Her reaction to him was on overload tonight. The romantic setting must be getting to her.

A waitress came to stand beside the table and popped the cork off a bottle of red wine. She presented a glass to Tanner. He sipped and nodded. She then poured each person at the table a glass.

Whitney liked their tablemates, Lucy and Rick. She had gotten to know Lucy a little during the trip to town but found Rick an interesting yet bookwormish type. Their conversation was steady and often drew laughter. Whitney felt herself relaxing. Midway through the meal she'd forgotten all her worry over whether or not she might fit in.

"I can't believe I've found someone as interested as me in growing violets," Lucy commented.

"Just goes to show you never know about people until you get to know them," Tanner said as he looked at Whitney. "We always get surprised."

Was he talking people in general or her in particular? How had she surprised him? Why would he be interested enough to notice? After all, she was only his matchmaker.

"Yeah, and after this weekend I'd be surprised if I get that promotion as Director of Infectious Diseases," Rick said.

Lucy placed her hand over his. "Now, you don't know that."

"I just have a feeling," Rick said.

"What do you mean?" Tanner asked.

Rick lifted his glass. "I don't think you need to worry. You're the perfect person for the cardiothoracic department. It's just something Malcolm remarked that Max had said."

Tanner turned in Charlotte's direction. She was laughing loudly. "He does seem distracted."

"Don't give up hope yet, honey," Lucy encouraged.

Rick shrugged and took a sip of his wine. "Let's talk about something else."

By then the salad had been removed and the entrée of prime rib and roasted potatoes with green beans was placed in front of them. As they ate they discussed a recent movie.

Whitney enjoyed the delicious food too much. Tanner smiled at her as she put the last bite in her mouth. "Good?"

"Yes."

"I like a woman who enjoys eating." Tanner's attention returned to his plate.

A sick feeling formed in Whitney's stomach. Her fork hit the edge of the plate with a clink. Tanner glanced at her. His expression turned from one of happiness to distress. His hand took hers under the table and squeezed. "Did I say something wrong?"

He truly looked perplexed. Whitney felt sorry for him. "No. I'm fine." She made herself smile. Would she ever reach the point where she didn't think every remark regarding her and food was a negative one?

Minutes later the waitress removed their plates and brought another with chocolate à la mode on it. Whitney stuck the tines of her fork in it and put a bite in her mouth. The shot of chocolate tasted wonderful but she took no more of the dessert. She saw Tanner look at her uneaten sweet but he said nothing.

With dinner finished, Marie stood. "Before we all go on our separate ways for the evening I'd like to give you a little idea of what we have planned for tomorrow. First, we're going on a hot-air balloon ride. We'll have to be up before daylight but I promise it'll be worth it. If you haven't seen Napa from the sky you haven't seen Napa. Cars will be outside the main entrance to take you to the field at six thirty." Charlotte groaned loudly as Marie continued, "The rest of the day is yours. Dinner is at eight beside the pool. Casual dress is fine. Malcolm and I have enjoyed having you here."

She and Tanner said their good-evenings to Lucy and Rick then thanked Marie and Malcolm for the nice dinner. Tanner pushed the door of the cellar open for her to precede him out. It had turned dark. The moon was big and full against the night sky and the air was cool.

"The hot-air balloon ride sounds awesome. I've always thought they were so beautiful." Whitney pulled the shawl up around her shoulders. Tanner helped her adjust it.

"It should be fun." Tanner's words didn't sound all that heartfelt. Whitney didn't have time to question him before he said, "It's a beautiful night. How about a walk?"

She wasn't sure she should take the chance on being alone with him on a moonlit night but after the meal she'd just eaten she could use some exercise. She wasn't looking forward to returning to the room where they would be closed up together. He had too much sex appeal to ignore. Feelings that had nothing to do with looking for a wife for him had crept in, feelings that would only break her heart in the long run if she were to let herself act on them. It might not be a safe idea but she agreed. "I guess so."

Tanner offered her his arm. She placed her fingers in the crook and he set a leisurely pace toward the rows of vines to the left of the winery. The paths between the rows were so well maintained the walking was easy.

The night was still enough for her to hear herself breathing. They had walked some distance away from the hotel when she said, "I love this. It makes you want to take off your shoes and run."

"Go ahead." Tanner's voice was as deep and smooth as the night.

Whitney glanced at him. Suddenly she felt like doing just that. He made her feel special. She kicked off her shoes, grabbed a handful of her dress and ran. The soft dirt, still warm from the sun, surrounded her toes. She threw up her arms and twirled.

A deep chuckle filled the air, bringing her to a halt. She looked at Tanner.

"Don't stop on my account."

She studied him for a moment. He looked handsome

and sturdy standing with his back to the moon as if he were a warrior of old. She wanted to reach out and take his smooth-shaven face in her hands and kiss him for all she was worth.

She didn't have to. He came to her, standing so close she could hear him breathe but he didn't touch her. "Whitney, I need to kiss you."

Needed to? Had anyone ever needed to kiss her? She stepped to him. His lips found hers. This was no practice kiss, this was a man wanting a woman and telling her so.

Tanner pulled her against him, lifting her until her toes barely met the ground. His tongue joined hers and danced a measure that Whitney recognized as theirs alone. She held on and took the spine-tingling, heart-revving and mind-blowing ride. Her arms circled his neck as her mouth begged in desperation for more. She clung to him.

Tanner broke away, inhaling before he took her lips again. This time his hands moved to cup her breasts. They tingled, became heavy. His arousal was evident between them. The pleasure of having Tanner touch her made her feel weak. She clung to him as if he were her lifeline.

In a low growl he said, "Let's go inside. I want you."

Whitney was tempted to throw caution away and act on the fiery emotions boiling within her. She'd had no business agreeing to a walk with Tanner. It was too romantic, too perfect, too much Tanner. He filled her thoughts, filled her days, and if this continued he would fill her heart. That would be a road to nothing but misery.

If she agreed to his request what would happen to her self-respect, her business? What would happen to what she wanted out of life? A husband who loved her. Someone who invested his life in hers, theirs. She wanted a loving marriage, something Tanner wasn't willing to give.

What was between them would only be a weekend fling. That wasn't enough.

"I can't." She stepped back, her mind forcing her body to move away when it yearned to cling to him. "I need to go in by myself."

"Are you running, Whitney?"

She looked at him. He stood with his legs apart and arms at his sides. "I guess you could call it that. I know when something isn't going to end well. We aren't meant for each other. We are looking for different things out of a relationship."

Tanner watched as Whitney became a shadow among the vines. He knew she was right. Heck, he wasn't even sure what she wanted was real. He'd seen his mother fawn over his father, but was that love or obsession? His father had certainly not cared for his mother in the same way. Was his son even capable of loving someone?

He followed Whitney at a distance, making sure she safely entered the front door of the château. Along the way he picked up her shoes. She had such tiny feet for a woman who had such a strong will.

Once again he was pushing when he'd said he wouldn't. He'd apologized to Whitney more than he had to anyone in his life and here he was needing to do it again.

He went to the library off the entrance hall and poured a drink. Taking a seat in a chair near a window, he nursed his drink, giving Whitney time to get ready for bed and for him to get his libido under control.

It was late when the sound of footsteps drew his mind away from the woman upstairs. He glanced behind him. Disappointment washed over him. It wasn't Whitney looking for him but Charlotte. He returned his attention to the window, hoping she hadn't seen him. Sadly, that wasn't the case.

"Why, Tanner, is that you? I thought you'd be upstairs with your plain little woman."

If his hackles hadn't already been up they would have stood on end at that remark. The need to defend Whitney ran hot and rapid through him. He made no attempt to keep the aversion out of his words. "You know, it's been a long time since it's been your business where I am or what I am doing."

"Or who you are doing, is my guess."

"Or that either. You've found who you want in Max. Leave me alone."

She sauntered toward him. "The question is, have you found what you want in Whitney?"

Had he? "That's between us. It has nothing to do with you."

Charlotte leaned toward him, giving him an impressive view of her full breasts. "You used to think I was pretty important."

"Those days are gone and I've moved on. Now, excuse me." He put his hands on her shoulders and pushed her away as he stood. "I have other people and things that interest me more now."

"Like that nondescript woman upstairs waiting patiently for your return."

What had he ever seen in her? "As a matter of fact, yes."

Charlotte stepped to him so fast he had no time to react. Her mouth found his. Forcing himself not to squeeze her waist to the point of pain, he set her away from him. "If you ever touch me again, I promise Max will learn in no uncertain terms what a witch you are." He didn't wait for her reaction.

When Tanner entered their bedroom Whitney was in the bed, asleep. One lone light near the sofa burned. On the couch was a pillow, sheet and blanket. Tanner looked longingly at the bed and the soft, warm woman in it. After muttering a few expletives that he was sure would make Whitney blush, he shook out the sheet and let it drop haphazardly over the sofa. By the size of the piece of furniture his feet were going to hang over one end. Removing his jacket and shirt, he threw them on a chair nearby. His hands went to his belt. Normally he slept in the raw but he would defer to Whitney's sensibilities and wear his underwear. She would just have to deal with them.

He was on the sofa, curled up the best he could, when a soft voice said, "Goodnight, Tanner."

Had she been watching him undress?

CHAPTER FIVE

WHITNEY LOOKED DOWN at Tanner sprawled across the sofa. He'd thrown the blanket off his chest. His head was on a too-small pillow and one leg rested along the back of the sofa. Despite the unusual position, he was snoring softly.

Their kiss in the vineyard had kept her awake into the early hours. The passion behind it still had her feeling fuzzy all over. She'd been kissed before but not with the magnitude of Tanner. It made her forget all her reasonable thoughts where he was concerned. For once in her life she understood that "heat of the moment" concept. Tanner, the cool night, the warmth of the earth beneath her feet, the yellow moon above had all conspired against her. She had to see that she didn't get into that position again.

She was thankful for the second of reality that had crept in, for she had no doubt she was on the fast track to heartache. She knew rejection too well. Most of her life had been that where men were concerned. As a chubby child, overweight teen and college student she'd always been picked on in some form. She wouldn't set herself up for disappointment. Anything she might feel for Tanner would turn into just that. Letting a simple kiss change her entire life was ridiculous. Only it hadn't been a *simple* kiss.

She'd known the second Tanner had entered the room. Her body vibrated with awareness when he was near. She probably should have let him know she wasn't asleep but instead she'd watched him remove his clothes. No doubt she had been invading his privacy but she'd been unable to help herself. Worse had been the urge to touch him. When she'd said goodnight she'd seen the small smile form on his lips. He must have liked the idea she'd been watching him. It had been an enticing show.

When the alarm had gone off she'd quickly turned it off. There had been no movement from Tanner's side of the room. She'd lain there listening to his soft snoring for a few minutes before she'd looked at the clock. They needed to get up and get moving. Marie would be expecting them.

Delaying no more, she reached out to touch Tanner then pulled her hand back. For just a second she wanted to admire him a little longer. His shoulders were wide and the muscles of his chest defined. He must work out when he could. A smattering of hair surrounded each nipple before it formed a line down the middle of his belly to dip under the elastic band of his boxers. Tanner's manhood rose high beneath the material.

She sucked in a breath that sounded loud in the almost silent room. What would it be like to be loved by him?

Heaven.

In a raspy voice Tanner said, "When you stare at a man in the morning, you should be prepared for what happens."

He grabbed her hand and jerked her down to him. Whitney's hands came to rest on the warm skin of his chest. Tanner kissed her. A now familiar heat built low in her. Without thinking, she leaned in for more. Before she could register what was happening he'd pushed her away. She quickly moved to sit on the end of the sofa where his feet were. A foot brushed her back as he came to a seated position as well.

Whitney blurted, "I was only trying to wake you. It's almost time for us to be downstairs."

He didn't look at her as he snarled, "Then go get dressed. I'll do the same."

"Are you always this grumpy in the morning?" she asked.

"No, just mad at myself. Now, go."

Was he mad because he'd kissed her? Even though she shouldn't, she'd like more. She'd promised herself when she'd gone to bed that their kissing was done. All he'd had to do was pull her against him and she'd forgotten that promise. What had happened to her self-respect?

She felt his gaze on her as she crossed the floor to the bathroom. A few minutes later when she opened the door, Tanner stood there wearing only a pair of well-worn jeans. He pushed past her, brushing her shoulder with his bare chest. "I need to shave then we can go."

"I like the stubbly look on you."

Tanner stopped and turned to her as if she had said something of world importance. "Then I'll leave it." He went to a chair and snatched up a sky blue polo shirt, pulling it over his head. She hated to see all that gorgeous physique disappear.

"Ready?"

"Yes." He held the door as she entered the hall. Thankfully his mood had improved since he'd woken.

Minutes later they were joining the others as they climbed into the limousines waiting in front of the hotel. Whitney sat beside Tanner, close enough that she could feel the tension in his body. She wasn't vain enough to think it had anything to do with her, so what was wrong?

True, she had led him on when she'd returned his kiss then ran, and again this morning, but he'd seemed to have forgiven her before they left their room. Yet now he was uptight again.

As she climbed out of the car, Tanner offered his hand and she accepted it. He didn't release it as they walked toward the six hot-air balloons waiting in a field.

"They're beautiful. I love the colors against the morning sky." Whitney couldn't contain her amazement and the excitement bubbling within her. When Tanner said nothing she glanced at him. His gaze was fixed on the balloons. "Don't you think so?"

"Uh, yeah."

A man greeted their group and gave each couple instructions on which balloon basket to climb into. Thankfully there was a stool she could use for help getting in the basket but she didn't need it. Strong, sure hands came around her waist. She glanced back to see Tanner standing behind her. He seemed to lift her with no real effort. He waited until she had swung her legs in and was standing before he climbed in himself.

Minutes later the pilot released the tether and the balloon lifted. She watched in fascination as the ground moved away from them as they floated into the blue morning sky. The other balloons slowly joined them. It was a sight to see. Two rainbow-colored balloons, two shaped like a sunflower, another like a bunch of grapes and theirs in a harlequin pattern all floated above the green valley lined with vineyards with mountains to one side. Picture-perfect. She closed her eyes and took a deep breath of the fresh air. This was turning into an amazing weekend.

She turned slightly, wanting to get Tanner's attention to point out something on the ground. One of his hands had a white-knuckled grip on a support while the other grasped the edge of the basket. His body was rigid and his face was pale. Compassion filled her. She diagnosed the problem right away. Tanner was afraid of heights. Knowing how proud he was and not wanting to embarrass him in front of the pilot, she shifted toward him and whispered, "You okay?"

"I'm fine."

That was a lie. "You don't like heights?"

He glared at her as if she had discovered a shameful secret. "No."

The word sounded forced. She placed her hand over his on the basket edge. "Do you mind if I stand close to you?"

Tanner barely nodded agreement.

"Look at that winery over there." Whitney pointed to one in the distance, hoping that would take his mind off how far up in the air they were. She continued to point out landmarks and Tanner slowly relaxed. He even made a comment or two about different views.

"Why didn't you say something? We didn't have to do this," she whispered, looking at him for an answer.

"I thought I could handle it."

She chuckled. "Stupid male ego." For the first time on the flight Tanner's eyes held no terror. He gave her a sickly grin but at least it was a step away from the grimace he'd been wearing.

"I guess you're right. Thanks for helping my ego remain intact, at least where the others are concerned. I may never recover my knighthood in your eyes, though."

"I wouldn't worry about that. Your knighthood is in good shape where I'm concerned." She'd seen the care he gave his patients. She'd also been protected and complimented by him. His armor was still shiny.

He whispered, "Even after last night?"

"Yes." What he didn't know was that, given a chance, she would have liked that kiss to happen all over again.

"I'm glad." He sounded truly relieved.

Too soon for Whitney they were back on the ground again. Tanner wasted no time in climbing out of the basket. He offered her his help. She didn't hesitated to place her hands on his shoulders and let him lift her. Swinging her legs out, she slid down Tanner's body.

He kissed her forehead. "Thank you."

Heat washed over her that had nothing to do with the sun. Tanner Locke had needed her. Not as a pretend girlfriend but as someone who understood and cared about him. Hadn't he had that before? Why wouldn't he want it all the time in his life? As they walked back to the limo her hand remained securely in his. She was going to enjoy the feel of him while she could.

On the ride back Tanner continued to hold her hand and the old confident Tanner had returned. He talked and laughed as they joined the others in the car. He continued to touch her as if she had become his lifeline on the balloon ride and he didn't want to let her go. The one time he did release her hand, his arm came up to rest on the seat behind her. For once she felt that the actions were genuine instead of for show.

Her feelings for him were getting the better of her. She wanted to shout, *No, no, no, you are headed for disaster*, but her body said, *Yes, yes, yes, I want more*. Her body was winning.

When their party once again stood in front of the château Marie announced, "There is a brunch set up in the library if you would like something to eat. The rest of the day is yours. Sleep, swim, golf, go into town. Do as you wish. Dinner is at eight."

Whitney said to Tanner as they trailed the others inside, "I'm not really hungry. I'm going up to check in with a few clients. Don't worry about me."

"If you don't mind, I'd like to come with you. I didn't get much sleep last night. I promise to be quiet while you work. We can eat later."

Guilt filled her. He probably hadn't got much rest because he'd been trying to fit his large frame on the small sofa. "I don't mind. It's your room too."

With a wry smile he said, "Thanks."

Had he not liked her statement? Did he want her to refer to it as their room?

They climbed the stairs and walked down the hall to their room with not a word between them. She hadn't meant to make him unhappy. The less restrained Tanner was fun. Cautiously she said, "Tanner?"

"Yeah?"

"Did I say something wrong?"

He stopped and faced her. "It's just that you're always putting walls up between us."

"Walls? What walls? The only one I know of is that you are my client."

Tanner looked around and then walked to the door to their room and opened it. She followed him in. He shut the door with quiet control. "What if I don't want to be your client anymore?" He focused on her as if her answer meant whether or not the world would come to an end for him.

"Then I'll be sorry to see your business go." And her contact with him.

His look was one of disbelief. "Just my business?"

"Tanner, I'm not very good with word games."

He stepped toward her. "I'm not playing a game. I want you. Badly. Haven't my kisses told you that?"

He wanted her? His kisses had made her know she wanted him. Didn't a man like Tanner just play with someone like her? "I guess so."

Tanner came toward her. One of his arms wrapped her waist, bringing her close but not so near she couldn't see his face. "How little experience have you had that you don't recognize when a man desires you? Can't survive an hour without touching you?"

She looked at the rug beneath their feet. "Truthfully, not much."

Her few times had been short and sweet. Steve had left her bed saying, "There's not enough room here for me to sleep well."

"May I show you how much I want you?" Tanner nibbled at her neck.

She turned, giving in to the divine pleasure. The mere idea of Tanner wanting her pushed every thought of self-preservation out of her mind. Just being desired by him was more than she'd ever dreamed of. "I guess so."

"'I guess so'?" he mumbled against her skin as he continued to leave little kisses across it. "I've had more encouraging invites."

"Then you might want to go and find them." She made an effort to leave his hold but he held her in place. "Or Charlotte."

He pulled back. There was a look of disbelief on his face. "I don't want them or Charlotte. I want *you*."

Tanner's gave her a gentle and chaste kiss on the lips. Then another. Another. He was testing and teaching at the same time. His lips brushed across hers until she couldn't help but rise on her toes, asking for more. When his mouth left hers she whimpered in disappointment. Eyes as dark as coffee studied her. There was a flare of light in them before both his arms circled her waist and jerked her against him. Tanner's mouth crushed hers.

Whitney's hands found a life of their own and pushed up his arms to circle his neck.

He didn't ask for entrance, his tongue took it. At first he teased until she joined him in the excitement of tasting, tempting and tantalizing. Whitney's heart thumped as her blood rushed to become a throbbing between her legs. She squirmed against him, unable to get close enough. Her fingers weaved through his silky hair, wanting to feel all of him. This was what she'd been wanting for days.

She had become someone she didn't recognize. Tanner made her feel special. Sensual. Confident. Wild.

Tanner's lips left hers and moved to the pulse point beneath her ear. His tongue flicked across it. She shuddered. He was jumbling her thoughts. They centered only on him. He held her mind and body in his control.

His hands moved up her sides to cup her breasts, gently fondling them. His fingers found a button of her shirt and opened it. He kissed the curve of a breast. She clung to his shoulders as her legs almost failed to hold her.

Tanner released another button, pushing her top away so that most of her bra was revealed. Fear drummed in her chest. She couldn't let him see more. Know. Her hands stopped his when they moved to the next button. "Close the curtains."

His head jerked up. "Why?"

"Tanner, I'm sorry. I don't think this is going to work." She didn't miss the flash of anger that entered his eyes before concern covered it.

He backed away and, taking her hand, he led her to the edge of the bed. Sitting, he pulled her down beside him. "Tell me."

Whitney looked down at his large feet and her smaller

ones beside them. They were so different. She the blend-into-the-crowd person, and he the shining star. How could he comprehend the pain she'd known? "You wouldn't understand."

His thumb rubbed the back of her hand. "Try me."

She'd seen him with Mr. Wilcox. His compassion, empathy. Could he?

"Please tell me. I know you like me as much as I like you. We're friends, right?"

He was right. They had at least become that. "I was heavy. Fat."

Tanner waited, as if there was more.

"That's part of the reason you didn't see me when we were in college. I wasn't one of those thin pretty girls you hung out with. You might not be interested in me now if I hadn't lost weight."

He shifted away. "You really don't have a very high opinion of me or yourself, do you? Has it occurred to you that I might have grown up? Can see beyond a woman's looks? Appreciate her intelligence? And you, can't you see what you have accomplished, not only in losing weight but starting your own business? You have a heart for people. Mr. Wilcox saw that. Marie as well. Is there some reason you think me incapable of doing so too?"

Whitney's heart swelled. She couldn't believe it. Tanner sounded hurt. "I didn't mean—"

"If I wanted anyone in my bed I could have Charlotte. You're my choice."

"You have no idea what it means to me to have you say that. But, you know, I have stretch marks. I still sag in places."

He gave her an incredulous look. Taking both her hands in his, he leaned toward her. "I don't care about that stuff. I want you. Just the way you are. I'm not going to close the curtains. I'm not going to let you do it either. You trust me or you don't."

"I don't know…"

He brushed her hair back from her face and cupped a cheek. His gaze never left her face. "Honey, I don't care about who you were. All I care about is the desirable woman you are right now. You're not running me off. I'm staying right here." He stood and kicked off his shoes. Pulling his shirt over his head, he let it drop to the floor. On the bed again he lay back on the pillows and crossed his feet. He patted the space beside him. "When you decide you want me, I have a spot for you. I'd be glad to share my nap with you anytime you're ready."

Could she trust him? Expose her vulnerability? What would she miss if she didn't? Minutes later Whitney watched as the dark fans of his eyelashes rested against his cheeks. She was tired too. They'd had an early morning. Maybe if she just lay down for a minute next to him she could accept what he offered.

If she did trust Tanner, act on her need, would she regret it?

Tanner woke to a warm body curled against him. Whitney lay spooned along him. At least that was a step forward. Except for the time she'd remarked about his facial hair and the moment in the balloon, had she shown him any real attention? Her kisses told him otherwise but she fenced him off when she wasn't in his arms.

It had been her choice to lie next to him. Progress. Good progress.

He brought his free arm over her waist and shifted toward her. Even now his libido was stirring, just being this close to her.

Whitney let out a small sigh as she wiggled her behind. He was in real trouble now. With a resolve he hadn't known he had, Tanner closed his eyes and went back to sleep.

The movement of the bed brought him awake again. Whitney had rolled to face him. She slowly opened her eyes.

His gaze met her green, unsure one and saw the second she registered where she was. "Whitney, if you don't want me to take you here and now in broad daylight, I would get off this bed," he said in a soft but firm voice.

She blinked then her look returned to his clear and confident. Her hand came up to rest on his chest. "What if I do?"

Her touch almost scorched his skin. "I want to see all of you. Appreciate everything about you." She waited so long to respond he was afraid all his desires would be dashed.

"Okay," she said softly.

Tanner reached to undo the button he'd undone earlier. His fingers moved to the next one then the next until he could push the shirt away from her shoulders. Sitting up, she let him remove it. He held her gaze as he reached around her and flipped the hook to her no-frills bra open.

She slowly let the bra drop to the floor.

"Now lie back so I can take in your beauty."

Tanner held her uncertain look as Whitney slowly lowered her head to the pillow. His gaze left hers to take in the view of her plump and perfect breasts. He touched the tip of one and heard the intake of her breath. His eyes lifted to her face. With her mouth forming an O and her eyes wide in wonder, he was sure Whitney was the most astonishing creature he'd ever known. "I don't know what you were worried about. You're beautiful."

"Don't look too close."

"Aw, honey, too late for that." His hand cupped a globe and lifted it so that he could take the nipple into his mouth. As he sucked and swirled his tongue, hissing sounds came from Whitney.

He raised his head. Her eyes were closed and she bit part of her bottom lip.

"Whitney."

Her eyes gradually opened. "Yes?"

"Please don't abuse that beautiful lip of yours. I wish to kiss it." He claimed her mouth as he continued enjoying the feel of her breast. She returned his kisses. Her hands traveled over his back and shoulders as if she were hungry for him. He sure hoped so because he was starting to hurt for her. "I need to see all of you."

The worried look returned to her eyes and she started to turn away from him. Tanner kissed her, stopping the move.

"You must think I'm some prima donna who is so uptight she can't let go enough to let a man see her."

"You certainly have nothing to be ashamed of. Don't you remember me being scared of heights this morning? You came to my rescue. I'm just coming to yours this time."

She looked at him then. "But you got in the balloon despite your fear."

"And aren't you here despite yours?"

She nodded.

He ran his hand along her ribs to her waist. "How about we do this together?" Tanner stood beside the bed and offered her a hand. Much to his delight, she didn't hesitate in taking it. As she stood he couldn't help but enjoy watching her ripe breasts moving freely. His gaze found hers. Whitney was waiting for his reaction. He took her hand and placed it on his length. "See what you're doing to me?"

A spark he'd only seen in her eyes when she was emotional about something he had said or done flared just before she stroked him softly.

Tanner stepped out of her reach. "Any more of that and I won't wait until you take off your clothes, I'll tear them off."

Her smile was a wicked one. His Whitney was gaining confidence. His Whitney? The idea was far more possessive than he liked.

With her hands at the button at her waist she said, "On three."

Tanner forgot all about his mental slip and watched her undo the button. He soon caught up with her actions and they both stood naked before each other.

"Whitney, look at me." He chuckled. "Not that part of me. Up here."

Her gaze rose to meet his. A delightful rosy color covered her cheeks.

"That wasn't so bad, was it?"

"No-o-o…"

"Now I'm going to look at you and you can look at me."

Whitney couldn't believe she was standing in a room naked before Tanner with the sun streaming through the windows. What had happened to her? Who was she becoming?

Trembling, she watched as Tanner's gaze left hers and started downward. His nose flared and his eyes darkened. With an index finger he lightly traced the curve of her hip. Almost reverently he said, "I see nothing that should be hidden."

Relief, desire and an emotion that went deeper filled Whitney. For once in her life she felt she measured up. She took that confidence and found her own pleasure. Studying Tanner's shoulders and chest, she let her look rove over his flat stomach to his slim hips. He stood strong and proud, and incredibly large. Her gaze continued down to his feet, where he wiggled his toes.

She looked at him and smiled. "There was a time I thought you had no sense of humor."

"I'm a man of many surprises. And right now I'm going to show you some of those." He grabbed her and lifted her onto the bed. "And I plan to touch every part of that lovely body."

"Shouldn't we get under the covers?"

"No. I want to experience you. Watch the light dance off your skin. See your expression as you climax."

"Oh!"

"I bet we can do much better than 'oh'…" Tanner kissed her deeply as his fingers caressed her breasts. Heat began to build. Involuntarily she flexed her hips.

Tanner continued to kiss her as his hand left her breast and moved to lie over her belly. Slowly, his hand lowered to her curls and over them. His lips moved over her cheek to nip at her earlobe. He whispered, "Open for me, beautiful Whitney."

She released the tension from her legs, let them part. Tanner didn't pause before he cupped her hot, throbbing center. A finger teased her, then pushed inside. Whitney bucked.

"Easy," Tanner said, then he kissed her and his tongue started making the same erotic motions as his finger.

Whitney sucked in a tight breath and arched her back. Tanner thrust his finger again and she wriggled against it. She squeezed her eyes closed. A heated swirl grew deep in her, built and curled into itself, tightening, growing. Tanner eased deeper and the spring popped. Pleasure flowed throughout her. She rode a sunbeam down with a sigh.

Her eyes opened and she looked into Tanner's grinning face. He teased, "You liked that, didn't you?"

"Mmm…"

"I think you'll like this as well." Tanner reached for the foil packet he'd pulled out of his wallet earlier and placed on the bedside table. He opened it and covered himself before he leaned over her, supporting his torso with his hands. Hers came to his shoulders. He kissed one of her breasts and she felt the pull deep in her center. Moving to the other nipple, he gave it the same attention. His length nudged her opening. He flexed his hips forward and Whitney allowed him passage. Tanner eased into her. With each push-pull her fingers contracted into the muscles of his upper back. With one final plunge he filled her completely.

After a few seconds Tanner withdrew and then pushed forward, then followed the same pattern until that fist of heat started tightening again. She squirmed, wanting more of him. He kissed her then pushed hard and sent her soaring once again. Whitney was on her way down when Tanner made three quick forward motions. He groaned deep in his throat then collapsed beside her.

His arm circled her waist, pulling her to him. He brushed the hair from her forehead. "That was far better than 'oh.'"

Whitney smiled. It was. Much better.

CHAPTER SIX

TANNER POPPED ANOTHER grape into his mouth and watched as Whitney bit into a cube of yellow cheese.

He wasn't by a long shot inexperienced where women were concerned, but he'd never enjoyed giving or watching a woman receive pleasure as much as he had with Whitney. She was so responsive to his touch. To his amazement he'd appreciated her to the point of pain. He wasn't used to that kind of connection. What was she doing to him?

She had crawled under the sheets as soon as she could, saying she was cold. When he'd gone to the bathroom she'd pulled on his shirt. Why was she so uptight about her body? What had happened to her? No one was perfect. Where had she gotten the idea he was only interested in looks? He certainly hadn't been focused on that aspect when he'd listed what he wanted in a wife.

He looked at Whitney. Wife? What kind would she make? She'd certainly represented herself well this weekend. He already knew she had a kind heart. Did she like kids?

"Do you want children?"

She gave him a quizzical look. "Yeah, why?"

"Just wondering." This wasn't a discussion they needed to get into right now. She'd been so unsure of their attraction he didn't want her to backslide to that point again.

He sat up. "As much as I hate it, I think we should make an appearance down by the pool."

Her face turned unsure.

"Something wrong? You didn't bring your suit?" He ran a finger over the top of her hand.

"I've got my suit." Whitney scooted off the bed.

"Then what's the problem?"

She stood beside the bed. "I just don't like wearing it."

"Why not? I bet you look cute in it." He liked the way she looked in his shirt.

"And I bet you need glasses."

He chuckled. Something he found he'd done more of around Whitney. "I'm a surgeon. Don't let the rumor I can't see get started."

A smile tugged at the corner of her mouth. "You go on without me."

"I don't think so." He leaned across the bed and reached out, letting the pad of his finger travel down the opening of the shirt. He reveled in her shiver. "Come on, for me." Tanner saw her indecision.

"And what're you going to do for me?" she came back in a saucy tone.

He wiggled his brows up and down. "What do you want?"

She looked at the ceiling, revealing her long creamy neck, then back at him. "I get to drive your car home."

"Done."

Whitney looked surprised. "I should have asked for something more."

He came to stand beside her. "Hey, I can count on one hand the number of times I've let someone drive my car. Three of those were my mechanic."

"The others?"

"My mother. My brother."

"Tell me about your mother." Whitney sat on the bed and patted the space beside her.

"Trying to stall about going to meet the others?"

"Maybe a little, but I do really want to know about your mother."

Tanner shifted around to sit beside her. He looked at the floor as he said, "She was a good mother. Did the usual things mothers do."

"No, tell me about her." Whitney leaned forward. "What does she like? Do? Her favorite things?"

His father, his father, his father. Tanner thought for a minute. "She likes sitcoms, pink lemonade, dressing up and going to the beach. But most of all she loved my father beyond reason. To the point it broke her heart."

Whitney's gaze was intent. "How's that?"

Tanner knew better than to start this conversation. He also knew Whitney wouldn't let it go. "She would do anything for him. Forgive him for anything, and he treated her like dirt. He had a traveling job that she hated. She desperately wanted him to stay at home. He refused. More than once I heard them fighting, her crying, and the next morning she was hugging and kissing him. She was always begging him to stay."

"That must have been hard on you."

"She just adored him. He could do no wrong. I've never understood why she stayed in the marriage. Let him treat her that way."

"She must have loved him deeply," Whitney said softly.

Tanner made a scoffing sound. "If that's love, I want none of it. Obsession was more like it. It wasn't healthy for her, or my brother and I. And my father didn't care one way or another." He could hear the anger building in his voice. "Look, that's enough on that subject. Let's go put in that appearance at the pool then we can find something else that we can do, just the two of us." He gave her a wolfish grin, took her hand and pulled her off the bed.

"Okay."

Despite him having seen all of her, she still went into the bathroom to change. When she returned she wore an orangey, flowy thing over her swimsuit. Her hair was pulled back at the nape of her neck. Going to the dresser nearby, she picked up the hat he'd bought her the day before in town.

He'd already put on his swim trunks and his polo shirt. "You ready?"

She nodded but there wasn't much enthusiasm in it.

Tanner reached out his hand and she placed hers in it. He pulled her to him and gave her a kiss. She had a smile on her face as they walked through the château. One that he knew he'd caused.

There was no one at the pool when they walked out of the hotel into the afternoon sunshine. Tanner not only heard Whitney's sigh of relief but saw her physically relax. He didn't mind them having the place to themselves, glad to have more time alone with her. His obsession with Whitney was starting to concern him. Was this how his mother had felt about his father?

No, no, no. He wouldn't care about anyone to that magnitude!

"I'm going in. Join me," Tanner said as he pulled his shirt over his head and threw it on a lounger.

"I think I'll sit in the sun for a few minutes. It feels good out here." Whitney took the lounger next to the one he'd tossed his shirt on. She lifted her feet and rested them on the cushion.

Whitney had pretty legs. Ones that had been wrapped around him only an hour ago. His body reacted to that thought. She'd already made it clear how she felt about public displays. He was going to make one of his own if she didn't get in the pool soon.

After swimming a few laps in the pool, he came to the edge where Whitney sat. Splashing water with accurate aim, he was rewarded with a yelp.

Whitney jerked forward and glared at him. "What do you think you're doing?"

Tanner grinned. "I'm lonely. Come in."

"After that I'd like to drown you!"

He pushed away from the side, backstroking to the middle of the pool. "Why don't you come in and try?"

Seconds later she stood, dropped her hat to the lounger, pulled the band from her hair, jerked the cover-up over her head and let it flutter to the chair. He liked this side of her. It reminded him of the Whitney he knew in bed.

He couldn't keep his eyes off her. Whitney wore a plain, navy one-piece suit that showed her curves to their best advantage. Her middle was charmingly rounded, which attested to the fact that she had once been heavy. It made her a real person instead of a stick figure.

There wasn't much time for him to admire her before she startled him by diving into the pool. Seconds later she was swimming toward him. He didn't move, thinking she was just swimming out to him. Instead, when she reached him she put a hand on his head and pushed him under the water.

Seconds later he came up, spluttering. "Hey, what was that for?"

"For splashing me." She had moved beyond his arm length.

He swam after her slowly, much as an animal sought its prey. "What if I dunk you?"

"I don't think you can so it doesn't matter." She moved farther away.

"Cocky, aren't you?"

She grinned. "You could call it that or maybe I'm just confident."

"I think I'll find out which." Tanner dove after her and to his surprise he came up empty-handed. As he surfaced he looked around. She was behind him in the deeper end of the pool.

Whitney just smiled. He'd be able to catch her against the wall. Diving again, he reached out and his hand skimmed one of her legs but couldn't hang on. Once again he came out of the water to glare at her. This time she was swimming toward the other end of the pool.

"I'd say *confident* was the word." She splashed toward him.

Now she was taunting him. He didn't know anyone who dared to do that. It seemed as if everything with Whitney was a new experience. This time he would have her. She was in the shallow end, easier to trap. As he came closer she moved to one side. He shifted to face her. She moved again. Tanner followed.

She giggled. It might have been the most pleasant sound he'd ever heard. They were playing like kids, something that he'd never seen his parents do. He laughed. "This time you're mine."

Whitney had a surprised look on her face for a second and he took advantage of that weakness to pounce. When he did she flipped onto her back and shoved a foot into his chest, pushing him away. Before he knew what had happened she was gone. Seconds later, her hand was on his head and he went under.

Tanner came up to her laughter and her taking a seat on the steps in the shallow end. "You've had enough?"

He swam to join her, sitting beside her. "You're good in the water."

"I've always liked it so when I decided to lose weight I started swimming for exercise. Even took a lifesaving course for the fun of it."

"I've been had."

"You started it." She pushed a handful of water toward him.

"I guess I did." This was nice. Just teasing each other. With his high-pressure job he didn't just have fun very often. "So what can I do to make it up to you?"

"Well, I'm already getting to drive your car, so how about you be my sex slave for a night?" A stricken look came over her face. "I'm sorry. I can't believe I said that."

Tanner shifted to one hip so he faced her. One hand went under the water to her calf then slid up her leg to her waist. Looking into her wide eyes, he said, "It would be my honor." His lips found hers.

The sound of someone clearing his throat broke them apart. It was Malcolm, standing at the other end of the pool. "I hate to interrupt, Tanner, but you and I haven't had much time to talk. I was wondering if we could do that now. Sorry, Whitney."

Tanner looked at her, unsure whether or not he wanted to leave her.

"Go on," she said quietly as her hand gently pushed against his chest. "This is what you came for. Wow him. I'll be fine. If I'm not here I'll be in the room when you get done."

It was nice to have someone being supportive of him, not just wanting something from him. He stood and climbed out of the pool. "I'll see you later then."

"Okay." She smiled. "I'm not going anywhere." She

looked at Malcolm. "You know Tanner really is a great doctor."

Tanner looked down at her and winked. "Thank you." For some reason he walked away thinking he could conquer the world.

Whitney went back to the room after a brisk swim that ended when Charlotte showed up. She shouldn't let her affect her life but Whitney was in a good mood and the woman would poison it. She'd just as soon read as spend time in Charlotte's presence. Sitting in the corner of the sofa with a book in her hand, Whitney was surprised when Tanner returned and came straight to her, giving her a kiss. Demonstrative actions from a man were something she wasn't used to. She rather liked them coming from Tanner.

When he pulled back and sat beside her she said, "That must have been a good meeting."

"Yes, it was. Malcolm said the board was pleased with my work. He and Marie really like you."

"I'm glad I could help." She just hated that they were not being truthful about their relationship. Even more, she wished it was true. She knew better than to let that happen yet she'd done it.

"How about we celebrate?"

"How're we going to do that? We're supposed to be at dinner in a couple of hours."

Tanner gave her a wicked grin. "I have a few ideas." He leaned toward her again. "To start how about we get it on here on the sofa?" He kissed her and his hand ran up her leg and under the sundress she was wearing. "Then we move to the floor."

"Floor?"

He nibbled behind her ear. "You can be on top if you want."

A flash of heat went through Whitney at the thought.

Boldly cupping her breast, Tanner said next to her lips in a voice that had turned rough with desire, "Then it'll be time for us to shower for dinner. I'll be glad to scrub your back."

Tanner took Whitney's hand and held it as they waited to fill their plates at the buffet dinner arranged in the grassy area surrounding the pool. She'd picked out a flowing blue-and-gray dress to wear and Tanner didn't even think to complain. He knew well what was under it. A satisfied smile he couldn't control came to his lips. They had celebrated just as he had suggested, to the point of exhaustion. Still he looked forward to taking her to bed later that night. Whitney was weaving a web around him that he wasn't sure he could find a way out of.

With plates filled, they were on their way to a table when his cell phone rang.

"I'll take that," Whitney said, reaching for his plate, "while you answer that."

Tanner gave her his plate and walked off so he could talk privately. "Locke."

"Williams here."

Tanner knew the minute he heard his physician assistant's voice that the call was important.

"We believe we have a heart for Mr. Wilcox," Williams said. "Won't know for sure for a few more hours but things look good. Thought you might want to do this one."

"I'll be there in an hour and a half. Keep me posted." Tanner rang off. As he walked back toward where Whitney was already sitting at a table, she turned and looked at him with concern.

She excused herself and met him. "Is everything okay?"

"No, but it will be, I hope. They think we have a heart for Mr. Wilcox. I've got to go back to town."

"Of course you do. Let's say our goodbyes to Malcolm and Marie. I can be packed in five minutes."

That's one of the many things he liked about Whitney— she didn't require convincing that his work was important. She understood and supported it. Other women he had dated had resented his job when it had interrupted their plans. His mother had certainly resented his father's job.

Less than ten minutes later he and Whitney were packed and going out the door of their room. Tanner stopped and looked back at the bed.

"Did you forget something?" Whitney asked.

"No, I was just thinking I had other plans for tonight." For once he was the one hating the interruption.

Whitney turned an appealing deep shade of red and headed down the hall.

Marie saw to it that his car was waiting outside the front door. As a bellboy loaded their baggage Tanner said to Whitney, "I'm sorry but this time I think I should drive. I promise you next time. If one of us gets a ticket, I want it to be me."

"I understand."

They were pulling out onto the main road when Tanner's phone rang. "I've got to get this." He put in his earbuds, not waiting for Whitney's response before he clicked the button.

Over the next few minutes he listened and gave instructions as they sped through the countryside and then onto the four-lane road back to San Francisco. He drove fast but not carelessly.

He rang off and glanced at Whitney. "I hope I'm not scaring you."

"No." And she appeared at ease.

"I hate it but I won't have time to take you home. I'll see that one of the security guards drives you."

"Would you mind if I stayed for the transplant? I think Mr. Wilcox needs someone in his corner. Maybe I could visit with him before he goes in."

Tanner glanced at her. "I think he'd like that."

A mile farther on his phone rang again and he spent the rest of the time on it with his team. Almost to the minute of the time he'd said he would arrive he eased into his parking space beneath the hospital. Whitney didn't wait on him to come around and open her door. She was at the trunk when he opened it to remove her bags.

"I'll put these in my office so that you can get them before you go home. I won't be leaving the hospital until I know that Mr. Wilcox is stable."

"I understand."

She walked beside him as they took the elevator up from the parking garage. They entered the hospital through a door that required him to swipe a card for it to open and rode another elevator up to the fifth floor. There they went down a couple of hallways and arrived at his office. Whitney waited outside as he set her bags inside the door and grabbed his lab coat.

"Now we'll go see Mr. Wilcox. He'll be in his room for a little while longer. I'll need to examine him then you may visit until I send someone to bring him to surgery."

"Will he be awake or will he have already taken some presurgery medicine?"

"He might be groggy from premeds but he should be awake enough to know who you are." Tanner started down the hall at a brisk pace. The retrieval team was on their way to get the heart. The clock was already ticking.

"Either way, I'll stay with him." Whitney hurried along beside him.

Soon they turned a corner and Tanner scanned his card again. Double doors opened. She followed him to the door of Mr. Wilcox's room. Tanner donned a mask and pulled his stethoscope from his pocket. Without looking at her or saying anything, he entered the room and closed the door. Now wasn't the time to think about what was happening between him and Whitney. He had a life to save.

Whitney was leaning against the wall opposite the room when he came out. He pulled off the mask and dropped it into a garbage can. "You can go in now. I told him I had brought someone to keep him company. I've got to go."

"I know."

He hated to leave her this way but if he kissed her… His focus had to remain on what was going to happen over the next few hours.

Whitney watched Tanner's long stride toward the double doors. He was a man on a mission. His shoulders were broad enough to carry the world. And he was about to do so with Mr. Wilcox's life. What would it be like to have Tanner watching over her with such single-mindedness?

They had shared far more than she had ever expected or anticipated. Tanner had opened up to her about his past. She was confident he didn't make a habit of telling people about his parents. Whitney felt honored he trusted her that much. No wonder Tanner felt the way he did about relationships. He'd never seen a healthy one up close.

But she knew what one looked like and that's what she wanted. To love and be loved. To have that closeness that came from understanding and caring. They were fundamentally different. Tanner wanted a business deal and she wanted happily-ever-after.

Whitney put on a mask then knocked lightly on Mr. Wilcox's door. Unsure if he was strong enough to call to her to come in, Whitney pushed the door open slightly. The lights were low in the room and the only sound came from the oxygen machine. Mr. Wilcox's eyes were closed. Maybe this wasn't such a good idea. She started to back out the door.

"Come in, young lady. It's nice to see you again."

Whitney smiled and said softly, "It's nice to see you too." She entered and closed the door before going to his bedside. She stood so he could see her without straining his neck. "I hear you have a big evening planned."

"That's what they're telling me. What brings you around at this time of night and on a weekend?"

"I was with Dr. Locke when he got the call about your heart." That made it sound like she and Tanner were a couple. That was the furthest thing from the truth. They'd enjoyed each other's bodies but there was no emotional attachment. "I thought you might like some company while you're waiting to go to the operating room."

"That's mighty nice of you. Pull up a chair."

Whitney tugged one of the bulky chairs around so she faced Mr. Wilcox and sat.

"So what were you and Dr. Locke doing this evening that I interrupted?"

Whitney was glad for the dim light to cover her blush. Making love everywhere they could. She couldn't say that. Making love? That's what she had been doing. Emotion was involved on her side. She was in love with Tanner. In love with a man who had no desire to love or be loved. She'd known better but there it was.

Whitney finally managed to get out, "We were in Napa for the weekend." One she would never forget.

"I'm sorry that I messed it up."

"Hey, getting a new heart is a big deal. Well worth messing a weekend up for."

"You're sweet. You remind me of my Milly. She always thought of others first. If she was here she would be holding my hand, telling me everything was going to be all right. She always saw the good side to everything."

"She sounds like a great person."

"She was." He said it as if he were thinking back over the years.

"Would you like me to hold your hand?" Whitney asked.

"That would be nice. I know it isn't very macho, but I'm a little scared."

Whitney pulled the chair closer to the bed. She took the thin hand of her new friend and held it gently. "That's understandable."

Half an hour later a nurse came in and flipped on the overhead lights. "Mr. Wilcox, Dr. Locke is ready for you in the OR."

Whitney stood and pushed the chair away from the bed. "I'm going to say bye now. I'll wait around and see how you're doing. I'll be by to visit again soon." She leaned over and gave the man a kiss on the forehead.

"And I'm going to look forward to dancing at your wedding."

That was an odd thing for him to say, especially since she'd said nothing about getting married, but she didn't question his statement. Maybe his mind was fuzzy.

The nurse gave her an odd look. "Dr. Locke said you could wait in the surgery waiting room on the first floor."

"Thank you," Whitney told the nurse. "See you soon, Mr. Wilcox."

Over the next few hours Whitney watched the weather channel on the TV in the waiting room, read a three-month-old magazine and dozed on and off, but otherwise remained anxious about what was happening in the operating room. She was concerned on two levels. Knowing what Mr. Wilcox meant to Tanner, she was sure he would take it hard if the transplant didn't go well. Then there was her fondness for the older man as well. With her nerves in a jumble, she also paced the room.

She'd been in the waiting room almost six hours when Tanner appeared at the door. He looked tired but it was wonderful to see him. He still wore his surgical cap and scrubs.

Whitney hurried toward him. "How's Mr. Wilcox?"

Tanner smiled. "He's in ICU and doing well."

Whitney hugged him and he returned it. "Now it's time for you to go home. I'll walk you to the front door and one of the security guys is going to drive you."

"What about you? You need to rest." Guilt washed over her. He'd had to sleep on the small sofa the night before, had been up early for the balloon ride and when he could have napped more they had been making love. Tanner had had little rest because of her.

He directed her toward the lobby door with his hand at her waist. "I'll be fine. I'm used to this."

The security man was waiting when they arrived. "What about my bags?"

"They're already in the van."

She grabbed his arm. "You'll let me know how Mr. Wilcox is doing?"

"I'll call you if there's any change," Tanner assured her. "Now go home and get some sleep." He gave her a hug and kissed her forehead.

By the time she was seated in the passenger seat of the hospital van Tanner had already disappeared. It was three in the morning and she paid little attention to what was going on around her on the way home. What had happened to her life? The one she understood? Tanner had entered it and spun it in a new direction. More than that, when he left, and he would, it would come crashing down. She was a woman in love who was destined for heartache.

Love. Heaven help her but she had stepped over the line. She had to stop this now. Next time she saw Tanner she would return his fee and give him the name of another matchmaker. She couldn't continue setting him up with other women. That would be more than her heart could take. Covering up her feelings would be impossible. If she told him now, maybe she would have a chance to recover, heal. But breaking it off would be the most painful thing she'd ever had to do.

It. There was no *it* between them. They'd just enjoyed sex as far as Tanner was concerned. What was there to break off? As far as he was concerned it would be no big deal while her heart would be crumbling.

Most of the day had come and gone when there was a knock on her front door. Whitney answered it to find Tanner standing there. Wearing the jeans and shirt he'd gone to the hospital in, he looked haggard.

"Hey," he said.

Concern gathered in her chest. "Is something wrong? Did something happen to Mr. Wilcox?"

"No, he's doing fine. Even asking when you're coming to see him again."

Relief filled her. So why was Tanner there? "That's good news."

"Can I come in?"

"Oh, yeah. Sure." She couldn't turn him away now.

Moving out of the entrance, she allowed Tanner to step in. He continued into the living room. Whitney closed the door and joined him.

"You look like you should be at home, getting some rest. Can I get you a cup of coffee?"

"At this time of the day maybe a soda or an iced tea." He was looking around the room as if evaluating it.

She waited, unsure if he would appreciate her shabby-chic style.

"Nice place. Comfortable. Like you."

Whitney wasn't sure that was a compliment but it didn't matter. Tanner would be gone from her life soon. "Thanks. I do have some iced tea made. Have a seat and I'll get a glass for you."

Gone only minutes, she returned to find Tanner with his head resting against the sofa back sound asleep. He looked out of place on the pink rose-printed fabric that covered the sofa, yet in an odd way he seemed to belong there as well. Pulling the thin white curtains over the windows to keep the sun from beaming in, she then took the crocheted throw, which her grandmother had made, off a nearby chair and covered him. The man had earned his rest.

She couldn't resist placing a kiss on his cheek. It was nice to have him near.

Tanner woke to the smell of something delicious. When was the last time he'd had a home-cooked meal? His mother used to prepare them in the hope his father would be home to eat them. Which had rarely happened.

Where was he? He looked at the blanket over him. *Whitney's.* The entire place reflected her. Simple, floral and comfy. All the things he hadn't had in his life until she'd come along.

Sitting up, he stretched, trying to remove the kink from his back. He'd been almost as surprised as her that he'd turned up on her doorstep. After leaving the hospital he'd just needed to see her. Whitney was like a balm to his tired spirit. Getting to his feet, he followed the smell down a hallway with a multitude of pictures on the wall. Many of them must be members of her family.

Humming, mixed with a song playing on the radio, came from the back of the house. He found Whitney standing in front of the kitchen sink. Her back was to him. Once again she wore a flowing dress but it was belted at the middle, giving her shape. The kitchen was yellow and had bright modern pictures of roosters on the walls.

He leaned against the door frame and watched her for a minute. What would it be like to come home from a hard day to this scene? Somehow life would be better just being a part of it.

A faster song filled the air and Whitney swung her hips to the music. She moved to the stove and must have seen him out of the corner of her eye. She turned. "Hey. Feeling better?"

He started toward her. "A little, but I'll be a lot better after this." Tanner pulled her to him and his mouth found hers. She briefly returned his kiss then stepped back.

Had something changed between them?

"I need to check our supper. I thought you might be hungry."

Was that all there was to it? He wasn't buying trouble until it came. "It smells wonderful. I'm starving. I've not had anything since we left the château."

"Really? That's not good for you."

He liked her being concerned. "I'm used to it."

"I guess with your profession you would be, but that doesn't mean it's healthy."

"I'm sorry I had to dump you off with Security. I know that wasn't a very gentlemanly thing to do."

Whitney held up a hand. "Stop apologizing for that. You had a more important job to do. I'm not so incapable that I can't take care of myself."

She was so insecure about her body and so confident about other areas of her life. "Not everyone thinks that way."

"Then they're wrong. Have a seat." She indicated the table. "The lasagna is ready."

Tanner took a seat in front of a square wooden table already set with mismatched plates and crockery. A glass of iced tea was there as well.

Whitney brought a steaming hot casserole dish to the table and placed it on a hot pad in the middle. She went back to the stove and returned with a basket of bread. She was half seated when she jumped up. "I forgot the salads." She hurried to the refrigerator.

She'd done all of this for him. He'd never dated anyone who showed they cared by cooking a meal. "You have gone to too much trouble. We could have gone out."

"I like to cook and don't eat out much." She put the salads beside their plates and then picked up his dinner plate and started spooning a portion of lasagna onto it. Placing it in front of him, she then put a small amount on her own.

"Where did you learn to cook?" Tanner picked up his fork.

"From my mother and grandmother. They said a way to a man's heart is through their stomach. I don't know if that's true but my father and grandfather seem happy enough."

Tanner put a forkful of the lasagna into his mouth. "If what they eat is anything as good as this then no wonder they're happy. This is delicious."

"Thanks."

Tanner filled his mouth again. The lasagna might be the best he had ever tasted. Whitney offered him the bread basket and he took a piece. Even that he savored. After eating in silence for a few minutes he said, "So tell me how you happened to live in one of the 'painted ladies' on 'postcard row.' It suits you, but they don't come on the market often."

"This one didn't come on the market. It was my grandparents'. They're letting me slowly buy it. They wanted something smaller and moved to a retirement community. I begged them to let me buy it."

"I have a nondescript place that I almost never see. When I marry, the first thing my wife will have to do is find us somewhere to live." What had made him bring up that subject? He poked at his salad full of fresh vegetables.

"Uh, there's something I'd like to talk to you about."

He didn't like the sound of that. Suddenly his food wasn't as appetizing. "What's going on?"

"About this weekend, I, uh, don't think I can be your matchmaker any longer." She reached into her pocket and pulled out a check. Placing it on the table, she pushed it toward him.

"What's this?"

"It's your fee and the amount you gave me to buy something to wear. I bought the dress with my own money."

"I see." And he did. But he wanted to hear her admit it. "So you're running out on me."

"No." She looked at her plate instead of him. "It's just

that I don't think I'm the right person to be doing your matchmaking."

"Probably not." Especially now that he had taken her to bed. And other places. He pushed the check back toward her. "I want you to keep this. You earned it."

Shock then hurt flickered over Whitney's face.

He reached for her hand but she put it in her lap. "I didn't mean it like that. I just meant that you had matched me and you helped me out this weekend. Nothing more."

"I don't want it." She acted as if he had offended her. Treated her as a woman for hire. Maybe in her mind he had. After all, he had promised he wouldn't turn the weekend into something physical and he'd broken that promise. His actions had put her in a vulnerable position both where her business was concerned and emotionally. He couldn't blame her for calling it quits between them. He didn't have to like it but he did understand.

Tanner reached for the check and shoved it in his pocket. "That's not all, is it?"

She didn't immediately answer. "Just that I don't expect anything from you. What happened between us was only because we were pretending to be a couple. I understand you're still looking for a wife."

When Whitney ran she did it in grand style.

He put his fork down and looked at her. "What if I want more to happen?"

"I don't think that's wise for either one of us. I'm not the affair type and that would only get in the way of you looking for the right wife." She refused to meet his look.

Tanner hated to admit it but she was right. He was already far too attached to her. "Then we part as friends?"

She glanced up at him. "Yes, of course." Her voice was a touch high. Was this more difficult for her than she was letting on?

"Well, then I guess I should be going. Thank you for the nap and the meal." He scooted the chair back and stood.

She did as well. "I'll call you with a name of a matchmaker after I have spoken to her. She'll be in touch."

Whitney made it sound like a business deal was being concluded. He didn't like that at all. It was far too civilized a conversation for what they had shared. A business contract was what it had been but Tanner had started thinking of their relationship as more. He walked down the hall toward the front door. Unhappy with the arrangement, he still couldn't disagree with Whitney.

It troubled him how much he disliked the idea of not seeing her again. What really got to him was that she was nothing like what he was looking for in a woman. He'd even had a difficult time making her understand what type of marriage he wanted. If they continued, he would only be using her. He admired her too much for that.

He stopped at the door. Whitney had followed him. He turned to look at her. "I've enjoyed getting to know you. You're a special woman." Tanner kissed her on the cheek and forced himself to open the door and walk out.

CHAPTER SEVEN

IT HAD BEEN a week since Whitney had let Tanner walk out of her house. What she'd wanted to do was beg him to stay. Telling herself not to listen to her practical side, even though she'd made the right decision. But there was still a gnawing pain in her chest. He could be a difficult and demanding man, but she loved it when he let loose and laughed. They'd had fun together. In more ways than one.

Without question she had done what needed to be done. But that didn't mean she didn't miss him. The day after their meal together, she'd called a woman in town who was also a matchmaker. As a professional courtesy Whitney had asked her to take Tanner on. When the other woman found out who Tanner was she had been more than willing to have him as a client. Now indirectly Whitney would be setting him up on dates. She didn't want him dating anyone. What she wished for was for Tanner to want only her. Open his heart to her.

She was relieved and disappointed in equal measure when Tanner didn't answer his phone. She left the new matchmaker's number and told him that the woman would be in touch soon. Her heart felt a stab of pain when she thought of Tanner meeting matches. Touching another woman. Kissing her. Maybe even taking her to bed. After disconnecting the line, she sat looking out the window at nothing. It would have been nice to hear his voice. This was much more difficult than she'd thought it would be.

As the days passed it wasn't easy but she managed to live through them. Had she made the correct decision? Could there be another way?

She was a grown woman who knew what she'd been getting into when she'd agreed to spend the weekend with him. He hadn't coerced her into bed. She'd gone willingly. Even now, when she missed him with every fiber of her being, she didn't regret it.

Almost daily she called the hospital to check on Mr. Wilcox. All reports were positive. He was now out of the ICU and in a room. Whitney couldn't put off going to visit him any longer. She wouldn't hide just because she was afraid that she might run into Tanner. She'd learned long ago that if she wanted to be emotionally healthy she had to face her fears. She'd done that a number of times when she had been heavy. This situation was no different. The sad thing was that she was desperate to see Tanner, yet she was also dodging him.

At the hospital she made it to Mr. Wilcox's floor without any sign of Tanner. She asked directions at the nursing station to Mr. Wilcox's room. As she walked away one of the nurses said to another, "That's the woman Dr. Locke was with."

The other responded, "Not his usual type at all."

"You're right about that."

Whitney didn't like being talked about. Most of her life had been spent worrying about what others had been saying about her. Old habits died hard.

After her knock, she was surprised to hear a strong voice invite her in. She certainly didn't expect Mr. Wilcox to be sitting up in bed, watching TV and eating a meal.

This didn't look like the same man she'd seen before the heart transplant. "Hey, Mr. Wilcox."

"Hello, young lady. It's so nice of you to come by."

Whitney stepped farther into the room. "Well, you look wonderful."

"I'm feeling grand except for a few aches and pains, but Doc Locke says those will go away soon."

Even the mention of Tanner's name made Whitney's heart beat faster. "I'm glad to see it. I've been calling every day to check up on you. If I had known you would be doing so well I would have been here sooner."

"New ticker is doing the job. This day is my best day so far. So come in and tell me all the news."

Whitney had a moment of panic. Had Tanner told him about them? No, he wouldn't have done that. Mr. Wilcox must be using it as a figure of speech. She came to stand beside the bed. "What news would you like to know?"

"I'd like to know what you have done to put such a sour look on my doctor's face."

There it was. Could Tanner really have been so upset over them not seeing each other? "I don't know what you're talking about."

Mr. Wilcox studied her a moment. "I think you do but that isn't a nosy old man's business. If you won't talk about that then tell me about yourself. I know you went to Berkeley but tell me what else you do."

Mr. Wilcox had a way of getting her to talk that few people had managed. But Tanner had as well. She even told Mr. Wilcox she was a matchmaker.

"You think you could find someone for me?"

"I'll be glad to see what I can do."

There was a quick knock and the door opened. Tanner came to an abrupt stop. Whitney's heart slammed against her chest wall. She'd stayed too long. She was unable to do anything more than sit in her chair and stare at him. Tanner was just as handsome and commanding as she remembered. Every fiber of her being ached to touch him. She'd missed him so.

"Whitney."

The sound of her name was so sweet coming off his lips. "Hi, Tanner." She pulled her gaze away from him and looked at Mr. Wilcox. "It's time for me to go."

Mr. Wilcox glanced from her to Tanner and back. Those old eyes missed nothing. "You will come back soon?"

Whitney put a hand on his arm. "You can count on it. I'm glad you're doing so well."

"I have to give part of that credit to Dr. Locke here. He's a great doctor."

"I know he is." She did. How could Tanner be anything but that? "Bye, now."

When she passed Tanner he reached out and caught her arm. His touch sent an electric shock though her. The simplest touch from him had her trembling. "Would you please wait for me in the hall until I'm done here? I won't be but a few minutes."

Whitney glanced at Mr. Wilcox. He was still watching them closely. She nodded to Tanner.

Minutes later Tanner joined her. He looked at her carefully. "How have you been?"

"Fine. And yourself?"

"Let's not talk here." He took her arm and led her around the corner to a small consulting room. Opening the door, he let her step in before he entered. The door closed.

"Tanner, I don't really have time—"

His hands cupped her face as his mouth captured the rest of her words. There was an edge of desperation to the kiss as his lips moved across hers. Yet he was holding back. His mouth left hers to run kisses over her cheek. "I've missed you."

Heaven help her, she craved him still. But they must be sensible. She gently pushed him away. "Tanner, we can't do this."

He let her go and moved away, giving her space, but still breathed deeply as if he was holding himself in check. "Forgive me. I couldn't help myself. Look, what I brought you in here for was to ask you if you would go out with me? I have two tickets to Jazz in the Park tomorrow night."

"Shouldn't you be taking one of your matches?"

"None of those have worked out. Besides, I enjoy your company. What do you say, Whitney? Go with me."

This time he was asking, not demanding, she do something with him. She knew better but she couldn't bring herself to turn him down. It didn't matter what the best thing to do was, she wanted to go. Wanted to spend time with Tanner. "What time should I expect you?"

A smile came to his lips. One that reached his eyes. He'd been worried she wouldn't go. "Seven. Don't eat dinner. I'll bring it." His phone buzzed. "I have to get this. I'll see you tomorrow night."

Whitney thought he might kiss her before he left and was disappointed when he didn't.

She had a date with Tanner. A real date.

Tanner had been out with a number of women but for some reason he was nervous about this date. Everything must be right. He enjoyed Whitney's company more than anyone's he'd ever known and he was going to do whatever it took to continue to see her, to have her in his life, permanently.

It had occurred to him that she was his match. The one he'd been looking for. She met all his criteria. Whitney enjoyed his company. She'd proven that over and over while they'd been in Napa. They were extremely compatible in bed. Which made her almost perfect. She wanted children, was a great cook, did well in social situations. What was not right about her? Their life together would be satisfying. He just needed to convince her of that.

He'd been planning to give her a little more time before he asked her out but, seeing her in Mr. Wilcox's room, he hadn't been able to wait. He'd missed her, longed for her. Before she'd been his matchmaker and now she wasn't. There was nothing stopping them from dating.

Now all he had to do was woo her, show her that they belonged together. Surely he could do that? Had that been what his mother had tried to do? But Tanner wasn't going to make the mistake his mother had. He wasn't going to fall in love. Somehow he and Whitney would make it work without that emotion.

The next afternoon after half an hour of indecision, Tanner settled on a light blue collared shirt and jeans with a navy jacket as his outfit for the evening. Dressy, yet casual. Before he left the hospital he made sure that he had two doctors taking his calls in case something came up. He didn't want any interruptions tonight.

He was at Whitney's promptly at seven in his freshly washed car. Why was he acting as if he were going to the prom? Because he wanted Whitney to see the possibilities between them.

Adjusting his collar for the third time and checking his hair in the mirror, Tanner climbed the steps to her front door carrying a small flowerpot. The lady at the flower shop had said she would love this one.

He rang the bell. No one came. Had Whitney forgotten? He pushed the button again. Waited. Relief washed over him when the knob turned and the door opened. Whitney looked amazing. She was dressed in a light pink sweater set and darker pink pants that skimmed her hips, and wore her hair down around her shoulders, and he'd never seen her look more beautiful.

"Wow."

She smiled. "Thanks. You look nice yourself."

He offered the potted plant in his hand. "I brought you a flower."

Whitney took it and gently touched one of the purple blooms. "It's beautiful. You remembered how much I like violets."

"I did." He'd won points.

"Come in while I find a home for this and get my purse."

Tanner would follow her anywhere. He'd never felt like this about a woman. Right now all he wanted to do was carry her upstairs to her bed. Hell, he'd settle for her sofa. But he wasn't going to do that. She deserved better than a rutting buck.

Instead of following her farther down the hall, he chose to remain near the door so he wouldn't be further tempted. She soon returned with purse in hand.

"I'm ready."

"Great. Let's go." He went out the door and waited on the steps as she locked up. Taking Whitney's elbow, he helped her down the steps. When she went to the passenger side of his car he redirected her to the driver's. "I promised you could drive. I thought you might like to tonight."

She grinned. "Really?"

He held the door open for her. "Really."

Whitney dropped her purse into the space behind her seat and climb in. She already had the car started before he was in his seat and buckled up. He groaned when she revved the motor.

She smiled. "This is going to be fun."

"You break it, you buy it, that's all I'm going to say."

"Oh, you're no fun." She pulled away from the curb.

Over the next few minutes Tanner sat back and enjoyed watching Whitney's facial expressions as she negotiated the narrow hilly streets of San Francisco in the powerful car. She was having fun. The evening was off to a good start.

When they were closer to the park he gave her directions about where to pull in and stop. He helped her out of the car and then went to the trunk and removed the picnic basket and blanket he had stored there.

"Nice. Fix that yourself?" Whitney asked.

He gave her a bashful look. "No, but I did call and order it."

She gave a bark of laughter. "If nothing else, you're honest."

"Yeah, about this, but I wasn't straight up with Malcolm and Marie. I plan to come clean the next time I see Malcolm."

They started toward the stage already set up in an open grassy area in the middle of the park. "Good. I felt bad about deceiving them."

They wouldn't be upset if he could tell them that he and Whitney really were a couple.

Finding a place where no one else would be sitting too close to them, he spread the blanket out. They took a seat on it. Opening the basket, Tanner unloaded the food. Tanner had requested raw vegetables with dip, ham and cheese rolls, fruit and wine.

"This is nice," Whitney said. "Who decided on the menu?"

"I did."

"Good choices." She bit into a carrot that she had pulled through vegetable dip.

More points.

They were just finishing their meal when the jazz band took the stage. After a couple of numbers Whitney shifted as if she couldn't get comfortable. Tanner moved so she could lean against him. He liked having her close.

"The music is wonderful. Thanks for inviting me," she said between songs.

"You're welcome."

She smelled of something fresh and natural. The temptation to kiss her neck was almost impossible to resist but he did.

For Tanner the concert was over too soon. He had to let go of Whitney.

He repacked the basket and she held it while he folded the blanket. When he was done he put it under one arm and took Whitney's hand. They followed the rest of the crowd toward the parking lot.

"Do you want to drive home?" Tanner asked as he stored the basket and blanket in the trunk of the car.

"No, I think I'll just enjoy the ride. You always seem to make it interesting." She settled into the passenger seat and laid her head back on the rest. Closing her eyes, she hummed a piece the band had played.

It was a sound he could get used to hearing all the time. Forty-five minutes later he said, "Whitney, you're home."

She rolled her head and looked at him. "I'm sorry. I went to sleep on you."

"No problem. I deal with people who are asleep all the time."

It took her a minute but she burst out laughing. "You know, there was a time I thought you were so uptight that you had no idea what a joke was."

"I could say the same about you."

She sat up and gave him an indulgent look. "I've never been uptight in my life."

"If you say so."

Whitney laid her head back again. Speaking more to the night sky than him, she said, "You know, I had such a crush on you in college."

"You did?" It couldn't be anything like the one he had on her right now.

"I don't think you ever noticed me. You never even spoke to me but, man, I was crazy about you."

Tanner liked the softness of her voice in the night. "I'm flattered. I'm sorry that I didn't notice."

"Hey, don't feel bad. I don't think we would have liked each other then."

"Why is that?" He turned in the seat to see her clearer in the dim light from her porch.

Whitney shrugged. "I just think we both needed to grow up. I sure did. A few more life experiences make us see things differently."

"So what do you think of me now?" he asked quietly. His future depended on her answer.

"I…uh… I…like you. Far more than I would have in college. You're a good guy."

More points. This was going from a good night to a great one. Was now the time to ask? With his chest tight with building hope, he said, "I've been thinking about this matchmaking stuff. You know, we're pretty good together. Great, in fact, I think. You're a good match for me. I don't want to look anymore. I'd like us to see where this will go."

She didn't say anything for so long Tanner was afraid he wasn't going to want to hear what she had to say when she did speak.

"Tanner, would you like to come in?"

Whitney knew what she was agreeing to. But she also knew what it was like not to have Tanner in her life. Just a week of it had been enough for her. She loved him. Maybe she could show him how to love. She wasn't going to let go of this opportunity. It might not come her way again.

Tanner was a good man. She'd seen that in his actions more than once. He had the ability to open his heart, she knew that with all of her own. She would find the key. There was no doubt that he was her perfect match as well.

They made it as far as her hallway where a small lamp burned before Tanner grabbed her. She let her purse fall as he nudged her back against the front door. "I've waited as long as I can." His mouth took hers in a kiss that said he wanted her here and now. Flexing his hips, he asked, "See what you do to me?"

Whitney's stomach fluttered in anticipation. She liked having that kind of power over him. She brought a leg up high along his as she kissed him deeply. This was where she belonged. The love would come.

Tanner stepped back and fumbled with the button of her slacks. When he couldn't release it she brushed his hand away. "Let me."

"I want you so badly I can't think." He nipped at her neck. Touching her everywhere.

This self-assured man was trembling with desire for her. It was a heady feeling. She flipped the button open and pushed her pants and panties to her feet, stepped out of them and kicked them away. Seconds later Tanner's jeans and underwear joined hers on the throw rug on the floor.

His hands skimmed up her thighs to grip her hips and lift her. "Put your legs around me."

Wrapping her arms around his neck, Whitney obeyed. His gaze held hers as he slowly lowered her until he filled her. Heat, raw and sharp, pooled at her center. Bracing her against the door, Tanner thrust and withdrew.

Whitney wiggled as the sensation rose, turning the heat into a burning flame. Her fingers bit into his shoulder muscles through the fabric of his shirt. She might die with pleasure. Tanner plunged again as his mouth plundered hers. The need grew, built on itself until she could stand it no longer. She threw her head back and screamed her ecstasy.

Tanner held her in place and drove into her until he groaned his own release against her neck.

He steadied her as her feet reached the floor then swept her into his arms. "Bedroom."

"Upstairs, room on the right."

The morning sun woke Whitney. She stretched. Her hand touched the space where Tanner had slept. She smiled. He would return. So this was how a woman well loved and in love felt.

Tanner did love her. He just didn't recognize it for what it was. He would one day soon. He must. She would show him what giving love instead of demanding love was all about. With time he would come to recognize the difference between what his parents had had and what they had. She couldn't believe any different.

At daylight he'd woken her and kissed her thoroughly. "I have an early case. I'll see you this evening."

Then he was gone. She was well aware that she had to

share him with his job but she would have liked to wake up with him next to her. Maybe tomorrow. Those were the type of demands she couldn't make. He would balk at them immediately. Too clingy.

Whitney went through the day with a smile on her face. She forced herself to review some client information but her thoughts kept returning to Tanner.

That evening she was in the kitchen when the doorbell rang. Hurrying down the hall, she opened the door. Tanner waited there with a smile on his face and a bag in his hand. He stepped inside and closed the door before swooping her up into his arms. His lips found hers for a hungry kiss.

When he pulled away he said, "I've been looking forward to that all day."

"You get an A+ for greetings. You hungry?"

"Yeah. For you." He took her hand and led her upstairs.

Sometime later they came down again and went to the kitchen for dinner. Whitney could get used to this. While she placed the food on the table Tanner poured their drinks.

"How's Mr. Wilcox doing?" Whitney asked as they ate.

"I think I'll be able to send him home in a few days." Tanner cut his pork chop.

"That's great. I'm so happy for him. Did you know that he asked me to find him a match?"

Tanner looked at her. "Really?"

"He did."

"I hope he finds one as good as I have." Tanner grinned at her.

She liked being his match.

After cleaning the kitchen, they spent the rest of the

evening watching TV, with Whitney curled up in Tanner's arms.

"I missed you," he said softy. "Please don't push me away again."

"And I missed you." She gave him a kiss.

The rest of the week continued much as the way that evening had gone. Tanner had to work late a couple of nights but Whitney was waiting on him with a smile and a warm meal when he came *home*.

The first night he'd been late she'd been wearing a long comfortable gown. When they'd made it upstairs to her bedroom, Tanner had pulled it off over her head and dropped it in the trash can.

"No more granny gowns. I'm going to buy you something that flatters that sexy body of yours."

Tanner's attention always made her feel sexy and appealing. For once in her life she was going to buy some skimpy lingerie.

After their first night back together Tanner had brought over a bag of his clothes. A few days later she'd cleaned out a drawer for him and given him space in the closet. Their relationship was moving fast but she hadn't been happier. Still, there was the nagging voice that whispered when she wasn't busy, *Will he ever say he loves you?* She pushed it away with, "I haven't said it either, but that doesn't mean it isn't true."

Friday evening they were eating Chinese takeout when Whitney said, "My grandfather has a birthday party Sunday afternoon. Would you like to come with me?"

"Sure. Why haven't you said something about it before now?"

She fiddled with her chopsticks. "I wasn't sure how you would feel about meeting my family so soon."

Tanner took her hand. "You and I are a team. I'd love to meet your family."

Team? She wanted him to see them as a couple but she'd settle for team right now. "Mom and Dad will be there. My sister and her family. Some cousins."

"I'm game," he said, and went back to eating.

Sunday morning he had to go to the hospital for an emergency. "I'll meet you at your grandparents'. Text me the address," Tanner said before he gave her a quick kiss goodbye.

She didn't like showing up at her grandparents' without Tanner, but he had said he would make it if he could. Even though they had only been together a week she felt lost without him. Her heart swelled just knowing he came home to her every day.

They were just singing "Happy Birthday" when there was a knock on the door. One of her cousins answered and called her name.

"Yes."

"Your Tanner is here."

Her Tanner. Whitney liked the sound of that. She met him at the door. He put his arm around her waist and gave it a squeeze. "Sorry, I'm so late. Case was worse than I thought."

She smiled. "I understand."

"That's one of the many things I like about you, you always do." He gave her a quick kiss.

Why couldn't that *like* have been *love*? "Come meet my parents and grandparents."

"Lead the way."

CHAPTER EIGHT

TANNER WASN'T USED to all the noise and excitement, the laughter, of a big family get-together. He decided he liked it. What he remembered about family parties growing up was that they were elaborate and his mother had often ended up breaking down in tears because his father hadn't shown up. They had not been happy affairs.

Whitney took his hand and led him into a dining room where everyone was standing around a table. He stood behind her in the crowded space. Sitting at the end was a balding, white-haired man. Next to him was a woman of about the same age who was cutting cake and placing it on plates then handing them to a younger woman who added scoops of ice cream.

"Harold, how much ice cream do you want?" the woman asked.

"Six scoops," Whitney's grandfather said.

"Harold! Even on your birthday that is too much," the woman cutting the cake scolded.

Whitney's grandfather reached for her hand and kissed the back of it. "It's my birthday, sweetheart."

She turned and looked at the woman with the ice-cream scoop. "Make it three."

"That's what I wanted anyway." Whitney's grandfather grinned.

"They're my grandparents." Whitney pointed to the older couple. "That's my mom helping with the ice cream. I'll introduce you in a minute." The love Whitney had for them was evident in her voice.

Didn't she use that same note when she spoke to him? He would have to think about that later.

"Okay, now that the birthday boy has had his share, pass the cake and ice cream around," Whitney's grandmother instructed.

Everyone did as they were told except for a few of the young kids, who grabbed theirs and disappeared into another room or outside. Soon Whitney and he had their share. Most of the others left to sit elsewhere, leaving room at the table for them. Whitney headed toward her grandfather and took a seat near him. Tanner slid into the one beside her.

"Paps and Memaw, I'd like for you to meet Tanner Locke."

"Hello, sir. It's nice to meet you. And happy birthday," Tanner said to her grandfather.

The older man gave him a long look then said in a teasing tone, "You must be the guy who has put the smile on Whitney's face."

Tanner glanced at Whitney to find her blushing. "I hope so."

"And this is my mom, Delores. Where's Daddy?"

"He's outside, getting some more chairs," Delores answered.

As if he knew they were talking about him, a man with the same coloring as Whitney entered the room. "I gave the chairs to those out on the lawn."

Delores smiled at him. "Thanks, honey. What would I do without you? Have you met Whitney's friend?"

Tanner had every intention of being more than her

friend but he would accept that title for now. He stood and offered his hand. "Hello, Mr. Thomason. Tanner Locke."

Her father accepted his hand. "Hi, Tanner. Joe Thomason. Nice to meet you."

"You too, sir."

"Joe, I saved you some cake and ice cream." Delores placed a plate in front of an empty chair across from Tanner.

Joe took the chair and smiled at his wife. "Thanks." He then turned to Tanner again. "Whitney says you're a heart surgeon. Interesting profession."

"I am. And most of the time it is." Tanner took a forkful of cake.

"It would be nice to have a doctor in the family." Joe grinned at his daughter.

"Daddy!" Whitney's voice went up an octave.

What would it be like to be a member of this family? Whitney must have really cast a spell over him. There was something rare in the air around these people, in the way they looked at one another and interacted. Rare at least in his experience. It made him want to be included. He couldn't remember that ever happening before.

When Whitney touched him he knew the feeling. Like on the balloon. Her smile alone made his life better. What was that element? Some would call it a connection. Others compatibility. Knowing Whitney, she would say it was love. Was it something he knew how to give? But if he did it would make him too vulnerable, weak like his mother.

His family, his mother and father's relationship had been so dysfunctional that he never thought of himself as wanting, or capable of being in, a loving unit. Whitney's family made him feel a little uncomfortable as well. As if he was looking in on something he had no knowledge of.

Over the next hour he met the rest of her relations, discussed baseball with her brother-in-law and listened to a conversation between her father and uncle about the best way to grill a chicken. When Whitney put her hand on his shoulder and said it was time to go, he had to admit he was ready. He wasn't sure he really fit in here.

They were inside saying their goodbyes when one of Whitney's nephews came running into the house. "There's something wrong with Papa Joe."

Whitney was ahead of Tanner as they rushed out of the house. Family members surrounded her father. She pushed through two of them to where he sat in one of the folding chairs. He was clutching his left arm.

"Michelle, get the baby aspirin." Whitney glanced at him. "He had some arrhythmia a few years back."

Tanner said to the man standing beside him, "Go to the convertible down there." He pointed down the street. "And bring me the black bag behind the seat." Tanner handed him his keys. "Everyone, please move back a step or two. Whitney, call 911. Even if this is arrhythmia he still needs to be checked out at the hospital."

Whitney pulled out her phone.

The man returned with the bag and Tanner located his stethoscope. "Mr. Thomason, I'm going to give you a listen. Just remain still. Everything is going to be fine. Whitney, I'm going to give you some information and I want you to tell the operator to relay it to the ambulance EMTs."

"I'm ready."

"Give them my name and tell them that I am on-site." She did as he requested while he listened to Mr. Thomason's heart. There was no question it was an arrhythmia issue. The man might require a procedure this time. "Tell them to patch you through to the EMTs."

Whitney relayed the message. Her voice didn't waver. She was a tough cookie even in an emergency.

Michelle returned with the aspirin in her hand and Mrs. Thomason on her heels.

Whitney said to Michelle, "Give three to Tanner."

She was even knowledgeable enough about her father's care to know what he needed in case of an emergency. Whitney took care of those she loved.

Tanner took the tablets from Michelle. "Mr. Thomason, I need you to chew these and swallow them. Make sure they go down."

"I'll get some water," someone said.

"No water. It could cause him to choke." Or if he required emergency surgery, he shouldn't have anything in his stomach.

"Joe, Joe, are you all right?" Mrs. Thomason sobbed as she pushed through the group and rushed to Mr. Thomason.

"Michelle, take care of Mother," Whitney clipped.

Her sister did as Whitney said, putting her arm around her mother and pulling her away a few steps. "Mom, back up and let Tanner see about Daddy."

Tanner knew the answer to the question before he asked but he had to anyway. "Mr. Thomason, are you on any medication?"

"He is. The information is in my purse. I'll get it," Mrs. Thomason said. She pulled away from Michelle's arm and headed for the house.

"Tanner, the EMTs are on the line," Whitney said from close beside him.

"Good. Tell them the patient is responsive. Three eighty-one-milligram aspirin given." He waited until Whitney had repeated his words. "Heart rate one hundred and sixty-seven. BP one-eight-four over ninety. Respirations forty-five." He pressed Mr. Thomason's index fingernail while she spoke. "Little discoloration of nail."

Whitney repeated the information.

Her mother returned with the medication list and handed it to him. He reviewed it then passed it along to Whitney. "Let the EMTs know. If you can't pronounce it, spell it out."

Tanner did another round of vitals as Whitney read out the medicine names and dosages to the EMTs. Mr. Thomason appeared stable but Tanner still wouldn't be comfortable until he was at the hospital and some tests were run.

The sound of the siren from the approaching ambulance soon filled the air. Tanner looked up and scanned the concerned family group around him. "I need everyone to move way back. Give the EMTs room to work." Thankfully everyone did as he asked.

Minutes later he spoke to one of the EMTs then let them do what they were well trained to do. After they had Mr. Thomason in the ambulance, Tanner conferred with the ER doctor who would be accepting his patient at the hospital. Soon Mr. Thomason was on his way. Tanner put his supplies back in his bag and found Whitney with her mother.

"I'm going to drive Mother to the hospital," Whitney said.

She really had been cool during an emergency. Many people would have fallen apart if a family member had been in trouble. Whitney had followed his directions to the letter without any questions. She was someone he could depend on during a crisis.

"Why don't I drive you both? We can come back to get my car later," Tanner offered.

Whitney gave him a grateful look that included something he wasn't sure he was willing to put a name to.

"Thank you."

Three hours later, Whitney was standing in the hospital at the foot of her father's bed. He had an oxygen cannula under his nose and had an IV in his arm but otherwise looked no worse for the scare he had put his family through. A monitor on a pole nearby continually checked his heart rate.

"I knew you bringing home a doctor was going to be a benefit," her father said with a wink.

Whitney was just glad Tanner had stepped out to speak to her father's cardiologist and hadn't heard that statement.

"I don't like Tanner because he's a doctor, Dad. He's fun to be around, nice, caring and good to me."

Her father looked at her for a moment. "Sounds like a woman in love to me."

She was. Deeply. "There's a lot to love about him."

Her father grinned as he looked over her shoulder.

Whitney turned to find Tanner standing there. Had he heard what she had said? Would he run now, knowing how she felt? She tried to read Tanner's face but there was no indication he had heard her. If she did tell him how she felt, would he even give them a chance?

She'd had no doubt that he was a thorough doctor and a compassionate one. With Mr. Wilcox she had seen some of those attributes but today with her father she'd seen firsthand how he could command a difficult situation. He had been magnificent. Someone she could lean on in a time of trouble.

Tanner came to stand beside her. "You're all set, Mr.

Thomason. I'll be in to check on you in the morning. If you need anything, just ask."

"Thanks for your help today. I don't usually make such a scene when my daughter brings home a man for the first time."

Tanner grinned. "I'm glad to know I'm special." He looked at Whitney's mother. "Delores, are you sure you're going to be okay here tonight? Have everything you need?"

"I'll be just fine. I wouldn't sleep if I went home anyway," her mother assured him, placing a hand on her husband's arm and looking at him adoringly.

Tanner seemed unnaturally focused on her parents, as if he was watching every detail of their interaction. Did their obvious affection make him feel nervous?

"Then Whitney and I will see you first thing in the morning," Tanner said.

He really was great. Tanner didn't have to go with her. She kissed both of her parents. "Call if you need anything."

As she and Tanner drove through the early evening toward her grandparents' house Whitney reached over and rested her hand on his thigh. "Thank you for saving my father's life today."

"I don't know that I did that but you're welcome. I was pretty impressed by the cool head you kept. I've had nurses who showed less control in an emergency. If you ever want to give up matchmaking, I recommend you consider nursing or med school."

Whitney chuckled. "I think you're giving me too much credit but it's nice to hear praise."

Tanner pulled her parents' car into her grandparents' drive. He turned to look at her. "You should hear praise all the time. You're wonderful."

"You're pretty wonderful yourself." Her hand cupped

his cheek and she gave him a kiss that held all the love she felt.

When they broke apart he wore a strange expression. Had Tanner sensed what she was offering him? They continued to look at each other. Had something subtly changed between them? Did she dare to hope he felt the love she did?

Tanner broke the spell of the moment with, "I guess we'd better go in and give your grandparents a report."

An hour later, she was driving her parents' car back to their house while Tanner followed her. She pulled it in the garage. Whitney had promised to pack her mother some clothes and her father a pair of pajamas and a few personal items. Tanner came inside to wait while she gathered things.

"So how long have your parents been married?" he asked from the living room.

"Thirty-one—no, thirty-two years." She stuck her head out of her parents' bedroom. "Why?"

"They just seem so happy together."

"They are," Whitney said from inside the bedroom.

"My parents fought all the time. I don't remember them being able to stay in the same room together over half an hour. They certainly couldn't stay in a hospital room together. Your parents must really love each other."

Whitney's heart filled with optimism. Tanner did recognize love. She stepped out of the room. "Yeah, they do."

Tanner was standing in front of a picture of her entire family. "No wonder you didn't understand why I didn't list that as necessary in my match."

"It was hard for me to understand at the time. Now that you have told me about your parents I sort of understand. But that doesn't mean that you can't have love in your life." She looked directly at him. "I want what my parents have."

It took a moment before he said, "I can't promise that. I'm not even sure I know how to love like that."

Whitney stepped closer. "Maybe I can help you learn."

That night they walked hand and hand up the stairs to what was now their bedroom. When Whitney started to undress Tanner pushed her hands away. "Let me." He slowly removed her clothes, kissing each piece of flesh he exposed. With all her clothes on the floor, he quickly removed his. Tanner took her hand and led her to the bed.

"You are so amazing." He gently caressed her lips.

Whitney cupped his face with both her hands and kissed him with all the love she felt.

Tanner lifted her to the bed and joined her without breaking the contact. When they broke apart, he lay on his side and looked down at her. As his eyes raked her body, Whitney trembled. Tanner's look found hers, held.

"I don't know what you're doing to me, but I like who I am around you."

Whitney smiled. She knew what it was. Love.

Tanner kissed her again. When it went deeper Whitney nudged him to his back. She brought her lips to his chest over his heart. He inhaled sharply. Whitney captured his hands and held them at his sides. She kissed the curve of his neck and slowly slid over him. He moaned his pleasure. She continued to work her way up him, enjoying her skin touching his. She placed a kiss on his ear, eyebrow and finally his lips. She released his hands. He brought them to her hips, caressing her. He gently lifted her then slowly lowered her, joining them.

Their movements were deliberate and calm, yet there was an intensity between them they'd not had before. There was nothing of the frenzied coupling Tanner normally preferred. This time it was as if he was marking her as his.

Afterward, they lay in each other's arms for a long time without either of them speaking. Hope blossomed in Whitney.

The next few weeks passed much as the others had. For Tanner life was better than it had ever been yet there was something off he couldn't name.

After their lovemaking the night Whitney's father had gone into the hospital something had changed between them. The smiles Whitney gave him had an extra brightness to them. She touched him for no reason when she was walking by. She was waiting when he came home no matter what the time. The pleasure he found in bed was pure bliss and went beyond anything he'd ever experienced. Yet something nagged at him. As if he was missing something.

Whitney's father was home and doing well. He'd only visited with him once since he'd been released but Whitney gave Tanner a report each evening of his progress. When was the last time he had spoken to his father? Five years? Even his mother he only talked to a couple of times a year. The closeness, real caring, he saw in Whitney's family was a foreign concept for him.

All the attributes he appreciated most in Whitney he could see in some form in her parents. It made him uneasy on a level he didn't understand. Would Whitney continue to be happy with him? Would she demand more? Start treating him as his mother had his father?

Mr. Wilcox had been discharged the day after Mr. Thomason had been admitted. Mr. Wilcox's new heart was doing well. A friend had come to pick him up and had promised to see that he made it to his appointments.

"That young lady of ours came by to see me earlier this morning." Mr. Wilcox climbed into the wheelchair the orderly held for him.

Of course Whitney had.

Even with her father sick she wouldn't forget about someone else.

"She's a keeper. She has a big heart. To be loved by someone like that is a special thing. I know. I had it and miss it every day."

"Whitney is special." Tanner meant that. The more he was with her the more he found another facet of her personality he liked. It disturbed him that his emotional attachment was growing. He didn't want to think about that. Emotional attachment was something that he'd never wanted or planned to have.

They had been together almost two months when Tanner said at dinner one night, "We've been invited to a cocktail party on Friday evening at Malcolm and Marie's."

"We have?" Whitney sounded unsure.

"Will you go?"

"Do you really need me to?"

Hadn't she gotten past her fear of social situations after their weekend in Napa? "There'll be questions if you don't."

"Those events are just not my thing."

"But you were great in Napa. You don't give yourself enough credit. What's the problem?"

She left the table and walked to the kitchen sink, then confronted him. "The problem is that for over half my life I was made fun of or looked down on for my weight. I wasn't invited to or included in parties. Now I just plain don't care to be around those kinds of people. Up until a few years ago no one in that group would have given me the time of day."

"Why, Whitney Thomason, I had no idea you were such a snob."

"I am not! What I don't do is put myself in situations where I know I'll be made to feel inadequate."

Tanner turned in his chair to face her. "Did Malcolm and Marie make you feel that way in Napa?"

"Well, no." She crossed her arms over her chest.

"Do I make you feel that way?"

She backed up to the counter. "No-o-o… But not all the people are like you and the Jarvises."

"So you're going to let others control what you do in life?" Whitney winced. Tanner could tell that shot had hit its mark.

"No, but I don't have to be around them."

"I'll be there with you. Don't you trust me to support you?"

She came toward him. "I do, but I just think you'd be better off at those events without some insecure woman to worry about."

He faced her. "Has it occurred to you that I might need your support at the party? That social situations might not be my 'thing' either?"

"Why would you need my support? You're a successful heart surgeon, you're gorgeous and intelligent—who wouldn't enjoy your company?"

"Apparently you." Tanner sounded hurt, which he was. "I'm still trying to get that promotion. Making small talk is a little nerve-racking for me as well."

Whitney studied him for a minute. "I had no idea you felt that way. You seem to have so much confidence wherever you go."

"Now you know another one of my secrets."

She came back to the table and just before she sat he

grabbed her and pulled her onto his lap. "So will you go with me?"

"I guess we're in it together."

Tanner kissed her. "About that gorgeous and intelligent remark, you really think so?"

She slapped his shoulder. "Now you're just fishing for compliments."

He chuckled. "That's because I like hearing you say them. They sound extra good coming out of your pretty mouth."

"Maybe for another kiss I could say more."

"For a kiss you don't have to say anything." His mouth found hers.

Whitney didn't make a habit of buying new clothes often but she had found that her wardrobe had almost completely changed since she and Tanner had started seeing each other. He liked to see her in clothes that fit her form and she'd taken to wearing less baggy clothes. Even her nightclothes, if she wore any, were flimsy gowns with lace and bows that had little substance. Tanner had slowly seen to it that all her granny gowns went out with the trash. She didn't mind. In fact, she rather liked the person she was becoming with Tanner.

On her own initiative, she went shopping for a dress for the cocktail party. She found a simply cut black A-line that she felt confident wearing. At home that evening, Tanner only added to her self-assurance when he saw her enter the living room where he was waiting.

He stood and came toward her. Taking her hand, he turned her around and whistled. "If I didn't need to show up for this party I'd say forget it and spend the rest of the night taking that dress off you."

"You do have a way of making a girl feel good." She kissed him. "You look superb yourself."

He did, dressed in his dark suit with a light blue tie. The man was almost too handsome to look at. It gave her a boost of confidence just being seen with him. But what she liked most about him couldn't be seen. Tanner was such a fine person.

An hour later they arrived at the Jarvises'. They were greeted warmly and Whitney was truly glad to see them both. She and Tanner had agreed on the way over that as soon as possible they would own up to their deception in Napa.

"Malcolm, Marie, Whitney and I owe you both an apology. Really me more than Whitney. I convinced her to pretend that she was my girlfriend in Napa when she was actually working as my matchmaker."

"But you're both here together now so it must have worked." Marie smiled broadly.

Tanner put his arm around Whitney's waist and brought her close. "Yes, it did."

"Then no harm was done." Malcolm patted him on the back.

"Did I hear someone say something about a matchmaker?"

Whitney cringed at the sound of Charlotte's voice. Squaring her shoulders, she turned and faced the woman. "I'm a matchmaker."

"Who needs a matchmaker?" Charlotte's voice held disgust.

Malcolm said, "Apparently Marie and I did. We met though a matchmaking service."

The look on Charlotte's face was almost comical. "If you'll excuse me, I think Max is looking for me."

Charlotte left to the sound of two couples' laughter.

Whitney couldn't help feeling both vindicated and sorry for her.

Tanner remained close throughout the rest of the evening and Whitney found she was enjoying herself. She liked the new person she was becoming. The one who felt good about her life.

She had excused herself and was in the hallway on the way to the restroom when she overheard some women talking in an alcove.

"I can't believe that woman Mark is with. She has an unbelievable body."

"Yeah. He went out and got him a thin one," another woman said.

"He divorced Mildred after she became so large," the first woman said. "I heard he said he needed someone who could help his career, not someone he wanted to hide."

Heat flooded Whitney. At one time that could have been her they were talking about.

A third voice said, "You're just saying that because he won't give you a second look."

Whitney shuddered. These were part of Tanner's social circle. Were these the type of people she would be forced into being around for the rest of her life?

"And that woman Tanner is with." Her tone held a note of disgust. "I know her name from somewhere. I just can't figure out where."

"Charlotte said she's a matchmaker. Can you imagine?"

"I know where I've seen her before. She went to college with me. She was President of the Literary Society. I knew I recognized her name. She used to be huge."

"A fat matchmaker," one of them cackled.

Whitney had heard that kind of talk before. She didn't like it any better now.

"She's not fat now."

"No, she isn't, but I wonder how she managed to snag that gorgeous Tanner. I wonder if he knows she was once so heavy."

Whitney had heard enough. She felt sick. Moisture filled her eyes. She wanted to get out of there. Turning, she headed down the hall again in search of Tanner.

As she reached him, he took one look at her and demanded, "What's wrong?"

"I'd like to go now." She worked not to have a quiver in her voice.

Tanner touched her arm. "Are you not feeling well?"

She pulled away. "You could say that."

A perplexed look came over his face. "Let's say our goodbyes to Malcolm and Marie then we can go."

"Why don't you do that for me? I'll wait for you in the car."

Tanner looked at her closely. "What's going on? You feeling ill?"

"I'll tell you when we get home." Whitney made her way toward the front door.

She had already called for the car by the time Tanner joined her. The valet pulled up in front of them before Tanner could start asking questions.

He helped her in then went around and slid into the driver's seat. They were out on the road when he asked, "Do you want to tell me what happened back there?"

CHAPTER NINE

TANNER'S TONE REMINDED Whitney too much of how he had sounded when he'd demanded that she go with him to Napa. He wasn't going to leave her any choice but to answer. "Can we please just talk about it when we get home?"

He glanced at her. "Okay, but I'll accept nothing short of a full explanation."

For the next three-quarters of an hour they said nothing. Tanner glanced at her a couple of times with concern. Which only made what she was going to have to say worse. Whitney searched for a way out of what she knew was coming. She was going to give up everything she had ever dreamed of or hoped for. A burning sensation rolled in her middle. Whitney crossed her arms over her stomach. She might truly be sick.

What could she do to stop herself from destroying her life? How could she not? She couldn't live thinking she was inadequate every time she and Tanner went out. That Tanner might one day be disappointed in her. Leave her. Those old insecurities she'd thought she'd put away when she had lost weight hadn't been far below the surface.

Anyway, Tanner had made it clear weeks ago when they had met to start looking for a mate for him that he was only interested in a mutually beneficial relationship.

Not love. She wanted love or nothing. There had not been one word about loving her in the weeks they had been together. There might never be. How was she supposed to gain his love if she couldn't even handle herself at one of his social gatherings without falling apart?

They weren't going to work. It was best to call it quits now before either one of them got in any deeper. Only it was too late for her. She loved him beyond measure.

At her house Tanner helped her out of the car. He followed her into the living room. She went to stand near the fireplace behind a chair. She needed it to provide her support.

Tanner stood in the middle of the room, waiting.

That nauseated feeling intensified. Only with a determination she would have sworn she didn't possess did Whitney meet his look. What she had to say must be said.

"Whitney, what happened?" There was alarm in his voice. "Are you okay?"

She sadly shook her head. "Tanner, we're not going to work."

"What?" He started toward her.

She put out a hand to stop him. "Us as a couple isn't going to work."

He came to an abrupt halt. "I thought we were working just fine until an hour ago. Now I'm just confused. Could you tell me what the problem is?"

What she wouldn't give to have him quit glaring at her. Hurt had seeped into his eyes. She said as clearly as she could, "I overheard some women talking about one of the ladies being fat. They even had something to say about me being with you. I can't tolerate that backbiting. I know that social events are important to your career but I can't do it. I spent too much of my life being treated as a second-class citizen. I won't go there again."

His look turned incredulous. "You've got to be kidding! All of this is about a few women being bitchy?"

She gripped the chair. How could she make him understand? A lifetime of people thinking you're less of a person because your body hung over a chair, your plate was piled full, your clothes baggy. Being judged and found wanting. Those emotions weren't easily pushed aside.

"It's more than that. I'm not who you need. I'll end up disappointing you. What if I gain weight? I can so easily. I have to watch it all the time."

He put out his hands as if pleading. "Hell, you're old enough and smart enough to know that people are the same everywhere. They're going to talk. What they say doesn't matter."

"I wish that was true. But it's hard for me to push away those old feelings of not being good enough. Your friends and associates are the type who used to put me down or, worse, not include me. I don't want to embarrass you. Be an embarrassment to you."

Tanner's hands had fallen to his sides and he all but shouted, "That's not going to happen."

"You don't know that." Whitney worked to keep her voice even and calm while her heart raced in her chest. "We're deluding ourselves. You hired me to find you the 'right match.' I'm not it."

"There has to be more to this than women talking. You couldn't possibly be that insecure. Or think so little of me. I've never said anything but positive things about your looks. I think you are beautiful." His disbelief circled around them like an angry animal.

"That's because you've never known what it's like, being an outsider," she said, unable to meet his blazing eyes.

"The hell I haven't." He stepped toward her. "What

do you think it was like to live with my parents? I never knew if my father was coming home or how crazy my mother would be when he did. My brother and I never had any idea what to expect. At least you had functional parents. A place to live where all the focus wasn't on what your parents wanted. You felt loved."

She gripped the chair, glad for its support. Maybe he did understand what it was like to have apprehensions but she wasn't going to keep putting herself into the kind of situation she'd been in tonight. "I don't know what you want from me."

"I was going to ask you to marry me."

Her look zeroed in on his. "What? As a business merger or a declaration of love?"

Tanner didn't come any closer. "You knew from our first meeting that love wasn't part of the deal."

And she had. But she had hoped he would change his mind. Would slowly come to know love through her actions toward him. "That's what you said."

He dipped his chin and cocked a brow. "You didn't believe me?"

"Yes, but I thought you'd change when you found the right woman."

His chuckle had no real humor to it. "Whitney, I know I've made it perfectly clear what I am looking for in a wife. I'm sure I've not misled you even once."

"That's just it. I want something you can't or won't give." She moved to stand beside the chair. "I love you and I want you to love me in return. You refuse. I won't settle for less. I've seen what a loving relationship can be with my grandparents and parents. I deserve the same.

"You do as well but you're so sure that it doesn't exist or that you'll be so dependent on another person for happiness that you push that happiness away. I've shown you love in every way I know how in the last few months. Mind, body and soul. Yet you won't accept it. I need someone in my life who wants me for more than laughs and companionship or good sex."

"I'll have you know that sex between us is better than good. And I want you to have my children. You would be a wonderful mother."

Whitney slowly shook her head, sadness overtaking her. "You just don't get it. The sex is so great because I'm making love to you. But I still won't bring a child into a loveless marriage. You're so fearful that you're going to end up acting like your mother that you can't let anyone in. The thing is that you act more like your father. Taking the love and life you could have and throwing it back in my face."

Tanner looked as if she'd socked him on the chin, dazed him. She had hit a nerve. A very exposed one. Whitney stepped back a pace. "I'm sorry. I shouldn't have said that."

As if performing a magic trick, Tanner made a transformation. Straightening his shoulders and with all the fire leaving his eyes, he smiled tightly at her. He shoved his hands in his pockets. His demeanor became as cold as the night air coming off the San Francisco Bay in winter. "You may be right about that. But this just proves that love isn't worth the hurt.

"Since we're being so open here, let me tell you a few things. Not everyone wants a pie-in-the-sky, everything-is-rosy marriage. Some people just want peace in their life. A haven to come home to where people coexist, have common interests and mutual respect. Maybe some people, you included, think that a loving marriage is the goal in life. Me, I don't know how to do that. And I've never said or implied that I did.

"Another thing. You can't punish me for what people did to you in your past. You can't live worried about what people might do and say now. You're not the person you were when you were heavy. It's rather vain for you to think everyone is judging you. People like your ex-fiancé disappoint others. I'm not your ex. I don't have to love you to be supportive and stand beside you. I think I have proved that more than once."

Whitney shrank back. He had proved his loyalty. Still, she wanted his heart.

"One more thing." He raised a finger in the air. "Not once have I ever said I give a damn about your weight. Even when I gave you a list of what I was looking for in a mate, I didn't once say anything about the woman being thin. All of that is in—" he pointed his finger at her "—your head.

"Don't bother asking me to leave. I'm gone. Throw my stuff in a bag. Put it on the front stoop. Text me and I'll come and get it. That way I won't ever bother you again."

Seconds later her front door closed with a shudder of the stained glass that coincided with her howl of agony.

It had been three weeks since Tanner had left Whitney's and he still didn't feel any better. He'd never been so blindsided in his life. Whitney's announcement that their relationship wasn't working had been news to him. She'd completely overreacted to what amounted to gossip. Those women didn't matter. People talked all the time. What mattered was what was best for Whitney and him. They enjoyed the same things, were great together in bed. Wanted the same things out of life. Maybe that wasn't exactly right. She wanted love, needed it from him. Did he even understand the emotion? Was he capable of giving it if he did?

He wanted to put his hand through a wall or shake Whitney until he shook some sense into her.

When he'd left her place he'd driven to his apartment, which he'd been thinking of selling because things between him and Whitney had been going so well. That was over. Entering the cold, sterile-looking place after staying in Whitney's warm and inviting home made him more depressed. She'd added vitality to his life.

More times than he could count he'd been hurt by his parents' actions but he had never felt this gnawing, snarling anger and frustration eating away at him that he had now. It affected every part of his life. Including his work. His staff was starting to give him looks and make hushed comments under their breath after he had given an order. He was trying to get a promotion and his staff was tiptoeing around him.

The nights were the worst. Especially when he did doze off and woke reaching for her on the other side of the bed. Most of the time he just paced the floor or stayed at the hospital. Eyedrops had become a staple because he never seemed to close his eyes. If he did, Whitney's smiling face invaded his mind. Her swishing her butt as she sang to a song while cooking dinner. Whitney's look of bliss as she found her release.

He slammed his hand down on his desk, making the pen beside it jump. This had to stop.

Punching the button on the desk phone, he ran back through the messages until he found hers, leaving him the name of the other matchmaker. It was time to move on.

The sound of Whitney's clear voice almost dissolved his resolve. He missed her with every fiber of his being. Even his clothes smelled of her.

He'd gone by her place. A bag had sat on the stoop, just as he'd requested. When he'd got it home and opened it,

the smell of her had wafted around him. He'd felt sucker
punched. Inside the bag had been his clothes, neatly
folded and arranged with care. She'd still been taking
care of him. The smell had lingered to the point where
he'd stuffed all the clothing back into the bag and taken
them to the cleaners.

Tanner picked up the pen and quickly jotted the number down that Whitney had left in the message. He didn't
want to have to listen twice. With a punch of his finger
he deleted the communication. That ended any temptation to hear it again.

He was tied in knots and it was time to get undone.
The first step was to call this new matchmaker and start
the process of finding someone who fit his requirements.
Someone who didn't see love as the main ingredient.
He would make the call as soon as he saw his afternoon
clinic patients. The first on the list was Mr. Wilcox. Whitney had even managed to take some of the pleasure out
of seeing the older man. Why had he let her permeate
his working life? He was paying for it dearly. And was
afraid he'd be doing so for a long time to come.

Tanner opened the door to the small but functional ex-
amination room. Mr. Wilcox sat on the exam table with
his shirt off. "Hello. How're you feeling?" Tanner asked.

"I'm fine except for the fact that I'm freezing to death.
You ask us to strip down then leave us in a cold room."

That was one of many things he liked about Mr. Wilcox. The man said what he thought. Not unlike Whitney.
"Sorry about that. Let me give you a listen then you can
get dressed."

Tanner pulled his stethoscope from around his neck.
Mr. Wilcox was doing well. His heart was working as
expected and so far there was no major rejection. Tanner
fully believed he would live many more years. Minutes

later he said, "You sound good. You can put your shirt on now." He gave Mr. Wilcox a steady hand to hold as he climbed down from the table.

Mr. Wilcox slid an arm into a sleeve of his shirt and said, "So how's your lady doing?"

The one subject Tanner didn't what to talk about. His lady. Whitney had been. He'd been happy then.

"She's fine."

Mr. Wilcox looked up from buttoning his shirt. "That doesn't sound so fine."

Tanner acted as if he was writing on the chart. "It's not. We broke up."

"I'm sorry to hear that. But you know the old saying, 'If it's worth having it's worth fighting for.' I would say that one is worth fighting for."

"I don't think it matters. We want two different things out of life."

Mr. Wilcox nodded with his lips pursed as if in thought. "That so? I think I'd be changing what I want to keep her."

Could he do that? Tell her that he loved her? Did he?

"It's good to see you, Mr. Wilcox. Call if you need us, otherwise I'll see you in two months."

"Sounds good. Hey, you know love isn't always easy but it's always worth it."

There was that word again. Love. That wasn't the kind of relationship he wanted. Yet there was an ache where his heart was that was saying differently.

His fourth patient for the afternoon was a middle-aged woman who had progressively gotten sicker and sicker. He would soon have to place her on the transplant list.

Tanner plastered on a congenial smile and entered the room. "Hello, Mrs. Culpepper."

"Hi, Dr. Locke. I'd like you to meet my husband, Henry."

The man with graying hair at his temples stood. He and Tanner shook hands.

"Do you mind if I give you a listen, Mrs. Culpepper?" Tanner said as he removed his stethoscope.

"That's what I'm here for." She smiled and sat straighter on the exam table.

Tanner listened carefully to the slow and sluggish organ in her chest. Even her breathing was taking on a more labored sound. "Give me a sec. I need to have a look at your X-rays." Tanner typed his security code into the computer and pulled up Mrs. Culpepper's chart. With another click the picture she had just taken in the X-ray department came up on the screen. There it was, the oversize heart of the thin woman sitting before him.

He looked at Mrs. Culpepper. "I'm going to let you get dressed and have you meet me down the hall in the conference room where we can talk more comfortably. Lisa, my nurse, will be in to show you the way."

A distressed look came over her face but she nodded and slid off the table to stand. Her husband hurried to help her.

A few minutes later Tanner entered a room furnished with a serviceable table and six chairs. His nurse assistant, Lisa, and the Culpeppers were already waiting for him. Tanner took a chair facing them. Mrs. Culpepper looked close to tears. She must fear what was coming. This was the least enjoyable part of Tanner's job. Mr. Culpepper placed a hand on hers resting on the table. He too must sense what Tanner was planning to say.

"It's time, isn't it?" Mrs. Culpepper said.

Tanner nodded. "It is."

Her husband gently squeezed her hand. "We'll get through this together. That's what we do."

She looked at him. The bond between them was obvious. "I know I can count on you."

Why had Tanner never noticed that in couples before? Since Whitney had come into his life he seemed to see loving couples everywhere where he'd seen none before. For the first time in his life he'd begun to want that. But he'd thrown it back in Whitney's face when she'd offered it.

"We'll start the process of getting you listed on the United Network for Organ Sharing today. There'll be further tests in the days ahead. Lisa will help you with those."

The couple's eyes glistened with moisture as they clung together.

Could the day get any worse? He'd bet everything he owned that Whitney would show that same loving concern if her husband was ill. Because she would love him. Their souls would be united. Would a wife based on his list care about him in the same way?

"So what do we need to do?" Mr. Culpepper asked.

The man saw his wife's health as a partnership. Why hadn't Tanner noticed that in his patients before? The Culpeppers couldn't be the only ones who felt that way. Had he just been choosing to ignore how people who loved each other acted? Was he so scared of loving or being loved that he was running from it? Wasn't that what Whitney had accused him of?

Could he live with someone who loved him without becoming emotionally invested himself? Not if he wanted Whitney. She would demand it of him. Could he give it? What he needed to understand was why his father had refused to accept it.

Half an hour later he left the Culpeppers with Lisa and returned to his office. He found the piece of paper he'd written the matchmaker's name on and crumbled it into a ball then tossed it into the trash. He already knew who his match was. Now all he had to do was be worthy of her. Find some way of meeting her halfway. That could only come from understanding why his parents had had such a dysfunctional relationship.

He picked up his phone. When a man answered Tanner said, "Dad. It's Tanner. Can I come down to see you this weekend?"

Tanner had driven faster than the speed limit, so he'd made good time on his way south on the coast road to Santa Barbara. He'd not seen his father in over five years and even then it had been brief and tense. There was no common ground for a relationship between them. That wouldn't change but Tanner needed to try to get some answers, a little understanding. There was no doubt he would be digging up painful memories but if he wanted to have the life he was dreaming of, finding that peace, he had to try to come to grips with his childhood.

Whitney had said he was like his father. The more he thought about it the more he tended to agree. So why was he like the man he disliked so much? Because he'd been so afraid of being hurt, like his mother had been?

His father had been surprised to hear from him. Rightfully so. There was a long pause when Tanner had asked if he could visit.

"Why?" had been his father's response.

"I have some questions I need answered."

Again there was a long pause. "Come on. I can't promise you'll like what you hear."

At least his father was willing to listen to the questions.

Tanner turned into his father's drive just before lunchtime. He had a simple one-story home that was well kept in a subdivision about five miles from the beach.

He and his father had agreed to go out to eat. Tanner felt they needed a neutral zone for the possibly tense discussion they were to have. His father had remarried while Tanner had been in med school but he had never met his new wife. Tanner had hardly stepped out of the car before his father exited the house and walked toward him. He was an older version of what Tanner saw in the mirror. He was like his father in more ways than one.

"Hello, Tanner."

"Hi, Dad. It's nice to see you." To his amazement Tanner actually meant it.

"Good to see you as well. The restaurant is just half a mile from here."

Was he protecting his wife from what might be said between them by not inviting Tanner in? "Okay. Would you like to ride with me?"

For a second Tanner thought his father might say no. "That'll work."

His father had picked a local place with plenty of room between the tables. Tanner was glad. They wouldn't easily be overheard. It wasn't until they were settled at their table, drinks served and orders taken, that Tanner said, "I have some questions about you and Mom."

Seeing his father's expression, Tanner was glad he'd requested a quiet spot off to the side. This discussion might be more difficult than he'd expected.

"Just what do you want to know?" His father fiddled with his napkin.

"Why you even married? Why were you never around? Did you even love her? Us?"

His father sighed deeply. "I should have had this discussion with you and Mark a long time ago but it was easier not to. I ought to have known it would happen one day. Yes, I loved your mother. Married her because I did. I've always loved you and Mark."

"So why did you and Mother always act like you were so unhappy?"

"Because we were. Your mother was so jealous. She smothered me. It wasn't that way so much at first. But as time went on she became obsessed. She'd accuse me of seeing other women. I wasn't but there was no convincing her. I tried to keep it all from you and your brother. We went to counseling but nothing worked. So when I had a chance to take a job traveling, I did, hoping that things would be better if I wasn't around so much. But that only made the situation worse when I came home. Her jealousy killed my love and then our marriage. I would have taken you and Mark with me but you were all she had. I feared she might take her life if I did that."

"You know that I hated you for how you treated her." Tanner couldn't keep his bitterness out of his voice. He'd lived with it too long.

"I know. But I thought it better for you to hate me than her."

His father had loved him enough to make that sacrifice. Was that the type of love Whitney had been showing him? She understood sacrificial love over possessive love. He'd still been the kid that couldn't see the difference.

"Dad, why have you never said anything? Mark and I have been adults for a long time."

He shrugged. "It wouldn't have changed anything."

"Yeah, it would have. I've had a wonderful woman in my life who I wasn't willing to love because I didn't think it was possible to have a marriage based on emotion."

There was a sheen of moisture in his father's eyes.

"Tanner, I never meant for you to feel that way. I'm sorry. Will you tell me about her?"

Over the next few minutes Tanner shared how he and Whitney had met. Why they had broken up.

"Life is too short to spend it without love," his father said.

"Another man told me the same thing recently."

His father met his look. "So what're you going to do?"

"Beg her to forgive me for being an idiot and shout from the Golden Gate Bridge that I love her."

His father's smile was genuine for the first time. "That sounds like a good start. Then tell her that every day for the rest of your life."

"I will."

During the meal they caught up on what they had missed in each other's lives. When they returned to his father's house he invited Tanner in to meet his wife. Tanner hesitated but then agreed.

"Julie, I'm home," his father called as they came in the front door.

The living room looked comfortable. Lived in, much like Whitney's. A place that made you feel welcome.

His father kissed the petite brown-haired woman on the cheek and put his arm around her waist when she joined them. That was something Tanner had never seen him do with his mother.

"Tanner, I'd like you to meet my wife, Julie. Julie, this is Tanner."

Julie surprised him by hugging him. Her smile was warm and inviting. "It's so nice to meet you. Your father brags about you all the time."

Tanner looked at his father, who shrugged and smiled affectionately at Julie. "Honey, don't tell all my secrets."

"Well, it's true. Why don't we sit down and I can find out if your father has been telling me the truth?"

Tanner couldn't help but smile. The warmth Julie exuded made him feel at ease. He liked her. She sat close to his father on the sofa and every so often she touched him when she was making a point. Julie obviously cared for his father. There was a happiness about him Tanner had never seen before. To his amazement Tanner was glad for him.

As Tanner was leaving his father called out, "Let me know how it goes with Whitney."

"I will." The relationship between his father and himself wasn't what it should be but they had made a step forward.

Now Tanner had to face Whitney. Could he possibly let go enough to admit how he felt about her? If he wanted Whitney, he'd have to. What sickened him was that he hadn't recognized her love when she'd given it. He'd had it right there in front of him and he hadn't grabbed it. After all, he did love her. Had for a long time.

Whitney had cried to the point of being sick. In the past there had been days when people had hurt her feelings and she'd been upset but nothing matched the agony she felt over the loss of Tanner. His absence was a void she couldn't fill.

She had managed to place Tanner's clothes in a bag and text him but it had almost torn her heart out. Against her better judgment she'd kept one of his T-shirts. It was an unhealthy thing to do but she'd become so accustomed to having him next to her in bed that she put the shirt under the spare pillow and pulled it out to smell it before she went to sleep. When she could sleep.

So much time had passed since she had spoken to her

parents they'd become concerned enough to check on her. When they did she gave them a blurry-eyed, tearful and painfully short version of what had happened. They were supportive and worried but in the end there wasn't anything they could do to help. As they were leaving her mother said, "We never know what life will give us. Never give up."

Whitney knew life sent you experiences and people that you never expected. Tanner had proved that. The problem was this time she was the one who had told Tanner to go. It had been the right decision but it still hurt.

In the middle of the second week she'd been in mourning for Tanner a new client called. That was the catalyst that started bringing her out of the darkness. She needed to keep herself busy for sanity's sake. To do that she was going to have to start clawing her way back to being a functioning adult again. She took a bath and washed her hair before sitting down at the computer. To her horror Tanner's profile was the first one to appear in her business file.

She looked at his smiling face for too long before she deleted it. She wouldn't need his profile any longer. Was he already dating other matches? The idea was crushing. But she had pushed him away. He was free to do as he pleased.

She kept repeating like a mantra that she had done it for their own good. Love was important to her. Necessary and nonnegotiable. For Tanner it was unimportant. He had issues that he needed to resolve. He'd stated clearly that he believed she did as well.

Hadn't she dealt with those long ago?

Whitney looked around the kitchen where bags of chips and dessert snack covers cluttered the table and counter. She'd turned to food again to sooth her stress and fear. Jumping up, she gathered the litter and uneaten junk food, cramming it in the garbage can. That too had to stop. Returning to her desk, she picked up her phone and punched in the number to speed dial the overeating support group she'd once attended. It was time to get her life back on track without Tanner.

Over the next two days she set up two socials and made an appointment to meet a new client. She didn't feel alive yet but at least she was making an effort.

Her client was a woman of about her own age. In fact, she looked familiar. Extremely attractive, she still seemed a little unsure of herself. She kept looking around as if she were expecting someone to catch her doing something she shouldn't. Her name was familiar too. Lauren Phillips.

High school. That was it! She'd been one of the popular girls. The one who'd got all the boys. Now she needed Whitney to help her make a match.

"I believe we went to high school together," Whitney said at their meeting.

Lauren studied her but there was no recognition in her eyes. "I'm sorry, I don't remember you. High school was a tough time for me. My parents were getting a divorce. I didn't pay much attention to anyone but myself."

"It's okay. We can't remember everyone." Whitney meant it. Before Tanner she would have been resentful of Lauren but now she understood too clearly that no matter how someone might act on the outside, they could still have problems. "So how can I help you?"

"I am looking for companionship. Someone who enjoys the same things I do," Lauren answered. "I want someone who's looking to get serious and settle down. All the guys I meet are just interested in my looks. I want someone who sees past that."

Whitney had had that with Tanner. What if she had waited longer? Maybe Tanner would have come around to loving her. He had certainly accepted her for who she was. Instead of giving him any real chance, she'd let her insecurities control her. How was she supposed to match other people when she couldn't handle her own? Her self-doubt had left her with nothing.

How he must hate her.

Whitney pushed through the glass door of the community center for the first time in years. It would be tough to join the Happier You support group again but these were her people and here she would be accepted without question. It had taken her years to admit she needed support when she'd lost weight. She'd started managing her eating again but what she had really been looking for had been the emotional care. The help for what had been behind her overeating. The Happier You group had given her that.

She walked down the hall to the classroom. Inside she found the circle of chairs she expected and a few people already in them. She smiled in their direction and took a seat. Another couple of people entered before Margaret, the facilitator, showed up.

"Whitney Thomason, is that you?"

"It is." Whitney stood and hugged the woman.

"So what brings you here tonight?"

"I guess just for a reminder of how far I've come," Whitney said.

"So it's like that?"

Whitney nodded.

An hour and a half later Whitney was feeling strong enough to face the world and Tanner as well. While others had been talking she had been formulating a plan. She would write Tanner a letter. Tell him that she was sorry for treating him the way she had.

She was on her way out of the room when Margaret called after her. Whitney turned.

"Hold on a minute. I want to ask you something."

Whitney waited until Margaret finished speaking to the last person and came to her. "What's up?"

"I was wondering if you would consider something," Margaret said.

"What's that?"

Margaret moved a chair back into place. "Taking over this group for me. I have a chance to start one over near my house but can't leave this one high and dry. I think you would be great at it."

Her lead a group? "Can I think about it? Get back to you?"

"Sure. Just don't take too long."

Whitney didn't know if she could. She had always been in the background. "I'll let you know something by next week."

"Perfect."

Whitney made it to the door before Margaret said, "You know, you've changed, Whitney. There is more confidence about you. And you look great. Whatever is causing it, keep doing it."

That was because of Tanner. He'd made her feel supported, confident. Even though she'd pushed him away, he had left her that gift.

"Thanks, Margaret."

At home that evening Whitney pulled out a piece of stationery. She was going to write that letter. After careful thought she decided that a text or email message was too impersonal. She had to show that she meant what she wrote, was making a true effort.

Dear Tanner...

She marked that out.

Tanner,
I want you to know that I'm sorry for the way I treated you. You did not deserve it. I should not have assumed the worst of you, your friends or colleagues. I should have accepted your support for what it was, just that.
Please know that in many ways you've helped me grow as a person, and for that I will always be grateful.
I wish you well always.
Whitney

She rubbed the moisture under her eyes as she reread the note. To the point with no emotion. Folding it perfectly, she slipped it into an envelope and addressed it to his hospital office. Not allowing herself to rethink it, she put it in the mailbox beside the front door for pickup the next day.

Now it was time to move on. The door with Tanner's name on it was closed.

CHAPTER TEN

TANNER ONLY HAD a few minutes before he was due in surgery to read the mail his secretary had left in a stack on his desk. He picked up a letter that looked out of place. His chest tightened. Whitney's handwriting. Why would she be writing to him? Tearing it open, he scanned the brief but sincere note.

His heart filled with hope. Maybe there was a chance with her after all. She was at least opening a door for him to approach. Now if he just knocked loud enough she'd have no choice but to let him in. He was going to start working on making that happen right away.

Tanner picked up the phone. When the man on the other end answered Tanner said, "Hey, Charlie, I need a favor."

"What's that?"

Tanner wasted no time in saying, "I need you to hire a matchmaker."

"I don't think my wife would like that." Charlie chuckled.

"No, I need you to pretend you need a matchmaker. I'll go in your place." Tanner couldn't afford for this to go wrong.

"You're not making any sense. Why can't you just do it?"

Tanner explained he wasn't sure that Whitney would meet him if he didn't surprise her. That he needed to get her to a public place so she was more likely to hear him out. "You do this for me and I'll take your calls for a month."

"Wow, you want this pretty bad."

"I do."

"Then it's a deal. What's the number?"

A few days later Charlie called back with a date and time at Café Lombard. "Good luck, man. She must be pretty special to go to this kind of trouble."

"She is. Thanks."

Three days later Malcolm stopped him in the hallway outside the CICU. "Tanner, can I have a word with you?"

"I've only got a second." He was due to meet Whitney in two hours and he wouldn't be late. Tanner was anxious and hoped Malcolm wouldn't be long-winded.

Malcolm smiled. "I wanted to give you a heads-up on this. The board met last night. You got the directorship."

Tanner should have been super excited but all he could think about was meeting Whitney. The directorship paled in comparison to winning Whitney back. He took a few steps backward, anxious to leave. "Thanks for letting me know."

Malcolm gave him a quizzical look. "Maybe you and Whitney would like to have dinner with us to celebrate."

"I'll let you know," Tanner called over his shoulder as he headed down the hall.

Two hours later Tanner sat at a table in the patio area of the café where he and Whitney had met his prospective matches. What would her reaction be when she saw him? Would she turn and walk away? Would she listen to him?

His pulse jumped. There she was. His heart swelled.

She looked beautiful. He'd missed her so much that it had almost become a tangible thing he carried.

Wearing a sky blue dress that fit her torso then flared gently around her legs, Whitney looked nothing like the dowdy shopkeeper of old. There was a spring in her step that was new. A sick feeling came over him. What had put that there? Had she found someone new? Maybe she wasn't missing him as much as he was her.

Tanner saw the second her step faltered as she crossed the street. She'd seen him. Their gazes met. He held his apprehension in check by sheer will. Standing, he never took his eyes off her. She continued toward him at a slower pace.

When she reached him he said, "Will you join me?"

"I have—" she cleared her throat "—to meet a client."

"I'm the client."

"What?" She looked as if she might run.

He quickly said, "I wasn't sure you'd meet me so I asked a friend to pretend to need a match."

She sighed and her shoulders slumped. "Tanner, I don't have time to waste with games."

"I'm not playing a game." It was his life they were talking about here. He pulled out a chair. "Please, join me for just a minute."

For a second he feared she was going to say no but she reluctantly sat, her hands clutching her purse. "What's this all about?"

"I was wondering if you could help me find someone to love and who will love me?"

Me. Me. Me. Whitney wanted to shout.

Did he mean it? Could she trust that she had heard him right? He had said love. Something he'd said he wouldn't give. Did she dare hope? She watched him closely. "What're you talking about? I thought we settled this weeks ago. I'm not the right matchmaker for you."

"You're usually not this slow to catch on," Tanner said with a smile.

"To what?" Now he was starting to irritate her.

"*You're* my perfect match. I'm telling you I *love* you. I hope you still feel the same about me."

Whitney's hands trembled. She could hardly breathe. She'd never thought she'd hear him say that. Could her dreams be coming true?

Tanner was looking at her with anticipation and a touch of uncertainty. Was he afraid she might turn him away? With his experience with love he might think it was something that came and went easily. Hers lasted forever.

She jumped to her feet and flung herself into his arms. His hands went to her waist, giving her a furious hug. Her arms circled his neck and her mouth found his. His kiss was all about acceptance and pleasure. But more than that—love.

As Tanner began deepening the kiss someone behind them said, "Excuse me."

They broke apart. Heat ran into Whitney's face. She looked at Tanner and he had a bashful look on his as well. They had both forgotten they were in a public place. Whitney eased back into her chair.

"Sorry," Tanner said to the young waitress. "She can't keep her hands off me."

"Tanner!"

He smiled and gave her an innocent look. "It's true. Would you like something?"

Whitney glanced at the waitress then said to Tanner, "What I'd really like to do is go home."

He asked, "I'm invited?"

Whitney smiled brightly. "You are. We need to talk."

"I agree." Tanner stood and dug in his pocket, pulling out a bill. After giving it to the surprised waitress, he offered a hand to Whitney.

Grinning and feeling like the sun was shining just for her, Whitney slipped her hand into Tanner's larger secure one. They made their way around a few tables and out to the sidewalk. Tanner led her down the street toward where his car was parked.

"Where's your car?"

"I took a streetcar and walked," she said.

They continued down the hill and Tanner said, "Thank you for your letter."

"It was the least I could do. I was pretty ugly to you." She'd spend the rest of her life making that up to him.

Opening the car door for her, Tanner said, "That you were."

She gave him a teasing swat on the arm. "But you deserved it."

"We'll discuss that more when we get to your house." He pulled out of his parking space and headed up the street. When he had moved into the rhythm of the traffic he took her hand and placed it on his thigh under his. She'd come home. It felt so good to have his touch again. But they still had things to discuss.

It didn't take long until Tanner slid the car to a stop in front of her house. She climbed out as he did and met him on the sidewalk. "Would you rather walk awhile or go inside to talk?"

"I think we'd better walk." Tanner took her hand again. "If I get you behind a closed door my mind is going to be on other things besides talking."

Tanner's raspy voice sent a shiver down her spine. "Walk it is."

They started up the sidewalk along the grassy knoll across the street from her home.

"Whitney, I'm sorry I've been such an idiot. The truth is I've been in love with you since you came to my rescue in the balloon. I just didn't want to admit it. My parents and what I saw in their marriage screwed me up."

"No more than the insecurities I carry around with me because I was once fat."

"Yeah, but my issues weren't even based on facts. It turns out that my father loved my mother. She was just so jealous that she killed it."

Whitney stopped and looked at him. "How did you find that out?"

"I went to see my father the other weekend. We had lunch together. He didn't much want to answer my questions but he did. Turns out he's been protecting my mother all along."

"Really?"

"Yeah. He let my brother and me believe he was the bad guy so that we wouldn't blame my mother. He wanted us to love her." There was acceptance in his voice she'd not heard when he'd spoken of his parents before.

"It takes a special person to sacrifice themselves for another." She started up the sidewalk again.

"I hadn't thought about it like that. It figures a woman with a big heart herself would see it that way." Tanner squeezed her hand.

Whitney gave him a sympathetic look. "But she wasn't all that bighearted when she sent you out the door, blaming you for all the things she didn't like about herself."

He smiled at her. "I don't remember you doing that."

Could she ever say sorry enough? "Well, I do. That's what it boiled down to. I was finding a way out so I wouldn't have to face situations I wasn't comfortable in."

"We all dodge those."

"I know. But not everyone judges others with such broad strokes." She hated to admit that she had done that.

"You have good reason."

"Maybe but it's time to grow up and face my past and not automatically think the worst of people." It would still be hard for her in some social situations but now she was aware of her shortcomings so maybe she could make some changes.

"What brought on this reevaluation?" He sounded as if he really wanted to know.

"Would you believe that the most popular girl in my high school class came to me for help? It turns out the beautiful people of the world all have problems too. I realized after she left that I was the lucky one."

"Why?" Tanner turned and they headed back toward her house.

"Because my issues were ones that I could control. I just had to be willing to do it. I went back to my eating disorder class. I'm even going to become a facilitator. I want to help others through my experiences."

"That's great. I know you'll be good at that. You've certainly taught me a thing or two."

She looked at the handsome face she'd missed so much. "Have I, now? I can't imagine me teaching you anything."

Tanner stopped and brought her into his arms. "You've done something no one else could do."

"What's that?"

"Shown me how to love and be loved." He kissed her gently.

"Do you really love me?"

Tanner grinned. "Did you hear me say it?"

"I did, but I'd like to hear it again."

"I love you, Whitney." She had no doubt he meant it.

"And I love you with all my heart."

Tanner pulled her close. "That's more than I've ever deserved. Now, if you don't mind I'd like to go back to your house and show you just how much I love you."

Whitney rested her head against his chest. "I can't think of anything that I would like more."

EPILOGUE

IT HAD BEEN nothing but blue sky and sunshine at the Garonne Winery and Château. Whitney couldn't have asked for a more perfect wedding day. She had walked between two rows of grapevines to where Tanner stood on the exact spot where they had shared their first real kiss.

They had chosen to share their own vows. Tanner's were so full of love that Whitney hurt with the poignancy of them. For a man who'd said he knew nothing about love, he was a quick study. Once he'd learned to feel and say the words, he never stopped.

She was surrounded by her family and friends, all smiling and enjoying a good time in the cellar of the winery where the reception was being held. Marie and Malcolm had insisted on taking care of the wedding details when she and Tanner had told them they wished to marry at the winery. Marie had tastefully taken Whitney's wishes and created a day to remember.

To both her surprise and Tanner's as well, his parents attended. There was a tenseness to their meeting but otherwise there was nothing but blessings for the bride and groom. Tanner had asked his brother, Mark, to be best man and he had accepted. They had grown closer during the weeks before the wedding. For that, Whitney was grateful.

"What's the bride doing over here by herself?" Mr. Wilcox asked.

"Just thinking about how happy I am."

The band started up a new tune.

"May I have this dance, Mrs. Locke?" Mr. Wilcox made a slight bow her direction.

She liked the sound of her new name. "I'd be honored."

He led her in a box step around the open area surrounded by tables. "I told you I would be dancing at your wedding."

Whitney smiled. "You did but I didn't believe it."

They made one more turn before Tanner tapped Mr. Wilcox on the shoulder. "Mind if I break in? I'd like to dance with my beautiful wife."

Mr. Wilcox gave her hand to Tanner and kissed her on the cheek. "Life and love are fragile things. Treasure them. Not all of us get a second chance."

"So I have learned." Tanner looked into her eyes. "Now that I recognize it, and have it, I'm never going to let it go."

* * * * *

If you enjoyed this story, check out these
other great reads from Susan Carlisle

THE DOCTOR'S SLEIGH BELL PROPOSAL
WHITE WEDDING FOR A SOUTHERN BELLE
MARRIED FOR THE BOSS'S BABY
ONE NIGHT BEFORE CHRISTMAS

All available now!

SAVED BY
DOCTOR DREAMY

BY
DIANNE DRAKE

Published in Great Britain 2017
By Mills & Boon, an imprint of HarperCollins*Publishers*
1 London Bridge Street, London, SE1 9GF

© 2017 Dianne Despain

ISBN: 978-0-263-92650-7

Our policy is to use papers that are natural, renewable and recyclable products and made from wood grown in sustainable forests. The logging and manufacturing processes conform to the legal environmental regulations of the country of origin.

Printed and bound in Spain
by CPI, Barcelona

Dear Reader,

Thanks so much for coming back to read another of my books. This story, *Saved by Doctor Dreamy*, is set in one of my favourite places—Costa Rica. As I'm a former nurse it interests me, because the healthcare system deals with modern medicine as well as jungle medicine, which is very much part of the culture. In my story Juliette and Damien have to meet in the middle of both medical worlds to find out what's best suited to them.

I read an article about nursing practices in the 1800s, and added some of those elements to *Saved by Doctor Dreamy*. Medical conditions around the world vary, and what's modern in one society is primitive in another. We see that in the little hospital where my characters work. They face harsh conditions because they have no other choices, and make tough decisions based on what they have.

I love writing about difficult hospital conditions, and have incorporated that theme into several of my previous books—because what better time is there to bring two people together than when facing hardship?

Again, I appreciate you reading *Saved by Doctor Dreamy*, and I'll be back shortly with another book!

As always, wishing you health and happiness,

Dianne

Books by Dianne Drake

Mills & Boon Medical Romance

Deep South Docs

A Home for the Hot-Shot Doc
A Doctor's Confession

A Child to Heal Their Hearts
Tortured by Her Touch
Doctor, Mummy...Wife?
The Nurse and the Single Dad

Visit the Author Profile page
at millsandboon.co.uk for more titles.

CHAPTER ONE

THE NIGHT WAS STILL. No howler monkeys sitting up in the trees yelling their heads off. No loud birds calling into the darkness. Damien doubted if there was even a panther on the prowl anywhere near here. It was kind of eerie actually, since he was used to the noise. First, the city noise in Seattle, where he grew up. Then Chicago, Miami, New York. Back to Seattle. And finally, the noise of the Costa Rican jungle, where he'd come to settle.

Noise was his friend. It comforted him, reassured him that he was still alive. Something he hadn't felt in a long, long time. And when it surrounded him, it was home and safety and all the things that kept him sane and focused on the life he was living now.

When Damien had come to the jungle he'd been pleasantly surprised by the noisiness of it all. It was as loud as any city, but in a different way. He'd traded in people for animals and honking cars for wind rustling through the vegetation. Now that he was used to the sounds there, he counted on them to surround him, to cradle him in a contented solitude. But tonight was different. He felt so… isolated, so out of touch with his reality. So lonely. Alone in the city—alone in the jungle. It was all the same. All of it bringing a sense of despair that caught up with him from time to time.

This despair of his had been a problem over the years. People didn't understand it. Didn't want to. Most of the time he didn't want to understand it either, because when he did he'd overcompensate. Do things he might not normally do. Like getting engaged to someone he wouldn't have normally given a second thought to.

But Daniel understood this about him. Daniel—he was the only one, and he'd never ridiculed Damien for what other people thought was ridiculous. Of course, he and Daniel had the twin-connection thing going on, and that was something that never failed him.

Damien and Daniel Caldwell. Two of a kind—well, not so much. They looked alike, with a few notable exceptions like hair length and beard. Daniel was the clean-shaven, short-haired version, while Damien was the long-haired, scruffy-bearded one. But they were both six foot one, had the same brown eyes, same dimples that women seemed to adore. Same general build. Apart from their outward looks, though, they couldn't have been more different. Restlessness and the need to keep moving were Damien's trademarks while contented domesticity and a quiet lifestyle were his brother's. Which Damien envied, as he'd always figured that by the time he was thirty-five he'd have something in his life more stable than what he had. Something substantial. Yet that hadn't happened.

It's too quiet tonight, Damien scribbled into a short letter to his brother. *It feels like it's going to eat me alive.* He'd seen Daniel a few months ago. Gone back to the States for Daniel's wedding. And it was a happy reunion, not like the time before that when he'd been called home to support his brother through his first wife's death. But Daniel had moved on now. He had a happy life, a happy family. Lucky, *lucky* man.

The work is good, though, bro. It keeps me busy pretty much all the time. Keeps me out of trouble. So how's your new life fitting into your work schedule?

Daniel's life—a nice dream. Even though, deep down, Damien didn't want strings to bind him to one place, one lifestyle. Rather, he needed to do what he wanted, when he wanted, with no one to account to. And space to think, to reevaluate. Or was that another of his overcompensations? Anyway, he had that now, although he'd had to come to the remote jungles of Costa Rica to find it. In that remoteness, however, he'd found a freedom he'd never really had before.

And remote it was. Isolated from all the everyday conveniences that Costa Rica's large cities offered. Not even attractive to the never-ending flow of expats who were discovering the charms of this newly modernizing Central American country.

Most of the time Damien thrived on the isolation, not that he was, by nature, a solitary kind of man. Because he wasn't. Or at least didn't used to be. In his former life, he'd liked fast cars, nice condos and beautiful women. In fact, he'd thrived on those things before he'd escaped them. Now, the lure of the jungle had trapped him in a self-imposed celibacy, and that wasn't just of a sexual nature. It was a celibacy from worldly matters. A total abstinence from anything that wasn't directed specifically toward him. A time to figure out where he was going next in his life. Or if he was even going to go anywhere else at all.

In the meantime, Damien didn't regret turning his back on his old life in order to take off on this new one. In ways he'd never expected, it suited him.

*Say hello to Zoey for me, and tell her I'm glad she
joined the family. And give Maddie a kiss from her
Uncle Damien.*

Damien scrawled his initials at the bottom of the letter,
stuck it in an envelope and addressed it. Maybe sometime in the next week or so he'd head into Cima de la
Montaña to stock up on some basic necessities and mail
the letter. Call his parents if he got near enough to a cell
tower. And find a damned hamburger!

"We need you back in the hospital, Doctor," Alegria
Diaz called through his open window. She was his only
trained nurse—a woman who'd left the jungle to seek a
higher education. Which, in these parts, was a rarity as
the people here didn't usually venture too far out into
the world.

"What is it?" he called back, bending down to pull
on his boots.

"Stomachache. Nothing serious. But he wouldn't listen to me. Said he had to see *el médico*."

El médico. The doctor. Yes, that was him. The doctor
who directed one trained nurse, one semiretired, burned-
out plastic surgeon and a handful of willing, if not experienced, volunteers.

"Let me put my shirt back on and comb my hair, and
I'll be right over." A year ago his world had been very
large. Penthouse. Sports car. Today it was very small. A
one-room hut twenty paces from the hospital. A borrowed
pickup truck that worked as often as it didn't.

Damien donned a cotton T-shirt, pulled his hair back
and rubber-banded it into a small ponytail, and headed
out the door. Being on call 24/7 wasn't necessarily the
best schedule, but that was the life he'd accepted for himself and it was also the life he was determined to stick

with. For how long? At least until he figured out what his next life would be. Or if he'd finally stumbled upon the life he wanted.

"I wanted to give him an antacid," Alegria told him as he entered through the door of El Hospital Bombacopsis, which sat central in the tiny village of Bombacopsis.

"But he refused it?" Damien asked, stopping just inside the door.

"He said a *resbaladera* would fix him."

Resbaladera—a rice and barley drink. "Well, we don't serve that here and, even if we did, I've never heard that it has any medicinal benefits for a stomachache."

Alegria smiled up at him. She was a petite woman, small in frame, short in height. Dark skin, black hair, dark eyes. Mother of three, grandmother of one. "He won't take an antacid from you," she warned.

"And yesterday he wouldn't take an aspirin from me when he had a headache. So why's he here in the first place, if he refuses medical treatment?"

"Señor Segura takes sick twice a year, when his wife goes off to San José to visit her sister."

"She leaves, and he catches a cold and comes to the hospital." Damien chuckled.

"Rosalita is a good cook here. He likes her food."

"Well, apparently he ate too much of it tonight, since he's sick at his stomach."

Alegria shrugged. "He's hard to control once you put a plate of *casado* in front of him."

Casado—rice, black beans, plantains, salad, tortillas and meat. One of Damien's favorite Costa Rican meals. But he didn't go all glutton on it the way Señor Segura apparently had. "Well, *casado* or not, I'm going to check him out, and if this turns out to be a simple stomachache from overeating I'm going to give him an antacid and tell Rosalita to cut back on his portions."

"He won't like that," Alegria said.

"And I don't like having my evening interrupted by a patient who refuses to do what his nurse tells him."

"Whatever you say, Doctor." Alegria scooted off to fetch the antacid while Damien approached his cantankerous patient.

"I hear you won't take the medicine my nurse wanted to give you."

"It's no good," Señor Segura said. "Won't cure what's wrong with me."

"But a rice and barley drink will?"

"That's what my Guadalupe always gives me when I don't feel so well."

"Well, Guadalupe is visiting her sister now, which means we're the ones who are going to have to make you feel better." Damien bent down and prodded the man's belly, then had a listen to his belly sounds through a stethoscope. He checked the chart for the vital signs Alegria had already recorded, then took a look down Señor Segura's throat. Nothing struck him as serious so he signaled Alegria to bring the antacid over to the bedside. "OK, you're sick. But it's only because you ate too much. My nurse is going to give you a couple of tablets to chew that will make you feel better."

"The tablets are no good. I want *resbaladera* like my Guadalupe makes."

Damien refused to let this man try his patience, which was going to happen very quickly if he didn't get this situation resolved. It was a simple matter, though. Two antacid tablets would work wonders, if he could convince Señor Segura to give in. "I don't have *resbaladera* here, and we're not going to make it specifically for you." They had neither the means nor the money to make special accommodations for one patient.

"Then I'll stay sick until I get better, or die!"

"You're not going to die from a stomachache," Damien reassured him.

"And I'm not going to die because I wouldn't take your pills."

So there it was. The standoff. It happened sometimes, when the village folk here insisted on sticking to their traditional ways. He didn't particularly like giving in, when he knew that what he was trying to prescribe would help. But in cases like Señor Segura's, where the cure didn't much matter one way or another, he found it easier to concede the battle and save his arguments for something more important.

"Well, if you're refusing the tablets, that's up to you. But just keep in mind that your stomachache could last through the night."

"Then let it," Señor Segura said belligerently. Then he looked over at Alegria. "And you can save those pills for somebody else."

Alegria looked to Damien for instruction. "Put them back," Damien told her.

"Yes, Doctor," she said, frowning at Señor Segura. "As you wish."

What he wished was that he had more space, better equipment, more trained staff and up-to-date medicines. In reality, though, he had a wood-frame, ten-bed hospital that afforded no luxuries whatsoever and a one-room, no-frills clinic just off the entrance to the ward. It was an austere setup, and he had to do the best with it that he could. But the facility's lack was turning into his lack of proper service, as he didn't have much to offer anyone. Basic needs were about all he could meet. Of course, it was his choice to trade in a lucrative general surgery practice in Seattle for all of this. So he wasn't complaining. More like, he was wishing.

One day, he thought to himself as he took a quick look at the only other patient currently admitted to the hospital. She was a young girl with a broken leg whose parents couldn't look after her properly and still tend to their other nine children. So he'd set her leg, then admitted her, and wasn't exactly sure what to do with her other than let her occupy space until someone more critical needed the bed.

"She's fine," Alegria told him before he took his place at the bedside. "I checked her an hour ago and she's sound asleep."

Damien nodded and smiled. The only thing that would turn this worthless evening into something worthwhile would be to shut himself in his clinic and take a nap on the exam table. Sure, it was the lazy way out, since his real bed was only a few steps away. But his exam room was closer, and he was suddenly bone-tired. And his exam table came with a certain appeal he couldn't, at this moment, deny. So Damien veered off to the clinic, shut the door behind him and was almost asleep before he stretched out on the exam room table.

"Like I've been telling you for the past several weeks, I don't want a position in administration here at your hospital. I don't want to be your sidekick. I don't want to be put through the daily grind of budgets and salaries and supply orders!"

Juliette Allen took a seat across the massive mahogany desk from her father, Alexander, and leaned forward. "And, most of all, I don't want to be involved in anything that smacks of nepotism." Standing up to her dad was something she should have done years ago, but first her schooling, then her work had overtaken her, thrown her into a rut. Made her complacent. Then one day she woke up in the same bedroom she'd spent thirty-three years waking up in, had breakfast at the same table she'd always had breakfast at, and walked out the front door she'd always walked out of. Suddenly, she'd felt stifled. Felt the habits of her life closing in around her, choking her. And that's what her life had turned into—one big habit.

"This isn't nepotism, Juliette," Alexander said patiently. "It's about me promoting the most qualified person to the position."

"But I didn't apply for the position!" She was too young to be a director of medical operations in a large hospital. The person filling that spot needed years more experience than she had and she knew that. What she also knew was that this was her father's way of keeping her under his thumb. "And I think it's presumptuous of you to submit an application on my behalf."

"You're qualified, Juliette. And you have a very promising future."

"I direct the family care clinic, another position you arranged for me."

"And your clinic is one of the best operated in this hospital." Dr. Alexander Allen was a large man, formidable in his appearance, very sharp, very direct. "This is a good opportunity for you, and I don't understand why you're resisting me."

"Because I haven't paid my dues, because I don't have enough experience to direct the medical workings of an entire hospital." The problem was, she'd always given in to her father. Juliette's mother had died giving birth to her, and he'd never remarried, so it had always been just the two of them, which made it easy for him to control her with guilt over causing her mother's death. Plus she was also consumed by the guilt of knowing that if she left him he wouldn't fare so well on his own. For all his intelligence and power in the medical world, her father was insecure in his private world. Juliette's mother had done *everything* for him, then it fell to Juliette to do the same.

Juliette adored her dad, despite the position he'd put her in. He'd been a very good father to her, always making sure she had everything she wanted and needed. *More* than she wanted and needed, actually. And she'd become accustomed to that opulent lifestyle, loved everything about it, which was why this was so difficult now. She was tied to the man in a way most thirty-three-year-old women were not tied to their fathers. Which was why her dad found it so easy to make his demands then sit back and watch her comply. "I just can't do this, Dad," she said, finally sitting back in her chair. "And I hope you can respect my position."

"You're seriously in jeopardy of missing your opportunity to promote yourself out of your current job, Juliette. When I was a young man, in a situation much like the one you're in, I was always the first person in line to apply for any position that would further my career."

"But you've always told me that your ultimate career goal was to do what you're doing now—run an entire hospital. You, yourself, said you weren't cut out for everyday patient care."

"And my drive to get ahead has provided you with a good life. Don't you forget that."

"I'm not denying it, Dad. I appreciate all you've done for me and I love the life you've given me. But it's time for me to guide my career without your help." Something she should have done the day she'd entered medical school, except she hadn't even broken away from him then. She'd stayed at home, gone to the university and medical school where her father taught because it was easier for him. And while that wasn't necessarily her first choice, she always succumbed to her father when he started his argument with: "Your mother died giving birth to you and you can't even begin to understand how rough that's been on me, trying to take care of you, trying to be a good father—"

It was the argument he'd used time and time again when he thought he was about to lose her, the one that made her feel guilty, the one that always caused her to cave. But not this time. She'd made the decision first, then acted on it before she told him. And *this* time she was resolved to break away, because if she didn't she'd end up living the life he lived. Alone. Substituting work for a real life.

"And it's not about going into an administrative position, Dad." Now she had to drop the *real* bomb, and it wasn't going to be easy. "In fact, I have something somewhat administrative in mind for what I want to do next."

"Why do I have a feeling that what you're about to tell me is something I'm not going to like?" He looked straight across at his daughter. "I'm right, am I not?"

Juliette squared all five foot six of herself in her chair and looked straight back at him. "You're right. And there's no easy way to put this." She stopped, waiting for him to say something, but when he didn't she continued. "I'm going to resign from my position here at the hospital, Dad. In fact, I'm going to turn in my one-month notice tomorrow and have a talk with Personnel on how to replace me."

"You're leaving," he stated. "Just turning your back

on everything you've accomplished here and walking out the door."

"I'm not turning my back on it, and I may come back someday. But right now, I've got to do something on my own, something you didn't just hand me. And whether you want to admit it or not, all my promotions have been gifts. I didn't earn them the way I should have."

"But you've worked hard in every position you've had, and you've shown very good judgment and skill in everything you've done."

"A lot of doctors can do that, Dad. I just happened to be the one whose father was Chief of Staff."

"So you're quitting because I'm Chief of Staff?"

"No, I'm quitting because I'm the chief of staff's daughter."

"Have I really piled that many unrealistic expectations on you? Because if I have, I can back off."

"It's not about backing off. It's about letting go." She didn't want to hurt him, but he did have to understand that it was time for her to spread her wings. Test new waters. Take a different path. "I— *We* have to do it. It's time."

"But can't you let go and still work here?"

"No." She shut her eyes for a moment, bracing herself for the rest of this. "I've accepted another position."

"Another hospital? There aren't any better hospitals in Indianapolis than Memorial."

"It's not a hospital, and it's not in Indianapolis." She swallowed hard. "I'm going to Costa Rica."

"The hell you are!" he bellowed. "What are you thinking, Juliette?"

She knew this was hard on him, and she'd considered leading up to this little by little. But her dad was hard-headed, and he was as apt to shut out the hints she might drop as he was to listen to them. Quite honestly, Alexander Allen heard only what he wanted to hear.

"What I'm thinking is that I've already made arrangements for a place to stay, and I'll be leaving one month from Friday."

"To do what?"

Now, this was where it became even more difficult. "I'm going to head up a medical recruitment agency."

Her dad opened up his mouth to respond, but shut it again when nothing came out.

"The goal is to find first-rate medical personnel to bring there. Costa Rica, and even Central America as a whole, can't supply the existing demand for medical professionals so they're recruiting from universities and hospitals all over the world, and I'm going to be in charge of United States recruitment."

"I know about medical recruitment. Lost a top-rate radiologist to Thailand a couple of years ago."

"So you know how important it is to put the best people in situations where they can help a hospital or, in Costa Rica's case, provide the best quality of care they can to the greatest number of people."

"Which leaves people like me in the position of having to find a new radiologist or transplant surgeon or oncologist, depending on who you're recruiting away from me."

"But you're already in an easier position to find the best doctors to fill your positions. You have easier access to the medical schools, a never-ending supply of residents to fill any number of positions in the hospital and you have connections to every major hospital in the country. These are things Costa Rica doesn't have, so in order for them to find the best qualified professionals they have to reach out differently than you do. Which, in this case, will be through me."

It was an exciting new venture for her and, while she wouldn't be offering direct medical care herself, she envisioned herself involved in a great, beneficial service. And all she ever wanted to be as a doctor was someone who benefited her patients, and by providing the patients in Costa Rica with good health-care practitioners she'd be helping more patients than she'd ever be able to help as a single practitioner in a clinic. In fact, when she thought about how many lives only one single recruited doctor could improve, she was overwhelmed. And when she thought of how many practitioners she would recruit and how many patients they would touch, it boggled her mind. "It's an important job, Dad. And I'm excited about it."

"Excited or not, you're throwing away a good medical career. You were a fine *hospital* physician, Juliette. In whatever capacity you chose."

"You were, too, once upon a time, but you traded that in for a desk and thousand-dollar business suits. So don't just sit there and accuse me of leaving medicine, because I'm not doing anything that you haven't already done."

"But in Costa Rica? Why there? Why not investigate something *different* closer to home, if you're hell-bent on getting out of Memorial. Maybe medical research. We've got one of the world's largest facilities just a few miles from here. Or maybe teaching. I mean, we've got, arguably, one of the best medical schools in the country right at our back door."

"But I don't want to teach, and I especially don't want to do research. I also don't want to work for an insurance company or provide medical care for a national sports franchise. What I want, Dad, is to find something that excites me. Something that offers a large group of people medical services they might not otherwise get.

Something that will help an entire country improve its standard of care."

"There's nothing I can do to change your mind?" her dad asked, sounding as if the wind had finally been knocked out of his sails.

Juliette shook her head. "No, Dad. There's not. I've been looking into the details of my new position for weeks now, and I'm truly convinced this is something I want to do at this point in my life."

"Well, I'm going to leave your position open for a while. Staff it with a temp, in case you get to Costa Rica and decide your new job isn't for you. That way, you'll have a place to come back to, just in case."

Her dad was a handsome, vital man, and she hoped that once she was gone, and he didn't have anybody else to depend on, he might actually go out and get a life for himself. Maybe get married. Or travel. Or sail around the world the way he used to talk about when she was a little girl. In some ways, Juliette felt as if she'd been holding him back. She still lived with him, worked with him, was someone to keep him company when no one else was around. It was an easy way for both of them but she believed that so much togetherness had stunted them both. She didn't date, hadn't dated very much as a whole, thanks to her work commitments, and she'd certainly never gone out and looked for employment outside of what her father had handed her.

Yes, that was all easy. But now it was over. It was time for her to move on. "If I do come back to Indianapolis in the future, I won't be coming back to Memorial because I don't think it's a good idea that we work together anymore. We need to be separate, and if I'm here at Memorial that's not going to happen."

"Is this about something I've done to you, Juliette?" he asked, sounding like a totally defeated man.

"No, Dad. It's about something I haven't done for myself." And about everything she wanted to do for herself in the future.

One month down, and so far she was enjoying her new job. She'd had the opportunity to interview sixteen potential candidates for open positions in various hospitals. Seven doctors, three registered nurses, three respiratory therapists, a physical therapist and two X-ray technicians, one of whom specialized in mammograms. And there were another ten on her list for the upcoming two weeks. The bonus was, she loved Costa Rica. What she'd seen of it so far was beautiful. The people were nice. The food good. The only thing was, her lifestyle was a bit more subdued than what she was used to. She didn't have a nice shiny Jaguar to drive, but a tiny, used compact car provided by the agency. And her flat—not exactly luxurious like her home back in Indiana, but she was getting used to smaller, no-frills quarters and cheaper furniture. It was a drastic lifestyle change, she did have to admit, but she was doing the best she could with what she had.

Perhaps the most drastic change, though—the one thing she hadn't counted on—was that she missed direct patient care in a big way. She'd reconciled herself to experiencing some withdrawal before she'd come here, but what she'd been feeling was overwhelming as she'd never considered that stepping away from it would take such an emotional toll on her. But it had. She was restless. When she didn't stop herself, her mind wandered back to the days when she'd been involved directly in patient care. And it wasn't that she didn't like her job, because she did, and she had no intention of walking away from it. But she could physically, as well as emotionally, feel the lack in herself and she was afraid it was something that was only going to continue growing if she didn't find a fix for it.

"Are you sure you want to go through with this?" Cynthia Jurgensen, her office mate as well as her roommate, asked her. Like Juliette, Cynthia was a medical recruiter. Her recruitment area was the Scandinavian countries, as she had a heritage there. And, like Juliette, Cynthia had experienced the thrill of being called to a new adventure.

"Well, the note I found posted on the internet says the scheduling is flexible, so I'm hoping to work it out that I can commute in Friday night after I leave work here, and come home either late Sunday night or early Monday morning, before I'm due back on this job."

"But it's in the jungle, Juliette. The jungle!"

"And it's going to allow me to be involved with direct patient care again. I'm just hoping it's enough to satisfy me."

"Well, you can do whatever you want, but leave me here in the city, with all my conveniences."

San José was a large city, not unlike any large city anywhere. Juliette's transition here had been minimal as she really hadn't had time to get out and explore much of anything. So maybe her first real venture out, into the jungle of all places, was a bit more than most people would like, but the only thing Juliette could see was an opportunity to be a practicing doctor again. A doctor by the name of Damien Caldwell had advertised and, come tomorrow, she was going to go knocking on his door.

"Could you get one of the volunteers to take the linens home and wash them?" Damien asked Alegria. The hospital's sheets and pillowcases were a motley assortment, most everything coming as donations from the locals. "Oh, and instruct Rosalita on the particulars of a mechanical diet. I'm admitting Hector Araya later on, and he has difficulty chewing and swallowing since he had his stroke, so we need to adjust his diet accordingly."

Back in Seattle, Damien's workload never came close to anything having to do with linens and food but here in Bombacopsis, everything in the hospital fell under his direct supervision. This morning, for instance, during his one and only break for the day, he'd even found himself fluffing pillows and passing out cups of water to the five patients now admitted. He didn't mind the extra work, actually. It was just all a part of the job here. But he wondered if having another trained medical staffer come in, at least part-time, would ease some of the burden. That was why, when he'd gone to Cima de la Montaña last week to mail his letter to Daniel, he'd found a computer and posted a help-wanted ad on one of the local public sites.

> *Low pay, or possibly no pay.*
> *Lousy hours and hard work.*
> *Nice patients desperately in need of more medical help.*

That was all his ad said, other than where to find him. *No phone service. Come in person.*

OK, so it might not have been the most appealing of ads. But it was honest, as the last thing he wanted was to have someone make that long trek into the jungle only to discover that their expectations fell nowhere within the scope of the position he was offering.

"There's a woman outside who says she wants to see you," Alegria said as she rushed by him, her arms full of bedsheets, on her way to change the five beds with patients in them.

"Can't one of the volunteers do that for you?" Damien asked her. "Or Dr. Perkins?"

"Dr. Perkins is off on a house call right now, and I have only two volunteers on today. One is cleaning the clinic, and the other is scrubbing potatoes for dinner. So it's either you or me and, since the woman outside looks determined to get in, I think I'll change the sheets and leave that woman up to you."

"Fine," Damien said, setting aside the chart he'd been writing in. "I'll go see what she wants. Is she a local, by the way?"

Alegria shook her head. "She's one of yours."

"Mine?"

"From the United States, I think. Or maybe Canada. Couldn't tell from her accent."

So a woman, possibly from North America somewhere, had braved the jungle to come calling. At first he wondered if she was some kind of pharmaceutical rep who'd seen the word *hospital* attached to this place and actually thought she might find a sale here. As if he had the budget to go after the newest, and always the most expensive, drugs. *Nah.* He was totally off the radar for that. So, could it be Nancy? Was she running after him, trying to convince him to give up his frugal ways and come back to her?

Been there, done that one. Found out he couldn't tolerate the snobs. And if there ever was a snob, it was his ex-fiancée.

"I'm Juliette Allen," the voice behind him announced.

Damien spun around and encountered the most stunning brown eyes he'd ever seen in his life. "I'm Damien Caldwell," he said, extending his hand to shake hers.

"And I wasn't expecting you." But, whoever she was, he was glad she'd come. Tall, long auburn hair pulled back into a ponytail, ample curves, nice legs—nice everything. Yes, he was definitely glad.

"Your ad said to come in person, so here I am—in person."

In person, and in very good form, he thought. "Then you're applying for a position?" Frankly, she wasn't what he'd expected. Rather, he'd expected someone like George Perkins, a doctor who was in the middle of a career burnout, trying to figure out what to do with the rest of his life.

"Only part-time. I can give you my weekends, if you need me."

"Weekends are good. But what are you? I mean, am I hiring a nurse, a respiratory therapist or what?"

"A physician. I'm a family practice doctor. Directed a hospital practice back in Indiana."

"But you're here now, asking me for work?" From director of a hospital practice to this? It didn't make sense. "And you only want a couple days a week?"

"That's all I have free. The rest of my time goes to recruiting medical personnel to come to Costa Rica."

Now it was beginning to make some sense. She aided one of the country's fastest growing industries in her real life and wanted to be a do-gooder in her off time. Well, if the do-gooder had the skills, he'd take them for those two days. The rest of her time didn't matter to him in the least. "You can provide references?" he asked, not that he cared much to have a look at them, but the question seemed like the right one to ask.

"Whatever you need to see."

"And you understand the conditions here? And the

fact that I might not have enough money left over in my budget to pay you all the time—or ever?"

"It's not about the money."

Yep. She was definitely a do-gooder. "So what's it about, Juliette?"

"I like patient care, and I don't get to do that in my current position. I guess you can say I'm just trying to get back to where I started."

Well, that was as good a reason as any. And, in spite of himself, he liked her. Liked her no-nonsense attitude. "So, if I hire you, when can you start?"

"I'm here now, and I don't have to be back at my other job until Monday. I packed a bag, just in case I stayed, so I'm ready to work whenever you want me to start."

"How about now? I have some beds that need changing and a nurse who's doing that but who has other things to do. So, can you change a bed, Juliette?"

CHAPTER TWO

COULD SHE CHANGE a bed? Sad to say, she hadn't made very many beds in her life. Back home, she and her dad had a housekeeper who did that for them. Twice a week, fresh sheets on every bed in the house, whether or not the bed had been slept on. At her dad's insistence. Oh, and brand-new linens ordered from the finest catalogs once every few months.

That was her life then, all of it courtesy of a very generous and doting father, and she'd found nothing extraordinary about it as it had been everything she'd grown used to. Her dad had always told her it was his duty to spoil her, and she'd believed that. Now, today, living in San José, and in keeping with what she was accustomed to, she and Cynthia rented a flat that came with limited maid service. It cost them more to secure that particular amenity in their living quarters, but having someone else do the everyday chores was well worth the extra money. So, at thirty-three, Juliette was a novice at this, and pretty much every other domestic skill most people her age had long since acquired. But how difficult could it be to change a silly bed? She was smart, and capable. And if she could cure illnesses, she could surely slap a sheet onto the bed.

Easier said than done, Juliette discovered after she'd

stripped the first bed, then laid a clean sheet on top of it. Tuck in the edges, fold under the corners, make sure there were no wrinkles—

She struggled through her mental procedural list, thought she was doing a fairly good job of it, all things considered. That was, until she noticed the sizable wrinkle that sprang up in the middle of the bed and crept all the way to the right side. How had that gotten there? she wondered as she tugged at the sheet from the opposite side, trying to smooth it out and, in effect, making the darned thing even worse.

"That could be uncomfortable, if you're the one who has to sleep on it," Damien commented from the end of the bed, where he was standing, arms folded across his chest, watching her struggle. "Causes creases in the skin if you lay on it too long."

"I intend to straighten it out. Maybe remake the bed." Actually, that was a lie. Her real intent was still to pat it down as much as she could, then move on to the next bed and hope the future occupant of this particular bed didn't have a problem with wrinkles.

"You know you've been working on this first bed for ten minutes now? Alegria would have had all five beds changed in that amount of time, and been halfway through giving a patient a bed bath. So what's holding you up? Because I have other things for you to do if you ever get done here."

"This is taking a little longer because I'm used to fitted sheets," she said defensively. Her response didn't make any sense, not to her, probably not to Damien, but it was the best she could come up with, other than the truth, which was that she just didn't do beds. How lame would that sound? Top-notch doctor felled by a simple bedsheet.

"Fitted sheets—nope, no such luxuries around here. In

fact, our sheets are all donations from some of the locals. *Used* bedsheets, Juliette. The very best we have to offer. Rough-texture, well-worn hand-me-downs. But I'll bet you're used to a nice silk, or even an Egyptian cotton, maybe a fifteen-hundred thread count? You know, the very best the market has to offer."

Who would have guessed Damien knew sheets? But, apparently, he did. And, amazingly, what he'd described was exactly what she had on her bed back home. Nice, soft, dreadfully expensive sheets covering a huge Victorian, dark cherrywood, four-poster antique of a bed. Her bed and sheets—luxuries she'd thought she couldn't live without until she'd come to Costa Rica, where such luxuries were scarce, and only for those who could afford to have them imported. Which her father would do for her, gladly, if she asked him. Although she'd never ask, as that would build up his hopes that she was already getting tired of her life in Costa Rica and wanted her old life back. Back home. Same as before. Returning to her old job. Taking the position as her father's chief administrative officer. Yes, that was the way his mind would run through it, all because she wanted better bedsheets.

OK, so she was a bit spoiled. She'd admit it if anyone— Damien—cared to ask but, since he wasn't asking, she wasn't telling. Not a blessed thing! "The sheet you're describing would have cost a hundred and twenty times more than all the sheets in this ward put together. And that would be just one sheet."

"Ah! A lady with a passion for sheets." Damien arched mocking eyebrows. "I hope that same passion extends to your medicine."

"You mean a lady *doctor* who's being interrupted while she's trying to do her job." She regarded him for a moment. Well-muscled body. Three or four days' growth of stubble on his face. Over-the-collar hair, which he'd pulled back into a ponytail, not too unlike her own, only much, much shorter. Really nice dimples when he smiled. Sexy dimples. Kissable dimples… Juliette shook her head to clear the train wreck going on inside and went back to assessing her overall opinion of Damien Caldwell. He was stunningly handsome, which he probably knew, and probably used it to his advantage. Insufferably rude. Intelligent. Good doctor.

"Does it bother you that I'm watching?" he asked.

"What bothers me is that you think you know all about me through my bedsheets. You're judging me, aren't you? You know, poor little rich girl. Never changed a bedsheet in her life. That's what you're thinking, isn't it?" Judging her based on what she owned and not what she could do as a doctor.

"I wasn't but, now that you brought it up, I could. Especially if you *do* own Egyptian cotton."

"What I do or do not own has no bearing on the job here. And if you want to stand there speculating on something as unimportant as my sheets, be my guest. Speculate to your heart's content. But keep it to yourself because I need to get these beds changed and I *don't* need any distractions while I'm doing it."

The ad she'd read about this job should have warned her that it came with a pompous boss because he was, indeed, pompous. Full of himself. Someone who probably took delight in the struggles of others. "And in the meantime I'm going to smooth this stupid wrinkle so I can get on to the next bed."

"Well, if you ever get done here, I've got a patient coming into the clinic in a little while who has a possible case of gout in his left big toe. Could you take a look at him when he arrives?"

Gout. A painful inflammatory process, starting in the big toe in about half of all diagnosed cases. "I don't suppose we can test for hyperuricemia, can we?" Hyperuricemia was a build-up of uric acid in the blood. With elevated levels, its presence could precipitate an onset of gout.

"Nope. Haven't got the proper equipment to do much more than a simple CBC." Complete blood count. "And we do those sparingly because they cost us money we don't have."

"Then how do we diagnose him, or anybody else, for that matter, if we don't have the tests at our disposal?"

"The old-fashioned way. We apply common sense. In this particular case, you assess to see if it's swollen or red. You ask him if it hurts, then find out how and when. Also, you take into account the fact that the patient's a male, and we all know that men are more susceptible to gout than women. So that's another indicator. And the pain exists *only* in his big toe. Add it all up and you've got...gout." He took a big sweeping bow with his pronouncement, as if he was the lead character in a show on Broadway.

Juliette noticed his grand gesture, but chose to ignore it. "OK, it's gout. I'll probably agree with you once I've had a look at him. But, apart from that, what kind of drugs do you have on hand to treat him with? Nonsteroidal anti-inflammatories? Steroids? Colchicine? Maybe allopurinol?"

"Aspirin," he stated flatly.

"Aspirin? That's it?" Understaffed, understocked— what kind of place was this?

"We're limited here to the basics and that's pretty much how we have to conduct business every day. We start on the most simple level we can offer and hope that's good enough."

"What else do you have besides aspirin?"

"Antacids, penicillin, a lot of different topical ointments for bug bites, rashes and whatever else happens to a person's skin. A couple of different kinds of injectable anesthetic agents. Nitroglycerine. Cough syrup. Some antimicrobials. Antimalarials—mostly quinidine. A very small supply of codeine. Oh, and a handful of various other drugs that we can coerce from an occasional outsider who wanders through. When you have time, take a look. We keep the drugs in the locked closet just outside the clinic door."

"Are any of these expired drugs?"

"Hey, we take what we can get. So if it's not *too* expired, we accept it and, believe me, we're glad to get it. One person's expired drug may be another person's salvation."

"Isn't that dangerous?"

He shook his head. "I check with the pharmaceutical company before I use it. I mean, commercial expiration date is one thing, but some drugs have usable life left beyond their shelf life."

"But you do turn away some drugs that are expired?"

"Of course I do. I'm not going to put a patient at risk with an expired drug that's not usable."

"So when you call these pharmaceutical companies, don't they offer to stock you with new drugs?"

"All the time. But who the hell can afford *that* around here?" Damien shrugged. "Like I say, I check it to make sure it's safe, then I use it if it is, and thank my lucky stars I have it to use."

She hadn't expected anything lavish, but she also hadn't expected this much impoverishment. Of course, she knew little clinics like this operated all over the world, barely keeping their doors open, scraping and bowing to get whatever they had. But, in her other life, those were only stories, not a real situation as it applied to her. Now, though, she was in the heart of make-do medicine and nothing in her education or experience had taught her how to get along within its confines.

"How do you learn to get by the way you do?" she asked Damien. "With all these limitations and hardships?"

He studied her for a moment, then smiled. "Most of it you simply make up as you go. I was a general surgeon in Seattle. Worked in one of the largest hospitals in the city—a teaching hospital. So I had residents and medical students at my disposal, every piece of modern equipment known to the medical world, my OR was second to none."

"And you gave it all up for this?" It was an admirable thing to do, but the question that plagued her about that was how anyone could go from so modern to so primitive? She'd done a little internet research on Damien before she'd come here, and he had a sterling reputation. He'd received all kinds of recognition for his achievements in surgery, and he'd won awards. So what made a person trade it for a handful of expired medicines and good guesses instead of proper tests and up-to-date drugs?

Maybe he had a father who ran the hospital, Juliette thought, as her own reasons for leaving her hospital practice crossed her mind.

"This isn't so bad once you get used to it," he said.

"But how do you get used to it? Especially when it's so completely different from your medical background?"

"You look at the people you're treating and understand that they need and deserve the best care you can give them, just the way that patients in any hospital anywhere else do. Only out here you're the only one to do it. I think that's the hardest part to get used to—the fact that there's no one else to fall back on. No equipment, no tests or drugs, no excuses…

"It scared me when I first got here until I came to terms with how I was going to have to rely on myself and all my skills and knowledge. That didn't make working in this hospital any easier, but it did put things into proper perspective."

"You've gotten used to it, haven't you?"

"Let's just say that I've learned to work with the knowledge that the best I can hope for is what I have on hand at the moment, and the people here who want medical help are grateful for whatever I have to offer. They don't take it for granted the way society in general has come to take much of its medical care for granted. So, once you understand that, you can get used to just about anything this type of practice will hand you."

"Then you don't really look forward, do you?"

"Can't afford to. If I did, I'd probably get really disappointed, because anything forward from this point is the same as anything looking backward. Nothing changes and, in practical terms, it probably never will."

"But you chose a jungle practice over what you had for some reason. Was it a conscious choice, or did you come here with expectation of one thing and get handed something else?"

"I got recruited to one of the leading hospitals by someone like you. They wanted my surgical skills and they came up with a pretty nice package to offer me. Since I've never stayed in any one position too long—"

"Why not?" she interrupted.

"Because there's always something else out there. Something I haven't tried yet. Something that might be better than what I've had." Something to distract him from the fact that he'd never found what he wanted.

"In other words, you're never contented?"

"In other words, I like to change up my life every now and then. Which is why I came here to Costa Rica. The country is recruiting doctors, the whole medical industry is competing in a worldwide arena and it sounded exciting. Probably like it did to you when they came calling on you. And I'm assuming they did come calling."

"Something like that." But her motive in coming here wasn't because she was restless, or that she simply needed a change in pace. Her acceptance came because she needed to expand herself in new directions. Someplace far, far away from her father.

"Well, anyway—they did a hard recruit on me. Kept coming back for about a year, until I finally decided to give it a shot."

"So you *did* work in one of the hospitals in San José?"

"For about a month. The timing was perfect. I'd just ended a personal relationship, which made me restless to go someplace, do something else. You know, running away. Which actually has been my habit for most of my adult life." Damien grinned. "Anyway, they offered, eventually I accepted, and it took me about a week to figure out I hated it."

"Why?"

"Because it was just like what I'd left. Brought back old memories of my last hospital, of how my former fiancée thought I should be more than a general surgeon, of how my future father-in-law said that being a general surgeon was so working class. Like there's something wrong with being working class! I'd always loved working for a living but that one criticism so totally changed me, there were times I didn't even recognize myself.

Tried to be what my future family considered their equal. Put on airs I didn't have a right to. Drowned myself in a lifestyle that I didn't like, just to play the perfect part." He shook his head. "I really needed something different after I got through all that. Got it all sorted—who I *really* was, what I *really* wanted to do with my life. So one day I saw an ad where a little jungle hospital needed a doctor…"

"Like the ad you placed?" He had so much baggage in his past, she wondered how he'd gotten past it to reach this point in his life. It took a lot of strength to get from where he used to be to where he was now. A strength she wished she had for herself.

Damien chuckled. "The *same* ad."

"The *exact* same ad?" she asked him.

"One and the same. No pay, hard work, long hours. Nothing like I'd ever been involved with before. So, since I'd come to Costa Rica seeking a new adventure—hell, what's more of an adventure than this?"

"Maybe a hospital with Egyptian cotton sheets?" Everyone had something to run away from, she supposed. He did. She did. It was lucky for both of them that their need to run away had coincided with a place for them to go. Whether running into each other would turn out to be a good thing remained to be seen.

"I've lowered my expectations these past few months. If I have *any* bedsheets, I'm happy."

"But they didn't train you in medical school to be concerned about the sheets."

"And they didn't train *you* in medical school how to be a recruiter. Which makes me wonder if it's a good fit for you since you came knocking on my humble little door, wanting something different than what you already had.

Ever think you made the wrong choice, that you belong back in your old life?"

OK, based on the little bit she knew about him, this was the Damien she'd expected. Not the one who almost garnered her admiration, but the one who annoyed her. "I made a very good choice coming to Costa Rica, regardless of what you think!" He was beginning to sound like her father. *Bad choice, Juliette. Think about it. You'll come to your senses.* "Not that it's any of your business."

"In my hospital, it *is* my business. Everything here is my business, including you. Because you working here affects everything else around you, and I have to protect the hospital's interests."

"What's your point?" she snapped.

"That's for you to figure out. Which, I'm sure, will happen in time."

"There's nothing to figure out. I accepted a position that brings first-rate medical professionals here. It's an honorable job and I like it. It's…important."

"I'm not saying that it's not. With the need to improve medical conditions expanding, I'm sure it's becoming a very important position. But is it important *enough* to you? Or is patient care more important?"

"Why can't both be important to me?"

"In my experience, I've found that we poor mortals don't always do a good job of dividing ourselves."

"That's assuming I'm divided."

"Well, I suppose only you know if that's the case." Damien stepped away from the bed. "Anyway, your patient will be here shortly, so I'd suggest you figure out some way to expedite those bedsheets so you can go be a *real* doctor." With that, he spun around and started walking away.

"Are you always so rude?" she asked him while he

was still within earshot. He was not only rude, he was also nosy, presumptuous and out of line.

Damien stopped and turned back to face her. "I do it rather well, don't you think?"

Struggling with simple bedsheets, the way she was doing right now, was almost cute. It was painfully obvious, though, that this was a chore far beyond her capabilities. Or one she'd never before practiced. Which reminded Damien of days gone by, and one of the reasons he was here in the jungle, hiding away from civilization. Juliette was obviously a rich girl, probably out on her own in the world for the very first time and, once upon a time, he'd almost married a rich girl who probably still wasn't out in the world.

Spoiled was the word that always came to mind when he thought about Nancy. It was a word he wanted to apply to Juliette as well, but the determination he could see in her stopped him short of going that far. The fact was, Nancy would have never set foot in his jungle clinic and Juliette was here, fighting to make a difference. Which didn't exactly fit his perception of a rich girl.

OK, he had a bias. He admitted it. Hated that he'd just shown a bit of it to Juliette, by raising the doubt that she could cut it here. But it was well deserved, considering how he'd endured months of spoiled behavior from a woman he'd planned on marrying. Not that Nancy had ever played spoiled rich girl when it was just the two of them. No, she'd been sweet and attentive, convincing him she was the one to settle down for. Or in *Juliette's* case, *she* was the one he needed here to help him.

But in the end, Nancy had told him he could never be enough for her. He couldn't give her enough, as her demands had grown larger. More time. More attention.

More of everything. He'd tried. He'd honestly tried. Bought her everything she wanted, which put him into deep debt. Cut back his hours at the hospital to spend more time with her, which almost cost him his job. No matter what he'd done, though, it hadn't been adequate. So he'd tried harder, and always failed.

As far as Juliette working here—could that be enough for her? Or was he overthinking this thing? Truth was, he was wary. With Nancy, the vicious circle he'd got himself trapped in had played against his self-esteem and it hadn't helped when her parents told him that he'd always be struggling, that he'd never have enough to give her what she deserved. Things. Lots and lots of material things. And social status. Even with his surgeon's salary and his position at the hospital, and all the awards he'd won, they were right. At least, he'd thought so at the time.

Anyway, she'd moved out of his apartment and gone home, straight into Mommy's and Daddy's arms. As far as he knew, two years later, she was still there, dwelling quite happily as their spoiled-rotten daughter. Probably waiting for Daddy to fix her up with a man who fit the family image. A man who could give her the things Damien could not.

Which, admittedly, stung. He'd reeled from the breakup for weeks, wondering what he could have done differently. Wondering why he'd thought he was good enough for Nancy when, obviously, he was not. Wondering why he'd chosen Nancy in the first place.

So, was Juliette that spoiled? Would she spend a day or an entire weekend here, only to discover that it wasn't enough for her? Would she walk away when she realized he couldn't give her proper bedsheets, let alone a proper bed? Bottom line—he needed her here. Recruits didn't come knocking every day when he advertised. And when they did show up, they usually turned right back around and left. In fact, other than George Perkins, she'd been the first doctor in his entire year here to show any real interest in staying. And he needed her skills. But could he count on her coming through, the way he'd counted on Nancy before she'd let him down?

He didn't know, couldn't tell. Juliette was obviously of upper means and, yes, that did have a huge bearing on the way he was feeling so uneasy about her motives or dedication. But there was also something about her that caused him to believe that her upper means hadn't knocked something basic out of her. She was a hard worker and, so far, she hadn't complained about the menial tasks. Time would tell what she was really made of, he supposed. For now, he was simply trying to keep an open mind. Because for some reason other than his need of her medical skills, a reason he couldn't quite put his finger on, he wanted her to stay. Maybe for a change of scenery? Or to break the monotony? He honestly didn't know.

"You've only got just the one exam room in the clinic?" Juliette asked him, once all the beds were made.

"The clinic was originally my living quarters. One room for everything. But I built a divider so there would be a waiting room on one side and an exam room on the other. That's all there was room for."

"Then where do you sleep?" she asked him.

"In a hut next door. Another one-room setup. Not as nice as the hospital, though."

Juliette cringed. "I hate to ask, but where will I stay when I'm here?"

Ah, yes. The first test. No sheets, no bed—no room of her own. This is where it began, he supposed. Or ended. "Well, I've got two choices. You could stay here in the hospital, use an empty bed and hope we don't get so busy you'll have to give it up. We'll partition it off for you to give you some privacy. And the perk there is that the hospital has running water, a shower, a bathroom. Or, if you don't like that idea, you can shack with me. And the drawbacks there are—I don't have running water, don't have a bathroom or a shower. I have to come into the hospital for all that. Oh, and rumor has it that I might snore." He cringed, waiting for what he believed would be the inevitable.

"So if I choose your hut, I'd be what? Sleeping in bed with you?"

"No, I'm a little more gentlemanly than that. I'd give you the bed, and I'd take the floor." Said with some forced humor, since humor was all he had to offer at the moment.

"But in the same room?"

"Kind of like the student years, when you'd crash in the on-call room, no matter who was sleeping next to you. You did sleep in an on-call, didn't you?" Somehow, he could picture Juliette as the type who would lock the on-call door behind her and keep the room all to herself.

"I did," she said hesitantly. "When I had to."

"So let me guess. You didn't like it."

"It was necessary, when I was pulling twenty-four-hour shifts. But did I like it? Not particularly."

"How did I know that?" he asked, still waiting for the curtain to fall on this little act he was putting on. Who was he kidding here? Girls accustomed to silk sheets liked silk. And he sure as hell didn't have anything silk.

"You *didn't* know that," she said, expelling an exasperated sigh. "You're just into making snap judgments about me. All of them negative. Do you *ever* see anything positive in *any* situation, Damien?"

Maybe she was right. Maybe he was so used to looking for the negative that he wouldn't recognize a ray of something positive if it walked right up and slapped him in the face. Damn, he didn't mean to be like that. But something about Juliette poked at him. It was almost like he was trying to push her away. From what? He had no clue. "Look, I'll try to be more positive, OK?"

"Don't put yourself out on my account. I'm a big girl. I can take it." She squared herself up to her full five-foot-six frame and stared him down. "And I think I'll just stay in the hospital, all things considered." Narrowing her eyes, she went on, "I *hate* snoring. And, just for the record, Damien, you're not going to scare me off. I came here so I could stay better in touch with patient care, and I don't intend to back out of it, no matter how hard you're trying to push me away."

"I'm not trying to push you away," he defended.

"Sure you are. Don't know why, don't particularly care. Just let me do my job here, and we'll get along. OK?"

Well, she certainly was driven. He liked that. Liked it a lot. "Look, if you want privacy, you can have my hut on the weekends you're here, and I'll stay in the hospital."

"The weekends I'm here will be every weekend."

"You're sure of that? Because it's a long, tough drive to get here, and I don't have anything to make your life, or your work, easier when you're here."

"I'm adaptable, Damien. I'll make do."

He wanted to trust that she would. "Look, we can finish talking about your housing options later on, over dinner. But, right now, Señor Mendez is waiting in the clinic. Remember, gout? Oh, and I'm going to go make a house call. I have a patient who's a week over her due date, and she's getting pretty anxious to have her baby."

"Borrow my car. Take her for a ride on that bumpy road into town. That should induce something."

So she had a sense of humor. Even though she made her offer with a straight face, Damien laughed. "Might work better if I borrow a cart and a donkey from one of the locals."

"They actually have donkey carts here?" she asked in full amazement.

"It's called traveling in style. A modern convenience if the cart is fairly new and the donkey is reasonably young." He stopped himself short of ridiculing the kind of car she probably had back home. A sleek sports model, most likely. Shiny and silver. Convertible. Her hair let down from its ponytail and blowing in the breeze. Nope, he had to stop this. It was going too far, almost daydreaming about her the way he was. "Anyway, I'll probably be back before you're done with Señor Mendez's toe."

"Will Alegria be able to unlock the medicine cabinet for me?"

Before he answered, he fished through the pocket of his khaki cargo shorts until he found a key. "Here, take mine. Just make sure you give it back before you leave here—when? Sunday night? Monday morning?"

"Haven't decided yet. I guess it will depend on the workload."

He dropped the key into her outstretched hand. "Well, next time I get to Cima de la Montaña I'll have a key made for you." Provided she lasted that long. In a lot of ways, he hoped she did because, in spite of himself, and especially in spite of all his doubts, he liked her.

CHAPTER THREE

"HOW WAS YOUR gout patient?" Damien asked Juliette on his way back into the hospital. She was coming out of the clinic, looking somewhat perplexed. "It *was* gout, wasn't it?"

"It was gout," Juliette confirmed. "I was concerned about his age, though. He seems too young to be afflicted with it."

"I thought so, too, but the people here live hard lives. They age faster than normal."

"And he's had a complete physical?"

"Before he presented with gout symptoms?" Damien shook his head. "Getting people around here to submit to physicals when they don't have any particular symptoms isn't easy, but about six months ago Señor Mendez did come in. Nothing out of the ordinary turned up."

"Well, I gave him aspirin like you told me to. But there was something else going on. I think Señor Mendez was high on some kind of drug. At least, that's the way he seemed. Slurred speech, slow movements. Do you know if he indulges?"

Damien laughed. "A lot of the locals indulge. I'm surprised Señor Mendez would, though. He's pretty straight. Doesn't drink that I know of. Doesn't do drugs—at least, I didn't think he did. And, even if he did, it surprises me that he would go out in public that way because he's a very polite, private, gentle man who spends every last penny he has to support his family. But I guess you never know what goes on behind closed doors, do you?"

"Is it really that common around here?"

"Ganja—marijuana—is cheap, and easily available."

"So what do you do if they come in here stoned?"

"Treat them for what they came in for, and ignore the rest. I'm just the doctor here. I don't get involved in anything else."

"Then you won't report him?"

"If he's not bothering me, there's no reason to. My personal policy is, if someone needs help they get help, in spite of all the external factors that might otherwise cause problems. In other words, if he's stoned, you treat him, anyway. The rest of it's none of my business."

"That's decent of you."

"I aim to be decent to my patients. They've got enough hardships to face in their daily lives without me adding to them."

"But do you condone it?"

"Nope. I'm a law-abiding citizen wherever I go, and the Costa Rican law makes ganja illegal, so I respect that."

"Then you, personally, don't indulge?"

"Never have, never will. Don't smoke, either. Drink only in moderation. Work out regularly. Eat a balanced diet. You know, all good things for my body." A body that seemed to be aging too quickly since he'd come to Costa Rica. Of course, that was about the hard work here. So were the new creases in his face and the pair of glasses he was now forced to wear any time he wanted to read. Most people wouldn't consider him old, as he overtook his thirty-sixth birthday in a few weeks. But some days he just felt old—older than dirt. "Keeps me in good working condition."

"Well, I just wanted to let you know the condition of your patient."

"And I appreciate that. But I'm not really concerned about it. At least, not right now."

"When does that point change for you, Damien?"

"When I see someone's drug use as a potential danger to themselves or others. That's when I'll step in. But again, only as a doctor."

"We always had to note it in our chart at the hospital," she said. "And if it was too bad, we were supposed to alert Security."

"Did you ever?"

"Once. Then I had regrets, because he really wasn't that bad. But I was new, still blindly loyal to hospital policy, probably more so than to the patient. Of course, that changed pretty quickly, the more involved I became with my patients."

"So you were a true, big hospital loyalist?"

"Still am. But I'm more practical about it now. But you've got to understand that I was raised by a true hospital loyalist—the chief of staff, and those were the kinds of concerns he always brought home with him. What was best for the hospital was always his main concern, right after the kind of patient care we were giving."

"So your daddy's a big shot in a big hospital?" Given her rich girl background, that didn't surprise him.

"That's one way of putting it, I suppose. But to me he was always just my dad. A man who went to work, worked long, hard hours and came home to tuck me in every night. It never occurred to me that he was so important in terms of an entire medical community until I was probably ten or eleven and he took me to work with him to see what he did during the day."

"Did it impress you?"

"Not so much then. I think I was more impressed by all the desserts in the cafeteria than I was by my father's position in the hospital. Of course, the older I got the more I realized just what a *big deal* he was."

"But you have no aspirations for something like that for yourself?"

"I had my shot at it. Dad offered me a promotion into administration a couple of months ago."

"So let me guess. You chose Costa Rica instead. Was it to run away from Daddy?" Probably her first real act of rebellion in a very laid-out life.

"You say that like it was a derogatory thing to do."

"Was it?" he asked her.

Juliette shook her head. "I like to think of Costa Rica as something necessary in my career development. In my personal development, as well. Also, I didn't feel as though I'd earned the job. I think promoting me was simply my dad's way of ensuring that I'd stay around for a while. Or forever, if he had his way about it. I mean, my dad always wins. No matter what it is, he finds a way to win, and I was tired of always having my ideas and hopes and desires tossed into that lottery."

Actually, that was admirable. "So you *did* want to get away from Daddy." He liked the kind of spirit it must have taken for her to make that much of a change in her life—a life that was, apparently, very sheltered. Something Nancy would have never done for anyone, for any reason.

"I wanted to get away from all the usual trappings and…"

"Make it on your own merits rather than resting on the laurels your dad created for you?"

"Do you challenge all the women you come into contact with, or is it just *me* who challenges *you*?"

He thought about that for a moment, wondering if his leftover resentment of Nancy did, adversely, affect his relationships with women. Certainly, he hadn't dated since Nancy. Not once. Not even tempted. No one-night stands. No quick meet-ups at the coffee shop. No phone calls, texting or any other sort of personal communications. In fact, if anything, he assiduously avoided *everything* that came close to putting him into a relationship of any sort with any woman—young, old or somewhere in between.

"Actually, you haven't challenged me yet. But I'm sure you're waiting for the right opportunity."

Juliette laughed. "You won't see it coming," she warned him. "And you'll be caught so far off guard, you won't know what hit you."

Now, that was something he could foresee happening. Juliette had a very disarming way about her, and he had every inclination to believe that she was good at the sneak attack. Of course, he was the one who'd placed himself directly in her line of fire, and he still didn't understand why he'd done that. But he was there, nonetheless, actually looking forward to her first barrage of arrows. "Sounds like the lady has a plan."

"My only plan is to take the next patient, who's coming through the door right now." She gave him a devious smile. "Unless you're really into doing some stitches today." A snap diagnosis made with the assumption that underneath the bloody towel the mother was holding over her son's hand lay something that needed stitching. "You *do* have a suture kit, don't you?"

He turned around, also looked at the people coming through the hospital door. Diego Cruz and his mother, Elena. This wasn't the first time Diego had needed stitches, and it wouldn't be the last as Diego was an active little boy who was pretty much left to run wild through Bombacopsis while his mother cooked and cleaned and sewed for other villagers.

Elena was one of Damien's regular hospital volunteers as well, which took even more time away from Diego. "If you mean needles and thread, yep, I've got them." He waved at Diego, who gave him a limp wave in return.

"Regulars?"

Damien chuckled as he bent to greet the little boy. "One of our best. So, Diego. What happened here?"

"I fell," the child confessed.

"From the top of the gate at the church," Elena volunteered.

"Were you trying to break in again?" Damien asked him, fighting to keep a straight face.

"Only for a drink of water."

"You couldn't go home for that?"

"It was too far." Diego looked up at Juliette and turned on a rather charming smile. "And the water at the church is holy, which is good for me. It makes me grow stronger."

"Well, you weren't strong enough to keep yourself from falling off the gate, were you?" Damien took the towel off the boy's hand and had a look. It wasn't a bad cut, not too deep, but deep enough that it would take about four or five stitches. The same number of stitches he'd had in his other hand a month ago, when he'd tried to remove the log bridge that crossed the village creek, and had gotten hung up on it.

"That's because I didn't have my drink yet."

Diego reminded Damien a lot of himself when he'd been that age. He and his twin, Daniel, were always getting into some kind of trouble. Nothing serious, but usually with some consequence like a broken arm, a sprained ankle, multiple areas of stitches. "You seem to have all the answers, Diego," he said, finally giving way to a laugh.

"I try, el doctor Damien," Diego responded earnestly.

"Well, here's the deal. I'm going to go get you that drink of water, from the hospital faucet, *not* from the church. And, while you're waiting for me to bring it back to you, el doctor Juliette is going to take care of your hand. Which means you're going to get stitches like you had last month. Remember?"

Diego nodded his head. "They hurt," he said, looking up at his mother as if she was going to stop the procedure. "Do I have to?" he asked her.

"You have to do whatever el doctor Damien says," his mother told him. "He's the boss."

For a moment Diego looked defeated. Then he perked right back up. "But el doctor Damien won't hurt me much. That's what he promised me last time."

"Hey, Diego. This one could have hurt a lot more if you'd cut something other than your hand," Damien said. He raised up and looked at Juliette. "Suture material's in the third drawer in the clinic cabinet. Oh, and I do have xylocaine to deaden the pain. I keep a fair stock of it on hand, thanks to Diego, here. He's our main consumer."

"Sure you don't want to do this, since you and Diego seemed to have built a rapport?" she asked. "He might trust you more."

"No, I'll let you do it. Even at the tender age of ten, our man here has an eye for the pretty ladies, and I'm sure he'd much rather have you taking care of him. Isn't that right, Diego?"

Once again, Diego turned his smile on for Juliette. "Right," he said, scooting past his mother and stepping closer to Juliette. "El doctor Juliette is very pretty."

Damien shrugged. "Like I said…"

"OK, Romeo," Juliette said to Diego, as she took his unwounded hand and led him into the exam room. "Let's see what we can do about fixing this up."

"My name is Diego, *not* Romeo!" he said defiantly.

"Where she comes from, they mean the same thing," Damien said from the doorway.

Juliette flashed Damien a knowing look. "Where I come from, grown women never have to worry about advances from ten-year-old boys."

"Almost eleven," Diego corrected. He closed his eyes while Juliette swabbed his hand clean in order to take a closer look at his cut.

"Does it hurt much?" Juliette asked, accepting a cotton gauze pad Damien had fished out of a drawer for her.

"No," Diego said. But the slight tentativeness in his voice said otherwise.

"Diego is one tough little kid," Damien said, on his way to the closet to fetch the xylocaine. "And the shot that el doctor Juliette is about to give him won't hurt at all, will it, Diego?"

This time his tentativeness was full-blown. "No," he said, pulling back his hand slightly.

"You going to break into the church again, Diego? Because this is the second time in a month and it's not going to be too long before Padre Benicio comes after you."

Diego's eyes opened wide. "Will he hurt me?" he asked.

"No, he won't hurt you. But he'll make you do chores, like washing the windows, or cleaning up the church garden." Damien recalled how he and Daniel had been the recipient of such chores from time to time. "And if you come in here hurt again because you've done something bad, I'm going to make you pay for your medical treatment with some chores here. Like painting the fence outside, or scrubbing the floors."

"I think he means it, Diego," Juliette said as she turned to hide the smile crossing her face. "By the way, does he need a tetanus shot? And I'm assuming you *do* offer that?"

"I *do* offer that, as a matter of fact. But Diego is up-to-date. I got him a couple of months ago when he got into a fight with a fence of chicken wire." Damien liked Diego. A lot. He was a smart kid. Resourceful. Bright in school. Knew how to get along in his own little world. But he didn't have a father, which meant his mother had to work doubly hard to support her small family. That, more than anything else, contributed to the mischief that always seemed to find Diego. The kid simply had too much time on his hands.

"Hey, Diego," Damien said, suddenly finding a little bit of inspiration, "I have an idea. Are you interested?"

"Maybe," Diego said, not even noticing that Juliette was preparing the syringe to give him the xylocaine shot.

"OK, well…" Damien blinked, sympathizing with the kid while Juliette stuck the needle into his hand. The hand was sensitive and that shot had to hurt, but Diego merely flinched and bit down on his lower lip. "Want a job?"

"A job, el doctor Damien?"

"Yes, a job. Here, in the hospital."

"For real money?"

Out of his own pocket, if he had to, Damien decided. This kid needed better direction. That was something he could do, without too much effort. "Real money."

Juliette threaded the suture needle and turned Diego's hand at a more convenient angle before she proceeded to start stitching. "You could make beds," she suggested, smiling over at Damien.

"No, I have something better than that in mind," Damien responded, smiling back.

"Could I be el doctor Diego?" Diego asked.

"Not until you're older, and have had more schooling. But you could be the person in charge of el doctor Damien's files."

Juliette raised amused eyebrows. "Now, that seems like a fitting job. And a very important one."

Damien nodded his agreement. "I can teach Diego how to alphabetize, then he can keep things filed away in proper order. I mean, we do it the old-fashioned way here. Paper notes put into folders, sorted and put away in the file cabinet. Everything completely organized."

"I can organize," Diego said.

"Do you even know what organized means?" Juliette asked him.

"No, but el doctor Damien will teach me."

She looked at Damien. "He has a lot of confidence in you."

Truth was, Damien had a lot of confidence in Diego. He wanted to be a good kid, and he tried hard to do it, but too many times his circumstances simply got in his way. Damien's own father had been the influence that had kept him from becoming too out of control, and Damien hoped he could be that same influence for Diego.

"Elena," he directed at Diego's mother. "Is it all right that Diego works for me?"

"That would be very good," she said, excitement registering on her face. "He responds very well to you and maybe this will help keep him out of trouble."

"Good, then I'll make out a schedule in a little while, and maybe Diego could start working tomorrow. OK with you, Diego?" he asked, shifting his attention back to the boy.

"For real money!" Diego exclaimed, as Juliette sank her first stitch.

Damien gave him a thumbs-up.

"Maybe I'll buy a car!" Diego exclaimed, grinning from ear to ear.

"You have real money to give him?" Juliette asked Damien, after Diego had gone skipping out of the hospital, bragging to one of the volunteers on the way that he was going to have a *real* job here, at the hospital.

"I have a little bit of money put away. And it won't take much to keep Diego happy. Five hundred *colónes* a week come to little less than a dollar, and that's not going to break my bank."

Juliette was impressed. More than impressed; she was touched by the way he'd handled Diego. He was a natural with children. And his love of children shone through so brilliantly it almost surprised her, as she hadn't expected to see that from him. "Do you have kids of your own?" she asked him.

"Never married, never had children."

"Is that your avowed way of life, or just something that has occurred because of your restless lifestyle? Because, if you ever truly settled down, I think you'd make a wonderful dad."

"Not a wonderful husband, too?" he asked, grinning at her.

He did have his good qualities. Juliette was beginning to see that. But did he have enough to make him good husband material? For her, the answer was no. For someone else—it all depended on what they wanted, or didn't want, in a husband. "Since you've never been married, there's no way to tell. And, personally, I'd never get that involved with you to find out."

"Never?" he asked.

"Outside of a professional relationship, *never*."

"That's harsh."

"But honest." She knew he was teasing her now, and that was a side of him she quite liked. Apart from his ability with children, maybe there were some other re-deemable qualities in him after all.

"Said by a lady who, if I'm not mistaken, has never been married herself."

"Never married. No regrets about it, either."

"For now," he countered.

"For now, maybe for the rest of my life." She didn't think about it much, to be honest. What was the point? If it happened, it happened. If didn't, it didn't. Dwelling on the *what ifs* didn't get her anywhere.

"Because you want more than any man could possi-bly give you?"

"Because I want what I want, and I haven't found it yet." It was a simple statement, but oh, so true. She hadn't come close to finding what she wanted. Funny thing was, she couldn't exactly define what it was. Couldn't put it into a mental checklist, couldn't even put it down on paper it was so vague to her. Yet she truly believed that if the man who fit her undefined list came into her life, everything would become crystal clear to her. She'd know him. She'd see the qualities that, until that very moment, had been nothing but a nebulous notion.

The day passed fairly quickly, and Damien was glad to see that it was finally turning into night. People had wan-dered in and out all day long, none of them with serious complaints, but now he expected they would stay home, coming to the hospital only if it was an emergency. Kicking back in a chair in the hospital waiting room, he put his feet up on a small side table, clasped his hands behind his neck and stretched back, sighing. "We don't usually see too much action at night. The people here like to eat a good dinner and go to bed early."

"The *arroz con pollo* certainly qualifies as a good dinner," Juliette commented, taking a seat across from Damien. "I love chicken and rice. Probably could eat it every few days."

"Which is how often you're going to get it here. The hospital is pretty limited in its culinary offerings, and we rely mostly on what the locals donate to us. They all raise chickens, rice is cheap, so—*arroz con pollo* happens a lot."

"Maybe I can get Rosalita's recipe for it. My roommate and I trade off on the cooking chores, and most of the time I just fix sandwiches and salads. She might enjoy something different from me, for a change."

"Do you like to cook?"

Juliette shook her head. "I've always had someone to do the cooking for me. Or I ate out. But now I work such crazy hours, it's easier to stay in to eat, because when I finally do get home I'm not inclined to go back out just for food."

"So you had a maid to change your bed, *and* a cook to fix your meals. Any other servants?"

"They weren't servants, Damien. Nobody calls them that! They were just employees. People who worked for us."

"Then I stand corrected. Did you have other people who worked for you?"

"Just a gardener, and he was only part-time."

"And someone to tend your pool?"

"We had a pool," she admitted. "And someone did tend to it."

"So we're up to four people who worked for you. Anybody else? Maybe a tailor for your dad, or a personal assistant to keep your calendar organized."

"OK, so we hired people to work for us. What of it?"

"Nothing, really. I'm just trying to determine the extent of your wealth." It was late, he was tired, yet here he was, baiting her again. Something about Juliette brought that out in him; he didn't want to be intentionally cruel to her, but his need to raise her hackles just seemed to ooze out of him, no matter how hard he tried to stop.

"And here I thought you were trying to be civil with me." Juliette pushed herself up out of the chair. "Look, I'm not in the mood to go another round with you tonight. So, I'm just going out to the ward, find myself an empty bed and go to sleep. If you need me— You know what? I don't want you coming to get me. Send one of the volunteers to do it."

"It was an honest question, Juliette. I was simply trying to find out more about you." *Yeah, right.* More like he was just trying to find out how far he could push her before she pushed back. In a sense, it was vital to her work here and how much he could throw at her before she resisted him. Of course, it was also about taunting her, which was something he was going to have to quit doing. If he wanted her to come back, and he did, he needed to be nicer to her. Needed to quit testing her. Most of all, he needed to stop comparing her to Nancy because she definitely *wasn't* anything like Nancy.

"Well, I'm not in the mood for your honesty."

Damien did like the way she stood up for herself. "But honesty is one of my best virtues. I don't lie. Not about anything. And if I want to know something, I ask."

"Well, you can ask me anything you want, professionally. But my personal life is out of it because you've prejudged who I am and what I am, and I can't see you being the type who changes his mind once it's made up."

She was right about that. "OK, so let me be honest here. I have a bias against wealthy people. More specifically, spoiled rich girls." So now she knew. In a way that was good, as it gave them a base to work from. And he really did want a better footing with Juliette, no matter how much he acted toward the contrary.

"You think I'm spoiled?"

"Are you?" he asked.

Juliette huffed out an impatient breath. "I've had advantages most other people don't have, and I'll admit that. And I'll also admit that I've enjoyed the privilege that comes from my father's wealth. So to you that may scream spoiled, but to me it says normal. Everything that I've achieved or had or done is normal to me. If you think that's being spoiled, then think it. It's not worth the effort of trying to change your mind, because I simply don't care what you think of me personally. Go ahead and label me all you want, if that's what makes you feel good. But don't waste my time pointing it out to me, because I've got better things to worry about. Like the job I intend to do here, no matter how bad you treat me."

She was red and fiery when she was angry. And sexy as hell! He liked that. Liked it a lot. "Look, I have these preconceived ideas, right or wrong, and for those, I do apologize. I'm trying to get that under control. But I also have an irascible personality that needs attention, which I haven't had time to give it."

"Irascible?"

"You know. Hot-tempered. Irritable."

"Yes, I've noticed. And you freely admit that?"

"I do because, like I said, I'm honest."

"Do you like being irascible?"

"Not so much." Especially now. But it overtook him and sometimes he couldn't control it. Like with Juliette. It was part of his restlessness, he supposed.

"Then stop it. You're a smart man. You're capable of getting a grip on yourself, if you want to. So quit acting like you're so mean because, deep down, I don't think you really are. It's only a defense mechanism, Damien. Against what, I don't know. Don't want to know. But if you keep putting people off, the way you do, you're going to wind up in a Costa Rican jungle with no friends, and no place to go. That could turn out to be very sad for you."

She was softening now, her flare of anger dying down. This smoother side of her was so attractive, all he wanted to do was stay in that place, at that time, and stare at her. But there was a part of Juliette that scared him—the part that was so easily digging beneath his surface to discover who he really was. Most of the time, he kept that face hidden. Didn't want people getting close because, in his experience, people who could find the vulnerable place had the power to hurt. Nancy had hurt him. In spite of all the things he'd seen in her, and all the qualms he'd had about marrying someone coming from an indulged, wealthy background, he'd still planned a life with her. In fact, he'd tried hard to make the changes she'd needed to see in him, changes he didn't necessarily want to make but had made, nonetheless, because that was what she'd wanted.

In essence, he'd been true to Nancy but he hadn't been true to himself. No way was he going to do that again, so it was easier to push people away before they expected something of him. "There could be worse things than ending up here without friends and no place to go," he said, even though a big chunk of him didn't believe that.

"Look, Damien. You're fighting some kind of battle here, and apparently you've decided to drag me into it. But I never fight. Not with you, not with anybody. All I want is for you to lay off the snide remarks and let me do my work. You don't have to like me, I don't have to like you. And it seems we're starting out that way, which doesn't make a working relationship easy, but since I'm only going to be here a couple days a week, our feelings about each other shouldn't get in the way. If you want to run me off, don't do it because I rub you the wrong way. Or because I'm wealthy. Do it because my work isn't good enough. Do it because I have a lousy bedside manner. Do it because I'm not as good of a doctor as you need. But don't do it because of personal issues. OK? Oh, and don't cop out to an excuse like your self-admitted irascible nature because, frankly, I don't care what you are by nature. All I want is a good supervisor. Someone who will help me when I need it, and leave me alone when I don't. And someone who doesn't ridicule me because I don't know how to make a bed."

Man, oh, man, *had* he been wrong when he'd compared Juliette to Nancy. Nancy would have never stood up to him like that. She was quiet, always ran to Daddy and Daddy did the talking. And she would have never been as passionate about anything the way Juliette was passionate about working here.

"You know. We're both tired. We've had a long day and we've got another long day ahead of us tomorrow. This is new to you, and you're new to me, both of which are going to take some getting used to. So maybe we should just stop this right here. You can go get some sleep. I'll hang around for another hour or so, do some final bed checks, turn the rest of the night over to George Perkins and go back to my hut and grab a couple hours of sleep. Then we'll regroup in the morning and see what we've got."

"Who's George Perkins?" she asked.

"My other doctor here. Plastic surgeon, good man. A little burned-out on medicine, but working his way back in."

"Burned-out?"

"He substituted work for life." The way *he* did. "Lost his wife over it, but one of the women here—let's just say that the love of a good woman has worked miracles for him. He's finding a new purpose."

"Well, here's to the good women," she said.

"They are out there, I suppose."

"You *suppose*?"

"Did I offend you again?"

"Actually, you didn't. And you didn't surprise me, either."

"Good. Then I don't have anything else to apologize for."

"Maybe, before you do, I should just go find myself a bed and stay away from you for a while."

If there was any way he could make this situation any more tense between them he sure couldn't come up with what it might be. It was as if to open his mouth was to say something he didn't intend to say. Hell of it was, he couldn't seem to stop himself. But tomorrow—ah, yes, the great unknown tomorrow. He wanted to think that come tomorrow he'd do better. Truth was, though, he didn't know if he could.

"Look, I've got a couple of room dividers stashed in the supply closet. Let me go get them and section you off from the rest of the ward. It's not much in the way of privacy, but it's the best I've got."

Juliette nodded her agreement and managed a polite smile. "Tomorrow will be better," she told him.

He hoped that would be true. "Let's keep our fingers crossed."

"So what time do you want me on in the morning?"

Damien checked his watch. It was almost midnight now, and breakfast would be served at seven thirty. "I'll have George wake you up at six. That should give you enough time to shower and get ready."

"Get ready for what?"

"Didn't I tell you? Rosalita doesn't come in until it's time to cook the noon meal. We all pitch in so I'm putting you in charge of the kitchen for breakfast."

"You've got to be kidding!"

Damien smiled at her. "It beats bedsheets, doesn't it?"

CHAPTER FOUR

JULIETTE TOSSED AND turned for almost an hour before she finally dozed off. The bed was lumpy, the sheets scratchy and the patient down the row from her snored like a buzz saw. None of that mattered much, as her mind was focused on Damien. Images of him popped up behind her eyelids when she closed her eyes, thoughts of him sent her brain into overload, instantly awakening every synapse in her body. But why?

Well, she wasn't sure. Maybe because he was an enigma of a man. It was as if he ran hot and cold, minute to minute. Nice then cutting, all in a flash. To say the least, it was peculiar behavior. But she wasn't going to criticize him for it, even though in the span of only one day she'd become the target of his off-and-on belligerence, as if something was boiling just underneath his surface. She didn't have to look too hard to see it.

"You're Juliette, aren't you?" A man with a very thick Boston accent poked his head in around her partition. "Damien told me to wake you up if I needed help."

"What time is it?" she asked groggily.

"A little after two. And I hate to disturb you like this, but one of us has got to go down the road and deliver a baby while the other one stays here and looks after the hospital."

"Are you George Perkins?" she asked as she tried to shake her single hour of sleep off her stiff body.

"Yes," he said. "George Perkins, plastic surgeon in the States, GP in the jungle, at your service. Pleased to make your acquaintance, Juliette. Sorry this comes at such a bad time but, in my experience, most of the babies I've delivered here have preferred to make their grand entrance in the middle of the night."

Juliette switched on her bedside light to have a good look at him. He was a distinguished man with silver hair and a full gray beard. He sported a crisp linen shirt and a neatly pressed pair of khaki trousers, looking very much as if he could have stepped right off the pages of a fashion magazine. All in all, he was a good-looking gent. And he looked…happy. Something she'd never seen in her father, and had never even seen in herself when she looked in the mirror. "Damien didn't mention that I was to be on call tonight. Is it posted somewhere that I should have noticed?"

"Damien doesn't mention a lot of things. You'll get used to that if you stay with us for very long. Also, we don't post things around here because most of the volunteers barely speak English and they sure as heck can't read it. So, everything's passed down directly, from person to person. As for taking calls at night, in my current situation which, in case Damien didn't tell you, is I'm living with a very lovely village woman and I prefer working nights while Carmelita and her children are sleeping, so no one really has to take calls then, unless I'm taking a night off. I'm just hoping that you'll stand in as my backup right now because I don't want to go wake Damien up to help me. He was on thirty-six hours straight before tonight, and he needs his rest."

Juliette blew out a deep breath and sat up. "So what do you want me to do? Deliver a baby, or watch the hospital?"

"Do you like babies?" he asked her. "Because if you do, I'd rather stay here and attend to a couple of my regulars who like to come see me in the middle of the night."

"Sure, no problem." Juliette swung her legs over the side of the bed and stood up. Normally, at home, she'd be wearing pajamas. But here, in the jungle, she'd brought a pair of scrubs along as she didn't know what she'd be doing and scrubs were good everyday work clothes, as well as stand-in pajamas. "Where can I find the mother-to-be?"

"Down this road until you get to the church. Turn left at that intersection, go another block, then turn right. She'll be in the third house on the left. The best landmark I can give you is a rusted-out old pickup truck in her front yard, and the house should be well lit, as half the village usually turns out for a birth." He held out a flashlight. "No streetlights," he said sheepishly.

House calls by flashlight. Couldn't say she'd ever done anything like that before, but there was a first time for everything. So she took the light from him and switched it on to make sure the batteries were good. They were. "Any complications? Anything I should know about before I go?"

"Her name is Maria Salas, and this is her third child so it should be a fairly easy birth. She hasn't been in labor long, according to her husband, but he thinks the baby is coming quickly. Apparently, she has a history of fast births."

"Then I should get going," Juliette said, bending down to pull on her sneakers. "Do you have a medical kit with maternity supplies I can take along with me?"

"I put it by the front door before I came to get you. It

should have everything you need for a straightforward birth. But if you run into any complications, have one of Maria's family members run and fetch Damien."

"Will do." Juliette pushed herself off the bed and headed immediately toward the door. She was finally awake, still feeling a little sluggish, though, as one hour hadn't been enough to shake off her tiredness. "Should we try to get her into the hospital for this? Because I'm not sure a home delivery is the safest thing to do." Also, as director of a clinic, she'd never made a house call in her life, flashlight or not, and, while she was looking forward to the experience, it also made her a little nervous going so far outside of what she'd ever done. But that was what they did here, and she was part of it now. So it was what she did, too.

"Sure. Bring her in, if she can make it. But I doubt that's going to work out for you because most of the women here prefer home births. You know, have the baby then getting back onto whatever they were doing before it came."

That was a stamina Juliette admired. As for her, though, if she ever had a baby, she wanted it in a modern hospital with all the latest equipment. Wanted an anesthesiologist on hand to give her an epidural for the pain. Wanted fetal monitors, and heart monitors, and blood pressure monitors. Soft lights and soft music in the delivery room.

"Well, whatever happens, if she's as fast about it as you've been led to believe, maybe I'll be able to get back here in time to grab another couple hours of sleep."

"Or you can sleep in the morning, when Damien comes on."

Right. And listen to Damien taunt her about that for the next several weeks. *What did you do? Come to the jungle just to sleep?*

Juliette grabbed the rucksack by the door and fairly ran out and on down the street, flashing her light along the path, making the proper turns where she needed and continuing on until she came to the rusty old truck standing in Maria's front yard. It was surrounded by several people, who were all talking quite loudly, as if they were having a party. Indeed, half the village seemed to be there, as George had said.

"The baby's coming out now," one of the men told her. "My new grandchild."

"And it's going to be a big baby. Maria always has big babies," an older woman added.

Juliette's first thought was gestational diabetes. It was a condition that put the mother and child at some degree of risk, and usually resulted in larger than the average baby. But hadn't Damien been seeing Maria? Surely, he would have noticed such a condition and prepared for it. Also, George would have mentioned it to her. So Juliette put that notion out of her head, preferring to think that Maria had received excellent prenatal care from Damien. In spite of his attitude, everything she'd seen and read about him told her he was a good doctor. "Thank you," she said, scooting past all the gathered people and hurrying through Maria's open front door.

The lights were bright inside, revealing a clean but cluttered little house. Judging from the knickknacks, toys, books, small appliances and clothing strewn everywhere, the Salas family never came across an object of any sort that they couldn't collect. "Where is she?" she asked one of the five people huddled among the clutter.

"Back bedroom, left side of the hall. Go through the kitchen." The man pointed to a narrow pathway winding its way through a corridor of old chairs, tables and lamps.

Juliette squeezed through the maze and stopped just

short of entering the kitchen. "What are *you* doing here?" she asked.

Damien, who was sitting in an old chrome chair at the kitchen table, smiled up at her. "Same thing you are, I guess."

"They came and got you, too?"

He shrugged. "I'm her doctor. Who else would they call?"

"Me."

"Not sure why they'd do that, seeing as how you've never even met Maria."

"George Perkins woke me up. Told me to get down here."

"George overreacts sometimes."

"Like sending me here in the middle of the night when I could be back at the hospital, sleeping?"

"I could be saying the same thing. But I started to realize, probably in my first couple of days here, that people's needs were always going to supersede my sleep. Comes with the territory."

"Well, that's too bad for you, I suppose."

"I'm used to it." He stretched back in his chair. "Anyway, Maria's fully dilated, fully effaced. Pushing it out as we speak."

"Then shouldn't you be in there, delivering the baby instead of sitting here, casually talking about it?" Frankly, she was shocked that he wasn't more involved at this stage.

"I'd like to be, but Maria's mother and grandmother are in there, along with her two sisters, a couple of cousins and an aunt. There's really no room for anyone else."

"You mean no room for a doctor?"

"She's already got plenty of help standing by. She doesn't need a doctor."

He was being so blithely unconcerned about this, it surprised her. "But haven't you been seeing her all along?"

"I was here earlier today, as a matter of fact. Kind of thought the baby would be coming in the next day or so."

"And yet you're sitting here, doing nothing."

"Actually, I'm sitting here, waiting to take over if she starts having problems. That's the only reason they called us in—as backups. Luckily, though, she's progressing through a normal delivery quite nicely. Oh, and I do poke my head in the door every few minutes to check on how things are going."

"So who's going to actually deliver the baby?"

"Her grandmother. She's delivered more babies than I have. I know she delivered Maria's first two. Oh, and just last week she delivered her neighbor's baby." He shrugged. "Lady's got a lot of experience, and she resents anybody barging in who doesn't belong there. In Irene's opinion, *we* do not belong there."

"Then she's a midwife," Juliette stated, relieved that someone with experience and knowledge was taking over.

"Of sorts. I mean she's not trained or anything like that. She's just always available to do something she's been doing for sixty years."

Sixty years? That alarmed Juliette. "How old is she?"

"Not sure, since she doesn't go to doctors or hospitals, and we don't have her records. But I'm guessing she's somewhere around eighty, give or take a few years."

"Eighty and still delivering babies? Why do you allow that, Damien? You're the doctor in this village. Shouldn't you have some say in the medical concerns of the people who live here?"

"Normally, I do. But when it comes to childbirth, the

women here gang up on me and keep me at a distance. It's their tradition to rally around their mothers in labor and see to the delivery. They've been doing it for more years than the two of us combined have been here on this earth. So who am I to intrude?"

Juliette pushed her hair back from her face. Tonight, it wasn't banded up in a ponytail. "Do you think they'd mind if I looked in?"

"As another woman, or as a doctor?"

"Why can't I be both?"

Damien laughed. "You really can't be that naive, can you?"

"What do you mean by that?"

"These people practiced their folk medicine long before anything remotely modern came in and took over, and so many of the older ones still hold on to their old ways. They'll tolerate us when they need us, but otherwise they'll resist the hell out of what we try to offer them because they consider that an insult. People trust what they know, and resist anything new to them. The fine art of healing is included in that."

From somewhere behind the wall to her right, the quiet voices of people chattering were beginning to grow louder, and Juliette wondered if that was a sign of imminent birth. The ladies in the room with Maria were getting excited. She could almost picture them huddling around the bed, talking, as Maria was assuming the position to deliver. All so casual. "Well, resistance or not, I'm going to go take a peek."

"Or you could sit down with me here, have a nice *refresco*—" Damien held up a glass of blended fruit and ice in salute "—and wait."

"Or you could go back home and go to bed, since I'm here now," she suggested. "George said you pulled thirty-six hours straight, so I think you need the sleep more than I do."

"I appreciate the offer, but I think I'll stay since I've been with Maria through this entire pregnancy. And she did ask me, specifically, if I would check the baby after it's born." He held his *refresco* out to her. "Papaya and passion fruit. Really good. Want a sip?"

What she wanted was to go deliver a baby, but seeing as how that wasn't going to happen, she still wanted to get into Maria's bedroom and watch what was going on. Hitching her rucksack higher onto her shoulder, she passed by Damien, whose feet were now propped up on the chair opposite him, and headed on back through the kitchen. "I'll let you know if it's a boy or girl," she said before she stepped into the back hall.

"It's a boy," he called after her.

"You did some testing to find out?" Juliette asked, clearly surprised that he'd go to such lengths for someone who wanted as little medical intervention as possible.

"No tests. Just a guess. And I'm usually pretty good at guessing. Got my last five deliveries right. No reason to break that winning streak now."

"You're that confident, are you?"

In answer, he picked up his *refresco*, took a sip, then said, "Yep!"

Damn, he was sexy, sitting there in all his casual, cocky glory. She really didn't want to think that of him, and maybe her guard was let down because she was so tired but, God help her, she was beginning to like Damien. Not enough to fall for him, in spite of his somewhat unusual charm, but enough to tolerate his ways.

"Can I come in?" she asked, pushing open Maria's bedroom door.

The women in the room all turned to look at her—all

but the oldest one, who was seated at the end of the bed, obviously ready to deliver a baby. "Who are you?" one of the women asked.

"Juliette Allen. El doctor Juliette Allen."

"No doctor needed here," the woman at the end of the bed said quite sternly.

"That's what el doctor Damien told me, so I'm not here as a doctor. I'm just here to watch. And if you need someone else to help…"

"Irene needs no help," another one of the women informed her.

Juliette sighed. If Damien were here, he'd be enjoying this rejection. "I won't get in the way."

"Don't get in the way somewhere else," Irene, Maria's grandmother, said. "Maria doesn't need a stranger here."

Struggling to be patient, Juliette smiled, and backed her way over to the door, where she stopped and simply stood, without saying another word. Apparently that was good enough for the women, as they turned their attention back to Maria, who was bearing down in a hard push.

"Push harder," Irene encouraged her.

"I can't," the pregnant woman moaned. "Can't push. Can't…breathe. Getting too tired."

When Juliette heard this, she was instantly on alert. "Maybe reposition her," she suggested. "Get her head up a little higher. More like she's sitting rather than laying."

Her suggestion was greeted with frowns from everyone in the room. "My grandmother knows how high she's supposed to sit," one of the younger women said, her voice curt.

Before Juliette could respond, a scream from Maria ripped through the room. "I can't do this!" she cried. "The baby's not coming."

This was more than Juliette could take, and she pushed

her way through the crowd in the room and went straight to Irene's side to bend down and take a look. But what she saw was no progression toward birth. No crowning whatsoever. "How long has she been in heavy labor?" Juliette asked the woman.

"Not long enough," the woman responded belligerently.

"I *mean* in hours. How long in hours?"

"About one," one of the women called out.

"And it's been heavy like this since the beginning?" Contractions coming almost one after another.

"She always has her babies fast," Irene conceded. "But I think this one is taking too long. I'm worried I don't see the baby's head yet."

"Can I take a look?" Juliette asked, slinging her rucksack down onto the floor, then opening it up to grab out a blood pressure cuff. Damn, she wished she was back in her clinic, where she could hook up a fetal monitor, because her greatest fear right now was that the baby was in distress and she had no way to observe it.

"Maria's having trouble. So if you could move over and let me get a look at her..."

Irene hesitated for a moment, then nodded and moved aside. "You can help her?"

"I'm going to try," Juliette said, taking her position at the end of the bed. "Could you hold back the sheets for me, so I've got a little more room to maneuver?" It wasn't really necessary, but she wanted to include Irene since she was such a vital part of childbirth here in Bombacopsis, and all the women in the village respected her. There was no way Juliette wanted to dismiss Irene and diminish her in the eyes of all the people who trusted her. "And also make sure Maria stays in position?"

Irene agreed readily, and moved into her place next to Juliette, where she did everything Juliette asked.

"It's good we have you here," the old woman finally said, after Juliette had completed her initial exam. "El doctor Damien is good enough, but this should be left up to a woman."

Juliette smiled, hoping that this might be the beginning of the village accepting something they'd never before seen—a female doctor.

"Did I hear my name mentioned?" Damien asked, poking his head through the door.

"Just in that the ladies here believe this is no place for a man," Juliette returned. Then continued, "But I do need some help, in spite of that."

"What's going on?" he asked, stepping fully into the room.

"We have an obstructed labor in progress," Juliette called over the increasing noise of the women surrounding her. "In spite of Maria's strong contractions, her labor isn't progressing."

Juliette pumped up her blood pressure cuff and tried to hear the dull thudding of Maria's heartbeat after she placed the bell of her stethoscope underneath the cuff. "Her blood pressure is high," she called out. "As best as I can tell." Then she felt Maria's belly, pressed down on it to determine the position of the baby. "Baby's in normal position. But not progressing down the birth canal."

"She needs to push again," Irene shouted over the crowd.

"Pushing's not going to help now," Juliette explained. "The baby's ready to come. But it's not, and trying to push now is only going to make things worse. Put the baby at some risk."

The noise of the women was growing louder, deafening, fraying Juliette's already frayed nerves. Maria was in trouble, she needed Damien to help her with this and she couldn't even communicate with him, the ladies were so loud. Pressure mounting. Maria moaning even louder. Ladies getting frantic. More pressure—

"Damien!" she finally yelled. "Can we get these people out of here? I can't do what I need to do with everybody hovering over me, shouting the way they are." She was trying her best to shut out all the confusion going on around her, but alarm for Maria's lack of pushing out the baby was making everybody crazy, including her. "We've got a problem going on, and I can't do what I need to do with everyone hovering over me." Her own anxiety for Maria and her baby was increasing.

"Give me a couple of seconds," Damien called back to her.

She couldn't see him, as the door was at such an angle it wasn't in her line of sight. But she felt reassured just having him in the room. She felt even more reassured when each of the women started to leave the room. Whatever Damien was saying to them was working, and she was glad for that as Maria had turned a pasty white and was slowly sinking into total exhaustion.

"What have we got?" Damien asked, once all the ladies, with the exception of Irene, had exited.

"Nothing. Absolutely nothing."

"Her contractions?" Damien approached the bed and took Maria's pulse.

"Strong and almost continuous. The baby should be coming out now, and I'm getting worried that it's not."

He nodded, and immediately tore into the rucksack he was carrying, producing, in just a matter of seconds, a scalpel, a sterile drape, forceps and a handheld suction device. "Six minutes," he said, as he grabbed a bottle of sterile wash and pulled the sheet off Maria's belly.

"What?" Juliette asked him.

"I can do an emergency C-section in six minutes from the time I get her sedated. Faster, if I have to. So, stand on the opposite side of me, and let's get this thing done." Then, to Maria, "Maria! Can you hear me? It's el doctor Damien, and I'm going to get your baby out of you right now. But I'm going to have to make a little cut in your belly to do so." He looked over at Juliette. "How long will it take you to get an IV going?"

"Not long," she said, immediately plowing through her medical rucksack to find the necessary equipment. Tubing, needle, IV drip solution. "What are we going to put in it?"

"I've got ketamine."

"Ketamine?" she asked. "You didn't mention that in your drug list."

"Because it's hard for me to come by and I put the little bit I do have back for emergencies."

Resourceful, she thought. Ketamine was a valuable property. "Well, a low-dose application of ketamine will work, since this baby's going to be out of her before the ketamine can cross the blood barrier," she said, as she readied to stick the IV catheter in Maria's arm. In no time at all, the IV was started, and Juliette handed Irene the bag of drip solution to hold above the head of the bed so the medication would run down into Maria's vein, while she piggybacked on a pouch of ketamine. As soon as the medications were both in place, Juliette opened up the port to let them pass through the tubing into Maria's body. It took only a couple of minutes for the anesthetization of Maria Salas to commence. "Ready?" she finally asked Damien, noting that he'd prepped the incision site whilst she started the IV.

"Put a clock on it," he said, poised to make the first incision through Maria's abdomen.

Juliette did, and Damien was right. Six minutes and

ten seconds into the procedure and he was handing over a brand-new baby for her to check. "A boy," she said.

"I was right," Damien said, grinning. "And he's a big one. I'm guessing nine or ten pounds."

"Closer to ten," Juliette said, as she turned her attention to baby Salas while Damien finished up with Maria. First she did the normal suctioning—mouth, nose. Then she took a towel and wrapped it around the baby, poking him gently, trying to get him to cry.

"Is he OK?" Damien asked, looking over at Juliette for a moment.

"Well, I don't have any equipment to do a proper evaluation, but he's breathing and his heart is beating."

"But he's not crying?" Damien asked.

"Not yet."

"Pinch him gently. Just a little one to see what you get." Damien grabbed up a pre-threaded suture and began to stitch up Maria's incision. But he took a second to look over at Juliette as she gave the baby a slight tweak on the bottom of his left foot. And got no response.

So she switched to tickling. Tickled a little spot on the baby's upper arm and ran her fingers down his arm lightly to his wrist, then waited for a second when he didn't respond, and tried it again. This time, baby Salas sucked in a lungful of air and let out with a royal scream.

"Good work," Damien said, without looking up at Juliette.

"How's Maria?"

"Hanging in there."

"Want me to finish closing for you?" she asked, handing the baby over to Manuela—Maria's sister—who'd snuck back into the room to be by her sister's side.

"No, I'm good. But what you can do is go outside and tell someone in the yard to run over to the hospital and fetch a stretcher. Then round up some volunteers to carry Maria over once I get through here."

"You OK?" Juliette asked before she left the room.

He finally looked up at Juliette, his brown eyes twinkling and his smile spreading from ear to ear. "I just delivered a baby. That always makes me OK."

"We do good work together," Damien commented as he and Juliette walked back to the hospital, arm in arm in the dark, leaning heavily on one another. He was tired. Almost too tired to function. But Maria and the baby were probably being settled into the hospital by now, so he had to take one more look at them before he dragged himself back to his hut for what was left of the night.

"It was a pretty slick delivery," Juliette admitted. "My first C-section since I assisted in one during my residency. Then later, in *my* clinic, I referred all my pregnancies to the obstetrics department."

"Well, around here you get to do it all. Bandage a stubbed toe, remove an infected appendix, treat malaria, remedy a bad heartburn. You know, jack-of-all-trades."

"So, I know you're a surgeon, but did you learn these other things in your training, or do you just learn as you go?"

Truthfully, it had been a culture shock coming here. No matter where he'd worked prior to this, he'd always surrounded himself with a security blanket in that he'd kept strictly to his general surgery, never wandering very far from it. Then this, where he had to wander in all different directions.

"It's been a huge learning curve. And yeah, a lot of it I do make up as I go. But the people here are patient with me."

"Do you consult outsiders? You know, friends or colleagues from your old days?"

"Not so much. We don't have great access to the outside world. Although, if I need to know something bad enough, I'll go into Cima de la Montaña and scare up an internet connection." They walked on by his hut, where he took a wistful glance at the front door, wishing he was back in there right now, sleeping peacefully in his uncomfortable bed. "And I did have several of my medical references shipped down to me, so I've always got those to fall back on, even though they're pretty outdated."

"Well, if there's ever anything you want me to look up for you, let me know and I'll do it when I go back to San José, then I'll get the answer back to you next time I come."

"Are you really coming back?" he asked her. "I mean, your first day has been pretty tough so far, and I haven't exactly been welcoming." That was putting it mildly. He'd been downright awful, which he regretted as Juliette was a real trooper. She'd come here first thing this morning, pitched right in and done everything that needed to be done. More, actually. She'd spotted the problem in Maria's labor, and the way she had assisted with the C-section was downright amazing!

"Have you been trying to get rid of me? Is that why you've been so rude? Because I thought you needed someone else here."

They entered the hospital where, down the hall in the ward, George Perkins was settling Maria Salas into bed. Irene, her grandmother, had seated herself in a chair next to the bed and was holding the baby. Maria's husband, Alvaro, was standing at the foot of the bed along with five other people Damien assumed were relatives or close friends. "I do need someone here. I just wasn't expecting...you."

"What were you expecting?" she asked him.

"I'm not sure, really. Maybe someone close to retirement age, or someone's who's basically burned out the way George was. The thing is, when you have very little to offer, you can't expect your pick of the profession to come knocking on your door. Then when you showed up here—well, you're closer to the pick of the profession, and I simply didn't expect that. It caught me off guard. Gave me some hope I'm probably not entitled to have."

"So you immediately turned rude, because you didn't think you deserved someone like me, with my background and skills?"

"I immediately turned defensive, because I thought there was no way in hell I'd get to keep you here after you'd seen what I had to offer." It was too late, he was too tired. Otherwise, he wouldn't be standing here confessing to things that were true but would otherwise never be admitted to. In the course of one day, Juliette had softened him. Whether that was a good thing remained to be seen.

Time would tell, he supposed. "Before we go look at Maria, would you care for a cup of hot tea? Herbal, so it won't keep you awake."

"Want me to make it?" she asked him.

Damien shook his head. "A cup of tea is the least I can do for you. Oh, and Juliette, how about you take my hut for the rest of the night so you can get some sleep? I think it's going to be pretty busy, and pretty noisy, in here."

"But you need sleep worse than I do."

"I've got my exam table."

"Which is ungodly uncomfortable. No, you go back to your hut and I'll stay here."

"And here, I'm trying to be nice to you."

Juliette shook her head, then smiled. "Don't be too nice, because if you are I'm afraid I won't recognize you."

And that was the problem. He wanted her to recognize him.

CHAPTER FIVE

"IT WAS BUSY," Juliette said to Cynthia over a typical Costa Rican breakfast called *gallo pinto*, made of black beans and rice. Some restaurants made it with bacon, eggs, ham and a number of other ingredients, but Juliette preferred hers plain, as her appetite was never large in the morning. "A lot of people come in with general complaints, and that takes up most of the time. So I saw gout, bug bites, a broken finger—those kinds of things. But I also assisted in an emergency C-section, which was a good opportunity for me to learn since all my pregnant ladies at the hospital back in Indiana got referred to the obstetrics clinic."

Cynthia snapped her head up and looked across the table at Juliette. "You did a C-section? How? Because what I've been gathering is that your little hospital isn't equipped to do much of anything."

"It's not. But that didn't matter, because we did it at the patient's home." She took a sip of coffee then sat the mug back down on the table. This had become her morning routine.

A small portion of *gallo pinto* and coffee in the tiny little restaurant down the block from her flat. It was cheap, filling, and once she'd gotten used to the starchy heaviness that early in the day, she'd actually grown to like the concoction.

"It was a little dicey, since I've never assisted in a C-section outside my residency, but Damien was there and he's a skilled surgeon so Maria—the patient—was in good hands."

"Is he cute?"

"Who?"

"Damien. What's he look like? Tall, dark and handsome? Great body? Nice smile? Soft hands?"

"Whoa," Juliette said, thrusting out her hand to stop her friend. "I was too busy working to pay *that* kind of attention to him." Nice words, not exactly true, however, as she *had* paid a little attention to him. And while Damien wasn't the physical type she'd always been attracted to, something about his blatant rawness was appealing. Sexy. "Actually, he *is* tall, dark and handsome. I did notice that much." With drop-dead gorgeous brown eyes, and a beautiful smile punctuated by the most appealing dimples she'd ever seen on a man. "And I have an idea that in his real surroundings, he's probably a bad boy."

Cynthia's eyes lit up. "Maybe I'll have to go out there with you sometime. I *really* like bad boys."

"He'll put you to work," Juliette warned. "Make you change beds."

"As long as *his* bed is included in that, I won't mind."

It almost put Juliette off, seeing how her friend was reacting to a man she'd never met, let alone seen.

"He's grumpy."

"So?"

"I mean, *really* grumpy."

"Yeah, but there are ways to soothe the savage beast."

"Aren't you engaged or something?"

A dreamy look overtook Cynthia's eyes. "To my one and only. But a girl can still look, can't she?"

Actually, Juliette didn't know since she'd never been one who was much into looking. Something else always got in the way, always took up her time and energy.

"Look, I need to get on into work. I've got a prospective GI doc coming in about half an hour, and I want to take him over to the hospital and show him around, so he'll have time to acquaint himself with the facility before his interview." She also just needed to get away from Cynthia for a little, to clear her head. To put some proper perspective on why she felt the way she did where Damien was concerned. "So why don't you finish up here, and I'll see you when you get to work."

"Do you have a thing for him, Juliette?" Cynthia asked bluntly.

"A thing?" There was no *thing* going on with her— except maybe a smidge of fascination. And that didn't qualify as a *thing*, did it?

"You know—something going on. Or maybe just a feeling. Because I think you're mad at me right now because I teased you about him."

Cynthia's reaction to Damien might have been teasing but, for a reason Juliette didn't understand, it had struck a raw nerve in her. "I'm not mad at you, and I don't have a *thing* with, or for, Damien." Said a little too vehemently, she was afraid. Which she was sure Cynthia would misinterpret.

"Well, I was just joking with you. I mean, I've got Carlos and I'm not looking to get involved with anyone else. Not even your Damien."

"He's not *my* Damien, and I'm not looking to get involved with him, either."

"Then you two didn't hit it off?"

Juliette shook her head. "He's a talented doctor, which I respect, but apart from that…" She shrugged. "He's just not my type." A sentiment that wasn't necessarily true, if she took into account all the many times she'd thought about him since she'd come back to San José just this morning. "Besides, I don't have time for a personal life. Between my two jobs, I barely have time to sleep."

"And whose fault is that? Aren't you the one who works the late hours and, as often as not, goes in early? And aren't you the one who always goes out of her way to help clients in ways not required of our job?"

What Cynthia said was true. But, in her own defense, these were the things she did to make sure the people who were trusting her to make a perfect medical match for them got everything they hoped for. She took her job seriously—as seriously as Damien took his job in his impoverished little jungle hospital. As seriously as her dad took his job in a large, university teaching hospital. "I'm just doing the best I can."

"And not enjoying your life while you're doing it. You're going to get tired of living that way, Juliette," Cynthia warned. "When I first came here, I was just like you—too dedicated. It almost burned me out. But eventually I began to back away from it and find a life outside of my work."

"You fell in love with a doctor at one of the hospitals," Juliette replied, smiling. "That'll give you a new life."

"If you let it. And, from what I can see of you, you're not letting it."

"I've barely been here a month, Cynthia. I hardly know my way around my desk yet."

"Well, keep your mind open to this jungle doctor. Your eyes lit up when you mentioned him." Cynthia shoved back from the little table for two and stood. "In the meantime, I think I'll go in a little early with you, and give Carlos a call."

"Didn't he just leave the flat like two hours ago?"

"Maybe he did, but I miss him already."

"Spoken like a woman in love," she said to Cynthia.

Of course, for Juliette, love was only an idea, a notion. Something that sounded beautiful. But she'd never been in love. Never pictured herself as someone who was lovable, as no one had ever fallen in love with her. Of course she wasn't sure she'd ever given anyone the chance. She'd been too busy, between her work and her father. In some ways, she was turning into him—always striving to take on more work, then hiding behind it in lieu of a real life. Building block upon block, which turned into a fortress. Well, she was finding herself more and more cloistered inside that fortress every day, wanting to get out of it. And Costa Rica was her out. Falling in love with someone, though, was the best out she could think of. But she didn't know if that would happen.

"Well, just give it time," Cynthia said. "Maybe you'll find the love of your life here, in Costa Rica, too."

Wishful thinking as she didn't know where to look for it. She was too inexperienced when it came to love. Embarrassed by the fact that, at thirty-three, she didn't know a thing about it. Saddened by the fact that she might have let it pass her by without even seeing it.

"Quit looking at the road, Damien," George Perkins said as he was changing a bandage on Alfonso Valverde, the local mechanic. He'd been working on a truck manifold and received a nasty burn, which he hadn't treated at the time. Now it was infected and the infection had spread from his thumb to his entire hand. "She'll get here when she gets here."

"I expected her an hour ago," Damien said, fighting to keep his eyes off the front window.

"Maybe she had car trouble. Or got swallowed up in one of the potholes on the way out here. Or maybe a jaguar…" George grinned up at Damien. "Or maybe she's just late."

"Or decided she didn't want to come."

"Without getting word to you?" George shook his head. "She doesn't seem the type. Of course, I really don't know what type she is, so maybe I'm not the one who should be telling you to quit looking."

Fat lot of help that was! He'd spent the whole week thinking about Juliette, planning on ways to make this weekend better for her. Of course, he'd also spent the week reminding himself of all the reasons he didn't want to get involved with a rich girl again. And he stretched that involvement to include working with her.

"Well, I'm going to run down the street and see Padre Benicio. He hasn't been feeling well for the last couple of days and since he refuses to come into the hospital, the hospital's going to him."

"Tell him for me that Carmelita and I want to get married in a few weeks, so he'd better get over what's ailing him, because I don't want a sick priest anywhere near me on my wedding day."

"It's allergies," Damien said. "He's not contagious."

"Well, I don't want him sneezing his allergies all over my bride."

"You're actually going to go through with it?"

George taped the end of the bandage and put on his reading glasses to make a close inspection of his work. "I'm almost sixty, so why wait? She's given me a second chance at life."

"Well, I wish you and Carmelita the best of luck. And, for what it's worth, I think you're a great couple. She's good for you." The man had so much faith in the power of love it almost made Damien want to believe again.

"Sorry I'm late," Juliette called from the doorway. "I didn't get away from San José as early as I'd hoped to."

Without turning to face her, Damien said, "You're late? I didn't notice."

George shook his head, rolled his eyes and gave Damien a pat on the shoulder as he walked out the door. "Good luck with Damien," he said to Juliette. "He's in a mood tonight."

"Another mood?" Juliette asked.

"My mood's no better or worse than it ever is," Damien replied, slinging his medical rucksack over his shoulder.

"Something I've looked forward to all week," Juliette replied. "So, are you going out on a house call?"

"I am. And George's off tonight, so the hospital is all yours for now."

"But you're coming back, aren't you?"

"Eventually." Actually, he wanted to get back as quickly as he could, but that would make him seem anxious, maybe even desperate. So, to avoid anything that made him look the least bit interested in Juliette, he decided to take the long road home, stop at the village café for a bite to eat— he had a taste tonight for *arreglados*, a tiny sandwich filled with meat and salad—then afterward he might wander on over to see how Javier Rojas was responding to the new medication he'd prescribed for him: cyclobenzaprine, a drug used for treating the muscle spasms he was having in his back. Anything to keep him away for a while. Anything to give him time to think about some unexpected feelings he was having. Unexpected, and quick, as he'd known her only a week.

"And if I need help while you're gone?"

"Alegria's on tonight. Right now she's gathering up

the hospital gowns from the lady who washes them for us, but she should be back here in about fifteen minutes."

Damn! This wasn't the way he'd envisioned the evening starting out. Every single day this past week he'd come up with a new scenario. He and Juliette would pitch in together and check every patient in the hospital. He and Juliette would have a nice meal together before they started work. He and Juliette would simply sit down together and have a pleasant chat. The list of scenarios went on and on, yet here he was, leaving her all alone. No *he and Juliette* anything!

"So you want me to make beds again?"

"Actually, what I'd like is for you to make a bedside check of all the patients. You know, get their vital signs, assess them for whatever we're treating them for, address wounds, that sort of thing. Oh, and we've got seven patients admitted right now. Nothing seriously wrong with any of them, so you shouldn't have a tough evening."

"How's Maria Salas and her baby doing?"

"Maria's doing fine. So is Alejandro, her baby. We sent them home day before yesterday, and she's due back in here tomorrow so we can make sure nothing's going wrong with her incision." He paused, and frowned. "You know, to save her the trip over here, I might just stop by her house this evening to take a look." At the rate he was going, he'd be lucky to get back to the hospital by midnight.

"Well, it looks like I've got a busy night ahead of me. Guess I should get to work." Instead of heading into the hospital ward, though, she turned and started walking toward the clinic.

"Where are you going?" Damien asked her.

"I ran into Padre Benicio on the way in. He's got a terrible cough, and he said he's coming down with a sore throat now. So I'm going to go take a look at him. He's in the clinic right now, waiting for me."

"How'd you get him here when I've been trying for days, and he's refused me every time?"

"Simple. I asked." Juliette smiled, and shrugged. "What can I say? I have good powers of persuasion."

"That's all it took?"

"Well, that, and I also promised to pick up a book for him when I get back to San José."

"So, you're bribing a priest. Guess I never thought of that."

"Actually I didn't either, but he laid the opportunity out there by mentioning a book he'd like to have, and I grabbed it."

"Well, your new *bribed* friend has allergies," Damien said, chuckling. "He's allergic to the flowers on the trumpet tree. They produce these lovely white flowers that go perfectly with a bat's nocturnal activities. The flower is closed up during the day and opens only at night, revealing its pollen-releasing stamen, which attracts the bats. Padre Benicio is allergic to the pollen."

"You had him tested for that?"

Damien shook his head. "Nope. Just applied common sense. He's improved during the day, pretty much to the point that he functions normally. But at night all hell breaks loose with his allergies. Which means that it's related to something that comes up every night. The trumpet trees are blooming right now, and since that happens at night—" He shrugged. "Common sense."

"Ah, yes, the standard at El Hospital Bombacopsis."

"Hey, it works! When you don't have the proper equipment at your disposal, you learn to rely on your own instincts or gut reactions."

"If you trust yourself that much."

Juliette was a confident woman. Somehow, he didn't see her as someone who wouldn't trust herself.

"It's a class they should probably offer in medical school, because there are a lot of doctors, all over the world, who are treating by the seat of their pants, the way we do here."

"Well, Padre Benicio is a lucky man since his diagnosis does make common sense. Like Señor Mendez and his gout."

Damien nodded. "We do the best we can with what we've got."

"And, apparently, you've got a good gut instinct. Anyway, how are you treating Padre Benicio?"

"Diphenhydramine."

"That's it? Something over the counter?"

"It's all I have on hand, and I wouldn't have even had that if not for the generosity of someone who passed through the village a month ago and left their bottle of it behind. Unopened, and well in advance of its expiration date, in case you're interested."

"Is it working?"

Damien shook his head. "Nope. Which is why Padre Benicio calls me over to the rectory every couple of nights. He keeps hoping we've got some relief for him."

"Which you don't." Juliette frowned. "Damien, you can't just let him go untreated, especially if he's really suffering from this. And, judging from what I saw of him outside, he is."

"I'm not going to let him go untreated. In fact, I'm going into Cima de la Montaña sometime this week, and when I'm there I'll get on a computer and order something that might work better for him. Maybe a steroidal nasal spray and an inhaler for his wheezing."

"How long will that take?"

"After I get it ordered, it'll probably take a week or so to get it to Cima de la Montaña, then another few days for me to go pick it up. So probably going on two weeks, total."

"That's too long. Let me pick up something in San José when I go back, and bring it with me next week. That'll shave off a week, which isn't great, but it's better than him having to wait for two."

She'd bring it back with her? Meaning she was coming back again? That gave Damien another week to get it right with Juliette. Another week to fret over how he was going to do that.

"Your gout is acting up again, Señor Mendez?" Juliette showed him into the clinic and pointed to the exam table. "Go ahead and have a seat, then take your shoe and sock off." Once again, the man didn't seem quite right, and her first inclination was to ask him about it. But she thought back to what Damien had said about treating the patients as they came. That was the hospital policy, so she'd follow it.

"Hurting bad tonight. I thought you could give me something for the pain so I can sleep better."

"You're not sleeping well?"

"My legs shake. They keep me up."

She wasn't getting a good feeling about this. "Can you take your trousers down so I can look at your legs?"

"Could el doctor Damien look at my legs?" the man asked.

"He's not going to be back for a while."

"I can wait," Señor Mendez said.

But *she* couldn't. She'd been on duty two hours already, and still hadn't gotten around to doing a general patient assessment. And there were other things that had to be attended to, so a shy patient was the last thing she needed right now.

"Maybe I can just rest on this table. It would feel good on my back."

"Your back hurts, too?" That plus the fact that his speech was definitely slurred tonight.

"Sometimes when I get tired. But it goes away after I rest."

"Do you ever feel any tingling in your face, or arms, or legs?" This was sounding even worse.

"Yes, but it always goes away."

"Do you get dizzy?"

"When I stand up too fast. Sometimes when I stand in one place too long."

Alarm was beginning to prickle up her spine. "I really need for you to take your trousers down. Just your trousers, nothing else." If she'd made an error in diagnosing him the first time, she wanted to be the one to correct it. "This will only take a minute."

Reluctantly, Señor Mendez slid off the end of the exam table, unfastened his belt and let his trousers drop to the floor. Juliette noticed that the man was staring intently at the ceiling. "Can you get back up on the table now?"

Exhaling a heavy sigh, Señor Mendez crawled back up on the table, and still stared upward. He clearly didn't like being in this position in front of a woman.

"I'm going to poke you in the leg, in several places, and I want you to tell me if what you feel is sharp or dull." She pulled a probe from a supply drawer and went to work. "OK, sharp or dull?" she asked, taking her first poke at the man's leg. When he responded that it felt dull, she went onto another site, then another and another, until she was pretty well convinced that he had an overall numbness in both legs. "You can pull up your trousers now," she said, as she dropped the probe back into the drawer, feeling totally discouraged by what she suspected.

"Am I sick?" he asked her.

"Do you smoke ganja?"

"No. Never."

Too bad he didn't, because she was now hoping he did. That would have been an easy diagnosis. This, unfortunately, wasn't going to be easy. "Do you still work?"

"Every day. I work on a farm, tending the cows. Sometimes I go to pick coffee beans."

"And the tingling you get, or your occasional dizziness, does that ever stop that?"

"No. I work hard every day. But it tires me out now that I'm getting older."

"How old are you?" she asked.

"Thirty."

Younger than her! All the other symptoms, plus gout—meaning compromised immune system—Juliette felt as if she'd just swallowed a heavy lump of dough that had plunked right down in the bottom of her stomach. "Look, I'm going to give you some ibuprofen for the pain." From the bottles she'd brought to donate to the drug supply. "That should help you tonight, but I want you to come back to the hospital tomorrow. Will you do that?"

"Early, *señorita*. Before I go to work."

"That's fine. I'll be here, and el doctor Damien should be back by then." She hoped.

Actually, it was two hours later when el doctor Damien finally wandered through the door. "Anything happen while I was out?" he asked, heading straight into the exam room and dropping down onto the exam table, laying back and cupping his hands under his head.

"Señor Mendez came in for his gout again."

"What did you do for him?"

"Gave him ibuprofen and sent him home."

"We have ibuprofen now?"

"Ibuprofen and another supply of penicillin. One of my hospitals donated it to me."

"Then you come with some advantages. I'm impressed."

"Well, if a few drugs impresses you, prepare yourself to be wowed, as I also come with a new diagnosis for Señor Mendez."

Damien frowned. "He doesn't have gout?"

"Oh, he has gout, all right. But he's thirty years old, Damien. Remember when we talked over our concern about him being too young for it?"

"Absolutely. But he denied having anything wrong with him when I did his physical. So with this gout—there's nothing else we can do except treat him for what he presented with. And hope that if he does start having other symptoms he'd tell us." He paused for a moment, then frowned. "Are there other symptoms now?"

"Now, and probably for quite some time. He has dizzy spells. His legs are marginally numb. He has slurred speech—the slurred speech I attributed to marijuana use. He gets tired too easily for someone his age, and his legs get too jerky for him to sleep."

Damien sat up and sighed heavily. "Damn," he muttered. "He never mentioned any of this. Not a word of it."

"My sentiments, too," she said, clearly frustrated by the situation.

"Well, we've got to take care of it," Damien said. "And I sure as hell don't know how we're going to go about it, since this isn't going to get fixed with a gut reaction and a penicillin pill. Any suggestions?"

"We need to get him into a hospital in San José, and I'm not going to be the one to convince him to do it. The man didn't even want to drop his trousers for me to take a look at his legs."

"Then I'll just tell him he has to go."

"And get him there, how?"

"Any number of the villagers will loan me a truck or a car."

"You mean you'd drive him in yourself?"

"I made the original mistake, didn't I?"

"It's not a mistake when a patient holds something back. We're only human, Damien. We can only see so much. And when a patient doesn't tell you what to look for, doesn't tell you what else is going wrong with him, how can you be expected to diagnose him with multiple sclerosis, or anything else, for that matter?"

"But he told you."

"I had to pry it out of him. But I'm used to prying it out of patients. That's a good bit of what a family practice is about. As a surgeon, you don't have to do that prying. The diagnosis has already been made by the time the patient reaches you, and all you have to do is patch, fix or remove something. So don't beat yourself up over this, because it was his choice not to disclose."

"Ugly diagnosis, all the same," Damien said, sliding off the exam table. "And how the hell am I supposed to treat that condition out here?"

"There are drugs…"

"Which no one can afford."

"And there are therapies we could do right here to treat some of the underlying dysfunctions that will occur. You know, exercises for cognition, various disciplines for weakness, those sorts of things."

"None of which I'm qualified to do."

"Come on, Damien. I'm trying to look on the bright side here. Señor Mendez isn't without hope."

"Hope comes in the form of convenience, Juliette. Which we're fresh out of here."

"So what do you want to do? Just sit back and watch him deteriorate because there's no hope? Oh, and feel sorry for yourself in the process because you have limitations?" She knew how he was feeling, as she was feeling the very same way. But this hospital needed Damien to function normally and, right now, she was the only one who could snap him out of his frustration.

"I don't feel sorry for myself."

"Then you're angry with yourself."

"Don't I have a right to be?"

"Damien, you chose to work in a very limited hospital. You knew, coming in, that you wouldn't have any kind of modern medicine at your disposal, yet you stayed here because you wanted to help. Give yourself some credit for that. Most doctors would have walked away because it was too difficult. But you stayed, and you do make a difference."

"Couldn't prove it right now."

"You know what? We need to pick up from right here and move forward, because that's what Señor Mendez needs us to do. No matter how he was diagnosed prior to this, and no matter how he'll be diagnosed after this, he's got a tough life ahead of him and you and George and I are the only ones who are going to get him through it."

"You say that like you intend on being in it for the long haul."

"Honestly, I don't know what I intend for my own personal long haul, but I'm in it right now and I intend on doing everything I can to help my patient. Which includes making arrangements at one of the hospitals for all the proper tests to be done. So, how are we going to accomplish that?"

Damien ran a frustrated hand through his hair. "You make the hospital arrangements this week and I'll bring him into San José next Friday, drop him off for the weekend to have his tests. Then I'll pick you up and bring you back to Bombacopsis to save you the drive, and take you back to San José Monday morning, when I go to fetch Señor Mendez."

Juliette was relieved that Damien was finally beginning to turn his inward guilt into the outward process that would accomplish what Señor Mendez needed. She appreciated the effort it took to do that.

"Look, Damien. Neither of us has really made a mistake yet. Señor Mendez is in early symptoms, and his condition might well have gone unnoticed for years. What we did was just treat what we saw, which is, really, all we can do when we don't have the proper facilities to do anything more. I feel horrible that I mistook his symptoms for drug use, but I can't let that stop me from moving forward with a different treatment. And you can't let it stop you because all you saw was gout. You diagnosed that properly."

"And you went from there and diagnosed multiple sclerosis."

"Because, in my specialty, I have to connect the dots. I look at a broad spectrum of symptoms to figure out what's going on. Relate one thing to another until I get it worked out. As a surgeon, you don't do that so much. You fix the specific thing you were called on to fix."

"But I'm not a surgeon here."

"Sure you are. Once a surgeon, always a surgeon. You were trained to think like a surgeon, and you were trained to act like a surgeon. That's what saved Maria Salas and her baby last week."

"Why are you trying so hard to cheer me up?"

"Because I have something else to tell you. Something you're not going to like. And I wanted to soften the blow."

He frowned. "What?"

"I didn't get around to doing patient assessments. I've been too busy." She knew it really wasn't a big deal, but she hoped her little distraction from Señor Mendez would defuse the moment.

"That's it?" His face melted into a smile. "You're confessing that you didn't follow my orders?"

"Something like that."

"Should I fire you?" he asked.

"That's an option. Or you could go help me do it now."

Damien laughed. "In spite of my bad mood and your naïveté, we're pretty good together, aren't we?" He stepped toward her, reached out and stroked her cheek, then simply stared at her for a moment. A long stare. A deep stare.

For an instant she thought he might kiss her and, for that same instant, she thought she might want him to. But he didn't. He simply smiled, stepped back, then walked away. And she was left wondering where a kiss might have taken them.

CHAPTER SIX

"NICE OFFICE," DAMIEN SAID, twisting around to see Juliette's entire suite. It was in a newer building, in a posh neighborhood, surrounded by other posh buildings and, for a moment, he almost envied her all this civilization. But only for a moment. He'd bought into this kind of a trap once before, and learned his lesson the hard way. "And you're in charge?"

"Just the United States division. I have five people working directly for me, and the office has another couple of recruiters who have their own staff."

"I'm impressed. But you ran a family practice clinic in Indianapolis, so how does that translate into this?"

"It's where I got my administrative experience. I recruited doctors and other medical personnel to my clinic, and it was a large practice, with thirty-six doctors on staff, as well as the associated professionals needed to fill the other positions."

"Sounds like a big job."

"On top of my own practice, it was. But it was necessary to maintain the quality of the care we offered. The best care coming from the best professionals."

"So, does your position here entail a lot of paperwork?" Personally, he hated paperwork. Hated all those details that had nothing to do with the actual medicine he was practicing. Which was why his jungle hospital was turning out to be a nice relief. With the exception of charting patient notes, there was no other paperwork involved. No insurance claims to fill out, no requisitions or vouchers to deal with. No nothing. And it was nice. So nice, in fact, he wondered if he could ever go back to a proper hospital and deal with all the superfluous things outside the actual patient care.

"Paperwork!" She snorted a laugh. "About half my job is the paperwork."

"And you like that?"

"No. I hate it. But I have to do it."

So she was diligent in her job, in spite of hating part of it. That was an admirable quality, one he, himself, didn't possess.

You have a week of charting to catch up on, Damien. Fill out the correct requisitions, Dr. Caldwell. Did you forget to submit an insurance justification for the treatment you prescribed?

Yep, he sure did hate all that. "Which makes a jungle hospital seem all the more attractive."

"Who are you trying to convince?" she asked.

"Don't need to convince anybody but myself, and I'm already convinced."

"As in staying there forever?"

"I don't commit to forever. Not in anything. A couple years is about as far as I'll go." And that was a year longer than it used to be. Of course, he was getting older. Not quite so eager to pick up and move so often.

Damien walked over to a fish tank that encompassed one entire wall, and stared in at the emerald catfish, a particularly shy little creature that was trying its best to hide from him. "So, how often do you get out of here?" he asked, as he was already beginning to feel a little shut in by his surroundings, a condition, he expected, resulting from spending the past year in the wide-open spaces.

"Every day. Sometimes several times in a day, going back and forth between the various hospitals. The job keeps me on the move."

"And you like it?" He turned around to face Juliette, taking particular note of the feminine way in which she dressed—a long crinkly cotton skirt in tones of green, blue and purple topped by a gauzy white blouse. Nice look. One he wasn't used to seeing on her.

"Actually, I do. I wasn't sure about it at first, since it's so different from anything I've ever done. But once I got really involved in the work— All I'm doing is dealing with the means to provide outstanding patient care, Damien. It's really quite gratifying, especially when you get to see the results of your work the way I do."

"Meaning, you follow the people you place?"

"For a little while. To make sure they're the best fit for the job, to make sure they're adjusting to their new position."

"Then why work for me? I mean, it's a long drive, and you get no rewards for doing what you do. Wouldn't it have been easier to take a part-time position here, in San José, in one of the hospitals you work with?"

"I did try to find something here before I came to you, but nothing seemed to fit into my schedule. The hospitals all wanted more than a couple days a week from me, and several of them insisted I'd have to take calls. Which I can't do, since I have to deal with people at all hours of the day and night. Except weekends."

It seemed to Damien that Juliette's life worked out to be very tough, as she didn't have any personal time scheduled into it for herself.

"Anyway—I got Señor Mendez settled into the hospital, so I'm ready to head back to Bombacopsis anytime you're ready to leave."

"How's he doing?"

"Understandably frightened. But bearing up."

"Well, I've been talking to a couple of specialists here, and if he does come back with a multiple sclerosis diagnosis, I think there are some things we can do to treat him. It's a difficult outlook, but not an impossible one. By the way, I need to stop at one of the hospitals on our way out. Just for a few minutes. Do you mind?" She grabbed a knee-length white lab coat off the peg by the door, then slung her overnight bag over her shoulder. "I have a new recruit there, an ophthalmologist, and I want to stop by to see how she's doing."

"I can do that for you," Cynthia said, stepping into the office. Her eyes immediately went to Damien, and she opened them wide in frank appreciation. "And I'll bet you're Damien, aren't you?"

"Last time I checked," he said, extending his hand to her. "And you are?"

"Cynthia Jurgensen."

"Doctor extraordinaire," Juliette supplied.

"Well, Cynthia, it's nice to meet you. Do you and Juliette go way back?"

"We only just met when we came here. I preceded her by a while, then trained her."

"When you weren't busy swooning on the phone to Carlos," Juliette teased. Then explained to Damien, "Carlos Herrera—her fiancé."

"The cardiologist?" Damien asked.

Cynthia beamed with pride. "You know him?"

"Vaguely. I made a referral to him a few months back. Good man!"

"He's the reason Cynthia's going to stay permanently in Costa Rica." She shrugged. "What we do for love, eh?"

"And you wouldn't stay if you fell in love with someone here?" Damien asked Juliette.

"Would you?" she asked in return.

That was a good question. One he couldn't answer, as he didn't anticipate love anymore. If it happened, it happened. If it didn't, he wasn't going to worry about it. Past experience had taught him it took up too much time, and time was a commodity he simply didn't have enough of these days.

"Look, I think we need to get going. It's a long trip back to Bombacopsis, and if we need to stop at the hospital first…"

"I said I could do that," Cynthia interjected.

Juliette shook her head. "I really have to do this myself, since she's there on my recommendation."

"You just can't stay away from it, can you?" he asked, smiling.

"What?"

"The patient experience—which, I might add, implies that you're in the wrong position since for you it always goes back to the patient."

"Just like my father," she said, half under her breath. This was something she didn't want in her life—another man trying to dominate her. Her father had always dominated, and it seemed as if Damien was trying to. But she'd finally resisted her father and, compared to him, Damien was a piece of cake. So let him bring it on. She was finally ready for it!

"Did you ever consider that your father might be right?"

"I like my job finding new medical talent, Damien. And I like the hours I put in at your hospital. The rest of it's none of your business." With all the newfound confidence she could muster, Juliette opened the office door and stepped into the hall. "So, are you coming, or would you rather stand there and think of even more ways to insult me?"

Damien chuckled as he followed Juliette into the hall. "So, have I gone and set you off even before we start out?"

"I can resist you, Damien Caldwell. Try anything you want, but I can resist you!"

Juliette threw her lab coat into the seat next to her, tilted her head back against the headrest and closed her eyes. "Finally done for the week," she said as Damien engaged the truck he'd borrowed and began the journey back to Bombacopsis. "And I think the people I've brought here are, overall, working out pretty well."

"You've got good instincts."

"Thank you," she said. "That's about the nicest thing you've ever said to me." She was starting out her weekend tired. It had been a long, grueling week—so many interviews to conduct, so many contacts to make, so much paperwork to do. Physically, her work hadn't been demanding. Not like what she was used to in her clinic back in Indianapolis. But she was exhausted, nonetheless. Probably just emotional fatigue, high heat, high humidity, she told herself as the noise of the cranky truck motor sputtered her to sleep.

"Juliette?"

She felt the gentle nudging on her arm, but resisted opening her eyes.

"I need to make a stop in Cima de la Montaña to see if I have any mail. Is that OK?"

Damien's voice was so soothing she simply wanted to melt into it. "That's fine," she mumbled.

"Then I want to make a house call. I have a patient who has just moved there from Bombacopsis, and he wants me to check his daughter. It sounds like infected tonsils. It's going to be a little delay, so I wanted to make sure you're up to it."

"I'm fine, Damien," she said, twisting in her seat to face the direction from which his voice was coming, yet still refusing to open her eyes.

"You've been sleeping," he said.

"Not sleeping. Just—resting my eyes." Too bad she couldn't rest her head on his shoulder.

"Well, your eyes have been resting a good two hours now, and you were resting so hard I began to wonder if you were sleeping, or dead."

"Two hours?" Her eyes shot open at this. "Are you serious?"

"Two hours, soft snoring, occasional mumbling."

She never took naps. Never! No matter how tired she got. For her to nap the way she had wasn't a good thing, and to do it in front of Damien? "I don't snore!" she said, sitting up straight in the seat.

"OK, so maybe it wasn't snoring so much as it was moaning."

"And I don't moan in my sleep. Neither do I mumble!"

"Well, somebody in this truck was fully invested in sleep sounds and, since I've been driving, I hope to God that wasn't me. So, are you feeling better now?"

"I was feeling fine to begin with. Just a little tired. Crazy week…"

"We all have them," he said sympathetically.

"Why are you being so nice to me?" she asked. "It's not like you, which has got me worried."

"Actually, you're the one who has me worried."

"Why? Because I took a nap?"

"Napping is fine. Fitful napping is a symptom."

"It is if you're sick. But I'm not sick."

Damien stopped the truck in front of a tiny wood-sided house and opened the driver's-side door. "Look, we've still got another hour before we're back in Bombacopsis. You look like you've been hit by a freight train, so why don't you get yourself another hour's worth of sleep?"

"A freight train? You sure have mastered the art of flattery."

"OK, maybe not a freight train. But at least a donkey cart." He grinned in at her. "Is that better?"

Juliette leaned her head back against the headrest once again, and shut her eyes. "Go do what you have to do, Damien. And if it takes you very long, you should have enough time to come up with your next round of insults. Or do you already have them stored up for me?"

He chuckled. "You do bring out the best in me."

"Thank heavens it's the best, because I'd really hate to see the worst." She settled back into the seat with a little wriggle, then deliberately turned her face away from him. "Now, go away. Leave me alone."

"Sounds like a direct dismissal to me."

With that, Damien grabbed his medical bag from behind the seat, then shut the truck door. And suddenly the truck cab was quiet. Too quiet.

"Shoot," she said, opening her eyes, and twisting around to watch him walk up the dirt path to the house, where a very anxious woman stood on the porch, wringing her hands. "Double shoot."

Reaching behind her seat, she grabbed hold of her own medical bag, jumped out of the truck and followed Damien into the house. "I may look like a donkey cart hit me, but I'm all you've got. So, what do you want me to do?"

"I knew you couldn't resist," he said, grinning.

Of course she couldn't. Not Damien. Not patient care. And this was getting very frustrating.

"Her parents are going to bring Pabla in," Damien said, tossing a handful of mail onto the seat next to him. Letters from home, advertisements that had an uncanny way of finding him even in the jungle, a medical journal, a pharmaceutical catalog. All waiting for him in his local pickup box. "In fact, they'll probably beat us there."

"Isn't there a place here, in Cima de la Montaña, where she could have her tonsils removed?"

"There's a GP here, and he's actually pretty good. Young guy, with a lot of ideals. But he doesn't do surgery. So he sends his minor procedures over to me, and anything major into San José."

"Like you're set up to do even the minor procedures."

"We do the best we can. Dr. Villalobos, here in Cima de la Montaña. George and me—and even you—back in Bombacopsis. Also Frank Evigan, a chiropractor-turned-medic who practices out of a one-room hut about an hour and a half east of us. That's the real Costa Rica, Juliette, and it's nothing like the one you live in, where you have first-rate hospitals, normal medical amenities and highly trained doctors coming in from all over the world to be part of it."

"But you stick with it, in spite of the hardships."

"Somebody has to." And, for now, he was that appointed somebody. In truth, he was glad he was. After a year, he was rather fond of his little hospital in Bombacopsis, hardships and all.

"Do you ever want to go back to a surgical practice, Damien? In society—a big city?"

"At least twice a day. I loved what I did. Loved that my scalpel could cure people. But, unfortunately, I also had a brief love affair with a lifestyle I didn't have the means to support, even at the salary of a surgeon." Which turned out to be the reason Nancy had left him. Bye-bye, lifestyle… Bye-bye, Nancy. "But, ultimately, it got me in trouble."

"How?"

"I became greedy. Wanted more than I was entitled to."

"And you recognize that in yourself."

"What I recognized was that my boat got repossessed, and my car towed off because I couldn't afford it. What I also recognized was that the condo I'd bought was far too expensive for me, and the woman to whom I was engaged was far too rich to come down to my means."

"And so it ended?"

"Because she was rich, I wasn't, and I was trying to play a part that wasn't suited for me. Bottom line—I loved it for a while, until I discovered I really didn't love it at all. That it was just me trying to face up to the fact that my life was pretty shallow—except for my work."

"So, to compensate, you were trying to come up to her standards? Is that why you hate rich girls, because you couldn't?"

"Don't hate them. Just avoid them." But, to be fair, he was in a place in his life where he was avoiding *all* women. The one he'd had hadn't wanted him for who he was, and that had hurt. What had hurt just as much was how he'd been taken in by it, how he'd been so blind to it. Now, he just didn't trust himself enough to get involved with someone else.

"Or give them a hard time."

"By that, I assume you mean the hard time I give you." It was his natural instinct taking over. He knew that, and he was fighting hard to control it as Juliette didn't deserve his leftover resentment.

"You do give me a hard time, Damien."

"But you bear up."

"I shouldn't have to, though. And that's the point. I'm a good doctor. I'm working here free of charge. People who know me will say I'm a good person. I'm a dutiful daughter. But you don't see any of this because one look at me, and one failed bed-making attempt, and *all* you see is the rich girlfriend you used to have, which equates to you as bad. And that's where it all ends for you."

"It's not you, Juliette."

"No, it's your former fiancée, and I get that. But what *you* need to get is that whatever went wrong between you and her has nothing to do with me."

She was right, of course. But that didn't change the fact that he still had his fears. Was it a fear born out of envy, though? Had he tried to emulate Nancy's wealth because he envied it? Because, if that was the case, it didn't sit well with him. Didn't say much about his character, either.

"I don't underestimate you as a person, or as a doctor," he said, giving in to the idea that he was completely wrong in all this. "And if you're intent on continuing on at the hospital—"

"Intent on continuing on?" Juliette exploded. "If I'm intent on continuing on? Who do you think I am, Damien? Someone who just flits in and out at will?"

"Well, it *is* an awfully big leap for you."

"Like it was for you? Don't you think I can measure up to you?"

"Of course you measure up to me. It's just that I thought that with the hard time I've given you—"

"And are still giving me," she interrupted.

"OK, and am still giving you. And, coming from the background you do—"

"You mean pampered and spoiled?" she interrupted again.

Open mouth, insert foot once again. He was nothing but a big blunder where Juliette was concerned, and it was beginning to worry him that he might actually drive her away. "No, that's not it. What I'm trying to say is that, in my experience, people have good intentions at the start, but they become disillusioned pretty easily. Do you know how many people have showed up at the hospital, responding to my ads, the way you did, this past year?"

She shook her head.

"Seven, Juliette. Seven. *And only one stayed.* And he stayed because, at the time, he had nowhere else to go. So why should I expect that you're going to stay, because you *do* have someplace else to go."

"Because I gave you my word, Damien." Her voice softened. "Because I'm not like the rest of them." She reached over and gave his arm a squeeze. "And one day you're going to trust that."

"What I trust, Juliette, is that I'm living in a godforsaken jungle village because it's the only place I *can* live right now. It's the only place where I can just be myself. And there's nothing else to offer here."

"You offered me a job, and that's all I wanted. It's enough, Damien." She smiled at him. "Don't make it any more complicated than that, OK?"

He didn't deserve her niceness, but he was grateful for it. More than that, he was grateful to have her there beside him. In a life that had let him down as often as he'd let himself down, he had no reason to believe that Juliette would.

* * *

"Stop!" Juliette twisted around in her seat and stared out the window. "Over there, on the side of the road. Did you see him?"

"See who?" Damien asked, as he slammed his foot onto the brake.

"I don't know. Maybe a child. Maybe a small adult. I couldn't tell. But he was huddling in the bushes."

"Where?"

"About fifteen or sixteen meters back."

Damien engaged the truck into reverse and started to back up. "Tell me when to stop."

"Right across from that tree." She pointed to a fabulously large shaving brush tree. "And I didn't get a really clear look, but I did see something—someone. I'm sure of it."

Damien stopped the truck in the middle of the road, and they both hopped out. "Over there," she whispered, pointing to a particular clump of bushes that was moving, despite the fact that there was no wind.

"Are you sure it wasn't an animal? Because we do have big cats, and crocodiles. And killer ants."

"It wasn't a killer ant," she huffed out.

"Fine, I'll go take a look. You stay here in case, well…" He shrugged.

"It was a person, Damien. I'm sure of it."

"A person who's not coming out to greet us."

"Maybe he's injured."

"Maybe he doesn't like outsiders." Damien approached the bush, looked down for a moment, then turned back and signaled Juliette over. "Or maybe he's scared to death."

Juliette looked down, and blinked twice. There, concealed in the bushes, was a little boy. Dark skin. Scraggly black hair. Huge brown eyes rolled up at them. Quivering lip. Probably aged six or seven. "He's…"

"Lost," Damien said gently. "Probably confused." He took a step toward the child, and the child hunched down into himself even more. *"Cómo te llamas?"* he asked. What's your name?

The boy didn't respond, so Damien tried again. *"Hablas español?"*

The child didn't respond to that either, so Damien took another try.

"Hablas inglés?"

When a third response didn't come, Damien looked at Juliette and shrugged. "He's not admitting to speaking either Spanish or English, and he's not telling us his name, so I'm at a loss what to try next. Any ideas?"

"No. But I do know we can't leave him here like this."

"So what are we supposed to do with him?"

"Take him back to Bombacopsis with us, and ask if anyone there knows him. Or if anyone knows of someone whose child went missing."

"Or comb a thousand square miles of jungle to see if he's from an isolated family living God only knows where. Or see if we can get someone out from the Child Services Agency who will, no doubt, relocate him, put him in a group home and let him get lost among all the other lost children there. Or—we could leave him here and let his family come find him which, I'm sure, they will."

"That's not safe, Damien, and you know that! We can't leave him alone."

Damien shut his eyes and shook his head. "I know. But there's no guaranteeing that we could even get him in the truck, much less get him all the way back to Bombacopsis. He's not used to outsiders, Juliette. In fact, he's probably never even seen an outsider before."

"But that doesn't mean he's automatically afraid of us."

"No, it doesn't. But the people here aren't that trusting. At least, not until we prove ourselves to them. And he, most likely, is being raised by a family that avoids us."

"He's not running away from us, though. Just look at him. He's staying here, and I think that probably means he wants help."

"You've got some mothering instincts going, don't you?"

"That's a bad thing?"

"No, it's not. But I'm afraid it's the thing that's going to convince me to take this boy back to Bombacopsis with us, then figure out what to do with him once we get there. So, can you direct some of that mothering at him and get him into the truck, because I've got a tonsillectomy to perform, and I need to get back to the hospital as fast as I can?"

Good Lord, what was he doing, picking up a child off the side of the road? The sad truth was, there were a lot of children, on the sides of a lot of different roads. That was simply a fact of life. The other fact of life was that this little boy, if not rescued, stood a good chance of being found by someone who would force him into child labor on one of the plantations. Damn, he hated this! Hated the harsh existence that so many people were forced into.

"I can try." Juliette took a couple of steps closer to the child, then held out her hand to him. "I don't know if you can understand me," she said gently, "but I want to help you."

The boy pulled away from her, but made no attempt to run.

"I know you're scared. I would be, too, lost out here,

all alone in the jungle. But we want to take you someplace safe, someplace where there are people who can help us find your family." She continued to hold her hand out to him. "We really do want to help you."

"Said to the little boy who looks too afraid to accept help." Damien took another step closer to the child and held out *his* hand. *"Permítame ayudarle."* Let me help you.

Juliette stepped back, amazed by what happened next. The child took hold of Damien's hand and stood. No hesitation, no fear. It was as if the boy instinctively knew he could trust Damien. "Looks like you two are forming a bond," she said.

"OK, now what?" he asked, standing alongside the road, hand in hand with the little boy.

"We take him with us, like we discussed."

"Like *you* discussed," Damien said, leading the boy over to the truck. "I didn't discuss it."

"Your gruff side isn't working on me right now, Damien. I can see right through you, and what I'm seeing is a big softy."

"What you're seeing is total confusion. I don't know what to do about the kid."

"What I'm seeing is a man who's stepping up to something even though he's not sure about it."

Well, that much was true. He *wasn't* sure about it. Had never thought about taking on the responsibility for a child, never even for the short term. Didn't want that obligation because he was always sure there was someone else who could do it better than him. Daniel could do it better. He saw that with Maddie. Juliette could do it better. He saw that with this little boy. So, as for him stepping up to anything—best-case scenario was someone in Bombacopsis would know the boy and, by evening, Damien would have him reunited with his family. Worst-case scenario—well, Damien didn't want to think about that one. Didn't want to think about how happy Juliette looked sitting in the truck next to the boy. Didn't want to think about how that mothering instinct in her had turned him on.

Nope. He didn't want to think about any of that. In fact, all he wanted was to get back to the hospital and get on with Pabla's tonsillectomy. "Do you think he's hungry?" he asked Juliette. "Because I have a candy bar in my medical bag."

She smiled at him. "Yep, a big, *big* softy."

CHAPTER SEVEN

"In the exam room?" Juliette shook her head in amazement. "You're going to perform a tonsillectomy in the exam room?"

Damien looked over his shoulder into the waiting area, to check on the little boy they were calling Miguel for a lack of a real name, and shrugged. "I have an exam room, hospital ward, a storage shed out back and a one-room hut in which I live. Which one of those places do you think I should turn into an operating room?"

"OK, so I'm overreacting. I get it. But Damien, you need a real surgical suite if you intend on doing surgeries here. Even minor ones."

"How about I add that to my list of needs, not to be confused with my list of wants, not to be confused with my list of desires. Which you'll find in the filing cabinet, filed under *nonexistent*, since I don't even have the means to buy the paper to write that list on. The government doesn't fund me here, Juliette. The people who use my services do, when they can afford to. And when they can't they cook me food and wash my clothes and clean my hut. They're also the volunteers you see doing odd jobs around the hospital."

"But you do have some income, don't you?" She knew

that El Hospital Bombacopsis operated on a shoestring, but she'd never known just how short that shoestring was.

"Some. And I have my own personal money, which is seriously on the decline since it's all about expenditures now, and no income."

He was using his own money to fund the hospital? She knew Damien had it in him to be noble, but she was only now coming to realize just how noble he was. "Have you ever thought about trying to find a benefactor? I know that can't happen in any of the villages because the people are usually too poor, but you could go into San José, or even back to the United States. I'm sure someone somewhere would be willing to donate to your hospital." She'd seen generosity at work all her life, seen what it could do. So why couldn't some of that generosity she'd come to count on go toward this ragtag little operation?

"And what would I have to offer them in return? A plaque over the door dedicating the building to them—a dedication that most of the people here won't be able to read? Or maybe I could name one of the beds after them? I mean, people who donate money do so for a reason, and we're fresh out of reasons here. There's no glory in it, no bragging rights, no visibility. So why bother?"

"That's a little jaded, isn't it?"

Damien shrugged. "It's all I've ever seen."

"So it gets back to your aversion of the wealthy." A very limiting aversion as she knew people out there who would donate simply out of their need to make a difference and their desire to see less fortunate people receive good medical care. Her father was one of those people. She'd watched him write checks for worthy causes all her life.

"Well, if you happen to run into one of them, tell them my door is open to them 24/7. But don't hold your breath,

Juliette. This hospital's been operating hand to mouth for ten years, and none of them has ever shown up yet. And I'm not expecting that they ever will, even though your naive view of the world is telling you just the opposite."

"My view of the world is based on what I know—based on generosity I have seen all my life." And sure, she hadn't traveled as much as Damien had, or seen as much as he'd seen, but she trusted that people were basically good—something Damien apparently didn't trust, and that made her feel sad for him. To have so much to offer, and to keep it buried away under such deep resentment—it was a waste. "And I know people, Damien. Generous people I can contact in due course."

"You know people who keep themselves locked into a tight little clique. And I'm not criticizing you for that, Juliette, because I don't think you've ever had the opportunity to spread your wings and see what's out there in this world."

"But you have?"

Damien nodded.

"And what you've seen—it's all ugly?" Had the man never witnessed true generosity and goodness? Or was he just too wounded to accept that it could exist?

"Not ugly. Just harsh. And not as giving as you seem to think it is."

"Maybe that's because you've never taken the time in the right places to find beauty and happiness, and optimism. But I know it's out there, Damien. I've seen the good in so many people. You just have to look for it. Expect it."

"Like I have to look for donors for the hospital, and expect that out of the goodness of their hearts they'll want to help us here?" He shook his head. "I've gone knocking on dozens of doors, asking for donations, only to have them slammed in my face. Asked pharmaceutical companies for donations and been denied. Approached medical equipment companies for anything they want to get rid of and, as you can see from what we have around here, failed miserably at that, too. I've turned up too many rocks, Juliette, and I know what's underneath them—nothing!"

"Yet you're here, doing good, in spite of all your rejections. Going into debt, taking a physical beating, getting lashed emotionally more than you'll ever admit, and you dare to tell me there's no good?" She shook her head and smiled at him. "Nope. You're wrong about this, Damien. I'm looking at good right now, and you give me the hope that there's so much more of it out there to be found. All you have to do is look for it. And that doesn't mean just turning up rocks to see what crawls beneath them. Although I'm sure if you turn up enough rocks you're bound to find something good there, too."

"What in the world did I do to deserve little Miss Optimism?" he groaned.

"You ran an ad, remember? And if you didn't want optimism you should have stated, *Optimists and believers and people who have a general sunny outlook needn't apply.*"

"That's exactly what the ad said when I applied," George said as he walked into the hospital. "Which is what got him *me.*"

"And I'm glad to have you," Damien reminded him, smiling.

"Good thing, since I'm not leaving." George patted Damien on the shoulder as he walked by him and entered the exam. "Now, what about this tonsillectomy?"

This was an interesting dynamic, to say the very least, Juliette observed. Not just Damien and George, but the whole hospital and all its workings. And the more she was here, the more she was growing to like it.

"So while you two are operating, what do you want me to do?" she asked. "Oh, and, Damien. I'm not giving up on you and the whole donation thing. You *need* an operating room, and there's going to be a way to get it." Even if she had to fund it herself, which was actually an appealing idea.

"You're not going to be here long enough for that to happen. In fact, I probably won't, either."

"We'll just see about that," she said cheerfully.

"Stop that!" Damien said.

"What?"

"Being so damned optimistic."

"You afraid it's contagious?" She took the stethoscope off his neck and put it around her own. Damien responded by heaving out a defeated sigh, but the twinkle shining in his eyes spoke of something other than defeat. Juliette wasn't quite sure what she was reading there, but she liked it, whatever it was. "Now, tell me what I need to do."

He bent down and whispered in her ear, "I'm not taking your money," he warned, then straightened back up.

She smiled up at him. "Who said I was offering it?"

"Your eyes."

"You read all that in my eyes?"

"I read all kinds of things in your eyes," he said with a seductive arch of his eyebrows. "And I meant what I said."

"So what if I march in here with a brigade of contractors ready to build you a proper OR?"

"How well do you withstand punishment?"

A slow smile crossed her face. "What kind of punishment are you offering?"

"Juliette, I mean it…" he said, squaring his shoulders, trying to put on a rigid face. And failing.

She laughed. "Just tell me where you want me to work. OK?"

He shook his head in surrender. "Do you always win?"

"I don't know. I've never really tried. But I'm liking the feel of this."

"And I'm not."

"Then we agree to disagree. Good!"

"You're incorrigible," he accused, finally giving in to his own smile.

"I'm working really hard at it, so I hope so. Now, about my assignment…"

"Fine. You win—*this round.* But only because I need to get to work. So, for you—take care of Miguel for starters. Make sure he gets fed. Get him washed up, get his hair combed. Padre Benicio's going to come and take him to the festival so people there can see if they know him."

"And if no one does?"

"Then we give him a bed for the night, and approach the problem from a new perspective in the morning."

"If I'm attending to Miguel, who's going to look after the patients in the ward?"

Damien grinned. "You are."

It sure sounded as if it was all adding up to a busy night. Owing to the fact that she was already a little draggy, she wasn't sure how far her limited reserve of energy was going to take her. But she'd be darned if she'd let it show to Damien. For a reason she didn't understand, it was important that he saw her as capable in everything she attempted. His opinion of her mattered more than she wanted it to. "Then I guess I've got my work cut out for me, don't I?"

"Did I mention that you also need to supervise Diego?

He's coming in tonight to do some filing for me since his mother is going to be out, delivering meals to some of the village's shut-ins."

"Two little boys, several sick people—anything else? Any beds that need changing? Or windows that need washing? Floors needing a good scrubbing?"

Damien chuckled. "Well, you might have a few inebriated partygoers wander in later on. This is the first night of Festival del Café, a celebration of the good fortune they receive from their coffee crops. Singing, dancing, food, beer—they really know how to put on a good party and usually we get some of the casualties of that *fun*. But don't worry, I should be done with my tonsillectomy before anything gets too out of hand."

Juliette shook her head. Well, so much for the little nap she'd hoped to sneak in sometime during her shift. "Fine, I'll get myself ready."

"You don't sound so enthused."

"I'm just…just worried about Miguel," she said. "That's all." That plus a definite lack of sleep these past few days.

"Well, just keep your fingers crossed that someone at the festival knows him."

An hour later she was still keeping her fingers crossed, as Padre Benicio took hold of Miguel's hand and escorted him out of the hospital.

"Where's his *madre y padre*?" Diego asked. He was currently working in the G section of the file drawer, putting away folders and sorting the ones that were already in there.

"We don't know. That's why he's going out to the festival tonight. To see if anyone there knows who he is."

"Doesn't he know who he is?" Diego asked in all seriousness.

"He hasn't talked since we found him, so I have no idea if he knows who he is or not."

"Will he come here to work for el doctor Damien, the way I do?"

She wondered if Diego was fearful for his position here. He had such an affinity for Damien, much like the way Miguel did, that she suspected Diego was scared to death of being replaced. "I'm not sure what we're going to do yet, Diego. Right now, we're just hoping to find his parents." She was happy both boys responded so positively to Damien. And Damien was so kind to the boys, even though he tried to hide it. It was a side of him that made him sexy and likable and all kinds of other good things she didn't want to acknowledge.

"That would be good," the boy said. "Very good."

An hour after that, though, *very good* hadn't panned out, as Padre Benicio returned to the hospital with Miguel in hand. "No luck," he said to Juliette, who was in the middle of doing routine patient assessments.

Huddling over a patient who was being treated for general flu symptoms, she looked up at the priest and took her stethoscope earpieces out of her ears. "No one?" she asked him.

Padre Benicio, an older gent with a round belly, thinning brown hair and kind gray eyes, shook his head. "No one has heard about a missing child, either. And I talked to everybody in the streets."

"Well, I appreciate what you've done." What she didn't appreciate, though, was the outcome as her heart ached for the little boy. "So, what do you think we should do next? Does the church have some provision to take care of lost children?"

"In Bombacopsis, no. I could keep him in my cottage, if that would help you for a little while, but I think you're going to have to go to Child Services in Cima de la Montaña to see what they suggest."

She already knew what they'd suggest. Damien had pointed that out so clearly. "Or we can keep him here at the hospital for a few days and hope that someone from outside Bombacopsis comes in and recognizes him." How Damien would feel about this, she didn't know. But she suspected he'd be agreeable, in spite of the protest he might put up. "Leave him here for now, and I'll talk to Damien once he's out of surgery. If he doesn't want to keep Miguel here, one of us will bring him to you later on tonight."

"Do you understand any of this?" Padre Benicio asked Miguel.

The boy looked up at him but didn't answer, and Juliette sighed a weary sigh. "He hasn't said a word since we found him."

"I'm sure he'll speak when he's ready, won't you, Miguel?" Padre Benicio said, as he let go of Miguel's hand and backed toward the hospital door. "In the meantime, I'll be at the festival if you need me."

If she needed him. Truthfully, she didn't know what she needed. Miguel's parents, a nap, a few extra hours in the day to accomplish everything she needed to…

"No luck," she said to Damien, once she noticed that he'd emerged from the exam room. "Looks like Miguel's ours to take care of for the time being."

"What it looks like to me is that you need to take a break. You look exhausted." He held out his hand to Miguel, who scampered across the corridor to take hold of it.

"It's nothing that a good cup of coffee won't fix."

"Well, if I thought that was true, I'd send you down to the festival to get one. They serve extraordinary blends at several of the roadside vendor stalls. But I think your tiredness goes beyond that."

"Are you diagnosing me?" she asked him, touched that he was noticing her so closely.

"Just worrying about you. You're running yourself into the ground, and I think you need to go over to my hut, where it's quiet, and take a nap."

"You know what they say…"

"That you'll sleep when you're dead?"

She nodded. "I'll be fine, Damien. But I appreciate your concern." This was a nice moment between them and she didn't want it to end, but Miguel needed to get settled down for the night, and she wanted to get onto the rest of her patients. So, reluctantly, she turned her back on Damien and returned to the ward, to the patient who was suffering complications from an infected puncture he'd got when, trying to grab its fruit, he fell out of a milk tree.

As Juliette lifted the bandage on her patient's right leg, she caught a glimpse of Damien standing in the doorway to the ward. He was staring at her. Holding on to Miguel and staring. It made her nervous, caused her to become self-conscious. So she tried her best to turn her back to him, but she knew he was still staring. She could feel it igniting a flame up and down her spine.

So what was *this* all about? She'd encountered all kinds of people before, in all kinds of places, but none of them had ever affected her like Damien. None of them had ever made her go weak in the knees or caused her pulse to quicken. None of them had ever distracted her so much. And she was distracted, make no mistake about that. In fact, she was so distracted she almost put the soiled bandage back on her patient's leg. Almost—but she caught herself before she did. Chastised herself for the absentmindedness. Berated herself for the straying thoughts that were trying to grab hold of her.

The thing was, she wasn't even sure she liked Damien. That caused her the most concern. The man was affecting her in odd ways, ways she couldn't anticipate, and there were moments she couldn't even stand being in the same room with him. Of course, there were also moments when she wanted to be in the same room with him, in the same space, breathing the same breath. And those moments were seriously overtaking the other moments.

So maybe she did need that nap. Maybe it could cure her of whatever was ailing her. Only problem was, she wasn't sure there was a cure for *that*—*if that was, indeed what was happening.* Or if she even wanted to be cured if it was.

Pabla was sound asleep when Damien went to check on her. Doing nicely after her tonsillectomy. Juliette was in the bed next to the girl, sound asleep, as well. As much as he needed her help with the influx of partygoers from the festival trooping into the waiting room, he truly didn't want to disturb her. But George had gone home after the tonsillectomy, Alegria was off for the night and, with the exception of Miguel, who was bedded down in one of the ward beds, the patients already admitted and Diego, who was busy taking the names of potential new patients coming into the hospital, he was all by himself. And, from the looks of things, this was going to turn into one hell of a busy night.

"Juliette," he said quietly, still on the verge of not disturbing her.

"Do you need me?" she asked, looking up at him groggily for a moment, then bolting straight up in the bed.

"I didn't, did I?" she asked, rubbing her eyes, then her forehead.

"What? Take a nap?" The expression on her face was frantic, almost like a deer caught in the headlights. For a moment, all he wanted to do was reach out, take her hand, pull her close and hold her. Reassure her. But, of course, he didn't. Urges like that had no place here. No place in his life, either. If he did allow them to take hold of him, though, it would have been with Juliette. Right here. Right now. In his arms. Loving the feel of it. Savoring the emotional foreplay. Nice thoughts, but too distracting...

"I didn't mean to, Damien. I'm sorry." She pushed off the edge of the bed, stood and tugged her scrubs back into proper place. "I sat down, thinking I'd rest here next to Pabla for a minute, just to keep an eye on her, and I must have..." She looked over at the young girl who was sleeping peacefully in the next bed. "How long was I asleep?"

"About an hour."

"Why didn't you wake me up?"

"I assumed you needed the sleep. It happens, Juliette. We all get to that point where we just break down. I figured you'd reached that point." He reached over and squeezed her arm. "And you looked so peaceful I didn't have the heart to wake you up—until now, when I need your help."

She looked up at him. "Damien, I don't put in nearly as many hours as you do, and most of my work isn't that physically demanding. I shouldn't have been so exhausted."

He chuckled. "Why not? You're only human, like the rest of us."

"But I didn't come here to sleep. I'm still up to pulling off a few straight shifts without..." She frowned, and drew in a deep breath. "Maybe I'm getting too old to do this, and I'm just kidding myself thinking I still can."

"Juliette, are you feeling all right?" Something about her seemed a little off this evening, and he worried that her hours here at Bombacopsis were proving too much for her to handle. It was a different kind of medicine than she was used to, in a harsher environment than she'd ever dealt with. He'd had to make some physical adjustments when he'd first arrived or he'd have burned out too quickly. Better nutrition. Sleeping whenever he could. Asking for help when he needed it rather than plowing through by himself. Maybe that was all Juliette needed—some adjustments. He hoped so, anyway.

"I'm fine. Better now that I've wasted half the shift sleeping."

"Don't beat yourself up. I had a med student once who sat down on the side of the patient's bed to take an assessment, and fell asleep right there. When the nurse on the floor called me down to have a look at what she'd just found, I walked in on my med student all cozied up with his patient, snoring away like he didn't have a care in the world."

Juliette laughed. "What was the patient doing?"

"Looking stricken, and fighting not to get pushed out onto the floor."

"Well, if you ever catch me literally falling asleep on my patient, do me a favor and fire me on the spot so I don't have to go to the trouble of resigning."

Damien stepped closer to her and put his arm around her shoulders as they headed to the desk at the entry to the ward. They stopped for a second, Damien picked up the clipboard listing all the patients waiting to be seen and, with his arm still around her shoulders, they continued on toward the waiting room. "Are you good to take on a few patients? Because the festival is ending for the night and we've got them lining up for us now."

"What are the chief complaints?" she asked.

"Nothing serious, as far as I've seen. Mostly cuts, scrapes and bruises from too much merrymaking."

She stopped, then looked up at him, clear confusion written all over her face. "How?"

"Too much booze leads to shoving and hitting. Or people falling down or stumbling into things. Like I said, nothing serious. But what you get are a lot of the men who don't want to go home in their condition, don't want their wives or families to see what they've been up to, so they come here first. It's sort of a village tradition, I've been told."

"How long does this festival last?"

"Two nights."

They started to walk again. "Well, sounds like a fun evening."

"Diego's giving them all numbers as they come in. How about you take the evens and I'll take the odds? And we'll both keep an eye out for serious problems that need to be seen immediately."

"So you've got an eleven-year-old boy on triage?"

"Almost eleven." Damien chuckled. "And I'm betting this isn't exactly the way your father would run a hospital, is it?"

She laughed. "Damien, this isn't the way *anybody* would run a hospital." In spite of that, she was growing to love it here, every underfunded, understaffed minute of it.

"Miguel is not his name," George Perkins announced, stepping into the exam room. Juliette was busy on one side of it treating a patient for minor abrasions, while Damien was treating a head bump on the other side. "He's

Marco. Marco de los Santos. He's seven. And he has a little sister, Ivelis, who's four."

Damien snapped his gloves off, tossed them in the trash and escorted his patient to the door; his patient reached into his pocket, grabbed out a few *colónes*, enough to total about twenty cents in US currency, and handed them to Damien in exchange for his medical care. *"Gracias,"* the man mumbled, then hurried on his way.

Damien turned to George. "So you've found the family?"

"Not exactly," George said. "I found someone at the festival who knew who Miguel—Marco—was. Told us where to find his family. Actually, his grandmother. In the jungle, in a pretty isolated little community. Marco and Ivelis have lived there with her since their mother died a couple years ago, according to the neighbor. Anyway, I took a couple guys from town out there and found…"

"His grandmother?"

George nodded, but the expression on his face told Damien there was more to the story. "So what's the bad news?"

"I think you found Marco on the road because he'd gone looking for someone to help his grandmother."

"She's sick?"

"She's dead, Damien," George said, practically whispering, so not to be heard. "Little Ivelis was sitting in a chair next to the bed, while her grandmother was laying there…"

"Dear God!" Juliette gasped. "That must have been horrible for the poor child."

"So what did you do with Ivelis?" Damien asked.

"Brought her back to Bombacopsis with me. Carmelita is looking after her now, but we really can't keep her since there's not enough room in our cottage, not with Carmelita and me, and her three children."

"And the grandmother?" Juliette asked.

"Padre Benicio is going to see to a proper burial. He's also going to make arrangements for the children."

"What kind of arrangements?" Damien asked.

"They've got no one. At least that's what the neighbor said. So the *padre's* going to talk to someone in Child Services in Cima de la Montaña this coming week and—"

"And they'll get lost," Damien snapped. "Separated from each other, and lost!"

"You can't be sure of that, can you, Damien?" Juliette asked, helping her patient down from the exam table and showing him to the door.

"No, I can't be sure of anything. But what I know is that there are so many abandoned children in Central and South America that all the protective agencies are too overrun to be effective. And what I know is that so many of the children who go into protective care don't fare well, especially older children like Miguel—Marco."

"But what else can you do?" she asked him. "Could Padre Benicio find them an adoptive family? Would Child Services allow that?"

"They'd love it. But it's an almost impossible task. Adopting out one older child is difficult, and to ask someone to take in two of them—there are too few resources to conduct that kind of a search for anybody who'd be willing to do that. And it would have to be done from here, because Child Services are so busy just keeping these kids alive from day to day, they don't have time to do much else."

"Which is why so many of these children are put into the fields to work," Juliette said, discouragement thick in her voice.

Damn, he hated this. Hated it to hell, as there was

no real solution here for Marco and Ivelis. If only he'd just kept on going when Juliette had told him to stop, he wouldn't have known that these two children existed. Wouldn't have become involved in their lives. Ignorance would have been bliss for him in this whole situation. But not for Marco and Ivelis. And that's where his mind stopped and stayed—on the children. *Damn!* He *had* to find a way to help them.

"You'll figure it out, Damien," Juliette said, squeezing into the doorway next to him once George had left. "And you'll do the right thing by those children." She reached up and brushed his cheek. "I know you will." Then she scooted on by.

Damien watched her for a moment, the trace of her fingers still lingering on his cheek. How was it that someone he'd known for so short a time had made such an impression? But Juliette did make an impression, and it left him feeling—nice. Even happy.

"So tell me, Juliette, what's the right thing? Because I don't know," he said, following her through the ward, both on their way to do general assessments.

"I wish I could." She stopped, turned around to face him, then laid a reassuring hand on his arm. "I really wish I could."

He looked down at her, smiled wearily. Then kissed her. At first on the forehead. Then on the tip of her nose. Then full on her lips. A gentle kiss. A kiss of warmth and subdued passion. A kiss of need. It was a short kiss, though. Come and gone before he even realized what he'd done. But it left him feeling…stronger. And that was all he needed right now. Strength. Juliette's strength.

"I wish you could, too," he said, pulling her into his arms, and holding her tight to his chest.

CHAPTER EIGHT

THE WEEK HAD turned into a busy one for Juliette. She'd taken on twelve new placements, as well as spent time checking into various avenues of funding for Damien. Plus she'd met with a pharmaceutical representative who'd given her enough antibiotic samples to keep Damien's stock in decent supply for a few weeks. On top of that, she'd worried endlessly about Marco and Ivelis and what was going to happen to them. It was frustrating spending a whole week not knowing.

Given all the worrying, as well as all the other efforts expended on El Hospital Bombacopsis's behalf, she was coming to realize that she was getting too involved there. Too invested. But she couldn't help herself as the more she did, the more she wanted to do. To impress Damien, though? That thought had crossed her mind and she'd swept it aside as quickly as it had entered. Apart from Damien and any feelings she might be having for him, Juliette did like her short stay there every weekend. Liked the people. Especially liked the work.

Of course, there *was* that kiss. One simple kiss they hadn't talked about. One simple kiss that had caused her a week's worth of distraction. A kiss she could almost still feel on her lips.

"It's getting rough out there," she told Cynthia, as she

packed an overnight bag to throw into her car for her weekend trip to Bombacopsis.

"The work, or your feelings for that gorgeous Dr. Damien?"

"Neither one. It's the involvement with the people. It's like I'm turning into a permanent part of the whole operation."

"Isn't that what you wanted?"

"I wanted some patient interaction, on a limited basis. I didn't want to get myself involved in day-to-day lives, and look at me. I've packed the whole backseat of the car with supplies I've managed to scrounge up for them." She sighed. "And I want to spend more time there than I have to give them."

"Is that a bad thing?"

"I don't know." Maybe she belonged back in direct patient care on a full-time basis after all. Maybe both her father and Damien had been right about her all along. Two dominant men, both tugging at her life. She was trying to resist, but not sure she really wanted to anymore.

"Did you know that Damien is in town right now?" Cynthia asked her.

"He is?" That surprised her. Hurt her a little, too, as he hadn't thought to confide his plans to her. Not that he should have. But it would have been nice. Might have signaled something more than their brief kiss being only a whim. "Why?"

"He referred a patient to Carlos, and he came in to have a consult. I'm surprised no one told you about it."

"It's none of my business what goes on out there during the week." Brave words, to cover the fact that she was bothered.

"Yet when you leave here this afternoon, your car will be packed full of things that will be used to take care of matters you state are none of your business. And you spent hours on the phone this week, looking for contributions. How does that make sense, Juliette, if it isn't your business?"

"Damien does what he does, I do what I do. We meet up on the weekends and work together, and that's as far as it goes." The problem was, he was taking up too much space in her thoughts now. Encroaching in places she'd never thought could be encroached upon. Putting notions into a head that had been previously blissfully notion-free.

"But you do have a working relationship, so shouldn't that count for something?"

"He didn't want to see me, Cynthia. Or else he would have let me know he was here." Truthful words, but they stung, nonetheless. She was getting in way too deep. Sinking down into the bottom of an undefined process that appeared to have no way out. Was she falling in love with him? In love for the very first time in her life?

"Look, I've got an appointment in twenty minutes. It should take me about an hour and after that I'll be back in the office for a couple hours. So if you're here when I get back we'll talk, and if you're not I'll see you when I get back Monday. Oh, and tell Carlos I said hello, and ask him if he could please do something to secure the towel rod in the kitchen."

"You should invite Damien to stay sometime. Maybe *he* could fix your towel rod."

"Except Damien and I aren't like that."

"You should be," Cynthia said, as she followed Juliette out the front door. "And you could be if you wanted to."

"You don't know that." Juliette turned to make sure the door was locked, then headed down the hall to the elevator in a casual stroll, Cynthia at her side. "Besides,

Damien and I aren't really existing together under normal circumstances."

"Couldn't you make them normal?"

Could she? Honestly, Juliette wasn't sure what constituted normal with Damien. Wasn't sure he'd ever reveal that side of himself to her. Wasn't sure she'd recognize it if he did.

"Lunch?" Damien had promised himself he wasn't going to do this when he'd come to San José, and here he was, doing it, anyway. So what the hell was he thinking? Why was he trying to turn a perfectly good professional relationship into something else? "I was in the neighborhood, so I thought I'd stop by and ask."

Juliette spun around in her desk chair to face Damien. "I wasn't expecting you."

"I wasn't expecting me either, but here I am." Approaching something he wasn't sure he should approach. "So, since it's lunchtime, I thought…" He shrugged.

Something about seeing her away from the hospital—she looked different. Not as confident as he normally saw her. Not as happy. And the stress he saw on her face—he'd never seen that in Bombacopsis, even when they'd performed a C-section bedside. "Are you OK?" he asked.

"Why wouldn't I be?"

"I don't know. Maybe because you look tired."

She smiled. "I'm fine. Just preoccupied."

"Do you want me to hang around and drive you to Bombacopsis later on?" He knew it was a feeble attempt to get some alone time with her, but it was the best he could come up with.

"If you did, you'd have to drive me back Monday morning, and that would put you on the road for half a day, coming here, going back to the hospital. So, as much as I appreciate the offer, I'll be fine driving out later on. Oh, and thanks for the lunch offer. It would have been nice, but I've got an awful lot to do between now and when I leave later today. But next time you come to San José—"

He was disappointed, but he wasn't surprised. Had he wanted a date with her, he should have asked properly rather than simply showing up and expecting it.

"Damien, why didn't you tell me you were coming?"

"Probably because we don't have to account to each other for anything. That's part of our relationship." A lame excuse, if ever there was one. He hadn't told her because he didn't know how to face her. And he didn't know how to face her because he wasn't sure about his emotions anymore. Or his dwindling resolve.

"What relationship, Damien? I work for you and, apparently, that's as far as we go."

"Is this about me kissing you?"

"It was just a kiss, Damien. Kisses happen all the time for no good reason."

"So you think I kissed you for no good reason?"

Juliette shrugged. "I don't know. But in my experience I don't take those things lightly. Maybe in your experience you do. But it's bothered me all week, because I've wondered if you have something more on your mind than only a professional relationship."

"Is that what you think we're doing? Forging a personal relationship?" In his mind, he believed that was exactly what they were doing. In a most awkward way. In a way that couldn't possibly work out for either of them as they were both headed in such different directions.

"Is it?" Juliette shook her head, and rubbed the little crease forming between her eyes. "Look, I have a lot of work to do before I leave for Bombacopsis, and I don't need to be distracted by this awkward dynamic we always seem to have between us."

"In other words, you're asking me to leave." Something he couldn't disagree with, considering the circumstances.

"Yes, I am."

"But you'll be in to work later on?" OK, so he knew he was on the verge of driving her away, but it was as if every time he got near Juliette he felt the need to retreat from her. Problem was, his way of retreating was all tied up in pushing her away. And he really didn't want to do that. But something always took him over, forced him into doing things he didn't want to do, saying things he didn't want to say. Was it simply that he expected Juliette to do the same thing to him that Nancy had done? Was he really *that* unsure of himself?

"I made a commitment to help you at the hospital, and I'll honor that, unless you say otherwise. So yes, I'll be there."

He was glad. Glad she could get around him. Glad she persevered in spite of his efforts to keep his distance. "I appreciate what you do, Juliette," he said, heading to the office door.

"Not enough, Damien. You don't appreciate it enough."

"You're right. I probably don't."

"And that's your problem, not mine."

It *was* his problem. Especially since thinking about Juliette had started keeping him up at night.

The three-hour drive seemed to take forever this evening, and when Juliette reached the edge of Bombacopsis she'd never in all her life been so happy to see anyplace as she was this one. First off, she intended to apologize to Damien for making it sound as if he had to account to her for his activities. He didn't. And she didn't want him thinking that she expected it. She also wanted to apologize to him for misinterpreting their relationship when, clearly, he had no intention of having anything other than a professional one with her.

Of course, that meant she'd have to quit reading more into it than was there. The kiss meant nothing. The personal interactions meant nothing. She was a colleague to him and she'd have to accept that, despite her growing feelings, or she'd have to leave. But she didn't want to leave.

This was where her inexperience in love was showing, and it embarrassed her.

Proceeding slowly down the main road, dodging potholes and barefoot children darting back and forth across the road, she looked to see if Marco and Ivelis were among any of them. But they weren't. She'd meant to ask Damien about them earlier, but her muddled thoughts had gotten in the way. So now she'd spent the better part of her three-hour drive imagining ways she would approach Damien and, alternately, worrying about the kids.

"Where are they?" she asked immediately upon entering the hospital. "Marco and Ivelis? Have you sent them to Child Services?"

Damien, who was busy rummaging through the file cabinet next to the single dilapidated desk in the exam room, turned to look at her. "They're with George and Carmelita right now. They've been looking after them during the day, when I'm working, and I've been looking after them at night, when George is working. It's not the best situation, but it beats having them locked up in an institution."

"Child Services are good with that arrangement?"

"Child Services are good with anything that doesn't

add to their list. The kids are eating, they're being schooled at the church with the rest of the village's children, by Padre Benicio, and they have a roof over their heads—that puts them way ahead of the game, considering how things could be turning out for them."

"But it's only temporary, Damien. In the long term, what's going to happen to them?"

He shrugged. "Out here, you take it one day at a time. You know, get through the day and hope you make it to the next and, when you do, figure it out from there."

Would Damien actually take on the responsibility of tending to these children in the long term? Feed them, clothe them, continue them on at the school? *Love them?* In spite of his casual exterior, she saw a man who had great compassion, especially for children, so she was encouraged to believe that this could turn into a permanent situation. Damien as Dad. In an unexpected sort of way, it seemed to fit him.

"Look, Damien, I'm sorry for how I acted earlier. You're right. We don't have to account to each other for anything outside this job. But I was a little hurt. I mean, I'm not making a lot of friends in San José. Not enough time. And I suppose I thought we were becoming friends, then when you didn't tell me you'd be there, that just pointed out to me how wrong I was. I presumed too much."

"First, you didn't presume too much. We're friends, and I should have told you I'd be in town. That's what friends do, but I'm not very good at it. And second, I can't have a permanent relationship with you, Juliette," he said, quite directly. "Something other than friendship. If you thought I was leading in *that* direction, I'm sorry. I didn't intend that."

"Because I'm wealthy," she stated.

"No. It's because I'm not available. I came here to avoid those kinds of trappings, and I can't afford to get entangled again. I need space to sort my life. Space to figure out where I'm going and how I'm going to get there. Space to come to terms with what I've done in my past so I'm not doomed to repeat it in my future. Nancy, my biases, my envies—all the things that, for a time, turned me into someone I didn't want to be."

"And I take up your space?"

"In ways you probably wouldn't even understand."

"So that's it? We can be friends and colleagues. But that's all?" She wasn't surprised by the direction this conversation was going, but she didn't like it. Didn't like knowing that these strange, new feelings she was having were letting her down.

"Honestly, I don't know." He sighed heavily. "I didn't want you to make a difference in my life, other than in a professional way. But you're doing that, and I don't know what to do about it because it wasn't in my plan. I mean, I felt guilty as hell about not letting you know I'd be in San José, and I intended to do that because I was trying to distance myself from whatever it is we're doing."

"Because?"

"Because I'm trying *not* to fall in love with you."

Could that mean he *was* falling in love with her?

"Falling in love with me would be bad?" If this was the way love started, it was a lot more difficult than she'd ever imagined it to be.

"It's very bad because I don't want to get hung up on someone. I don't want to feel guilty when I decide to avoid a situation or don't meet personal expectations. I don't want to be distracted from the things I'm trying to accomplish both professionally and personally."

"I distract you?" This was leading to something depressing. She could feel it coming. And it scared her because the side of Damien she was seeing right now, the brutally honest side, was the one she desperately wanted in her life. But it frightened her because his truths were turning out to be painful.

"When I let you."

"Which leaves us what? Anything? Or do you intend on running another ad to replace me?" In and out, just like that. It was almost too much to comprehend. "What do you think?"

"What I think, Juliette, is that I'm better off alone. It suits me. Keeps me out of trouble. Keeps me from putting myself in the position that I might not do the best work I can do."

"Then that's the answer, isn't it? I'll go, and you can find somebody else to replace me. Someone who won't mess with your mind the way I, apparently, am." Better to do this now, before she got in any deeper. But she certainly hadn't counted on how much it would hurt. And it did hurt. And now she was feeling light-headed and dizzy. Nauseated. Headachy. "Well, if it's OK with you, I'll stay on until my replacement arrives." Stay on to endure more of an emotional beating. Because she did have her obligations here, and she wasn't going to let him defeat that in her. Not while she had a shred of pride still intact. "So go ahead and assign me my work for the evening, and I won't bother you."

"Juliette, I—"

She held out her hand to stop him. "Look, Damien. All I want is to do my job, and skip the rest of this. OK? Just let me work." Which was all she should have ever done in the first place. But, stupid her, she'd stepped in too far.

"Fine. I have two patients down in the village I need to see, and I want to drop an inhaler refill off to Padre

Benicio. Alegria is here, tending to some basic chores, and what I need you to do this evening is to admit Senõra Calderón when she shows up in a little while. She was complaining of symptoms that lead me to believe she might be diabetic, but when I tried to admit her earlier she insisted on going home and bathing first. So she should be back here anytime. Do an A1C—I have the test kit in the medicine cabinet. Also a general assessment for any signs of neuropathy, and take a comprehensive medical history. I mean, you know all this already, so I really don't need to tell you what has to be done. By the time you're finished, I should be back, and I'd like for the two of us to inventory our supplies—"

Business as usual, she thought. That was all she was to him—business as usual.

"—and then, after that, I want to check our medicines. Which should pretty well take us on into the night."

Couldn't he simply ask her not to go? Couldn't he say something to encourage her? Something? *Anything?* This was awkward. She felt it. He felt it. But there was nothing they could do about it. She was developing feelings for him, and she had no idea what he was developing for her, he was so back and forth about it.

"Anyway, I'll be back in a while." That was all he said. Then he walked out the door, and Juliette walked into the exam room, feeling numb.

Damn, he was stupid. She'd done all but admit to him that she loved him, and here he'd gone and thrown it right back in her face. How stupid could any one man get?

"Have you ever done something you knew you didn't want to do, but you did it, anyway?" he asked Padre Benicio.

The *padre* chuckled. "Too often, I'm afraid."

"I've got something good happening to me, and I know it's good, and I know I want it, but I'm doing everything I can to stop it because I don't know what kind of future I have. Whether it's here or someplace else. Whether it's as a jungle GP or a big-city surgeon. And if I don't know these things about me, how can I offer anything to anybody else?"

"Whose best interest do you have at heart in this?"

"Everybody's—nobody's. I don't know."

"Then maybe you should reevaluate this good thing that's happening to you and try to figure out if you want it badly enough to sort the rest of your life. Ask yourself what you're really afraid of. Because the jungle is a good place to hide, Damien. It has a way of sorting things for you, if you're not careful."

The *padre* was right, of course, as Damien wasn't sure he even knew how to go about *starting* to put his life in order, let alone proceeding through and finishing it. He was scared of changing his life, scared of changing himself, scared of coming to terms with what he *really* wanted. Which was Juliette. And now she was leaving. He'd pushed her too far. Pushed her in a direction he didn't want her taking. And he was the only one who could rectify that.

"Look, I've got to go try to straighten something out before it's too late." He prayed that he wasn't.

Hearing the approaching footsteps, Juliette looked up to greet her patient and was surprised to see Damien standing in the exam room doorway. "You just left," she said, trying to sound even when everything inside her was fluttering and flustering.

"I came back because I shouldn't have walked out and left things hanging between us, the way they are."

"You said what you wanted to say, Damien. What else is there?"

"That I don't want you to leave. That I look forward to Friday evenings, knowing that you're on your way here. That I don't know what to do with our friendship and I want you to try to help me figure it out."

This wasn't what she'd expected from him. Not at all. And she wasn't sure what to make of it. Wasn't sure of the way he swung back and forth.

"You know, I've never had a relationship other than friendship before."

"Never?"

She shook her head. "I've had casual dates, nothing serious, and no, I'm not a virgin. But anything that went beyond casual—" She shrugged. Life just hadn't permitted anything else for her, between her work commitments and the fear of what losing her might do to her father. Yes, dutiful doctor, dutiful daughter—all of it had caused her to miss out and now, here she was, practically clueless. "I don't know how to help you figure it out, Damien. If you want something more, you've got to figure out how to do it. And if you decide you really don't want anything other than what we've already got, that's fine. I'll accept it." Even though it would break her heart. "But the one thing you have to know is that if we go any further, I don't expect to be hurt."

"I wouldn't hurt you intentionally."

"But there are so many unintentional things you do. And sure, you have regrets and apologize, like you're doing now. But some things can't be undone. When you say the words, they can't be unsaid. Apologies may be accepted, Damien, but words still linger." OK, so she was putting it all on the line now, but what was there to lose except a little self-esteem?

"I didn't come here to fall in love, Juliette. I came to escape it. Had one serious experience with it, and it didn't work. And it scares me to think that I could go and do it again."

"I didn't come here to fall in love, either. I came to escape my father's dominance. I don't want to be dominated, don't want to be around anyone who believes he or she has that right."

"So where does that leave us?" he asked.

"It leaves us as two runaways with strong ideas of what we don't want, trying to define what we do want." And that pretty well summed it up. "We don't have to date, Damien. We don't have to get physical. We don't have to admit our feelings toward one another. But what we do have to do is realize that our friendship isn't just casual, nor is it just professional. If you can live with that—if *I* can live with that—then I can stay here. But if we can't live with what's apparently going to go unspoken, then I'll have to leave." It surprised her that she'd summoned the courage to say these things to him, but they needed to be said. And so far Damien hadn't made any effort to say them himself.

But she felt good about clearing the air. It gave her hope that even if she couldn't move forward with Damien, someday she might be able to move forward with someone else. Although she didn't think she'd ever find anyone who could compare to him. It was a thought that made her feel as if she'd just said her last goodbye to her best friend.

"I don't know what to say, Juliette. I mean, I appreciate your honesty. And I appreciate you."

He looked as if he were at a loss for something to latch on to. An explanation, a hope. It was something she'd never seen in him before.

"I don't want you to leave. I just don't... I just don't

know how to handle you being here. So for right now, how about we let this blow over and see what happens in the future. OK? You know, get past it, and see what we've got left."

"So what do you want from me, other than work? Or do you even want anything?"

"Damned if I know," he said, slamming his fist into the file cabinet so hard the sound resonated out the door and down the hall. "I had this plan. I was going to come here for a couple of years, get away from all the trappings that almost ruined me before, try to find my worth again. All of it just me, by myself. I mean, who the hell ever goes to the jungle to hide and comes across someone like you?"

She laughed. "It goes both ways, Damien. I didn't expect to come to the jungle to find *you*."

"But here we are. And this *thing* between us is driving me crazy because I don't even know what it is."

He *did* know what it was. She was sure of it. But he was dancing all around it, coming so close, then backing away. And it was frustrating that he wouldn't, or couldn't, admit it. Not to her, not even to himself. As much as Damien had tried pushing her away, he was pushing himself away even harder.

"Then, by all means, distance yourself, Damien. Think as much as you want, and I'll stay out of your way so you'll have even more time to think." She didn't want to be cross with him, but his hot-and-cold switch was confusing her so much she didn't know how else to react. This *thing*, as he called it, was getting complicated—for both of them.

"You want me to take them back to the hospital and get them something to eat?" Damien asked George. "I hate dumping all this responsibility on you and Carmelita."

The more he was around the children, the more he wanted to be around them. It was yet another new facet to his ever-baffling life.

George looked over at the two, who were playing in the churchyard, keeping a distance between themselves and the other children who were there for school. "We're good for dinner. How about we let them stay for that and I'll bring them back to the hospital in a couple of hours?"

Damien sighed. "I might be back by then, if I don't feel the sudden urge to get out of there and take another walk." Although walking, as he was doing now, wasn't a solution to what was bothering him. And what was bothering him was—him! He was disgusted with himself. Didn't know where all this uncertainty came from, as it was something new to him. Normally when he was interested in a woman he'd ask her out. They'd dine, dance, maybe make love at the end of the evening. Then he'd call her again, or he wouldn't. Whatever struck his fancy at the time. Of course, there was Nancy, and he'd thought she was the keeper.

But, in recent days, he'd even wondered about that. Wondered if his real motivation in that relationship was to prove to himself that he was worthy of climbing into higher circles, worthy of being embraced by the likes of Nancy's ilk more so than by Nancy, herself. Which made him pathetically lacking in character, and full of self-doubt. And it wasn't a stranger to him. He'd felt it recently when he'd gone to Daniel's wedding and saw what a wonderful life his brother had made for himself in the wake of a tragedy that many men would never overcome. He'd seen happiness and contentment and joy—things he'd never seen in himself. Things he'd never thought he could have, given his lifestyle choices. Things that made him desirous of something he didn't know how to get.

Home, family, all the trimmings—in other words, maturity. It was bound to happen at some point in his life, but he wasn't prepared for it the way it hit him. He'd actually looked forward to scaling back on his lifestyle, not running around so much, driving a family SUV rather than a sports car, maybe even mowing the yard on Saturday mornings. Yep, that was him. Craving the domestic after living the high life. But he'd picked the wrong person, and had actually convinced himself for a while that Nancy would do well living that life. Apparently, he'd been seeing things in her that just weren't there, though. Deluding himself. Which was why he'd come to the jungle. After Nancy, he'd needed to get away—from what he'd been, from what he'd hoped to become. Just get away from it all. Isolate himself from everything and try to figure out what was real in his world, because for so long nothing in his past had been.

"Are you and Juliette disagreeing again?" George asked, his eyes twinkling.

"Juliette and I aren't anything!"

"Maybe that's the problem," George said as he signaled Marco and Ivelis over to him. "Maybe you and Juliette should be doing something. Talking at the very least. Taking a walk together. Holding hands. Gazing into each other's eyes. You get the point anyway. I'll bring the kids back down to you later. Good luck with Juliette, by the way."

Talking? Walking, holding hands, gazing? Yes, good luck, but to whom?

Juliette looked at the results of the A1C test she had given Senõra Calderón and cringed. She was reading way above the normal for diabetes, which was a pretty good indication that the woman was afflicted. Damien had called it right and she wanted to consult with him to see what could be done to treat the woman, given that resources for diabetic treatment out here in the jungle were very limited. But he'd been gone for over an hour now, and she was beginning to wonder if he was coming back.

"I'd like to admit you to the hospital tonight, and have el doctor Damien talk to you when he returns."

"You can't talk to me? Because I like seeing a lady doctor."

That was flattering, especially in a village where old-school values prevailed and outsiders were viewed as intruders. Most notably, female outsiders. "El doctor Damien is going to be your doctor, not me, since I'm only here two days week. Which is why I want you to see *him*."

"Then I'll come back tomorrow when he's here. Right now he's at the Bombacopsis Taberna drinking *cerveza*, and he didn't look like he was going anywhere for a while." Senõra Calderón hopped off the exam table and went on her way, walking right by George, as he brought Marco and Ivelis into the hospital.

"Are you OK?" George asked Juliette on his way in the door.

"Just tired. Nothing big. What's the Bombacopsis Taberna?"

"The Bombacopsis Tavern."

"And *cerveza* is…?"

"Beer." He smiled sympathetically. "But he limits himself to one, just in case you were wondering. Oh, and Damien knows the kids are here."

"You talked to him?"

"Briefly, on my way here. He should be back anytime."

She wasn't going to hold her breath on that one. "So what am I supposed to do with them in the meantime?"

"Find them a bed and let them go to sleep. That seems to be the usual routine."

"That's a heck of a way for a child to live, isn't it?" Even though this arrangement was better than what they might have ended up with, she wanted better for them. Wanted them in a happy home. Normal life. Normal family.

"Damien means well, and I know he's trying to do right by them. And he *has* been building a partition in his hut so the kids can have their own room there. It's just that these things don't get done too quickly when your resources are limited."

Was Damien actually setting himself up in a family situation? She liked the idea of that. Liked it a lot. The light on him, bit by bit, was shining much brighter. And it notched up even more thirty minutes later, when he entered the hospital ward and went straight to the beds she'd sectioned off for the children. He stood there looking at them, while she stood there looking at him. The tender expression for them on his face—it made her heart melt. Made her heart swell at the same time. For this was the real Damien. The one who kept himself hidden under so many layers of uncertainty. The one he probably didn't even know existed. The one she'd gone and fallen in love with. And yes, it was love, in spite of all its obstacles.

CHAPTER NINE

RUBBING HIS EYES and shaking himself, trying to stay awake, Damien took one last look into the waiting room and finally, after sixteen hours of back-to-back patients, it was empty, except for Juliette, who'd taken a moment to sit down and rest. She'd apparently fallen asleep. But who could blame her? She needed it, and that was really all he wanted for himself, as well. Several hours of uninterrupted sleep.

To sleep, perchance to dream... Dreaming that impossible dream... Dreaming dreams no mortal ever dared...

Damn, he was getting punch-drunk now. He shook himself again. Harder this time, trying to throw it off. But random thoughts were running rampant through his brain, which meant he was no good for anything. Especially not for anything as far as the hospital was concerned. So as soon as George came in to take over the shift, he was going to go back in his own hut. Take the rest of the afternoon for himself—no children, no patients. Nothing but perfect peace and quiet. And sleep.

But first he had to tend to Marco and Ivelis. He'd walked them down to the church for morning school earlier, and now it was time to take them back to the hospital for lunch. When he arrived, Padre Benicio was standing in the doorway, waiting for him, holding the children's hands. Just seeing them there—it caused a lump in Damien's throat. He wanted so badly to have more time with them. Desperately wanted to take Marco out to play ball, and Ivelis to one of the local women who cut hair. Wanted to read to them. Sit down to a quiet meal with them and ask them about their day. Wanted to…be a father? *Did he really want to be a father?*

No. He couldn't—*could he?* He thought about that for a moment. Thought about all the changes he'd have to make to accommodate children in his life. About how much he enjoyed having them around—and what might happen to them if he didn't allow them to stay. That was the thought that sobered him. Made him sick to his stomach because he knew what was waiting for orphans like Marco and Ivelis, and it was bleak. How could he let those children step into the kind of life that awaited them outside Bombacopsis? Which meant—well, it meant a lot of things. Changes in his life. Changes in his outlook. Changes in ways he couldn't even anticipate.

Could he do it? Could he take on two children when he refused to take on a real relationship with Juliette? How did any of that make sense?

"Any new developments with the children?" he asked Padre Benicio.

"Nothing's changed. They don't talk, don't go outside to play when the other children do. They don't do anything. So I was wondering, do you think it's time to take them somewhere and have them examined? See if there's something psychological that can be treated? I know I'm not a doctor, but I am concerned that they might have a condition of some sort."

Damien shook his head. "The only condition they have is an overwhelming sadness for the loss of the only security they had in this world. I imagine they're scared to death and they're drowning in everything that's going on around them."

"They need a family, Damien. Two parents together, or a mother or father, separately. Someone to look after them properly, and not do what we're doing here—trotting them from place to place, person to person. Dropping them into situations they couldn't possibly understand."

"I know that and, believe me, I'm looking at ways to take care of them." One way, actually, and he wasn't yet sure about it. Wasn't sure about anything.

"Damien, Child Services isn't going to list them as a priority now, since they already have a roof over their heads, they're being fed, bathed and schooled. As far as the child authorities are concerned, these children are in a good situation. They're not going to change that, since they've got so many other children to deal with who are in horrible situations."

"I know," he said. "Their prospects aren't good."

"Unless they stay here, with you."

He shook his head. "I've been thinking about it. But sometimes I'm barely able to make it on my own as an adult, and I certainly shouldn't be dragging two children along into that. They're great kids, but they deserve better than me." That much was true. They did.

"They deserve to be happy, Damien, however that happens. And whoever that happens with. And I don't think what you consider to be a lack of stability would matter at all as long as you love them."

"Look, Padre. I'm doing the best I can, with what I have. It's not good enough, but it's all I can do. And I'm well aware of my limitations." The biggest one being how turning himself into a single dad scared him to death.

As much as he cared for those kids, he didn't know if he could do justice by them.

"We all have limitations, Damien. But the real measure of a person comes not in what he knows he can do, but in what he doesn't know he can do and still does in spite of himself. Think about that for a while. And, in the meantime, I'm going to go find a nice *casado* for lunch, then I'll come down to the hospital to get the kids and take them back to the church for afternoon school." He tipped his imaginary hat to Damien, and scooted out the door, leaving Damien standing there, with Marco on his left side and Ivelis on his right.

"Well, let's go see what Rosalita has fixed for your lunch." He extended a hand to each child, and the three of them wandered off toward the hospital, looking like a perfect little family.

"Juliette?" Damien gave her a little nudge. She was still asleep. Three hours now. And she was sitting up in one of the chairs in the waiting room, looking totally uncomfortable. He should have insisted she go to bed hours ago, but he hadn't had the heart to wake her. Now he wished he'd found that bed for her, as he could practically feel the stiff muscles she'd have when she did wake up. Which would be in about a minute since he wanted to make sure she got something to eat before Rosalita got busy with dinner preparations.

"Wake up, Juliette. We need to get some food in you." And he needed her company, if only for a few minutes. Missed it when he didn't have it.

"Not hungry," she mumbled, turning away from him without opening her eyes. "Let me sleep another few minutes."

"After you've eaten." He nudged her gently again, then

frowned. Stepped back. Took a good hard look at her. And his face blanched. "Juliette, do you understand what I'm saying to you?"

"Yes," she said, dropping her head to the left side, resting it on her shoulder. "And I'll get back to work in a minute."

"Juliette, listen to me. I want you to look at me. *Open up your eyes and look at me.*"

"They're brown, Damien. Dark brown. Nothing extraordinary." She opened her eyes wide for him to take a look. "See?"

Damien uttered an expletive and immediately reached down to feel her forehead. Then uttered another expletive. She was burning up! Fever, fatigue... "Do you have a headache?" he asked, grabbing his stethoscope out of his pocket and positioning it in his ears.

"Only because I haven't had enough sleep lately," she said, finally starting to rouse, starting to stand. But Damien pushed her gently back into her chair.

"Stay there while I listen," he instructed, sticking the bell of the stethoscope just slightly into the top of her scrub shirt.

"What?" she asked, her face beginning to register slight alarm. "What are you looking for?"

He held his finger up to his lips to shush her. Then listened, first to her lungs, then her heart, then her lungs from the back. "Any joint pains?" he asked when he'd finished his cursory exam. "Or vomiting?"

Now she looked totally alarmed. "What aren't you telling me?"

"Any joint pains or vomiting," he repeated, trying to sound as calm as he possibly could, when nothing inside him felt calm.

"No, and no. Now, tell me!"

"Before you came to Costa Rica, what were you vaccinated for?"

"Typhoid, Hep A and B, malaria…"

"And you're up-to-date?" He looked down at her. "With everything?"

"What's wrong with me, Damien?"

"I need blood tests to confirm…"

She bolted up out of her chair, but was struck by a sudden, severe dizziness, and almost toppled over. Toppled into Damien's arms instead and, rather than pushing away from him, stayed there as he wrapped his arms around her close. "Is it malaria?" she asked, her voice now trembling.

"Your eyes are jaundiced, Juliette. And the rest of your symptoms…" Damn, he hated this. Her onset was too fast. Her symptoms growing too severe far too soon before they should have. Nothing about this was as gradual as he'd seen before, and that worried him. Malaria was bad enough, but with this kind of reaction to it— "And you're showing all the usual symptoms." Of all the diseases he'd treated here, he hated malaria the most.

"I can't have malaria, Damien. I was vaccinated!"

Worldwide, malaria killed nearly half a million people every year and infected over two-hundred million.

Soon after he'd arrived in Bombacopsis, a small outbreak of it had taken eleven villagers. It had swooped in and killed them before he'd even known what was happening. But he didn't want Juliette to know that. Didn't want her to know that, right now, he was scared to death for her. "I'm afraid you do have it, sweetheart," he whispered gently, stroking her hair. Wiping the fever sweat on her face onto his shirtsleeve.

"Damien…" She nestled tighter into him.

"Shh," he said tenderly. "I'm going to take care of you."

"But if the vaccine didn't work…"

Then there was a good chance the limited antimalarial drugs he had on hand might not work, either. It was unthinkable. But he had to face it.

Damn, he wanted to take her to San José, put her in a proper hospital, hold her hand while she got cured there, but he was sure she couldn't make it that far. Especially now that she was starting to tremble in his arms. Hard trembling. Paroxysms. Soon to be a spiking fever, plummeting in the blink of an eye to a below-sustainable life temperature, then spiking back up and plummeting back down again. Over and over until coma. Then death—

No! That wasn't going to happen. He wouldn't let it. "It will work," he said, hating himself for giving her an empty promise. "I'll take care of you, Juliette. Whatever you need, whatever I have to do, I'll take care of you."

"Promise?" she whispered.

"Promise," he whispered back. But she didn't hear him as she'd slumped even harder against him, exhaling a long sigh.

Juliette remembered being swept up into Damien's arms, then being carried across the hall and placed gently down on the exam table. Remembered the tender way he'd examined her, started her IV, sponged her down with cool water, removed her fever-drenched clothing and put her into a hospital gown. She even remembered him carrying her out to a bed in the ward, and pulling the protective screens around her for privacy. After that, though, she remembered nothing. It was all a blank. A vague cloud in her mind that concealed something she couldn't find.

"How long have I been out?" she asked, as Damien appeared at her bedside, preparing to change her bedding.

"You're awake!" he said, his voice sounding almost excited.

"I think I am. Not sure, though." She reached up to brush the hair back from her face and saw the IV running in her right arm. Saw the old-fashioned green oxygen tank sitting next to her bed. Saw the darkness coming from the window above her head. "Is this still Sunday?" Sunday night. Late. Yes, it had to still be Sunday, as she remembered working earlier.

"It's Thursday," Damien said, setting the bed linens down on a chair. "Thursday night, almost midnight."

"No," she protested, shaking her head. "It's Sunday. I'm just tired from overworking."

"You're tired because you have malaria, sweetheart. And the last time you worked was four, almost five days ago."

Nowhere in her mind was she prepared to process this. Nowhere in her mind was she prepared to accept it. "Damien, I don't see how…" She shook her head. "You've got to be wrong. I haven't been sleeping for four days!"

"No, you weren't sleeping. Not exactly, anyway."

"I was unconscious? In a coma?"

Damien nodded, then sat down on the edge of her bed, and took hold of her hand. "You have malaria. An advanced case of it. And you collapsed Sunday night."

"But I remember Sunday night, and I wasn't feeling that bad." Medically, she understood this. Understood the gravity of it. But emotionally—she couldn't grasp it. She hadn't felt sick. Just tired. Down-to-the-bone tired. Nothing some proper rest wouldn't have cured. Malaria, though? "I don't recall that I had any symptoms."

"You didn't. Not up until just a few minutes before you collapsed."

"And you've been treating me with?"

"Quinine and doxycycline."

The same combination they would have used in any hospital in San José. But they'd had such a limited supply on hand. How had he sustained her for so long on what they had? "How?" she asked.

"I have my ways," he said, offering no further explanation, dipping his hand into his pocket to finger the exorbitant bill that came with an overnight express delivery out in the middle of a jungle. A bill he'd paid himself as the hospital had no funds for it.

But she wanted to know what they were. Not that it made a difference to her one way or another, but that was what her mind was fixed on now. She was fighting to make sense of things she couldn't... But the drugs—they made sense to her. She understood them, even though she understood little else. "Where did you get them, Damien?" she persisted.

"Why is it so important to you?" he asked.

"I don't know. I'm...confused. I can't think. Can't focus. But the drugs you used—I remember them, and I remember you didn't have enough of them. I wanted to bring you some. I remember that. I put it on my list of things I wanted to find for the hospital."

"You have a list?" he asked.

"Things you need." Things that she couldn't remember yet. But she did remember there was such a need here. A need she'd wanted to fix for some reason that had also vacated her memory.

"You never told me."

"I didn't?"

Damien shook his head.

"I should have. Don't know why I didn't." Was she involved here in something more than merely being a doctor? Juliette studied Damien's face for a moment. Was she involved with *him*?

"It'll come back to you, Juliette. In time. Your brain is suffering a trauma right now, with the malaria, but you're getting better."

"I hope so," she said, as her eyelids began to droop. "I really..." She didn't finish her sentence. Couldn't finish it, as she dropped back off to sleep.

So Damien waited until he was sure she wouldn't wake up, then changed the bedsheets underneath her, and kissed her on the forehead. "You've still got a way to go, Juliette," he whispered, as he pulled a sheet up over her frail body. "But you're going to make it. I promise, you're going to make it." Wishful thinking? Empty promise? He didn't know, as she was clearly not out of the woods yet. But hearing the words, even though he'd been the one to speak them, made him feel better.

Damien searched for twenty minutes before he found Marco and Ivelis. Twenty long, panicked minutes. Padre Benicio had brought them home from school, left them outside the hospital to play, and when Damien had gone to call them inside they were nowhere to be found. Frantically, he'd searched the property, looked in the supply shed, run to the church to see if they were there. But no one he'd asked knew where they were, no one had even seen them, leaving Damien to wonder if they were trying to get back to their home. Trying to get back to that one place where they felt secure.

He'd been so preoccupied with Juliette these past few days—caring for her, holding her hand, talking to her even though she was unconscious again. He hadn't meant to neglect the children, but he had, and he felt guilty as hell. Now, he was nearing nausea, he was so worried, as he headed back to the hospital. To think Padre Benicio had actually suggested to Damien that he keep the children! How could he, when he couldn't even keep an eye on them for a few minutes?

"No luck," he told George, as he entered through the hospital's front door. "I'm wondering if they're trying to go home."

George gave him a sympathetic smile. "There's something you need to see," he said, pointing into the ward. "Or two young people you need to see, rather."

"But I searched the ward first," Damien said, clearly perplexed.

"Not all the ward, you didn't."

"Then they've been here all along?" His heart felt suddenly lighter.

"Like I said, there's something you need to see." He gestured for Damien to follow him, and he stopped at the end of Juliette's bed, on the other side of the partition. "Take a look."

Damien pushed one of the partitions aside and there, standing next to Juliette's bed, were Marco and Ivelis. Just standing there, looking down at Juliette. Not moving. No facial expressions. Nothing. It was a curious sight. But a nice one. Juliette surrounded by children. It suited her, and he only wished she'd wake up again so she could see what he was seeing. "Thank you," he whispered to George, as George backed away then returned to the clinic.

Damien stepped closer to Juliette's bed, and stopped next to Marco. But he didn't say a word. Instead he just put his arm around the boy, and held out his other hand to Ivelis, who clasped on immediately. And they simply stood there together. For how long? Damien didn't know. A minute? An hour? An eternity? It really didn't matter, as he was so relieved that everything else around him faded into a blur and all his concentration was on this, right here, right now.

"Por qué la señora duerme tanto?" a tiny voice finally asked. Why does the lady sleep so much?

It was Marco asking. A voice of concern where previously there had been no voice.

A lump formed in Damien's throat, causing his own voice to go thick. *"Porque ella está muy enferma."* Because she's very sick, he answered, trying hard not to show how affected he was by one simple sentence. But he was affected, and it was strange that he would be, as he was trying hard not to care for these children. To be custodial, yes. But to care—

"Cuando ella va a despertar?" When will she wake up?

Damien bit down on his lip.

"No sé. Realmente, no sé." I don't know. I really don't know. Words he almost choked on.

Marco accepted this, and nodded. Then he reached out and took hold of Juliette's hand. But only for a moment before he turned and walked away from the bed, and Ivelis let go of Damien's hand and followed him.

And neither Marco nor Ivelis spoke during dinner. Or afterward, when they did their drawing assignment for school. Or later, when they went to bed.

But Damien didn't speak either as, for the first time in his life, he felt overwhelmed. Too overwhelmed to function. Too overwhelmed to speak. Too overwhelmed to make sense of anything. Except this. Seeing Marco's little hand in Juliette's—this was what Damien wanted. All of it. The whole picture. Everything he'd never wanted before. And everything he so badly wanted now, yet still wouldn't admit, for fear he couldn't have it.

* * *

"Where is she?" the booming voice demanded from outside, on the doorstep.

Damien, who was just then exiting the clinic, spun around to the door to face the man. "Who?" Actually, he did know. Who else would have trekked out into the middle of godforsaken nowhere in crisply pressed khaki pants and a blue cotton dress shirt to find Juliette, other than her father? Asking Padre Benicio to go to Cima de la Montaña to contact the man was one thing, but standing here now and facing him—it put fear in him. A new fear. A different fear. The fear that he would take Juliette back with him. That he would never see her again.

"My daughter, Juliette. Tell me this is the place, because I've had a hell of a time getting out here, and I hope I don't have to continue searching for her."

"She's here," Damien conceded, pointing to the open ward behind him. "First bed on the right."

"I don't understand," Alexander Allen said, still keeping his distance from the door. "What was she doing here? I'd been led to believe she was working for a company in San José, so how the hell did she end up here, with malaria?"

"How she ended up here is that she answered my ad. I needed another doctor to help me in the hospital, and Juliette was the one who came out here to do that. As for the malaria—this is Central America. People here get bitten by mosquitoes. Mosquitoes carry the parasite and Juliette was one of the unfortunate ones who had a vaccination against it that didn't work. Look, she's sleeping right now. In fact, she's slept for the past several days. A fitful sleep, sometimes so close to the verge of consciousness you think that she's simply going to open her eyes and smile as if nothing was wrong. So she might wake up if she hears your voice. Come in and talk to her." God knew he'd been talking, and talking, and getting nothing back from her.

"Has she been conscious at all, from the start of this?" Alexander asked.

"Briefly. I explained what was happening to her and how I was treating her, and I guess that's all she needed to hear because she went back to sleep and hasn't woken up since."

"What's her prognosis?" Alexander asked, sounding very stiff about it.

"Physically, she's stable."

"Her vitals are maintaining?"

"Pretty much. No major problems."

He nodded, as if taking it all under consideration. "And prior to her collapse, she was showing no symptoms?"

"She was tired, but around here we all get tired, so it didn't seem unusual."

"But you continued to allow her to work, even though you knew she was tired." Stated, not asked.

"That's just one of the facts of life in this hospital. We always work under difficult circumstances. Juliette knew that before she accepted the position, and she was good with it."

"Why this hospital, though? That's what I don't understand. She chose to work here when she could have had her choice of any proper medical institution in the world. So, what is it I'm not seeing?"

He wasn't seeing Juliette. Not at all. But Damien wasn't going to step into that mess. It wasn't his place. So, instead, he ignored the question, as it was Juliette's father's to answer.

"Juliette was sleeping lighter than she has been when I looked in on her a few minutes ago, so go on in and…"

"You're not worried that she's still unconscious?" Alexander interrupted.

"Worried as hell." Beyond worried. But that was something Alexander Allen didn't have to know. "But she's getting the correct medication, and we're taking good care of her, and waiting—which is all we can do."

"I want her transferred to another hospital. To *my* hospital."

"Against medical advice, Doctor. Juliette's in no condition to travel anywhere."

"With all due respect, she's not in any condition to stay here, either. In case you haven't noticed, her illness is not manifesting itself in the normal way, which means something, or someone, is going wrong. My intention with this, Doctor, is to save my daughter's life, *not* to spare your feelings."

The thin thread of civility between them was nearing its snapping point. And Damien was nearing his own snapping point. With the exception of the past few minutes, he'd spent most of an entire shift sitting at Juliette's bedside, holding her hand, wondering if someone else could do better by her. Wondering if, somehow, he'd gone wrong. Doubting himself. Doubting his decisions. And now, here was her father, practically throwing all Damien's doubts in his face. Accusing him of not being good enough, the way Nancy's father had done.

"Then we agree on something, since my intention is to save Juliette's life, and I don't give a damn about my feelings because they don't matter in this." His impassive facade was beginning to slip, and he wasn't sure what to do to put it back in place. Wasn't sure he even wanted to. Not for *this* man.

For the first time, Damien realized just why Juliette had been so keen to get away from her father. And Alexander Allen's wealth had nothing whatsoever to do with Damien's mounting hostility toward him. Which, surprisingly, was a step in a completely different direction for him. It made Damien wonder if it was not the wealth he hated so much as the way some people acted because of it. That eye-opener gave him a whole new perspective of Juliette. Caused him to see something in her that he'd refused to see before. The fact was, she wasn't spoiled, as he'd first assumed. She wasn't caught up in the trappings of wealth, but she was trying to escape the way her father was caught up in them. And he owed her an apology for that, and for all the other wrong assumptions he'd made. When she woke up—

"There's a chair next to Juliette's bed." One that was probably warm from all the hours he'd spent in it. "Please feel free to stay as long as you wish. We don't have visiting hours here. Oh, and if you'd like something to eat or drink, just ask. I'll be in and out for a while, as will my nurse, Alegria, and a couple of our volunteers."

With that, Damien turned and walked back into the empty clinic, and shut the door behind him, then slumped against it. He was so sick with worry over Juliette he could barely function, and part of him wanted her father to take her back home with him to get her other help. But part of him feared that once she was gone from Bombacopsis, he'd never see her again. That was the part he feared most. Because he loved Juliette. Pure and simple. He'd gone and done the thing he'd promised himself he wouldn't do and he was about to lose her, without ever having told her how he felt. That was the worst part— he'd never told her.

CHAPTER TEN

"YOUR FATHER WAS here today, Juliette. Did you hear him?" It was dark now, and Bombacopsis was staying away from the hospital. No minor complaints coming across the threshold, no major complaints in queue. They were staying away out of respect, and Damien appreciated that as he didn't want to leave Juliette's side. He also didn't have it in him to do any doctoring. Something about seeing Juliette lying there, so pale, so helpless— slipping away from him. "He's staying with one of the families in the village tonight, even though I don't think he's happy about the arrangement. But it was the best we could do for him.

"The hospital's quiet, too. No patients at the moment. Oh, and you'll be happy to hear that there are no other cases of malaria in the village. We asked people to come in to be checked, and George went out door-to-door the other day, and we're all good. So when you wake up and get back to work…" Wake up? Back to work? The words were so painful to say, he almost choked on them. "When you wake up and get back to work you won't have to be treating a crisis." Damien raised his hand to his forehead and rubbed the spot just above his nose, directly between his eyes, the spot where a relentless throb had set in and wouldn't let go. She'd been like this a week now and he felt so helpless. So damned helpless.

"Marco and Ivelis are fine. They've been in to see you every day, and Marco is actually beginning to talk a little bit. Not Ivelis, though, although sometimes I think she's right on the verge. Padre Benicio is keeping them up with their schooling, and he says they're both very bright. Apparently, Marco is good with numbers. Oh, and Ivelis—she's a budding artist. Draws lovely pictures. Anyway, they're staying with George and Carmelita until you get better. It's a little crowded but, with help from so many of the locals, it's working out. Everybody in Bombacopsis is concerned about you, Juliette."

Small talk. It was all just small talk, and he felt awkward about it because he wanted to tell her that he loved her. But he wanted her to hear it. Wanted to see her reaction when he said the words. Wanted her to laugh at him, or fight him, or kiss him. Wanted to look into her eyes to see if they reflected any love for him.

"Your dad's a formidable man, but you already know that, don't you. I hope you don't mind that I had him called to come see you. But I thought he needed to be here. Also, just in case you don't know where you are when you wake up, it's probably going to be back in Indianapolis. Your dad is making arrangements to have you transported there. He doesn't think we're doing enough for you here."

Damien took hold of Juliette's hand, and kissed the back of it. And he fought back the lump in his throat that was threatening to explode, because Juliette needed him to be strong right now. Strong enough for the both of them. "And I don't want you to go, Juliette. I don't ever want you to go. Which is why I need for you to wake up and tell me what *you* want. If you do that, sweetheart, I'll fight for it with everything I am. I promise."

"You don't have the right to keep her here," the voice from behind him said.

Damien twisted to see Alexander Allen looming over the foot of his daughter's bed. "But do you have the right to take her back to a place she doesn't want to go?"

"Legally, yes I do."

"What about morally? Have you ever, once, done anything for Juliette that she wanted, and not what you wanted for her?" He didn't want to have this argument with the man. Especially not with Juliette here. Whether or not she could hear, he didn't know. But he wanted to believe she could. Wanted to believe that his words were getting through to her on some level and making a difference. "Have you ever listened to her, Dr. Allen?"

"My whole life. And even though you think I'm being an ogre, all I want to do is what I believe is right for my daughter."

"What's right for Juliette is to wait until she wakes up to make the decisions herself."

"And in the meantime?"

"We talk to her and give her a reason to want to come back to us."

"That's not exactly a medical cure, is it?" Alexander Allen said. But his voice wasn't stern. Now, it was full of worry, and fear. The voice of a loving father.

"When she found out her vaccination hadn't worked, she was afraid the antimalarials we might give her wouldn't work, either. And I promised her they would." And she'd trusted him. Damn it, she'd trusted him!

"You had no way of knowing."

"But I shouldn't have promised."

"I'm sure my daughter needed to hear that promise from you." He stepped up to the bed and squeezed Damien's shoulder. "Look, son. I know you care for her. I think you might even be in love with her. But right now, I want to take her home. I've got an expert there—he's expecting her."

"Her body is weak, Dr. Allen. She's been unconscious for quite a while now and her overall condition may be stable, but the physical strain of putting her through what it would take to get her transported may be more than she's able to withstand." That, and the fact that he simply wanted her here. Wanted to be the one to take care of her. "In the end, I just want to do what's best for Juliette, and I think staying here's what's best."

"We both want what's best for Juliette, Dr. Caldwell. In my medical opinion, she's fit to travel. So, tomorrow morning, I'm returning to San José to arrange for an ambulance to come get her, and I'm also going to hire air transport to get us back to Indianapolis. If all goes as I hope it will, Juliette and I will be leaving the day after tomorrow. So spend your time with her now. Say what you have to say to her. I won't interrupt that. But do know that I'm taking her home with me, and I'm not going to be persuaded to change my mind."

Damien didn't respond to that. How could he? What was there to say?

"Remember when you first came here," Damien said to Juliette a little while later, after her father had gone. "And you promised that someday, someway, you were going to challenge me, and I wouldn't see it coming? Well, this is the challenge, Juliette. But I did see it coming when I sent for your father. I knew what he would do. The thing is, I think I know what you'd do, too. And you're going to have to wake up and do it, because I can't do it for you. Do you hear me, Juliette? Squeeze my hand if you hear me."

But she didn't squeeze his hand, and he was crushed. "OK, if you can't squeeze my hand, can you wiggle your toes, or open your eyes? Anything to give me a sign?" Yet still no sign, and he was crushed again. Maybe later—

Damien stretched his shoulders and rolled his neck to fight back the stiffness settling into his muscles, then he took a drink of water from the cup sitting on the bedside stand, and exhaled a deep breath. Bent down, kissed Juliette on the forehead, then tenderly, fully on her lips. "Did I ever tell you about the time my brother Daniel and I burned down the next door neighbor's shed?"

And so it went into the night. Damien talked until he was hoarse, while Juliette slept.

"You look terrible."

Damien bolted up in his chair, blinked open his eyes and looked around. He must have dozed off for a moment. And now he was a little off on his orientation. It was daylight, but barely. He'd been sleeping for—what? Maybe two hours. Then something—a voice? Had someone spoken to him? Was that what had startled him out of his sleep? Or was he dreaming it?

It sounded like Juliette but, looking over at her, he saw that her eyes were still closed.

"Morning, Juliette," he said, standing up to stretch his body. He looked a mess. His hair was in disarray. His scrubs wrinkled beyond recognition. His normal three-day stubble gone way beyond that. He needed to grab a shower, wash his hair, shave, put on some fresh clothes, grab a bite to eat since he couldn't remember the last time he'd been anywhere near a plate of food. Yes, he had a long list of things he needed to do, but hated to do, as they would take him away from Juliette longer than he wanted.

Damien bent down, kissed her on the forehead and took hold of her hand. "Juliette," he said, "I've got to go make myself presentable. But I won't be gone long. I promise. And while I'm gone, I'm going to have Alegria come in and bathe you, and change your linens—just so you'll know what's going on around you. Also, it's Friday morning, and you've been sleeping for eight days now." He'd oriented her first thing every morning, but he'd never, ever used the words *coma* or *unconscious*. *Asleep* sounded much more gentle—much more hopeful. And he needed some hope here. Desperately needed some hope.

Before he left Juliette, Damien pushed his chair back to the wall, then took a look out the window directly over Juliette's bed. It was beautiful out today. Sunny. Cheery. For a moment he thought about carrying Juliette outside, to let some of that sun sink into her body. Maybe she would feel its warmth. Maybe she would taste the difference between the stale hospital air and the fresh air out there. Of course, it was only a thought. A rather silly one at that. Fresh air and sunlight didn't cure malaria or, in Juliette's case, the toxic side effects of the drug used to treat malaria.

Bending down to kiss her once more before he left, he pushed the hair back from her face. "This won't take me long," he said, then turned away from the bed and headed to the opening between the two partitions set at the end of it.

"Could she comb my hair?"

Damien spun to face Juliette. But her eyes weren't open. "I'll ask her," he said cautiously, even though his heart was about to leap out of his chest. "Anything else you want?"

The reply came, but it seemed to take forever. "Water," she said eventually. "Dry throat."

Damien bit down hard on his lower lip, trying to control his emotions. "A few sips. It's been a while since you've had anything in your stomach, and I don't want you cramping up."

"I'm a doctor." Finally, she opened her eyes. "I know that."

"Juliette…" Damien choked out, stumbling back to her bedside and pulling her up into his arms. "We were so afraid… I was so afraid…" He moved back away from her. "Do you know how long you've been out?"

"You've been reminding me every day."

"You've heard me?"

She let out a weary sigh, and nodded. "I heard you sometimes." Then she closed her eyes and snuggled her head against his arm. "And like I said a few minutes ago, you look terrible."

She held out her hand to his, and he took hold. "Don't leave me yet, Damien. Please, just sit with me for a while."

"For as long as you want," he said, bending down to kiss her hand. "For as long as you want."

"You *know* my dad wasn't too happy about my staying here," Juliette said. She was sitting outside in the sun today, three days after she'd awoken, and she was greeting the many visitors who'd casually dropped by to say hello, bring her flowers or simply hang around hoping to help her out in any way they could. She was truly touched by the sentiment, and shocked to discover how highly regarded she was in Bombacopsis.

Damien, who'd pulled out a chair next to her, and was taking in the sun as well, smiled lazily. "He'll get over it."

"I'm glad he was here, though."

"I was afraid you'd hate me for sending for him."

Juliette laughed. "No. He needed to be here. It would have hurt him if you hadn't sent for him, and I really don't want him hurt. He loves me, Damien. And maybe he's a little too overprotective, but that's just the way he is."

"I know your dad means well, Juliette. I think he'd move heaven and earth to take care of you. And while we didn't necessarily agree on what was best for you, I think he's a good man."

"He *is* a good man," she agreed. "And a good doctor." She was touched by Damien's kind words, especially since her father and Damien had been on opposite ends of the debate on how to best take care of her.

"Well, all I know is, we both agreed that we wanted what was best for you, even though we wanted it done differently."

"Wouldn't it have been easier on you to let me go back with him?"

"No," he said quite simply. "I wanted you here."

But why did he want her here? Why wouldn't he just say the words? She knew he loved her. There was no doubt in her mind. But she wanted him to tell her, and she was afraid he never would. Yet she'd felt his kisses when she was somewhere smothered deep in her fog. Felt his hand holding hers. Heard the words, but never the right words. The words that would have soothed her heart.

"Well, it's a good thing I woke up and made the decision for myself."

"But staying in Costa Rica is going to be very difficult for you, especially now that you don't have a job here."

"Can you believe they'd do that to me?" she asked, sounding more angry than hurt.

"I don't think it was nice of them, but I can believe it. People look after their own best interests, and your employers needed to move on at a time when you couldn't. Would I have done that to you? No, I believe in loyalty. But you were apparently working for someone who didn't." Her company had laid her off days ago, after he'd sent Padre Benicio to call Cynthia and ask her to explain Juliette's absence to her employer. The director of her office had sent an impersonal note explaining his circumstances and said, if Juliette recovered sufficiently, she could reapply should another position come open. But, as he'd explained, he had too many medical professionals waiting in queue, and they had to be attended to immediately.

"Well, it stings. And more than that, it leaves me stranded here needing to find work or else I'll be forced to leave in ninety days, thanks to the visa requirements."

"And ninety days to find work may be unrealistic, considering that you'll still be recovering from your malaria and the hospitals here might not be so eager to take you on due to your medical situation. But maybe going home is what you need to do, considering how badly you responded to standard malaria treatment."

It almost sounded as if he wanted her to leave. Between losing her job, and now this…

"There are other cures, Damien. A whole host of other drugs I can try. And I still have the hospital here, if you'll let me work." Would he let her, though? Over the past couple of days, she'd given it a lot of thought then reconciled herself to the fact that here, with Damien, at this little hospital, was where she was happiest. What she didn't know, however, was if her being here made him happy. But since the rest of her world seemed to be crumbling at her feet right now, it seemed like the perfect time to find out if this little piece of it was, too.

"Will you let me stay and work for you?"

"But how would you support yourself since I can't pay you?" he asked.

This wasn't what she wanted to hear. No, what she

wanted to hear was him telling her how thrilled he'd be to have her stay, that he wanted it more than anything. That they could have a bright future together here. He hadn't said any of that, though. Hadn't even sounded close to anything hopeful. "Remember—I'm rich. I don't need for you to pay me."

"Could you actually work under these conditions, Juliette? I know you can do it for a couple days a week, but do you even realize what it's going to be like if you're here every day, all day? And there's no phone connection. No internet—"

And again, nothing hopeful. "I'm well aware of what you don't have here, Damien." This hurt. When she'd thought he loved her—had she mistaken that for something else? Something she didn't understand? Had she truly believed everything had changed between them when nothing had? Nothing at all?

Suddenly, Juliette felt tired. Overwhelmed. Sad. Didn't want to sit outside anymore. Didn't want to talk to Damien. Didn't even want to see him. Wanted to get away from him before the tears came. "I need to go back to my bed and rest," she said, scooting forward in her chair, ready to stand up.

Damien sprang immediately to his feet to help her, but she held out her hand to stop him. "I'm fine," she snapped. "I can do this by myself."

"You've only been awake three days, Juliette, and you're still weak." In spite of her protests, he stepped forward to take her arm. But she shook him off.

"I *said*, I can do this by myself." Brave words, even though her legs were still weak, and her back still ached from too much time flat in bed.

"Damn it, Juliette! What the hell's wrong?"

"Wrong? Do you want to know what's wrong, Damien? You're what's wrong. And I'm what's wrong."

"Why are we fighting?"

"Because that's what we do. We have since the first day I stepped into the hospital, and while I'd thought we'd gotten past that, apparently I was wrong." She took two steps toward the front entry to the hospital and her legs gave out on her, causing her to lurch forward. But Damien was there to catch her before she fell, and for a moment she clung to him, wishing that his desire to hold her came from something more than simply trying to keep her from hurting herself.

"Juliette, I—" he started, his voice almost in a whisper.

Why didn't he just tell her that he loved her? That would make everything right. But he was running out of chances, and she was running out of hope. Whatever was holding him back was still hanging on, and she didn't know how to break through it. Not even her near-death had broken through it.

"Look, Damien. I can't get out of here on my own yet, but I've decided to talk to Padre Benicio, to see if he can find someone to help me get back to San José. I'll have my dad help me from there. I think that's best for every-body concerned." For everybody but her. But falling in love with a man who kept himself hidden from love was impossible to deal with. She wasn't strong enough, now. Her defenses were gone. And, for the first time in her life, she found herself totally without direction.

It was time to go home.

"I think you should stay here for a while. The chil-dren need you—"

The children, but not Damien. "The children will be fine. They've got you, and you're turning into a great dad." She did hate to leave Marco and Ivelis. In fact, the idea that she'd never see them again was tearing her apart. It was amazing how quickly she'd come to love them. But they were great kids. So full of life and eagerness. So adaptable to their new situation. So easy to love. Juliette's throat tightened when she thought about walking away from them, but she couldn't allow the emotions she knew would come from that sad scene to stop her from doing what she had to do. The children would get along without her and, as much as Damien loved them, he would eventually adopt them. Maybe he didn't know that yet, but she did.

"But they huddle around you every minute they can."

Juliette smiled. "And they adore you, Damien. The thing is, I can't stay here only because the children need me, especially when I know they've got a wonderful life ahead of them."

"I want to keep them, Juliette, but I don't know how. They need more than I can provide them."

"Do you love them?" she asked.

He nodded. "It snuck up on me, but yes, I do."

He could admit his love for the children, but not for her. It hurt. "Then that's all they need. The rest will work itself out. See, you *need* to be a father, Damien. And once you realize that, you're going to discover some happiness you never thought you could have." But what he wouldn't realize was that he needed to be a husband. It was too late for that now, and she had to leave before her emotions affected the children. "Look, I won't be going for a couple days, because I'm not up to the travel yet, so I'll have plenty of time to say my proper goodbyes to Marco and Ivelis. And I'll be gentle about it, Damien, because I don't want to hurt them."

"You won't be coming back again, will you?"

His face was shielded from her, but she wanted to think it was covered with sadness.

"I think it's time for you to run your ad again. Now, if you'll help me back to bed, I really do need to rest." And fight back the tears that wanted to flow. And pray that her heart wouldn't hurt any more than it did at this moment.

Damien looked at the truck parked outside the hospital's front entrance, then turned his head away. He didn't want to see it, didn't want it to be here. But it was, and there was no denying the fact that Juliette was about to climb into that truck and leave his life for good. He'd struggled with this for two days now. Struggled from the moment she'd told him she was going until this very second. Why was he letting her do this? Why wasn't he trying to stop her?

Because she deserved better than this. And *this*, he was coming to realize, was where he was going to stay because, for the first time in his life, he fit. Anyplace else, he floundered. Either way, it wasn't enough to offer her.

Did he want her to stay? More than anything. Did he want to work with her and love her and marry her and raise an army of kids with her? He did, so much so that when he thought about life without her he couldn't breathe. Yet he couldn't ask. Didn't have that right because he knew that to have Juliette here would be to deprive her of a life where she truly belonged. Yes, she was a rich girl. And yes, she was used to privilege. But she wasn't spoiled by it. He'd been so wrong about that. So terribly wrong. But it was a wrong he couldn't right because, if he did, she would fall into his arms and tell him how much she loved him and if she did that he'd never be able to let her go. And, for Juliette's sake, she had to go.

"You know you're going to have to do something about

this, don't you?" George said. He was standing in the clinic door, watching Damien purposely turn his back to the hospital entrance.

"About what?" he said, even though he knew exactly what.

"How stupid can any one man be, Damien? You love her, she loves you—admit it to yourself, you damned fool, then admit it to her, and the rest will be easy."

"Easy?" Damien spun to face the man. "This isn't easy, George. And it can't be easy, no matter what I do. Juliette belongs in a different world, and in time she'll remember that. Then she'll resent me for telling her that I love her because that's what would hold her here. And I don't have the right to hold her because all I'll ever be able to give her is a run-down, underfunded little hospital and a hut with maybe enough room to add another room or two."

"The village will build you a proper house, Damien, if that's what's concerning you."

"Hell, they can build me a mansion. But that's still not good enough."

"What's 'good enough,' Damien, is what she wants. Have you ever asked her what she wants?"

Damien turned to look out the front door. The damned truck was still there, still waiting. Still breaking his heart. "Nobody has," he whispered. "Not her father. Not me."

"You're right," Juliette said, exiting the hospital ward. "Nobody has."

George walked over to Damien, squeezed him on the shoulder, then retreated back into the clinic and closed the door.

"Why is that, Damien?" Juliette asked. "Why didn't you ask me?"

"Because I was afraid you'd tell me."

"Do you really not want me here that much?" she asked.

"No. I really *do* want you here that much." This was, perhaps, the most honest thing he'd ever said to her. Maybe the most honest thing he'd ever said to anyone.

Juliette stepped up to him, her face to his back, but maintained a few inches of separation between them. "Then ask me, Damien. Ask me what I want."

He wanted to, but did he really have that right? "If I ask you, then what?"

"Then I'll know that, for the first time in my life, someone values me for who I am and not for who they want me to be."

Damien swallowed hard, then turned to face her. She was so close to him he could smell the scent of her shampoo—the shampoo she always brought with her for her weekends at Bombacopsis. The shampoo he'd grown to love. "What do you want, Juliette?" The most difficult words he'd ever uttered.

"I want to stay here, work in a little hospital where daily hardship is normal. Where I'll have to scrape for drugs and bandages. Where I'll have to make beds. And love a man who spends too much time worrying about the things he can't give me to fully understand what he *can* give me. Raise two lovely children who need both a mother and a father, and maybe add a couple more to the mix. Live in a hut, or a cottage, or a mansion or anywhere the man I love lives."

"And give up everything you've ever known?"

"Yet have so much more than I ever expected to have. See, Damien. The thing about falling in love is, it changes everything. Several weeks ago, when I first came here, I wasn't sure I wanted to stay. And, to be honest, I had to do some pretty stern talking to myself to get me back here that second weekend. I loved the work, but I wasn't particularly anxious to work with you. But, you know, falling in love replaced all that. It changed me so much that by the third week I was actually looking forward to seeing you. I'd spent my whole week away from you wanting to see you. And it wasn't only you. I wanted to be part of the work here. It made me feel vital, and necessary. Back in Indianapolis, I was…replaceable. Any number of people could have stepped into my job at a moment's notice, and my absence there would have never been noticed. But here—it's the first time I've ever been necessary for who I was and not for who my father was, or who he wanted me to be. Being necessary—that's the highest calling a doctor can have. And you know what, it doesn't matter that I can't just send someone down the hall for a CT scan or an endoscopy, and all I may have available to fix a serious gash is a simple stick-on bandage. What matters—the *only* thing that matters—is that you and your hospital allow me to be the doctor I always knew I could be." She reached up and stroked his cheek. "What I want, Damien, is the rest of my life with you, but I'm not sure you want the rest of your life with me."

"Do you know what you're saying, Juliette? Do you understand what a life with me will be like?"

"It'll be difficult. It will lack the advantages I'm used to. It will be nothing that I'd ever planned for myself. And it will be wonderful because I'll be facing the challenges alongside the man I love, if the man I love loves me enough to want me there." She looked deep into his eyes to see if the answer showed, and what she saw was a softening she'd never seen before. Tenderness. Love.

"The man you love does love you. But he's terrified that the life he's offering you won't be good enough. That, in time, you'll grow to resent it, and him." He sighed deeply, lamentably. "And I couldn't bear that, Juliette. Knowing that I couldn't give you enough to make you happy—"

"Damien, I know what will make me happy. For the first time, I truly know. And it's not going to change because all I want from you is to have you love me."

"Juliette, I do love you. More than I can express. But I can't give you…Egyptian cotton bedsheets. In fact, I'll be damned lucky to give you a proper bed."

"Do you think I really care about Egyptian sheets, or proper beds? I'm not that shallow, Damien. Are you still hung up by my wealth?"

"I know you're not shallow, and I got over my rich girl lunacy shortly after I met you. But to love you is to *want* to give you everything. That coming from a man who has nothing."

"A man who has nothing? How can you say that, Damien?"

"Because it's true."

"What's true is that, to me, *everything* is waking up every morning and seeing the man I love lying there next to me. *Everything* is raising two wonderful children with the man I love and someday giving him another couple. *Everything* is working by his side, fighting the odds with him and knowing that, together, we can't be beaten. *Everything* is who you are to me, Damien. Don't you understand that? *You* are everything."

"Juliette, I… I…" Words failed him, but his actions didn't as he lowered his face to Juliette's, and sealed their unspoken vow with a deep, eternal kiss. A kiss that Juliette melted into and knew that there she would find the rest of her life.

Damien and Daniel Caldwell looked the handsome pair, standing outside the village church in their matching suits and matching ties, mixing and mingling with the few remaining wedding guests. If it weren't for the fact that Damien's hair was long and his face scruffy with stubble, a look she adored on him, and Daniel was clean-shaven with short hair, they were absolutely as identical as Damien had told her they were. Same bright eyes, same dimples to die for, same smile. Zoey, her new sister-in-law, was a lucky woman to have Daniel, and Juliette was a lucky woman to have Damien.

Juliette looked out into the garden, where Marco and Ivelis were playing with their soon-to-be new cousin, Maddie—Daniel and Zoey's daughter—and Diego, who'd seemed to latch on to their lives and wouldn't let go. Marco's and Ivelis's adoption wouldn't be final for a while, but they were already a family, in spite of the children's legal status. And what an amazing family it was—a joining of what, at times, seemed almost insurmountable odds.

"You know this means you're a grandfather now, don't you?" she said to her dad.

Alexander Allen cleared his throat, straightened up rigidly. "I'm too young to be a grandfather," he said, trying to sound stern. But there was no real sternness there. Not from the man who'd packed an entire suitcase full of toys for his new grandchildren.

"Well, Grandpa, like it or not, that's who you are now. And, for the next two weeks, you're going to have an awful lot of time to perfect it." When her father assumed temporary medical duties at the hospital and also took over the care of Marco and Ivelis, while she and Damien slipped away to Hawaii for a honeymoon.

"I did tell you that I'm having a few supplies delivered here because I refuse to work under such primitive conditions. Oh, and antimalarials. I'm having every kind on the market shipped down here so you'll have them on hand, since you insist on living here with the mosquitoes."

"Bring in whatever makes you comfortable, because Damien and I expect you to come visit us several times a year, and when you're here you know you *are* going to be expected to work with us."

Alexander finally conceded a laugh. "I was right, you know. I always did say you'd be a great administrator. Just didn't expect it to be in—" he spread his arms wide to gesture the entire village "—this!"

"Well, get used to *this*, because it's now your home away from home. In the meantime, the village is throwing us a festival and Damien and I need to put in an appearance."

"Only an appearance?" Alexander questioned.

"Only an appearance," Damien confirmed. "They tend to overindulge a little during their festivals around here, and Juliette and I need to go back to the hospital and get ready to take care of about half the villagers who'll eventually come in sometime later on." He took hold of his wife's hand, then leaned down and kissed her on the cheek. "It's just one of the things we do around here."

"Mind if I join you?" Alexander asked. "My doctoring skills may be a little rusty but, since you really don't have anything to treat people with, I don't suppose anybody will notice."

"I'm in, too, bro," Daniel said, stepping into the mix with his wife. "And I'm serious about what I said. Zoey and I will be down here a couple times a year to help you out in the hospital."

"So I might as well get started tonight, too," Zoey said cheerfully. "If you could use a nurse on duty."

"We can always use a nurse on duty," Damien said.

In the distance, Juliette heard the sounds of the festival and smiled. This was going to be a great life. "Well, why don't you three head on over to the hospital, while Damien and I arrange for Padre Benicio to look after our children tonight, and we'll join you shortly. Oh, and scrubs are in the storage closet."

As Daniel, Zoey and Alexander set off together, Damien and Juliette stood in the road and watched after them for a bit. "This is good, Damien," Juliette said, turning to face him, and raising her arms to twist around his neck.

"Very good," he agreed, tilting her face up to his. "Very, *very* good."

And there, in the middle of the road, in a remote jungle village in the middle of Costa Rica, to the sound of revelers celebrating her marriage to Damien, Juliette kissed her husband with the first of a long lifetime of soul-shaking kisses. For the first time in her life, Juliette truly knew where she was meant to be.

* * * * *

*If you enjoyed this story, check out these
other great reads from Dianne Drake*

*THE NURSE AND THE SINGLE DAD
DOCTOR, MUMMY...WIFE?
TORTURED BY HER TOUCH
A HOME FOR THE HOT-SHOT DOC*

All available now!

MILLS & BOON®

MEDICAL ROMANCE™

THE ULTIMATE IN ROMANTIC MEDICAL DRAMA

A sneak peek at next month's titles...

In stores from 29th June 2017:

- **The Surrogate's Unexpected Miracle** – Alison Rober
  and **Convenient Marriage, Surprise Twins** – Amy Rutta

- **The Doctor's Secret Son** – Janice Lynn
  and **Reforming the Playboy** – Karin Baine

- **Their Double Baby Gift** – Louisa Heaton
  and **Saving Baby Amy** – Annie Claydon

Just can't wait?
Buy our books online before they hit the shops!
www.millsandboon.co.uk

Also available as eBooks.

0617/03

MILLS & BOON®

EXCLUSIVE EXTRACT

Lana Haole and the all-too tempting Dr Andrew
Tremblay agreed to a marriage of convenience… But
suddenly their convenient arrangement has become a
whole lot more!

Read on for a sneak preview of
CONVENIENT MARRIAGE, SURPRISE TWINS

Lana's request had caught him off guard, but he wasn't
displeased by it. Not at all. It was just that he couldn't.
He'd just never expected it from her. She was always so
careful, guarded, but the more time he was spending with
her, the more he realized a hot fiery passion burned beneath
the surface.

And that was something he wanted to explore, but he
had a sneaking suspicion that if he tasted this once, he
was going to want more and more. So, even though it
killed him, he left the room. Walked the beach, far away
from the wedding, to calm his senses, but it didn't work
because all he could think about was Lana's lips pressed
against his.

The feeling of her in his arms.

And her begging him to make love to her.

You can't.

Although he wanted to.

After what seemed like an eternity he returned to the
room. Hoping that everything had blown over, that she
might be already asleep even, but instead he saw her sitting
on the couch, a flute of champagne in her hand. She turned
to look at him when he shut the door and he could see the
tearstains on her cheeks.

Pain hit him hard.

He'd hurt her.

"Oh, I didn't expect you to come back," she said quietly and she wiped the tears from her face.

"I just needed a moment to myself."

"I see," she said quietly. Then she sighed. "Well, I think I'm going to turn in."

"Lana, I think we need to talk," he said.

"What is there to talk about?" She frowned. "You didn't want me and you have nothing to apologize about. I'm the one that wanted to step out of the boundaries we set. Not you."

"No, that's not it."

"What do you mean?" she asked, confused.

"I want you too, Lana. It's not for lack of desiring you. I want you. More than anything." And, though he knew that he shouldn't, he closed the distance between them and kissed her, fully expecting her to pull back from him the way that he had pulled from her, but she didn't. Instead she melted into his arms and he knew that he was a lost man.

Don't miss
CONVENIENT MARRIAGE, SURPRISE TWINS
by Amy Ruttan

Available July 2017
www.millsandboon.co.uk